WAR
OF THE
FAITH
INTO LIMINATUM

BOB VACANTI JR

North Carolina

War of the Faith: Into Liminatum
© 2025 Bob Vacanti, Jr. All rights reserved.

No part of this book may be reproduced in any form or by any means, electronic, mechanical, digital, photocopying or recording, except for the inclusion in a review, without permission in writing from the publisher.

This is a work of fiction. All the characters, names, incidents, organizations, and dialogue in this novel are either the products of the author's imagination or are used fictitiously.

Published in the United States by BQB Publishing
(an imprint of Boutique of Quality Books Publishing, Inc.)
www.bqbpublishing.com

979-8-88633-045-8 (p)
979-8-88633-046-5 (h)

Library of Congress Control Number: 2025936196

Book design by Robin Krauss, www.bookformatters.com
Cover design by Rebecca Lown, www.rebeccalowndesign.com

1st editor: Caleb Guard
2nd editor: Andrea Vande Vorde

I dedicate this book to the Author of All Creation, for whom I am eternally grateful, to my loving family, and to my cousin, Nick, whose insightful feedback and love of fantasy helped shape my world.

PROLOGUE

The Waldean Plateau was little known to the world of Essa, perched above vast wastelands and restless emerald seas. That is, until Day 25 by the 13th Moon, 1190 QE, when the Mad Prophet Judecca, having usurped the Empire of Gul'dan, sent his zealots to Waldea's southern shore. The brutal subjugation that followed nearly consumed Waldea.

Over the Great Chasm came a people known as The Trust, with their mechalurgical wonders never before seen, glimmering aircraft and blazing cannons. They helped Waldea repel the Gul'dani forces back across the Waters Emeralda, and shortly thereafter they disappeared.

Waldea barely survived the dreadful Holy War.

One generation has since passed in isolation. The Waldean Alliance, forged in the War, remains vigilant against the outsiders, or any sign of faith, the expression of which is forbidden.

This peace has come at the price of progress, yet the sudden return of The Trust is determined to set Waldea's fate once again into motion.

Many welcome this reunion, though some find it an ominous reminder of a past better left forgotten. What will become of their peace? Will the looming threat return?

PART I

CHAPTER

Lawrence Carlyle awoke in the dead of night. His crimson chamber was obscured by darkness, save for hints of gray light extending through three windows towering over his bedside. He nervously twisted the thin, salted-brown mustache upon his sweaty face and scanned the other muted shapes across the room, counting them one by one: the desk, the mirror, his wardrobe, a coatrack, an end table, and his most dear painting of his beloved, across from his bed. Oh, how he adored that gorgeous blue-eyed woman, who was always wrapped in long locks of radiant gold.

Lawrence breathed a deep sigh of relief. All remained as it always had. The lofty span of mountainside upon which his lavish home stood, stared ominously back through the windows. Its majestic countenance humbled him at once.

That's right, he thought, *just another dream on the precipice of that fateful mount. Dear Alma, whispers of your final words caused my stomach to sink. Such traitors did not deserve your ceaseless love! That wrathful king and his duplicitous wife, their betrayal of you and the tender woman beside you complete. Without regret, they cast you both into the deadly chasm, where that or any tragic tale would have normally ended. Yet, this time, you kept falling. You plummeted through glimmering pits of dancing quartz, deep into the bowels of the world. I could see each of you delivered gently adrift a sea of shifting jewels toward its cradled core. Others awaited your arrival, singing songs unheard, yet echoing endlessly in those crystalline halls.*

He remembered saying something in the last instant of his dream. Had his voice joined their silent concert? What were the damn words?

The moment vanished like footprints in a trail of dust, leaving a sense of unease and fatigue. He yawned up at the winged creatures ornately carved into corner posts upon the bed's canopy, the only witnesses to another night of daunted slumber. He nervously jostled, resisting their hypnotic gazes from lulling him back to sleep. He dreaded to return, yet he couldn't bear to forget. It was a dismal bargain. Would he relive that same heartache yet again, or risk losing his love to the fractious caverns of his memory?

Who could forget that captivating smile Alma wore, even in falling? he thought. *She and that other woman—Sancta, I believe she was called. Was I really so afraid then? Was she? If Alma reclaims me tonight, perhaps I will remember to ask.*

A sudden rattle against the windowpane sent the gangly man ducking into his sheets. He assured himself it must have been another poor fowl. When would those blasted things ever learn? The explanation didn't convince his pounding heart for a moment.

Soon, there was a second slam on the pane, and then another. Now wide awake, his body seized under the blanket as a steady clamor shook the entire room. He feared the wall of glass would shatter before long.

Even in waking, Lawrence could still hear Alma speaking in his head. *Know they linger this night, my dear Doctor.*

"Damn it," he cursed under his breath. "There was still time. I could swear it."

Please flee while you still may.

Several alarming shrieks pierced the air in high, dissonant pitches. Some were closer than others, more intense, none relenting. Lawrence spilled from his bed as indigo light bled starkly through the drapes. He could do nothing but tremble at the sound of them, at the sight of a stained room, himself included. The taint would not be wiped from his skin, nor would his sorrow leave him. He was reduced to a shivering knot curled on the floor, his wit having absconded. Both hands cradled the back of his neck as he remained prostrate, crying to anyone who would listen.

Alma's voice came to him again: *Those who pray idle are first to fall. Get up! They will come and take you, lest they find another . . .*

Slowly, he raised his head to the portrait hanging like a talisman to protect him. Almalinda's haunting eyes suggested he could not stay, that his safety there was no longer guaranteed. Her visage gripped him, lifted him up, led him to the door, and with great reluctance, delivered him from the chamber. More purple light infiltrated the multitude of windows lining the corridor of his personal wing atop the manor's fourth story. A quick glance through one window sent him crashing upon a long rug atop the glossy wooden floor as glowing apparitions peered in from the night. Their cold, skeletal frames floated like bones of shining silver draped in tatters. A pair of ghostly wisps hovered at each figure's shoulders, their forms like wheels within spinning wheels. The space around them hummed and warbled as they hung effortlessly in the air, lingering traces of their visage dancing in the turbulent wind.

Most notable were the thick strips of intense red light over each pair of eyes, buzzing in no particular direction. Their faces possessed no other features, not even a mouth from which came the dissonant screams.

Lawrence understood their terrible purpose at once. *It is just as she threatened. Future is never still. It has come.*

"That's not true!" screamed Lawrence, his eyes darting every which way. "Where are the others? Can no one hear my cries, or those of my tormentors?" As he crawled along the floor, that same blue-crimson hue bled from underneath each door he passed. He knew then his servants would not stir, for this light had a strange way over all it touched. And even if he was able to rouse them, those foolish enough to answer his call would surely regret it.

On the other hand, if he left them to sleep through the terror, they might awaken tomorrow spared from his curse, at least for a time.

Too many poor souls have already perished on my behalf, he thought. *You most tragically, lovely Alma, eternal mother to my daughter.*

His mind was swimming. Gwyndolyn! Yes, his daughter, too, must be left behind, very sadly so. He had carefully calculated every aspect of this fateful circumstance a hundred times over, and had long since decided against rushing to her side. Doing so now would only endanger her, not to mention cause her pain. Besides, he had but cryptic admonitions with which to console her. What could be said? That he had subjected her to something so dire that she had inherited a great sin from him, one she would now suffer in his stead? That she would hate him all the more? That part of him lamented ever bringing her into the world of Essa? No, he would protect her from that burden as long as he was able, as long as there was a chance.

There's always a chance, he thought. *I locked her away from them for a good reason. Let me be the one to plunge into peril.*

Certain the apparitions could see him even in hiding, he spun down a tower of stairs to the second story, tore across several adjoining halls while daemonic stares followed along outside. A minute later, he entered the foyer with its pair of polished, winding staircases and practically threw himself down the left set. This was his only chance to lure them away and hope to disappear under the cover of darkness. Scrambling across the antechamber as large as a ballroom, he found it also drowning in that haunting hue. Heavy, ironclad double doors waited on the other end, which he tackled with a clang. It took every bit of his strength to part them. Then, with one last tortured look backward, he quit his home.

Lavender skies glazed even the dim courtyard. To the right, Lawrence's geldtmares lingered anxiously in their stable, some poking long, beaked faces and tall, narrow antlers like barbed pikes out into the moonlight. Others bucked their six hooves as they paced in circles within the night's shade. Lawrence's servants may have slept through the early aurams, but these large, loyal beasts of burden could not ignore his plight. They bellowed in beautiful, high-pitched cries like silvery sousaphones, each mourning as their master scrambled for his life. If he chose, they would've gladly carried him beyond the estate, but there was no time to ready them, and the outer gate would only bar their egress.

His stamina had all but disappeared by the time he crashed against said gate, a tremendous structure practically two stories tall, the prison trapping him in this nightmare. He struggled in futility to scale the metal bars.

"Climb, damn it!" he screamed, his grip already beginning to fail. "I guess this is it." He could hear the warbled hum of his pursuers gather from behind, and judging by the disparate clash of buzzing that hovered over the rooftop, he knew they would be upon him soon. The fact that they took their sweet time made him all the more frantic. He knew he had nowhere left to go, as did they.

Lacking the strength or temerity to face them, he did what was natural and turned inward like the recluse he was. "I deserve this."

How many times must you be forgiven, my dear Lawrence?

Lawrence shook his head in resignation. "Of course. Sorry, my love. I've failed you and Gwynny once again."

Not all is lost. Even now, there are those who fight for us.

"Sancta, you mean? You always spoke so highly of her, yet she and I never had the pleasure of meeting."

You will soon, I promise you that. And if it still be her will, allow me to intercede on behalf of our daughter.

Just as the ghastly stalkers descended to claim him, Lawrence noticed another shadowy figure adorned in dark, taut wrappings watching the madness unfold from a distant treetop. With ashen hair flowing chaotic in the wind, the stranger also seemed acquainted with those apparitions hidden to most others in the world, silently witnessed them swarming upon the gate only to pull away just as quickly. They vanished into the indigo haze, leaving no trace or lingering sound, nothing at all. Dr. Lawrence Carlyle was no more.

CHAPTER 2

A southern light dawned across the Waldean Plateau. It was a day just like any other, with the Solstar lifting slowly into the southern sky on its way to greet Mount Greneva. Her jagged throne covered the northeastern corner of the region, more north than east, delivering every morn the same stream of fog, this stubborn gift smothering patches of forest below. Countless birds soared overhead, landing upon the tips of tall pines floating above the haze. Rooftops, both thatched and shingled, rose closer to the mountain's base, where the crashing of bromidic bells filled the streets. Soon after, residents slowly emerged from their homes, meeting the day as they always did, with a quiet lassitude. Each hardly noticed the fog as they shuffled about in the hapless city of Greneva.

Everyone but Gwyndolyn Carlyle. She was a distance above the city, staring down from a lonely manor carved neatly into the mountainside. Her home in that fifty-room estate, normally quiet and uneventful, was now filled with sounds of maids cleaning and henchmen hauling away all manner of sundries: furniture and chests, their contents unseen. Even her formerly elegant quarters had been stripped bare by the movers the day before, much to her consternation.

Sulking in her bed, she revisited her father's sudden disappearance a fortnight past, recalled waking to screams throughout the manor. Her entire company of servants had erupted into a frenzy, each searching feverishly for their master. Dr. Carlyle had left nary a trace.

Over the next several days, they pleaded for Greneva's Enforcers to find their man, but with no threads to pull, little more could be done. Not long afterward, the case closed entirely.

Overwhelmed by the news, Gwyndolyn watched despair creep through the halls and hearts of her father's subjects. At times, some were too aggrieved to fulfill their duties, and she could tell they increasingly desired to abandon the cursed place. Not that she could blame them. She overheard a few discussing what to do next, perhaps managing in their lord's stead, but most had already given up hope. It was ultimately decided to hail the true backers of the estate, something that shocked Gwyndolyn, considering she knew nothing of such individuals. These distant stakeholders, once aware of the doctor's disappearance, apparently wasted no time in making the appropriate preparations. It was only a few days later when they came to collect.

They have no right to take my father's things, Gwyndolyn thought presently. She sat upright in her bed, despondent, and looked where her mirror had once hung, imagining the tall, beautiful blonde youth that used to meet her there. All that remained now was a single mattress and some personal belongings. She stared listlessly about the unoccupied space, unable to sleep without drapes to guard against the tyrannical light. How countless the aurams she'd spent in that room, yet its current surroundings were no longer recognizable to her. The colors, textures, and warmth of the place had already begun to fade from memory.

Perhaps it was better that way, she thought. Despite living

in a manor considered lavish by any reasonable standard, most of her memories there were unpleasant, though they really had no right to be. Her meals were always painstakingly prepared, her baths soothing and warm, wardrobe exceptional, yet she had become numb to it all long ago. Her staff made every day dull, and controlled every aspect of her routine. She grew resentful of them, loathed how they doted on her like a child, yet loathed even more when they left her alone. And most of all, she hated that her life, however empty, garish, and dull, had been suddenly taken from her.

Of course, her first impulse was to blame Father for such unpleasant developments. Dr. Lawrence P. Carlyle, renowned Noetic Clinician, practicing arbiter of the people's wellness, had vanished without a trace. This was all Gwyndolyn knew.

That man is always off one place or another, she griped. *He's probably somewhere lost in his head again.*

To her, his absence itself was less of a concern than the inconvenience it caused. At least, that was what she told herself. Those around her were shocked, stressed, and full of despair, yet by the day of her departure, Gwyndolyn could not find it within herself to commiserate. She was more agitated than anything, maybe even a tinge baffled at times, but mostly, she was just numb.

After all, their relationship had been estranged for as long as she could remember, and what time they did share was usually part of some Noetic exercise. Servants seated Gwyndolyn upon a cold leather sofa in his study before leaving her alone with the tall, overbearing man in his usual white robe over a gray trench coat. For a time, he would pace in complete silence while she admired the countless, colorfully bound books on stained shelves and an exquisite portrait of her dearly departed mother just above the dark, oversized, wax-polished desk. It was easily the most ornate room of the entire manor, one she despised him for largely keeping to himself.

Eventually, he would begin with the same perfunctory "How do you feel today?" followed almost certainly with "What did you do today?" No matter how short or long her response, he would scribble endlessly on his parchment, occasionally pausing to cast a long, probative stare. Then he would ask seemingly unrelated questions pertaining to past memories, or the contents of dreams, his keen perceptions dissecting every mannerism, recollection, and lie. She knew he could always tell when she lied. All sense of time often fled the space, and she feared his barrage of questions would never end, only for him to abruptly summon the servants to send her away without another word. *I'm glad he's gone*, she pretended to convince herself. *He can stay away, for all I care.*

The news of her relocation, however, was a different story. She was completely beside herself with the few details available, and the scores of questions unanswered. She revisited each one again and again. Where would she go? Which of her servants would care for her in the meantime? Perhaps some long-lost relatives? She knew of no such persons. Who beyond these walls even knew she existed? When would she be able to return? She honestly had no clue. Her mind remained as nescient to the world as it had been the moment they arrived in Greneva many annums ago when she was but a small child.

She groaned into her pillow before deciding to face facts. There was no use in fretting anymore. Wrapped head to toe like a cadaver, her body slowly rose from the bed and staggered against the onerous light to catch a glimpse of the commotion unfolding below. The Solstar was never particularly kind to her complexion, but it felt especially vexing today bouncing off one of the Trust's hulking aero-freights. Given the size of this craft, it might not have safely fit within the confines of the courtyard had it required wings to fly. She hadn't the foggiest idea how it managed to without them. From her vantage point, each worker moving to and from the vessel looked like tiny children or overgrown insects by comparison. She wondered whether she, too, would be tossed into the massive mechalurge like another piece of cargo.

Despite the chaos outside, she could hear a clock somewhere in the distance chiming fourteen times. Soon after, a rap at the door announced Gwyndolyn's governess, a kindly, austere, older woman everyone referred to as simply Matron. Her formal attire consisted mostly of a prim blue dress, matching heels, and a white ribbon tying her short gray hair into a bun. Among all the servants, she was really the only one Gwyndolyn looked forward to seeing. Matron entered the room, paused to take one look at the mopey girl on the bed, and shut the door.

"My Lady, surely you remember my instructions from yesterday?" asked Matron with a stern stare while motioning for Gwyndolyn to quit the warm confines of her sheets. "You are expected downstairs. Let's not keep the others waiting, shall we?"

Rolling her eyes, Gwyndolyn reluctantly shed her cocoon. "Isn't it the job of this manor's staff to wait on me?"

"It is indeed, but soon, no longer. I have been by your side for many an annum now, but today, we must say goodbye."

"But why?"

"You know perfectly well—"

"No, I mean why don't you come with me? Wherever it is that I'm going?"

"Unfortunately, that won't be possible."

"With that attitude," chided Gwyndolyn with the Matron's favorite rejoinder. She let out a soft chuckle, then paused sadly. "Don't you care about me, Matron?"

"Of course I do, but it's simply a matter beyond my control. Come now. You are too old to conduct yourself in such a lousy manner."

"Lousy, indeed." Gwyndolyn's face pinched with grief. "So, where will you go then? Some place I cannot follow?"

"I'm afraid my future is just as much a mystery. Worry not. Your new caretaker will mind your business much better than I ever could."

"Who is it? Family?"

Matron slightly averted her attention. "She is well regarded in Greneva, a confidant of your father."

"She knows Father? Then that makes me feel *much* better. Speaking of which, he has been such a pain as of late. He's surely gone on another unannounced sojourn across the Plateau. Hopefully, they will find him soon so that I can get on with my life here at the manor. When they do, who can I expect to send for me?"

"It's hard to say when, or if, that will come to pass. We'll just have to see. For now, let's attack that tangle of frazzled hair."

Matron removed a brush from her pocket as Gwyndolyn braced herself. In a way, she was glad the mirror was not there to reveal the unsightly creature on her head, or the battle about to ensue. It was a painful struggle, and hard-fought, but Matron was ultimately the victor, as she always was, weaving the untangled locks into a loose braid tied low at the nape of her neck.

"That wasn't so bad now, was it? Arms up! I'll ready your favorite dress."

Gwyndolyn stepped through the lovely, once-white dress her mother used to wear, a bit old-fashioned, and frilly at the knees. After Matron had properly laced its backside from waist to shoulders, she lifted one of Gwyndolyn's feet, pulled up a long silken legging, and then the other. Next, Matron helped her step into a nice pair of black boots before removing the frilled, gray-on-gray stitched overcoat hanging from the door hook. "There's that look again. It's a perfectly fine coat."

Gwyndolyn disagreed wholeheartedly. It shared too close a resemblance to her father's attire. "What a dreadful article," she said, dusting the old thing off, despite it needing no such treatment. It was buttoned up and down a few times before she decided to keep it tight. "At least it still fits."

There was a knock at the door.

"We'll be right out!" shouted Matron.

Gwyndolyn nervously rubbed her sleeves over by the window, where she took one last glimpse at the world below before finally joining Matron at the door and abandoning the empty room once and for all.

Another servant wearing a white undershirt beneath a blue vest, with pants and a bow tie to match, entered to collect the rest of her belongings before escorting both toward the manor's entrance. Every room appeared barren without drapes or pictures on the walls, the occasional chandelier, or soft rugs once stretched down each glossy hall. The foyer looked similarly vacant, save for a few packers and a line of Gwyndolyn's servants waiting near metal double doors joined within an arch. They jumped to attention as their would-be heiress descended the right of the twin staircases.

With a heavy sigh, Matron stood before Gwyndolyn, searching carefully for the right words to lift the despondent girl's spirits. "We are so glad to have served you, Gwyndolyn.

You've become a fine young woman. Please do not fret over your father. I'm sure he'll turn up sooner or later." Gwyndolyn's eyes softened somewhat, but otherwise stared dead ahead. "Take care of yourself," said Matron.

"Farewell," said another maid with a teary eye. "Your belongings are packed and waiting outside."

"Very well," said Gwyndolyn plainly. A part of her wished to speak further, but this was the closest thing to a goodbye she could muster. They all shared a moment of discomfort before two of the servants finally turned to open the doors. She recoiled at once from the light bouncing off the right door.

This has already become a headache, she griped to herself while taking leave of the others.

The weather was a little too breezy for her liking that day, though perfect for the haulers toiling about in the courtyard. The young men carrying the estate's belongings into the aerofreight quickly caught her ire. She hated how nonchalantly they stole away every part of her life bit by bit with absolutely no care or consolation. Without warning, two men lifted a sofa clear over her head from behind, leaving a musty stench in their wake, which made her wince. Their sleeveless white jerseys under uniform brown overalls almost dripped with perspiration.

Somebody of her station found these strangers and their enterprise quite unappealing at first glance. However, some began to win her over in ways she was not fully aware. A strapping lad tipped his hat her way while engaged in a bit of banter with the fellows. She found the manner with which they mocked and ribbed each other uncouth and sometimes vile, though at times strangely endearing. Their various fetes of unbridled strength and relentless stamina were laudable, perhaps even desirable, though she would never admit such things aloud. Most striking of all, they actually seemed happy despite their lowly position, something that could not be said for herself. She had spent so much time locked away that she had never even known such men existed, yet their vitality was bright and sure as the day was long.

There was one among them who did not share this sense of purpose and gusto. This unimpressive man combed back slimy black hair under the shade of a tree while carefully watching the haulers. His petty, disdainful eyes were waiting for one of them to slip or slack off.

"You!" shouted the man. "Yes, you, by the crates. Be careful with that or it's coming out of your pay!"

Presently, he stood to meet Gwyndolyn, who was now walking through the courtyard. She completely ignored him, and was instead fixated on the proper middle-aged woman in a modest, neatly pressed gray skirt suit, who stood near a similarly fancy coach tending to a pair of geldtmares tied to a glossy black carriage. The woman's matching high heels seemed painful to wear, yet they accentuated her posture, which remained rigid and unflinching. She had brown hair that she wore in a tight bun, and over her beady eyes were thin-framed spectacles, which looked ready to fall from the edge of her nose. Gwyndolyn reluctantly approached her, somewhat put off by the way she meticulously scribbled onto a clipboard just like her father.

"Ms. Gwyndolyn Almalinda Carlyle, seventeen annums elden, hair blonde, eyes blue, five scores tall, 120 mass," she read from the parchment before staring up at her charge. "Good day. You will refer to me as Madam Gebhardt, or Madam. I have been tasked with escorting you to Greneva, where you will henceforth reside at my Common Ward Institute for wayward youths. There, you will be required to perform assorted daily chores, as well as study at the local Grenevan Academy. So long as my expectations are met, adequate accommodations will be provided. How does that sound?"

"Hmm, yes," answered Gwyndolyn dismissively, her gaze averted to glance at the lad who had greeted her from afar. He was currently showing off a nice flex after singularly lifting a considerable parcel.

They are much more interesting up close than from a window, she mused with a faint smile.

Gebhardt cleared her throat. "My child, it is not proper to gawk at the help. Besides, we are on a tight schedule, so please pay me your full attention."

Before she could continue, the manager approached from their flank, obnoxiously waving to ensure they would not overlook his presence.

Gebhardt did so regardless until her papers were in order. "Is there something I can do for you, gentle sir?"

Upon closer inspection, the man was lousy even in frame, barely fitting into a white button-up two sizes too large. One rolled sleeve unraveled as he reached for his papers, almost covering his entire left hand, knuckles and all. Neither would say, but his attempt to look professional came across somewhat foolish. Standing upright, he combed back his hair once again before handing his business over to Gebhardt.

"Yes, yes. Just sign here, and we'll get the girl out of your hair." The man then looked Gwyndolyn up and down with a naughty grin. "You know, we could always use another to haul goods. Have any experience handling parcels and packages?" he jested to his own delight.

Gwyndolyn gave him a sour look. "Have *you*?"

His smile faded. "Only one way to find out."

"I do apologize," interrupted Gebhardt, "but there really

must be some sort of mistake. It has been made perfectly clear that *I* am responsible for the girl." Pulling a feathered pen from her jacket pocket, she signed her own formal parchment and promptly handed it to the man.

"That's not my understanding," said the man dryly. After reviewing her document, he scrunched his nose at the woman. "Anyone can draft their own legalese, but what proof do you have that she belongs to you and not me?"

"Not that it's any of your business, but I have the correspondence right here." Gebhardt flashed her clipboard just long enough to show an elegant crest of three overlapping circles, one that seemed to hold great meaning to him. Gwyndolyn recalled the symbol from somewhere before, thought it looked like some sort of flower, or perhaps serpents circling each other. Before he had a proper chance to scrutinize the letter, Gebhardt abruptly retracted it.

"Something doesn't add up here," he said. "My father is the manager, you know! He surely would have informed me ahead of time. I'm afraid you must remain until I sort this out with him."

Gebhardt's eyebrow twitched ever so slightly. "As I have already stated, the matter has been settled. Besides, I highly doubt you require any more *baggage*. Good day, sir."

With that, she and Gwyndolyn turned to leave, only to be yanked back by the wrists. The man was apparently done being disregarded.

"Unhand me!" shouted Gwyndolyn with great indignation. The Madam's face remained as composed as before.

"I will tell you when our business is finished—" started the man with a huff, his ego wounded. "Quit resisting, or I will call the Enforcers and have you thrown in gaol!"

Before Gwyndolyn or the man even realized, Gebhardt's

feather pen had driven straight into the man's puny forearm. Stupefied, he watched blood spill to the ground as she wiped the instrument on his drooping sleeve.

"Come along, Gwyndolyn," ordered Gebhardt, though it took a moment for the girl to collect herself and follow.

"Cursed slag!" he cried in vain, while his men glanced with pitiable looks. Gwyndolyn could see how their indifference pained him all the more. "Get back to work, you ingrates! No more breaks until every piece is packed up and ready to go. You hear me?"

Back at the carriage, Gebhardt straightened her skirt, the amusement on her face poorly veiled. "Now, where were we?"

Gwyndolyn wondered whether she would've been better off with the sleazy man after all. Considering what had just transpired, she quickly fell in line. "When do we depart?"

"Immediately," answered Gebhardt while adjusting her drooping spectacles. "That is, after you have secured your provisions. Load them, and we will be on our way."

One of the men must've dropped it off a moment ago, thought Gwyndolyn. Again, she stared around for someone to offer assistance, but there was nary a servant in sight. For a second, she thought to ask one of the haulers to load it for her but correctly figured that opportunity had since passed.

"Now would be lovely, *my lady*."

Gwyndolyn sneered as the woman disappeared into the carriage. *Come now, you can handle this*, she assured herself while wringing her hands. Soon after, she tugged on the top of the trunk, which easily resisted her feeble attempt. She made another attempt with her body leaning at a steeper angle, only to fall when both boots slipped upon the gravel road. Aggravated, she lifted upright and circled the hulking leather box a few times while dusting her dress. Eventually, she tackled it sideways in hopes of pushing it toward the carriage, yet for all her effort, it only budged a few feet.

May I never find the dullard who carelessly overpacked my things, she brooded while looking once again to the haulers. She watched them carefully hoist and heave before mimicking their bent posture. This time, the luggage gave way easier than expected and practically toppled the girl under its weight. Holding steadfast, she waddled slowly toward the carriage, step by step, and rested the package on the lip of the rear compartment. Then, with a loud grunt, she finally stuffed her things away, eliciting cheers from some of the men in the distance. Her pride was brimming, yet both shaky legs humbly delivered her back around the carriage.

Inside, Madam Gebhardt was seated upon a cushioned booth of green velvet facing the rear, her notes neatly covering a polished wooden table bolted to the undercarriage. Gwyndolyn gracelessly spilled over the opposite booth, though her fellow passenger was apparently too busy to notice. Once properly seated, she stared at the fancy interior and found it needlessly ostentatious for such a small space. Impatience soon set in as she waited for their departure, but before she could make a fuss, Gebhardt rapped thrice on the wall without so much as lifting her gaze. Without delay, a crack of the whip launched their carriage out from the manor's gates down a winding road to the city below.

Gwyndolyn watched the path twist endlessly down and around Mount Greneva's jagged hills. An urge to double back filled her as though she'd forgotten something, but she knew the carriage would not return. Sadly, she watched the manor shrink considerably in the distance, and soon, a thick wall of trees blocked it completely from view. Slouching on the soft velvet seat, she closed her eyes and let out a sigh while Gebhardt poured through more paperwork.

"You seem distressed," said Gebhardt finally to the disheveled girl. "I suppose you would rather return?" Gwyndolyn didn't respond. "By now, your home is most likely locked up, though I'm sure those men would be absolutely delighted to have your company."

"What would a bunch of packers want with me? I haven't the constitution for such arduous toil."

Gebhardt dismissed the girl's naivete and continued on. "Believe me, there will be plenty for you to do at Common Ward. Unlike your previous arrangement, most people there don't have the luxury of being coddled. Life in Waldea has always been a struggle, but never so grueling as the many annums following Gul'dan's invasion, the War of the Faith, as it were. Both then and now, our continued survival is only made possible by the Waldean Alliance, not to mention more recent intervention from the Trust. With any luck, both will help us build a life worth living soon enough."

Gwyndolyn's gaze remained fixated on the trees as they passed by the window. "The Trust? That is what you call those men from before?"

"In small part, yes. Most Waldeans on this side of the Great Chasm are unaware of the Trust beyond what contributions they made during the War. Their way of life, political disposition, and even their homeland is not well known. Needless to say, they are a powerhouse commanding an overabundance of capital, including aero-freights like the one you saw back at the manor. Their so-called technalurgy makes our lives on the Plateau seem horribly poor in comparison. Well, most of us anyway."

It took a moment for Gwyndolyn to follow the Madam's meaning. "No longer. From what I gather, my wealth has been squandered, thanks in large part to my father."

"You remind me of him quite a bit."

"I beg your pardon?" asked Gwyndolyn, her eyes locking with Gebhardt's for the first time in the carriage.

"Yes, of that I am certain. Absolutely antisocial and easily agitated to a fault. It's shameful such a man kept to himself the way he did. I can only imagine the sorts of brilliant insight floating around his head."

"Brilliant? Not quite the word I would have chosen. More like obsessive. And, for the record, we are *nothing* alike."

"Could have fooled me," the shrewd woman replied, amused to finally have her guest's full attention. "If you care to know, we met a while back, annums after your family first moved to Greneva. It was then, while working together, we exchanged a more substantial correspondence. He was a man of few words, but we developed an understanding over time."

"What sort of work?"

"He performed assessments on some of Common Ward's more disturbed children, so we kept in touch." Gebhardt lifted her spectacles by the frame.

"More than I can say," said Gwyndolyn, her eyes rolling back toward the thick forest outside. "You know not of his whereabouts? Nothing at all? Surely, there must be some clue as to what happened to him."

"Sadly, I do not," Gebhardt conceded softly. She paused for a moment. "I realize you are upset about leaving home. Life at the Institute may be different from what you're—"

"I'm sure it will be fine," interrupted Gwyndolyn, her face swelling with grief. "My estate often felt more like a gaol than a home. I had half a mind to leave moons ago. The people there treated me like a mental case, surveilling me every waking moment. I struggle to recall a single fond memory from all the time I ever spent there."

"Oh, I'm sure that's not true. Not even one of your father?"

Gwyndolyn fought back tears. "My father was always more focused on his work, his legacy, himself. So, no. Nothing comes to mind."

"You're wrong, you know. He cared a great deal about you."

"Madam, who are you to claim such things?"

Gebhardt allowed a short respite before continuing: "A few moons ago, I received a letter from your father requesting I collect you in the event of his disappearance, malady, or death." She paused again, as if waiting for some response. "It was a strange communiqué indeed, rife with paranoia—of what, I cannot be sure. He alluded to matters of a 'great quickening' in Waldea, something that could no longer be forestalled. I honestly had no idea what the letter meant and originally dismissed its contents, but it seems something is indeed amiss. Arrangements were made the moment I learned he had suddenly vanished."

"What else? He must have mentioned something else."

"Tell me again how little you care of this man." Gebhardt cracked a smirk before shaking her head. "This is all I know for the moment. Only time will tell how his fate unfolds, but more importantly, yours at least has been made secure. Rest for now. We will arrive before long."

CHAPTER 3

Madam Gebhardt's words hung heavily over Gwyndolyn for the remainder of the trip. Was her fate secure? What did that mean? This time was spent in silence, save for the hypnotic rhythm of dashing geldtmares lulling her to sleep. They continued along a narrow dirt path carved through the forest for maybe an auram before the clopping noises outside transitioned to a more abrasive clacking. She awoke soon after, aggrieved that Gebhardt was still poring through her work.

What could be so important in those stacks of parchment? she wondered as she stared out the window.

They had finally emerged from the thicket of trees onto a cobblestone road between weathered, thatch-roof log cabins scattered among the upper outskirts of Greneva. These run-down neighborhoods appeared secluded, almost forgotten in the hillside compared to the street blocks coming into view. Further down the way were dense rows of stone buildings springing up two and three stories high, some with stained wooden frames, others painted white or green, most with gray and brown rooftops. New streetlights were posted on every corner with somewhat opaque white globes instead of the lantern boxes she remembered from her last visit two annums ago.

Continuing through the town square, they passed many shops sporting various goods and services, some less modest than others, all with different-colored banners and decor. The carriage proceeded at a trot's pace, slowed by waves of passersby crossing to and fro. The delay was most bothersome, but she was fascinated, if not a bit overwhelmed, to see so many bustling about. Even more fascinating was that some of the people seemed to stare back with interest as if they recognized her. Soon, a crowd followed behind while pointing and chatting among themselves. She imagined herself the talk of the town, that noble girl suddenly transported from the lap of luxury into Common Ward with nothing to her name. It was already too much to bear without the entire community involved. There came so many onlookers that Gwyndolyn eventually closed the drapes in an attempt to escape them.

Before long, the carriage crossed a small bridge over the stream running through town, its waters like a moat guarding the rickety metal gate ahead. A chiseled sign outside the gate read "Common Ward Institute." Gwyndolyn noticed a few armed men in black suits of armor waiting, but she thought little of it. She saw them nod to someone, presumably the coachman who scrambled to open both gates and then returned to take his carriage inside, where Madam Gebhardt and Gwyndolyn soon disembarked. A tall structure loomed overhead, much longer than wide, erected with countless bricks of pure gray stone. The building was unique among others in the city, replete with arched windows, grooved ramparts with exotic carvings, and what appeared to be two hollowed bell towers at the forefront. A large dome protruded from the rear section of the massive rooftop with a creaky weather vane that strangely looked out of style. The overall size was comparable to the manor, yet Gwyndolyn was unimpressed by the drab exterior and lines of wet laundry drooping between some of the windows.

From Common Ward's double doors exited a tall, distinguished man of middle age with chiseled features and wavy peppercorn hair. He was followed at the heel by scores of cheerful youths, their filthy, tattered clothes quite the contrast to his dark-green cape wrapped around shiny, obsidian armor. He wore an impressive cluster of medals upon his mail, and an elegantly sheathed blade at his waist. The wards absolutely adored him and were very sad to see him go, but with a heartfelt smile and wave, he bid them farewell.

"Madam," he greeted with a nod on his way to the gates, where the men in black waited patiently.

"Good General," responded Gebhardt simply as he passed. Neither seemed particularly surprised or pleased to see the other, though their interaction was cordial enough.

"Who was that?" asked Gwyndolyn once the man had fully taken his leave.

Without turning, Gebhardt answered, "Why, none other than Sigurd Dietrich, Regent-General of Greneva and head of the local Enforcers. No doubt on another goodwill visit to Common Ward. He's quite a hit with the children here, but never you mind about that." She turned with an arm extended. "Welcome to Common Ward. Let us get you situated, shall we?"

Gebhardt then motioned for some of the cleaner boys to carry their new ward-sister's belongings inside. A couple were more than happy to comply. After a quick stretch, they lifted the trunk and marched together with it toward the entrance. Gwyndolyn scoffed at how easily they hauled the hulking parcel, though she was relieved to no longer be burdened by it.

While they walked toward the building, Gwyndolyn carefully watched the wards as they ran about like loons in the patch of foreyard. She had never seen such a number of them. Boys with mason jars wrestled and scoured the mud for insects while girls skipped around, singing cheerful nothings with makeshift ribbons in hand and hair. Each possessed a sense of levity she had long since forgotten, the whimsical contentment forged within a puerile conception of the world. She envied—almost resented—their happiness, questioning how truly pleased they could be without parents or any modicum of affluence. In the end, her cynicism only served to remind that she had become one of them, that her station in life had suddenly plummeted. The very prospect saddened her.

Gradually, they traveled into the lobby, where more children of various ages happily cavorted in every direction. Several of the older wards approaching to greet their Madam didn't expect another guest and kept a wide berth from the cold, unfamiliar face. Gwyndolyn returned the courtesy, taking in their curious stares while still behind Gebhardt.

Not a very warm welcome, she thought as her attention shifted toward a handful of unruly rascals clearly up to no good. Some were roughhousing in the commons, others tossing a shiny, stitched ball from both sets of stairs on each side of the spacious chamber. Their shifting stares suggested each were eager to see how long they could act foolish, and so far today, they were uncontested.

"Those checking in or out, form a line!" shouted a wide, exasperated attendant woman from the main desk, a large, squared fortress currently surrounded in the center of the lobby. Her frumpy green dress flowed ever so slightly every time she twisted about. "I don't know where your dolly went, all right? Today is the fifteenth. Check the clock for time! Little miss, your knee will have to wait. Calm down, it's just a scrape. Boys, that gift from the General is for outside only!" The

Headmistress's arrival gave her a sudden fright. "Everyone, single file, please!"

One look at the Madam instantly brought the wards in line and those in the distance to stop as well. "My dear children, if only you always acted so orderly. Let's not set a bad example for Gwyndolyn here." With an extended hand, Gebhardt guided her forward to take her place in line. "For your edification, we must check in or out with the attendant orderly, without exception, and never after curfew. Sign clearly in full with a precise time."

When it was Gwyndolyn's turn, the attendant instructed her to sign a thick binder with *Day 15 by the 6th Moon, 1212.* neatly written at the top of the page. She found this exercise quite tedious and unnecessary, despite being accustomed to others keeping tabs on her. Nonetheless, she wrote her full name on the next available line. A nearby dial helped her document the time as well. After a quick review, the attendant initialed the entry and struck it with a fat stamp before motioning for the next child to step forward.

Gwyndolyn proceeded toward a commons area at the rear of the main hall and noticed many of her peers still observed her from afar. Still, she was more focused on the vast, open chamber with its high, vaulted spaces a couple of stories taller than before, not to mention the peculiar designs found throughout. She lifted her gaze beyond the side balconies of the second and third floors up to a beautiful dome decorated with faded tapestries. One depicted a castle on the mountaintop crumbling as an aggrieved king and queen watched light rise from a nearby chasm. These illustrations were all very breathtaking, though Gwyndolyn was completely oblivious to their ultimate significance.

Returning her attention to the lobby, she found several others gathered around a large bulletin board under the left-side staircase. Various duties were posted next to each child's name, which apparently alternated every fortnight. Small golden ribbons riddled a couple of names on the list, signifying overachievement, while many had at least a few, and some had none at all. She had never seen such a thing before and balked at performing menial tasks for scraps of cheap fabric. Perhaps some magnificent prize was in store for whoever toiled the most. Yet, she couldn't imagine what sort of incentive would drive these poor souls into servitude.

Just as she began to turn away, a name stood out at the bottom of the list: *Gwyndolyn Carlyle*.

"What is this about?" she asked with a hint of consternation. "I haven't been here for more than a few moments, and you already insist on putting me to work?"

Gebhardt dawned a slightly devilish grin. "Surely, you didn't expect to stay here without some contribution? Here you are." She handed Gwyndolyn a parchment from her clipboard. "I've prepared your itinerary for the coming week, plus a few preliminary chores. See also the letter of curriculum from the Academy."

Gwyndolyn winced at the paper. "Acquire academic supplies? Purchase foodstuffs for supper? Why, I wouldn't know the first place to look for such things." Several of the eavesdroppers were amused by her look of confusion.

"Calm yourself, dear," said Gebhardt. "Proctress Alberecht is waiting down the street at the Academy with everything you need. Ask her nicely, and I'm sure she'll point you to Market as well. But make haste! The day will end quicker than you think, and these children can become quite sour on an empty stomach."

Gwyndolyn realized she had yet to eat a single crumb of food all day. She skimmed the grocery list for the night's menu and was left disappointed. That disappointment became despair as she flipped the page to her lesson plan. Apparently, every single reading and exercise dating back over two moons was assigned to her, with only half the time given to complete it. This, compounded with the new material assigned, struck her as a foul injustice. Every bit of it was due next moon for each class to review in preparation for a heavy round of examinations. Without Matron's exemplary tutelage and plenty of free time to digest each lesson, Gwyndolyn feared her education would be rushed, if not utterly stifled. "I have no time for any of this!"

"You won't if you don't get moving!" snapped Gebhardt, pointing to the door. Gwyndolyn thought to have the last word, but fearing her list might be amended, swallowed her tongue. After another quick glance at the parchment, she dashed toward the exit, but just before she reached the tall wooden doors, a slightly perturbed Gebhardt cleared her throat.

"Forget something?" she asked as the attendant at the desk waved from afar.

Gwyndolyn was already sweating by the time she reached the Academy. These grounds were even less impressive than Common Ward. If not for another large stone placard by the road, and several students swapping notes outside, she wouldn't have believed the simple brick building was a place of learning at all. The boys sported solid green jackets with tanned trousers, while the girls wore a greater variety of attire, including white blouses over various lengths of verdant skirts. Stopping dead in her tracks, Gwyndolyn ogled the group's apparel from afar, astonished they all had coordinated their wardrobes. She fancied them members of some exclusive club and wondered how she might join their ranks.

She approached the entrance, yanking the doors by their steel-looped handles, but neither would budge. Determined to gain entry, she gave them a considerable tug, followed by a furious rattle, which set off one of the girls studying nearby.

"Cut out that racket! Don't you know class is out today?"

"How can that be?" Gwyndolyn hollered back. "I was told a proctress was expecting me."

One of the lads looked up from his text. "Somebody should be inside. Try the side doors. But keep it down, will you?"

Unsure which way he meant, Gwyndolyn nodded before checking the left side first. There was a row of windows, but no doors in sight. She peeked into several of the classrooms, hoping someone would spot her outside, but every room was empty, save for a bunch of wooden desks. While circling toward the back of the building, she let a pleasant thought play out in her mind, one of sitting in class, front and center, impressing the other students with her brilliant beauty and intellect. They whooped and applauded along with the instructor, who showered Gwyndolyn with adoration.

Unfortunately for her, the daydream abruptly ended as she yanked another pair of locked doors at the rear. Her normal reaction would be to scream for assistance, but remembering not to disturb, she stomped over to the remaining side, where the last set of doors opened into the Academy.

Inside, her eyes gradually adjusted to the dimly lit vestibule. More bulletin boards lined the walls, along with countless hooks for coats and bags. Further down the darkened path, a sudden burst of laughter echoed from afar, one she followed to its source. Peering through the classroom door, she found two girls about her age roughhousing with wet rags in hand. There was a taller, freckled girl with long, wavy red hair and an obscenely red ribbon around her neck, accompanied by a less notable brown-haired girl. Gwyndolyn found the redhead clearly the more attractive of the two. Their laughter stopped when they noticed Gwyndolyn peeking from the door.

"Hello?" greeted Gwyndolyn, entering the room. "I heard laughter down the hall. What, pray tell, is so amusing?"

"You mean aside from that thing you have on?" quipped the redhead while exchanging an awkward glance with her friend. "Bethany, have you ever seen such a dreadful dress?"

"I beg your pardon? This was my mother's finest vintage dress. It's priceless!"

The long, elegant gown, though currently faded after countless uses, had once shined a vibrant white. It may have been a bit too lavish for most others to appreciate, but she adored it, as she did her mother.

"No, Scarlet, I don't believe so, though I hope Mummy found something more respectable to wear," sneered Bethany.

Gwyndolyn crossed both arms in a huff. "You will do well to not mock the dead!"

Bethany's pale face recoiled with embarrassment, yet Scarlet didn't miss a beat. "That explains a lot, considering the look *died* annums ago," she heartlessly doubled down, her glare at Gwyndolyn expressing great pleasure in her complete lack of tact.

Gwyndolyn shot a pained glare at the fiery girl, resisting the urge to further lose her composure.

"Why are you even here?" shouted Bethany finally after the uncomfortable silence had a chance to subside. "In case you couldn't tell, class is not in session today, *obviously*."

"I have come to collect materials for tomorrow. One of you, be a dear and fetch the Proctress for me," ordered Gwyndolyn with a slight chuckle. "Tell her Gwyndolyn Carlyle sent you. She's expecting me, of course."

"What nerve, ordering the Mayor's daughter to fetch like a mongrel!" scoffed Bethany, apparently a bit of a brownnoser.

Scarlet approached Gwyndolyn with a wrinkled smirk on her face. "Gwyndolyn Carlyle, is it? That's right, now I remember. You're that snotty girl from those boring dinner parties I used to attend up in the mountains. That is, before your daddy disappeared. What a shame. In case you've forgotten, I am Scarlet Rothbard, daughter to the mayor of Greneva."

At that moment, Gwyndolyn remembered seeing some awkward redheaded girl gallivanting around the ballroom, usually not far from the Mayor's side. He always went on about how his beautiful daughter would make a great leader herself one day. Gwyndolyn had never cared much for the girl and kept her distance, although they would occasionally exchange nasty looks as their fathers chatted idly.

Bethany attempted to introduce herself as well but was silenced by Scarlet's hand.

"Surely, you remember me, don't you?" asked Scarlet.

Gwyndolyn began to smile as well. "Oh, certainly. It's nice to see you've finally filled out somewhat. Speaking of dresses, yours never seemed to fit right, if I recall."

Bethany saw Scarlet's face burn with rage and quickly leaped forward in her defense. "Proctress Alberecht isn't here, *obviously*, but there's the door. Why don't you go fetch her yourself?"

"Most unfortunate! And I thought you were here to give me a tour." Gwyndolyn's taunt succeeded in rustling their feathers. "Then again, scrubbing the floor suits you better, *obviously*."

More blood surged through Scarlet's freckled cheeks as she glanced down at the rag in her hand. "That does it!" she shrieked before lobbing the dripping wad of cloth straight at Gwyndolyn, who barely dodged it.

Gwyndolyn's eyes were like daggers, sharp and narrowed. "Try that again, and I'll slap the red from that frightful face of yours!" Her threat loudly reverberated throughout the Academy just as a woman came marching down the hall. She rushed into the classroom to find the girls prepared to battle. Bethany grew pale as she spotted the burly figure looming in the door.

"You will do no such thing!" the woman exploded, stomping her foot against the ground. "What is the meaning of this?" All three shook with horror at the brutish woman.

"Proctress!" cried out Bethany. "We were just cleaning, as you instructed, when this girl came looking for you. She started *shouting* orders and then threatened poor Scarlet."

"But that's not quite how it happened, ma'am," Gwyndolyn objected.

"I don't care what happened," declared Alberecht. "Your words told the tale as far as I could hear. There will be absolutely no violence in my classroom, understood?" Her fearsome eyes admonished the girls, causing each to begrudgingly nod, no one daring to challenge her authority. Walking to her desk, she pulled out a stack of books and binders. "I have prepared your materials per Madam Gebhardt's request. Now, if you have no further business here, I suggest you show yourself out."

Gwyndolyn conceded as Bethany and Scarlet made all sorts of vulgar faces from behind the Proctress. Once her things were gathered, she headed for the door, almost forgetting to ask for directions. "Would you point me to Market?"

The professor said nothing, waiting to see if this new girl had one bit of tact to show after her outburst. Gwyndolyn looked to the girls for some indication as to why her request was ignored, and judging by their surprised looks, she finally got the message. "I—I'm new in town, you see. Point me to Market—if you please, um, ma'am."

The woman let out a disappointed sigh. "Go downhill, and then bear west. There will be many people toiling wares and wandering about, so I'm sure you can find your way."

In a last-ditch effort to save face, Gwyndolyn slightly curtsied and turned to leave, pausing to the sound of a throat clearing. She didn't bother turning about. She knew exactly who was addressing her then.

"I'll see you around, Gwynny," said Scarlet, her venomous voice ever so slightly sweetened.

CHAPTER

4

Gwyndolyn managed to reach the marketplace just before the Solstar began its decline. Her previous encounter took longer than expected, so she hurried past several shops, none matching the one written on the parchment. In the interest of time, she asked passersby for directions, only to be brushed off. Many people rushed to get home themselves and were too preoccupied to help. She considered giving up altogether when a few young men came from across the way, having caught wind of a pretty new face in town.

"You new around here?" asked one as she looked around.

"Why the long face?" added another. He and the others practically jogged to keep up.

"I must find this place at once," answered Gwyndolyn without turning. "Gotta's Grocer, I think it was called."

"No problem! Right this way, miss," exclaimed the third lad, all too eager to please. She took off almost immediately without saying a word, and they followed close behind, bombarding her with small talk and flattery. "Why, you look awfully familiar."

The first jogged in front of her before responding. "Now that you mention it, I think so too. Miss, aren't you that Carlyle girl from the papers?" She offered no response. "I'm almost sure of it! You're quite the talk of the town as of late."

I knew it, she bemoaned without addressing the others.

Everybody was talking about her after all. She offered no supposition as to what exactly was being said. She didn't want to know. Thankfully, the desired store was coming up ahead. Once they reached the shop, she shot the poor saps a lousy smile and curtsy before quickly entering without them.

Inside the grocer, a stocky young man with wavy dark-copper hair greeted unenthusiastically as she grabbed a basket and scoured the aisles. His fiery cape and matching headband, considered flamboyant to many in Greneva, was balanced with a simple white shirt over tan trousers and heavy boots. The front of his rotund frame sported a large pouch discretely composed of many bagged compartments and a long metal chain wrapped several times under the waist. Though larger and older than Gwyndolyn, he was only a couple decums of age, barely two annums out of the Academy.

Behind the counter, he leaned forward in his chair over a book titled *Know Your Steele: Fundamentals of Metalurgy*. When his bushy brow lifted at something of interest, he took a match in one hand and a long, hollowed pipe in the other. Then he very carefully struck the match, dropped it into the pipe safely pointed away from him, and reveled as sparks of various hues burst forth in a swirl of beauty.

Gwyndolyn was briefly dazzled by the colorful display but returned to the task at hand before he looked to see if anyone had noticed. Grumbling, he buried himself back into the book.

Gwyndolyn had already finished collecting every item from the list: hen-cockel broth bullion, flour, white amaranth stalk and seeds, plus a few loaves of bread.

Thoroughly impressed by her accomplishment, she looked to see if anyone had noticed, which none had, and grumbled right out the door. Incidentally, she didn't think to pay for any of the goods, and why would she? The notion of possessing and exchanging tin was foreign to her, a girl who need only ring a bell to receive anything she desired.

Taking her leave, she stopped half a block outside to check her things when the shopkeeper suddenly exploded from the grocer in a huff. This sent her scrambling around the corner in a panic, as she could hear him scream. "Young lady! Where'd you run off to? Get back here now!"

She had no idea as to why he'd become so ornery, and she had no time to find out. Quickly retracing her path through the Market, most signs of life had since faded from the darkening streets with a few still rushing to conclude their business. One such individual was a youthful lad bartering with pelt merchants up ahead. His tall, solid frame, light-olive skin, and pitch-black hair caught her attention from afar, but one look at the smoldering pair of auburn eyes stopped Gwyndolyn dead in her tracks. Her gaze traveled from his dark-leather jacket over burgundy shirt down to the tan trousers, which matched a large satchel strapped over one shoulder. She had never seen anyone like him, and his rugged looks effortlessly mesmerized her in a manner she didn't fully comprehend.

Before she could gawk further, he parted ways with the merchants, but his handsome features burned into her mind as the final glimmers of day brought her back to rights. Even further behind schedule now, she resumed a mad dash to her new home at Common Ward.

Back in the shop, the grocer slumped back in his chair, and wiped a drop of sweat before it fell from his damp headband. He repeatedly rapped the book upon the table with his knuckled fist, trying frantically to recall the thief's appearance. Only a girl in a white dress came to mind, surely not enough to recognize in a crowd. Dripping with anxiety, he gripped both sides of his fat head. "That's coming out of my pay for sure."

"Did you say something, Leopold?" spoke a similarly portly woman in a white bandana and apron over brown dress stomping downstairs with keys jingling at her side. It was none other than the owner of Gotta's Grocers, Momma Gotta herself. "Time to close up! Did we get another customer?"

"Uh, a customer, right. Somebody stopped by a moment ago," stuttered Leopold, untying his headband to wipe every trace of sweat from his face.

"Feeling all right, hon? You seem a bit clammy at the gills. Get some sleep tonight, you hear? I expect you to be up bright and early to open—"

"Yes, Momma," replied Leopold a beat too soon. She tossed over the keys, which his fat fingers fumbled next to the pipe still out in the open.

"What's this?" she inquired, pointing at the choom pipe. Smoke still lingered in the air. "You smoking the loopy cheroot, boy? Explains why you're dressed like a fruitcake. You kids and your fashion these days. Could it hurt to wear something more respectable in my shop?"

Leopold was always bad at covering his tracks. "You see—I can explain," he fretted, his large forehead continuing to dampen.

Momma was not happy. "And that book of yours—not this again. How many times do I gotta tell you? There will be none of that garbage under my roof, period!"

"Damn it, Momma, be reasonable for once."

"Don't you 'Damn it, Momma' me. I know of your fascination with metal and flame. The whole dreaded block knows of your devilry. Remember the last time I humored this hobby of yours? Our shop almost burned down."

Leopold swore he would never live down that incident. "One time, Momma, annums ago! With a smithy in the back, we can make all sorts of things people need, sell 'em for a good price. Think about it! Tinder fuel, craft jars, cast-iron pots and pans, eating utensils—"

"Weapons, armor, and explosives, am I right?" she interrupted.

"You always said you wanted to try something new. Selling foodstuffs and the occasional tincture just won't cut it anymore. Why not use the open flame to flaunt your cooking, make something for the patrons?"

"Don't butter me, boy. Open flame? In my shop? Simply out of the question! Your crazy experiments have lost us enough already. Besides, what kind of momma would let you go down the same path that got your worthless father killed in the War? Sancta, save his soul!"

"Not that again!" Leopold shouted defiantly, something done very rarely in the face of his mother. "Would you knock this 'Sancta' nonsense off? It makes people uncomfortable, and you know talk like that is taboo. If you ask me, it just as much explains why we've been scraping along lately. And don't pretend like I haven't seen you sneaking around to those underground Sh'tama gatherings!"

"No harm in a blessing now and again, is there?"

"The law forbids it!" he screamed, surprised to see his stubborn mother shrink back slightly. "But that's not the point. If it weren't for people like Pa, we'd be praying for mercy under the heel of a madman, to a god we don't even believe in, might I add."

"That *you* don't believe in, son." She began poorly sweeping the floors. "It ain't all bad though—believing, I mean. Just because somebody took things too far. You know, a few prayers might've done your pa good. Gregor was always aching for a fight, but in the end, he got cut down fleeing like a godless coward."

"No shame in retreating when the odds are against you. It was the logical thing to do."

Momma stared up at the framed sketching of her husband hanging over the stairs. "A whole lotta good that did him, bless his heart."

Leopold refused to give up. "He was only following orders. General Dietrich—"

"I told you never to speak that bastard's name in this house! If there's anyone I blame more than your father, it's that man!" It had been a long time since Leopold saw Momma so fired up. "This conversation is over. Lock up and get to bed, understood?"

She snatched his choom pipe, flint case, pouch of mysterious powder, and metallurgic text, missing a second bag he had discreetly tucked under the counter. Then, with a stern yet concerned stare, she stomped back up the stairs and turned in for the night. It was typical for the woman to neglect her duties, especially when in such a bad mood, but he knew better than to complain. Pacing back and forth, he cleaned the rest of the floors until he could hear her snore exploding through the awning.

Somehow she's already out cold, he thought on his way to lock the entrance.

Suddenly, a light jig tapped on the door.

"We're closed," he said, "but feel free to come back in the morning." The same rhythm rapped at the door shortly after, this time much louder. Afraid Momma would hear, he opened the door, something she told him never to do after dark.

Outside, a young man in a dark-leather jacket stared Leopold straight in the face.

"Come on, Leo, you know the drill," he said, poking his almost-black head of hair through the door. "Are we doing this, or what?"

"Give me a few, Laerzo," whispered Leopold fiercely while shoving his friend back outside. "I still gotta close up shop. And would you keep it down? I will never see the light of day again if Momma finds out what we've been doing. Now scram and meet me at the usual spot."

"Yeah, yeah," said Laerzo in farewell.

Leopold gently set the keys down on the counter and grabbed his remaining bag on the way through the back room to his quarters. Therein, kneeling in the corner of the room, he quietly slid a couple of wooden wall panels to the side, revealing a metal chest. He had personally crafted it and hidden it a while back when Momma was away in Thannick. Its construction was of amateur quality, one of his early works, but he loved it all the same. Unlocking it with his personal key, he lit with excitement at the sturdy, one-handed, metal hammer laying inside, the end of its hilt welded with a loop. Grabbing the hammer, he hooked it into the first link of his chain belt, grabbed a rusty-brown jacket, and was on his way.

Despite wearing boots never intended for sprinting, Gwyndolyn pushed up the daunting final hill toward Common Ward, her arms aching from carrying the foodstuffs all this way. She came to the foreyard, which was once boisterous and full of revelry but was now completely still except for the creaking of the weather vane. Beads of sweat streamed down her face as she imagined rows of starving children banging their spoons on the table, chanting louder and louder for food. The attendant failed to flag her down, as she sped straight toward the dining area and crashed through the doors. To her relief, the children were all sitting patiently with food already laid out before them.

Madam Gebhardt stood at the rear of the room, staring first to Gwyndolyn and then the others. "Children, before you sup this evening, I have a special announcement. One of your dear brothers, Henery, has been welcomed into a humble home by a loving family in Thannick. Will you please stand, Henery?" A strapping young lad stood before the gasping children. "There you are. Sadly, he will take his leave of us and Common Ward soon, but let us give him a loving farewell as he begins a new life in the Heartland."

The wards all stood and clapped while Henery simply bowed. They seemed more pleased at the news than him, but nevertheless, the room was filled with joy. When the space had fallen quiet again, Gebhardt continued. "That having been said, let us give thanks!" Still standing, everyone placed a hand on their chests and recited the following in unison:

"O Waldea, Cradle of Commonwealths, on this day we give you thanks. Praise be this bountiful meal, procured by the Reapers, without whom our bodies would wither. Let this nourishment given keep our mighty plateau strong and free like the Enforcers who secure it. To Waldea! To the Alliance!"

Then they all were seated and began to feast. Gebhardt motioned for Gwyndolyn to join her at the head table.

"Did I . . . make it?" asked Gwyndolyn, short of breath.

"Not quite, but I see you've at least made the effort."

Gwyndolyn stared down at her groceries, then to the

children happily stuffing their faces. "The others are supping, but how?"

"You seem almost perturbed by that fact. I suppose I should've made myself clear. Those foodstuffs you gathered were actually for tomorrow." Gebhardt beamed at the sour look on Gwyndolyn's face. "Surely, you didn't think we'd put those poor souls to bed with empty stomachs?"

"You tricked me!"

"I only wondered how far you'd inconvenience yourself for another."

Gebhardt then snapped her fingers, and a plate was placed on the table, mostly hot greens and a meaty stew, along with a tall glass of water. The food looked simple and bland, certainly nothing Gwyndolyn was accustomed to eating back home, yet her belly growled eagerly. Taking a large wooden spoon in hand, she proceeded to inhale the entire meal in short order, pausing only to catch an occasional breath. The water was refreshing, but she didn't notice. It served only to wash the food down her throat.

When the plate had been sufficiently licked clean, she looked around for a second one to attack, or at the very least some dessert, but there was none. There was, however, another set of eyes, large and unyielding, watching from down the table, unbeknownst to her.

"I think that's quite enough for now," chuckled Gebhardt. "You have shown some promise today, but more work awaits you tomorrow. Go upstairs and get some rest." She handed Gwyndolyn a simple brass key. "Your room is up the left staircase to the fourth floor, and the last door on the right. There you will find your things, along with some clothes for tomorrow. Class starts shortly after dawn, so do not be late!"

Gwyndolyn excused herself and began the grueling climb upstairs while her legs were still able. There she stumbled into a narrow hallway, where several girls chatted idly before bed. They giggled at the sweaty, disheveled mess of her damp attire, though a nasty glare quickly sent each into their respective rooms.

At last, she arrived at her own, unlocked it, chucked her bag of books inside the blackened space before entering.

Moonlit contours gave her a bare impression of the room. To the right, a large mirror hung above a wooden desk and chair. To the left, a nightstand facing a window, and a bed along the far wall. The current lodgings were considerably more plain and cramped than the last, but it still felt like home in a way. She thought nothing of having the space to herself, though most other rooms at Common Ward usually housed two or more children. Falling into bed, she lit an oil lamp on the nightstand and leaned over to unpack her luggage when a ghastly figure caught her eye in the mirror.

"My hair!" she quietly cried in horror, noticing several new knots and a twig twisting through the locks of dusty blonde.

The creature has returned, she thought while spilling through her things. Brandishing an old yet beautifully crafted wooden brush bequeathed by Matron, she tugged through the mess on her head, the figure in the reflection groaning in pain. Soon, only Gwyndolyn remained. The old brush, however, did not bode as well, with more of its bristles worn or broken in the process. She wiped the fatigue from her baggy eyes, turning to peer out into the night. Darkness had fallen over the city, save for faint lights glimmering in the mountains.

It can't be, she thought to herself, but there was no mistake. Out the window, however far away, she saw her former estate along the mountainside. And if the lights were lit, then people still dwelled within. *How convenient*, she thought. Was this also that woman's doing? She could not decide whether it was a vindictive gesture or a terrible coincidence, but regardless, the sore sight would be there every day to remind her of what once had been. On the bed, she sat in resignation, unable to avert her eyes.

That point in the distance, coupled with her run-in with Scarlet, brought to mind the various social gatherings she was forced to attend back home at the behest of her father. Their guests had been the usual trifling dignitaries and socialites, including the Rothbards. Conversation was a boorish experience, fluctuating between the perks of privileged high society to lamenting the slightest inconvenience endured at the hands of incompetent servants, sometimes in the same breath. Speaking excessively or out of turn was greatly cautioned, so she would keep to herself, smiling arduously at those who cared to make eye contact, always in agreement with whatever tripe happened to leave their mouths.

Despite the mind-numbing triviality of the parties, most of the guests were bearable, apart from a group of peculiarly dressed men that always surrounded her father. Some were no doubt military men from the Waldean Alliance, dangling medals over one shoulder and a blade at either side. Others were beneficiaries of her father's work, whatever it happened to be. It was then she remembered the same flowering triplicate of circles adorned on their gray trench coats.

The Trust, she thought, recalling how they'd ogled her throughout the evenings with cold, calculating eyes. Whenever they did, she suspected they were talking about her, though it was difficult to know for sure. The men's preoccupation persisted for several minutes until her father proposed a toast or invited them outside for a smoke. None ever approached her, though many seemed eager. Fortunately for her, most promptly left as soon as the party began to unwind. Even sooner would her father disappear, moments before she was escorted to bed. Those were truly sleepless nights, for images lingered into early aurams of the men's eyes ever upon her.

Once again, she was left with nothing but contempt for her distant father, and the current situation only gave more reason to despise him. Shaking her head, she finally pulled away from the window to unpack the rest of her things. An old photograph was pulled from the luggage, one of her long-since-lost mother, whom she adored despite no clear recollection of the woman. Her beauty was effortless, breathtaking. Every bitter thought held for her father was accompanied by a lovely, though probably contrived, memory of her mother. Gwyndolyn's most cherished dreams were replete with the same heartfelt embrace, accompanied by melodious declarations of love. She worshipped the woman in the photo, dressed as she did, wore her hair similarly. Sometimes she would even talk to the photo and recite the name signed at the bottom: Almalinda. Suddenly, she looked up to find that very woman by her side in the mirror and began to weep. She was frightened at first but quickly became entranced by her mother's eyes.

"Why did you leave me with him? Why did you leave me all alone?" lamented Gwyndolyn.

You are not alone, my darling, said the woman. Overcome with weakness, Gwyndolyn quit the day, once again cradled in her mother's arms.

CHAPTER

Class began with a mighty slap to the chalkboard, the usual sign of another grueling auram ahead. Each startled classmate sat on edge, hoping to be spared from the enormous quandary on the board, as well as Proctress Alberecht, whose thick hands tightly gripped her ruler. Neither boded well for the students, as she was surely in a terrible mood, but some would leave unscathed if they played their hand right. A few unfortunate stragglers would not.

"Now, who will solve for zed?" Gwyndolyn heard somebody say despite having dozed off a few minutes into the session. "Miss Carlyle."

Gwyndolyn then faintly recognized what sounded like a collective sigh of relief, though in that moment, she was too tired to care. She let out a deep snore from the back of the room, a lifeless body warped over her desk. The Proctress, still vexed from the day before, did not bother introducing Gwyndolyn in any official capacity. She knew Scarlet and Bethany, the only two who were already acquainted, and who eagerly waited for the humiliation to begin. It took but a few moments more for Alberecht to pounce. "Gwyndolyn Carlyle!"

Gwyndolyn jerked awake with a smear of drool on her face. "What . . . Oh, I wasn't—" mumbled Gwyndolyn incoherently, gaping at her peers.

"Now that I have your attention, solve the equation on the

board, if you would be so kind. You've completed the work for today, I take it?"

Gwyndolyn had browsed the lesson on her way to class, though surely not long enough to tackle whatever mess was written on the wall. A familiar laughter echoed a few seats ahead.

Alberecht sneered at the addled student. "To the board, Miss Carlyle."

Lacking the strength or pretense to refuse, Gwyndolyn sluggishly rose from the desk, trying desperately to recall anything remotely familiar or useful at all. She wore the dark-green jacket provided yesterday in keeping with the dress code, though decided to wear her favorite white dress underneath. It was barely in line with typical decorum, and as a result, she received some sour looks from peers on the way up the aisle.

As she stared incredulously at the board, what few symbols she did happen to recognize were arranged in new ways, with none of the numbers seeming to cooperate. As far as she could tell, they had been written completely at random.

What does Proctress expect me to do? she griped to herself. *What could possibly be derived from this abomination?*

After a solid minute, every effort to decipher the massive formula had been in vain. She was too proud to concede defeat, however, and decided to take a shot in the dark. She drew a disproportionately large 5 on the board, much to the others' amusement.

Gwyndolyn would not turn to face them, though she could feel the multitude of eyes slowly burn into the back of her skull.

Perhaps I am a bit out of practice, she thought.

Alberecht seemed much less amused, though a patronizing smirk broke through her frumpy veneer as she scribbled something into her notes. Gwyndolyn could tell it was nothing good. "All right, that's quite enough," said Alberecht. "Who would like to lend her a hand?"

"Oh, ma'am, I would love to help," announced Scarlet disingenuously while Bethany veiled her delight behind the cover of a book.

"Wonderful! Please join her up front," said Alberecht, her frustration shifting to adulation. She scribbled some more, this time with a pleasant smile.

Still facing the board, Gwyndolyn's body convulsed as Scarlet approached from behind, erased the previous pitiful attempt, and began to rework the equation. Each step was executed with celerity and grace as the class watched their proctress's favorite student in action. A few moments later, the problem had been broken down so that even Gwyndolyn could understand. Scarlet finished with a subtle cheap shot, solving with an especially large 9, which garnered some snickering from her peers.

"Very good, Scarlet!" declared Albrecht, all pride in her profession suddenly restored. "I hope you were paying close attention, students. Miss Carlyle?"

Indeed, Gwyndolyn could not help but fixate on the big-headed, know-it-all classmate the entire time as a blinding hatred coursed through her being. "Yes, very much so," she said, her spurious smile fading quickly. She wondered how much brownnosing Scarlet had employed to afford such hubris, wondered whether any amount of flattery or pleasantry would earn herself any good graces here. Not with Scarlet around, not today, maybe never. Gwyndolyn didn't know which was worse, being utterly humiliated on her first day, or watching the teacher's pet puff with conceit. As she returned to her seat, she could hear Scarlet whisper, "Daddy too busy to help study?"

Gwyndolyn stood over the inked quill on her desk, clenched it tightly as she sat down and seethed until the bell rang into high dawn. This met the students well as they poured out the door, glad to have survived the Proctress for another day. Gwyndolyn was not so fortunate. She found Alberecht standing between her and the exit.

"Not so fast. That board isn't going to clean itself."

Lunch was already in full swing by the time Gwyndolyn managed to escape. All but a few scraps of food remained in the cafeterium, mostly biscuits and some manner of lumpy stew. The selection was stale and appalling, but she reluctantly loaded her plate with what appeared the most edible. Finding a place to eat proved equally miserable, as most seats were taken and those still available were guarded with demeaning looks. Several trendy classmates packed tightly around Scarlet in a corner table, while everyone else sat as close as their popularity would allow. Awkwardly enough, Bethany tried to join the conversation from an adjacent table. Gwyndolyn wanted to stay as far away from them as possible, however little she favored sitting next to the foul, clamorous kitchen.

She slouched into the nearest chair and choked down some biscuit bread. Unbeknownst to her, an oddly anxious yet pleasant girl stared from across the far side of the table, trying not to appear too conspicuous. Thin, mousy features hid behind round, abnormally large spectacles magnifying her brown eyes into almost comical proportions. Any forehead not eclipsed by the massive saucers was covered by brown bangs nearly as long as her bowl-shaped cut was short. Like most other girls at the Academy, she wore a nice short-sleeved white blouse buttoned high at the collar, and a green dress that extended past the knees. Light bouncing from her bulky glasses caught Gwyndolyn's attention before long. "Would . . . would you like some?" asked the girl, scooting closer while pointing to her pudding. "I've already had my fill, so it's no trouble."

Gwyndolyn poked a few times at the odorous, pale-brown goo. *At least it looks more appetizing than the slick on my plate*, she thought. With a nod and a slight smile she snatched the bowl and forced a spoonful of its contents down her throat.

"You're Gwyndolyn, right?" asked the girl with a pensive smile. "We've never met, but I've heard others talking about you." Gwyndolyn stole a quick glance, but then her eyes promptly returned to her plate. "Have you really been cooped up in the mountains all your life? If so, I hope you weren't terribly lonely." The girl paused again. "Oh! I forgot to introduce myself. I'm Maybel, tenth class here at the Academy." Again, there was no response, but Maybel soldiered through the silence with a seemingly effortless contentment, almost defiantly cheerful.

Gwyndolyn grimaced for a few moments before abruptly dropping her spoon on the tray. "How did Scarlet solve that equation so quickly? She made me look quite the fool."

"Goodness, that's rough," said Maybel after Gwyndolyn remembered to compose herself. "Having trouble on your first day?"

"Something like that."

Maybel's eye sparkled. "You know, I deal well with numbers and figures. It's no big deal, but my best marks are in the Arithmetics."

"How very impressive," replied Gwyndolyn with a lazy sarcasm.

"Oh, no! I didn't mean it like that." Maybel took a moment before trying again. "Is there any way I can help? With your studies, that is."

Gwyndolyn's attention perked. "Perhaps. Yes, I suppose that would be helpful." She lifted her heavy satchel full of texts onto the table. "I have so much to do, you see. Including some unfinished duties back home. At the Institute."

"Ah yes, you are at Common Ward!" declared Maybel. "I live there as well, on the second floor."

"Is that so?" asked Gwyndolyn, tilting her head inquisitively.

Maybel beamed a curious smile. "Yep, been there since I can remember. How do you like it so far?"

"I suppose it's acceptable, but the others there . . ." Gwyndolyn paused, briefly lost in thought. "They don't seem too pleased by my arrival."

"Don't worry about that. They're just getting to know you in their own way. Maybe I can help break the ice—that is, when they've had some time to adjust."

Gwyndolyn appreciated the gesture, though she didn't find it especially compelling coming from the girl. "Could you?"

"Well, can't say I'm close with many of them myself, but all of us wards look out for each other. We're family, for better or worse. You'll see!"

"I suppose I will," answered Gwyndolyn with a guarded smile just as the ringing bells prompted everyone to their next session. Grabbing her things, she stood to leave, and briefly turned to nod fondly at the chipper girl.

"It was nice meeting you," said Maybel, bowing with books cradled in her arms. "See you around."

CHAPTER

6

Time seemed to drag on endlessly through Proctor Perdue's mind-numbing lecture. This shriveled, elderly man with balding gray hair was clearly struggling to win, much less keep, the attention of his pupils. Fellow faculty members had recommended he retire annums ago, yet none could seem to find a suitable replacement for the marveled mind. Despite an amazing penchant for all things historical, Gwyndolyn overheard in passing that the haggard man was best known for putting most students to sleep, sometimes even himself.

On the verge of her second nap that day, Gwyndolyn understood this all too well. While she appreciated his soft voice and kindly demeanor, he sorely lacked the vigor exhibited by the other instructors. Especially now, as today's lecture broached a topic most students were already bored to death of covering—the War of the Faith, as it was called throughout the Plateau. Purdue spent most of his energy dithering about things a generation past which every Waldean with a pulse would know. Gwyndolyn too was aware of the peace Gul'dan destroyed with their fanatical invasion of Odgen's southern shores, though she didn't pay it much mind. Instead, she opted to stare blankly at an elaborate map of the region hanging on the wall. The last thing she pondered before nodding off was how long a trip through the Heartlands of Thannick would take to reach Stolgrum in the west. Some time later, the bell woke her and others to Perdue droning on about their most unexpected alliance with the Trust, and their mysterious disappearance after helping to defeat Gul'dan.

"Oh, remember we have a quiz tomorrow regarding Waldea's reconstruction after the War," he announced to the few students yet to take their leave.

Gwyndolyn stumbled into the halls, relieved to survive her first day at the Academy, however daunted she was by the remaining backlog of work. The reading alone would take a fortnight to complete, new assignments notwithstanding, and if the lessons were anywhere near as bland and irrelevant as the material covered today, she might very well die of boredom before the task was done. At the moment, the prospect didn't seem so bad, though she was much more preoccupied by another matter, something more subtle.

A quick glance around the hall revealed two girls discreetly mocking her from afar while several other students passed with dismissive stares. It was the same uniform coldness she felt back in the cafeteria. Her peers, it seemed, had unequivocally rejected her from the moment she set foot on school grounds. None bothered to greet and welcome her, not even so much as wave, but they were not ignoring her after all. She wished they were. Their condemnation gripped her with grief, wounded her confidence. Perhaps she had neglected to keep up appearances since coming to town, but looks alone would not garner such hostility—not that quickly, anyway.

It was then she remembered what Maybel had said earlier: "I heard others talking about you."

But who even knew to talk, and what tales would they tell? thought Gwyndolyn. The only person who came to mind was—

"Scarlet," she muttered low. *Has that girl already begun to plant seeds of discord? Have I been made into a dullard, some half-wit hillbilly? I will not let this stand.* With hands clenching to fists, she decided to head back downtown for some personal provisions. And once properly presentable, she was certain they would come flocking to her yet.

Turning the corner, she found Maybel waving eagerly from down the hall. This should have lifted Gwyndolyn's spirits, but it soon became apparent that her singular friend was a bit odd, with awkward mannerisms and a slightly puerile development. This observation did not sit well with her newfound insecurity. The others would surely disapprove of anyone found consorting with such an oddity. At present, she had no choice but to take her chances with the girl.

"You're late," whispered Gwyndolyn after pulling Maybel aside.

"I'm sorry. Are you ready to begin studying? If what you said earlier is true, we have a lot of ground to cover—"

"There has been a change of plans. I must be on my way to Market, but perhaps another time."

"Oh, I have a couple of errands to run down there as well. Would you like some company?"

The proposal caught Gwyndolyn off guard. "Well, I—won't really be there long, you know, just picking up a few things. A new brush, powders, a sewing kit if available." Having no real reason to refuse, she ultimately capitulated to the power of Maybel's cheerful disposition. "Fine, let's just be quick about it."

Making haste from the Academy, they reached the Market with plenty of day still hanging over Mount Greneva's lofty peeks. The streets were bustling with rows of vendors waving wares at onlookers dressed as properly as they could manage. Children pawed at colorfully bannered windows showcasing candy neatly stacked while their folks admired fine frock and frippery through adjacent panes. The crowds moved in waves unwittingly, sometimes nudging others into shops they could not afford, only to rejoin the mass of wandering desires largely unfulfilled. Life in Greneva had always been hard, being a product of the War and all, but most were happy just to scrape by as long as they could indulge every now and again.

Through the clamorous rabble, Gwyndolyn noticed a ping-ing of sweet sounds down the block from a procession of strange individuals wearing gray garb crossed between a robe and trench coat. They marched triple-file, a couple dozen strong, led by a conductor of sorts who flicked finely tuned, double-pronged pitchforks both short and tall in various tempos and intensities. These enchanting instruments caused surrounding lampposts to glow, quickly fascinating those nearby. Their melodies, though rich and unique, were not familiar to these parts. Every one of the figures wore sleek bands over their eyes like single-lensed goggles, the side of each device labeled VISI, which displayed vibrant images in motion. They did not speak, yet their song quickly attracted droves of bewildered bystanders.

Many of the youth followed along jubilantly; however, those fortunate enough to remember the War firsthand trembled as if living those terrible days anew. What they feared was not the procession itself but what it represented, or rather, what horrors came in its wake. Of the fearful bunch, concerned guardians pulled their children away while others persisted if only to witness the ominous spectacle. Some even shouted in protest, though their voices were easily drowned out by the ordered cacophony.

Gwyndolyn found it all quite unusual, yet she couldn't help

but fight for a closer look while Maybel trailed several paces behind.

The sluggish parade continued apace until an armed cadre standing ahead blocked their path. In times of strife, these Men of the Law were soldiers of the Waldean Alliance, but in peacetime, they were simply known as Enforcers. A signet engraved on their obsidian chestplates, the upward arch overlapping a downward dome, likened to a mountain being rooted in one's hand. Each wore a pair of dark slacks over black boots with a tightly sheathed blade at the waist. Some stood fast with stern glares and arms crossed, while others beat bully clubs against their palms as they approached the leading man.

Maybel managed to squeeze up next to Gwyndolyn just as the conductor brought his troupe to a halt. Both noticed strands of golden hair peeking from under a hood only he wore, and though they could not see behind the visor, he appeared younger and more vibrant than the rest. Unlike their typical gray attire, his shined a brilliant white, its hem laced with neon tubes glowing in a shifting array of color. Maybel appeared absolutely mesmerized by its resplendence.

With a wild smirk on his face, the conductor fearlessly stared down the Enforcers for a long moment until one moved too close for comfort. He then bashed the bottom of his long pitchfork to the ground, along with some of his cohorts, emitting a foul, unsettling tone that drove the official back in warning. Disquiet quickly grew among the captivated crowd as the Enforcers surprisingly made way for the procession to pass. Raising his pitchfork triumphantly overhead, the conductor instructed those in his employ to proceed, though they did so under careful surveillance.

Many assumed the Enforcers had buckled, though they were simply repositioning for the coming confrontation. Upon arriving in the spacious square downtown, the performers suddenly found themselves surrounded, with more men blocking the path once more. This time, they were joined by Chief Montgomery, deputy to the Regent-General of Greneva, though most just called him the Chief of Law. "Dispense with that incessant flicking!" ordered the chief.

The conductor gestured his troupe to abide before bowing to the men in black. "Greetings, Enforcers. What brings us together this glorious day?"

The others all bowed in unison, wands to hearts.

Chief Montgomery stepped forward. "There have been reports of an unauthorized procession through the city. I would say you folk fit that description quite nicely."

"That we do. What of it?"

"State your business at once."

"Does one need a reason to walk these streets?"

"When disrupting the public order, yes."

The young man's arm extended to the audience as if to include them in his company. "Curious, the public seemed orderly enough to me. Verily, each among us took part in this joyous procession. Would you stand against them all in kind?" Gwyndolyn noticed the exotic fibers of his robe light up in measured accordance with every syllable he spoke. The wondrous sight caused Maybel's bulbous eyes to light up as well.

"We'll ask the questions," barked another Enforcer. He clumsily spit some chew on the cobbled road, ground it with his boot. "Quite the outfits you've got there, all matching features and such. If I didn't know any better, I'd say this was a religious march."

"My man, to call those among us religious would be sheer folly. For you see, the religious wrap themselves in adherence to some Molder in the Shadows they will never meet. That is not our way. We distinguished members of the Trust do not seek out hidden makers, only that which can be perceived. Our convictions lie down the path of *true knowledge*."

The chief shook his head dismissively. "You claim this march is not for some Grand Exemplar?"

The conductor tilted his head with a laugh. "What would we call her? Lady Wisdom, perhaps. She practically makes us gods in our own rite."

"You heard him, sir!" a third Enforcer bellowed. "A cult, if I ever heard one!"

The conductor let out another quick chuckle. "But a joke, my friend. Our purpose here is simply to test and calibrate the lampposts recently installed in these parts. Nothing more, except maybe to spread a little cheer through otherwise dour streets."

"I don't believe you," said Chief Montgomery.

"That word. It rings a bit *religious*, does it not?"

"Silence! You have one more chance to state your true purpose here."

"Our purpose has been made abundantly clear. We humble members of the Trust—"

The chief pointed his club at the young man. "I don't care who you people are! The law is the law. Pursuant to Enforcer code 7 mark 11B, we command you stop this unlawful assembly at once."

The conductor's smile widened. "As you can clearly see, we have already stopped. And now it is you and yours who have disrupted the public order. What gives you the right which we have not?"

"I will not repeat myself!"

"Then don't."

The conductor's smile was almost goading them to approach, and a couple of Enforcers did just that. The first attacked, and though his club's swing was sure, he inexplicably missed his mark. The other's attempt was no more effective. He lost his balance altogether after the bludgeon seemingly traveled through its target. Completely unscathed, the conductor stared blankly at the staggering man as the previous Enforcer came back around from the right for another shot. The strike quickly met the ground. By now, it was becoming clear that some sort of trickery was at play, though none had ever seen anything like it. Both flummoxed aggressors had no choice but to retreat before long.

"What an unfortunate display," remarked the young man disingenuously. "Is this how Waldea greets her allies? Please allow me to expound upon our intentions if you are so desperate to know." With his declaration, the Trust struck another ominous tone before lifting their wailing wands on high.

In moments, the clouds above began to part, and from them descended a bulky, metallic vessel humming steadily over the widening crowd. Like many of the younger folks, Gwyndolyn had only recently seen these remarkable crafts appear in the sky, though she recalled Matron mention them soaring over the Great Chasm in the final days of the War a generation ago. Gwyndolyn found this particular ship similar to one of the aero-freights seen back at her estate, only smaller and a bit rounder, almost fishlike in shape.

Still hovering, the ship lowered a ramp for the Trust to board, though in the meantime, their leader remained to keep the Enforcers at bay. Just as they closed in to intercept him, he suddenly vanished in a flash of light that sent ripples of excitement through the crowd. Everyone eagerly looked for him while the vessel lifted skyward, and soon, the mysterious figure appeared once again, this time on its roof.

"Meek and downtrodden," he shouted, "hear me! Decams ago, Gul'dan arrived at your shores bearing the Sh'tama faith, and with it, promises of salvation. Yet, for all their sanctimonious bluster, they left you with nothing but death and suffering in the end. Though we across the Great Chasm on the mainland had no interest in burdening ourselves with your plight, the atrocities committed during that most Unholy War were too much to bear even from afar.

"And so, whether through pity or self-preservation, the Trust finally roused on Waldea's behalf. Just in time, too, for none among you would even be here today had we not intervened. Together with the Alliance, you were spared from Judecca's Conquest, but we could not unsee the looks of bloodlust still brimming among your faithful. Even before the conflict, the Sh'tama had made its course through the land, and sooner or later, we feared the War would be waged anew. Ultimately, our forces left you to pick up the pieces, and so have your miserable lives continued to crawl alone through the squalor.

"But our predecessors were misguided, and your suffering too long-lived! While we continued to rebuild and prosper all this time, your Polities, the varied Commonwealths of Waldea, have subdued you, suppressing every aspiration for something better. Mistaking fervor for faith, they hid away every last scrap of mechalurgical innovation left in our military's wake. In so doing, they unjustly bridled you with limitation. My friends, I feel your pain, for I was once a simple Grenevan like you, bound by misery. But no longer!"

"He's from Greneva?" asked Maybel.

"The Trust's renewed vision of prosperity," continued the conductor, "will render those long days of toil and strife into nothing but fleeting memories. I gaze upon a sea of disbelief, but fear not! Knowing is its own blessing; it does not require faith. Every wondrous advancement employed in the War, the mechalurgy of steam-powered wagons, geared cannons, fledgling aero-craft—all were but a preamble to the splendors of a new revolution. Even now you marvel at its wonders with no conception of how it works.

"I speak to you of technalurgy! Through it, the blind see clearly beyond the horizon, the enfeebled rise to withstand any burden, the ignorant wizened from the stupor of hopelessness. It has cast off the shackles of my ineptitude, given me new life. Its Light can transmute perception into reality, and very soon, even reunite us with the dead! This miracle is why I have come to you today, though I am not actually *here* at all."

With this, his likeness vanished again, giving the crowd quite a show as the Enforcers tried to force them back. Like most others, Gwyndolyn was shocked, though she noticed Maybel appeared less shocked and more curious, seemingly strangely cognizant of the presentation's true nature. Gwyndolyn watched her squint through her bulbous glasses as if able to see the conductor for what he was amid the flowing, flickering light, as if she could see right through him if she focused hard enough. The discovery hardly seemed a bother given her bright, inquisitive nature, but Gwyndolyn could tell the girl was dead set on learning everything there was to know about this extraordinary spectacle.

"Technalurgy..." whispered Maybel in awe.

Gwyndolyn, on the other hand, had grown wary of the entire thing. *Something is vaguely familiar about all this*, she thought. *Is it a premonition?* No, the procession didn't stand out so much as something about the men's glossy uniforms. Through some reticent impulse or emotion, she briefly recalled the gala back home, where similarly clad figures surrounded her father, their clinking glasses reminiscent of the humming in the air. It was a sensation she quickly buried back into the depths of her memory, though she could never fully forget.

Without warning, the conductor's likeness projected large above the vessel for all to see. "Curious how these Keepers of the Law act against every interest of the people while we seek to make your lives whole. What a shame that our work should be impeded by the likes of them! Sadly, we must say farewell, but I leave you with one simple question: Will you allow these men to keep Greneva down in the mire? Only time will tell. Goodbye for now!"

With this, the ship lifted away toward the mountains, leaving the Enforcers to deal with the excitable crowd. Many appeared to have been made quite ornery by the speech. The men in black saw this, locked into formation, and approached mere feet from where Gwyndolyn and Maybel stood.

Hearing shouting from every direction, Gwyndolyn felt a swelling pressure from the crowd as simple arguments quickly morphed into veiled threats. Both girls stared uncomfortably at one another, each realizing the impending danger but not knowing how to react. And before either could decide, a burly man burst between them, bowling both of them over while winding to throw the first punch. Gwyndolyn arose, shocked and shaken, but not as much as the Enforcer who got clocked square in the jaw and dropped to the cobbled road.

In a flash, Gwyndolyn was swept up in a scuffle of around fifty people—mostly men but some women, and not to mention the twenty Enforcers. Pressing through anyone who would budge, Gwyndolyn escaped through the crowd, noting the desperate expressions on everyone's faces, who had clearly long been aching for a fight. For a split second, it made her wonder at the conductor's words, whether they had rang true with the Grenevans. She heard the Chief of Law's deep, booming voice order his men to quell the mob, and with that, the brawl was on.

By then, Gwyndolyn had thankfully retreated, but turning, she realized Maybel had not followed. Staring back through the chaos, Gwyndolyn noticed her friend had been caught apart, forced into a line of surrender with her arms up. For a moment, she thought to intercede but panicked and fled when an Enforcer several paces away shouted her over. There was nothing she could do for Maybel then, and the last thing she wanted was to be in the papers again.

"Sorry, Maybel," she said, finally ridding herself of the commotion. Promising to check back later, she returned to the task at hand and traveled several blocks from the square toward a promising boutique along the eastern edge of the adjoining forest with a sign that read "Willow Creek Boutique." It seemed the perfect place to seek out her desired items, even if she didn't think to purchase them.

As she made her way over, however, Scarlet emerged from its doors with a handful of girls, Bethany included. Gwyndolyn was incensed by their sudden presence, yet undeterred from her destination, she veered closely behind a couple of strangers also approaching the shop. There, she listened to Scarlet prattle on about the limitations of their tawdry uniforms while offering questionable beauty tips. Bethany, always aiming to please, lapped up every word, shamefully praising her idol's obviously superior sense of fashion. Though Scarlet did love the attention, she rolled her eyes while quickly changing the subject.

Unfortunately for Gwyndolyn, it was not long before the strangers providing cover caught wind of their unwelcome guest and split, leaving her completely exposed. With nowhere left to hide, she expected to be discovered within seconds, though the girls were all too self-absorbed to notice her lurking nearby. Nauseated by their petty posturing and sorry banter, she decided to stroll around the block in hopes they would be gone when she returned.

The alleyway led to an area she found somewhat familiar, and for good reason. Gotta's Grocer was just around the corner, where she witnessed the portly young man from the other day shaking out a dusty rug. He was wearing the same flamboyant attire as before, but with a tan jersey. They unwittingly glanced in passing, and though neither recognized the other at first, the corner of her eye caught a glimpse of his incredulous double take. She was several paces away when she heard something heavy flop on the ground.

"Hey, you!" he shouted, to the surprise of her and a few other passersby. "Thought I wouldn't remember you? Ha! Guess again!"

She was caught completely off guard by the man's aggression. Flinching, her pace hastened as she continued down the street as calmly as she could.

Just keep moving, and things will be fine, she thought. *He's probably yelling at someone else anyway.*

On the contrary, his inflamed outbursts continued until half the block was looking directly her way. She refused to address his violent accusations, though another brief glance over her shoulder confirmed he was, indeed, following her.

In a rush of panic, she quickly rounded into another narrow road heading back toward the boutique. She ignored the jingling keys growing more pronounced from behind but briefly twirled toward a crashing sound, which was actually Leopold tripping over a woman taking out her rubbish. This gave her time to clear the alleyway into the open street, weaving between a smattering of people to give her pursuer the slip.

She might have too, if not for the girls blocking her way again, this time through her only clear avenue of escape. She leaned back around the way to find Leopold inching closer through several bystanders, though he hadn't spotted her just yet. Even worse, Scarlet's posse was beginning to move Gwyndolyn's way as well. With moments to spare, she quickly crossed the street while pulling part of her unbuttoned green uniform jacket over her face, then dove through a bush just as Leopold emerged from the crowd. He nearly toppled Scarlet and the others in the process, each pausing to wince at the sweaty mound of man before taking their leave in utter disgust.

Gwyndolyn may have narrowly escaped, but the ground immediately beyond the thick brush suddenly escaped as well, sending her twisting turbulently down into the forest. She landed at the bottom of a fairly steep hill with an audible thud, laying there for a moment before murmuring some garbled malediction. Every bit of wind had been ripped from her lungs, and nausea set in as she reeled from the nasty spill. She fought a terrible churning inside until her pained wheezes normalized into more steady, shallow breathing.

There was no telling if the man still gave chase, but she was unwilling to take any chances. Stumbling upright, she was only able to take a few steps farther until forced to rest again, this time behind a tree. Every breath remained a chore, and her sides ached in pulses, but at least nothing seemed sprung or shattered from the fall. After some time had passed, she considered heading back to Market but did not trust her legs enough to climb the hill. At any rate, it seemed unwise to return for the time being. She decided instead to trail along the hill, reenter town farther along the path, and find help. Maybel, she remembered, would hopefully be looking for her.

As she continued on, a small log cabin caught the corner of her eye from behind a distant patchwork of trees. Though not especially noteworthy, its secluded presence strangely drew her closer before long. She began to make out the nicely trimmed bushes outlining its foreyard when something suddenly whipped her violently upward by the left foot. The way it tightened around her boot suggested it was a rope, though her flipped dress made it almost impossible to see. Against her better judgment, she tried screaming out as her body dangled helplessly, but only sobs could escape her trembling lips. Being ensnared was terrifying in its own right, but she was more concerned somebody might see her exposed in such a compromising manner.

Just then, something rustled abruptly in a neighboring tree before landing nearby. She could make out the sound of footsteps approaching.

"Who's there? Let me down at once!" she cried at the boots peeking below into her narrow line of sight, but there was no response. In fact, the individual hadn't produced a single noise since halting before her. "What are you doing? Don't just stand there. Let me down!"

Only her pleas were left unanswered. She squirmed hysterically while horrible thoughts creeped through her mind, like some degenerate had arrived to put his hands on her. Her fear only intensified when he began rummaging through a bag suddenly dropped with a clank at his feet. She could see several tools, a few metal traps, some rope, and a bloodstained knife.

He is going to gut me after all, she thought.

Her heart pounded harder, faster with every passing moment, so much that she feared it would burst from her breast. As every breath became more difficult, she hoped to pass out before he went to work. Just as she began to fade, a shrill, deafening cry tore through the air.

CHAPTER 7

The lingering shriek haunted the air for some time. Its pitch was high like a teakettle, deafening like a storm. There was a certain metallic ringing in its undertone which sounded fowl-like, though Gwyndolyn knew of no fowl that could rattle an entire forest. It rendered time a strange thing with seconds passing as aurams. Her eyes were clenched shut all the while. She fixated on the echo far after it had faded, anything to distract her from the dread building in her breast.

Finally opening her eyes, she noticed the boots previously peeking into her narrow line of sight had suddenly disappeared, wondered if the man had fled from the terrible cry. If so, she thought, he must've been too afraid to take his bag of goodies with him. However, this was not the case. She heard a voice beckoning from afar, either from that man or another, reigniting her fear as she gasped ever harder for air. The voice was unfamiliar to her, but at least markedly different from the shopkeeper's. For this reason alone, she assumed it came from the cabin. The rope's constant spinning made it difficult to know for sure.

"Hey, there you are," said the voice, and soon there were two pairs of boots standing beneath her. "Not something you see every day. Aren't you going to introduce me to your new friend?" There was no response. "Didn't think so. Anyone ever tell you it's rude to keep a lady hanging?"

Gwyndolyn would have screamed if dangling there

hadn't made her so horribly lightheaded. She witnessed the newcomer's boots retreat, presumably to scale several branches of the tree that kept her. The other pair retreated again as well, though not far. She experienced a quick shaking through the rope, felt a sawing gradually sever bundles of fiber above.

It's about time they release me, she thought with equal parts relief and consternation, perhaps a sliver of gratitude as well—that is, until the rope snapped and sent her crashing to the ground.

She might have met it headfirst if not for the sturdy pair of arms catching her around the waist. This exceedingly awkward moment caused her to snap about as quickly as the rope, with both legs flailing about. And the moment one of her kicks connected, she was unceremoniously dropped on her head.

Gwyndolyn rose before the tall, sickly man standing over her, took in his long silver hair tied back into a tail, and the callous, apathetic look on his wiry face, which only served to wind her up again. Poised to give him a slap, she felt her hand grabbed by the other man from behind, and reflexively spun around to strike him instead. Before she could, he pulled her close to his chest with a fierce tug. Blushing, she could do nothing then but stare up at her assailant.

It was the strapping young lad in vermilion who'd been haggling the other day. "Calm down, yeah?" he sternly whispered while her body tussled like a netted fish. "I'll let you go if you promise to behave. We have a deal?"

Gwyndolyn didn't expect it, but his auburn stare into the blue of her eyes ignited a contradictory mess of emotions. Her defenses were up, but she felt safe in a way, almost happy.

Strangely and suddenly, something else roused within her, evoking her mother's visage from the other night.

He will never do, darling, said the voice with a hollow warmth. *You deserve better.*

This took Gwyndolyn by surprise, and out of disbelief, she shook her head.

This, the young man took as a no to his offer. "We're not here to harm you, honest! Let's start again, yeah? My name is Laerzo. Tell me yours."

"G-Gwyndolyn," she stuttered, still uncertain what had just transpired. "I am calm. Please release me, if you would."

"Gwyndolyn," he repeated, somewhat smitten with the name. He released her slowly with a smile on his face. "Sorry for putting you out like that. We have snares set for game. That is, me and Gustav Grimstad here. Some call him my partner in crime. Say hello to the pretty lady."

Gustav, as if accustomed to Laerzo's foolery, simply bowed with a hint of acrimony. Dark, faded clothing closely hugged his slightly gaunt yet sinewy physique, along with what appeared to be a bow-like device folding compact over his right wrist sleeve. Even more notable was the set of thick bandages crisscrossed diagonally at his neck, surprisingly white and well dressed. As he picked up the severed rope from the dirt, a few long locks of sterling gray fell over his pale face. Apparently agitated by the trap's destruction, he made his way over to Laerzo and tossed the piece of rope at his feet.

"Criminals. Splendid," said Gwyndolyn while approaching Gustav cautiously, her finger pointed at his face. "This creeper just stood idle without uttering a single word. I thought the absolute worst!" She then leaned in uncomfortably close, gawking tactlessly at the bandages twisting around his throat.

"What ails you, Miscreant? Someone clip your collar? Or are you perhaps damaged in some . . . *other* respect?"

Laerzo quickly stepped in to defend his friend. "Hey now, no need for that. Gustav's not simple, if I take your meaning. Just the strong and silent type. It's been like this since we first met annums ago. He never told, and I never asked. It just works out better that way. As for the bandages, I'm not sure about those either, now that you mention it. But enough about him! I'm more interested in your story. What's a lass like you doing romping around in the forest?"

Gwyndolyn ran shaky fingers through her dirty hair for a moment while collecting her thoughts. "I cannot say for sure. It was very unexpected, to say the least. Some crazed man chased me down the street for no reason at all! I managed to lose him through the bushes, but also lost my footing in the process. Had quite the fall. And before I knew it, I found myself strung up like a ham."

"That trap was not meant for you, yeah? You see, we hunt game to peddle pelts and meats for a living. Do a pretty good job of it too, I must say." With a brazen smirk, Laerzo briefly glanced at Gustav, then back to Gwyndolyn. "You happen to be the largest thing we've scored in some time! Quite impressive, really."

"Oh, it is all very amusing, isn't it?" asked Gwyndolyn while trying to hide a smirk. "It's no wonder you took your sweet time getting me down."

"Hey, come on. It wasn't like that at all," Laerzo played down almost convincingly.

Before she had the chance to hear his explanation, the two of them were startled by another sudden shriek piercing the sky like the one from before. They twisted toward Gustav holding a long, steel whistle to his lips, and his keen eyes fixed upon multiple pairs of tall, sharp ears jutting from the distant brush like daggers. Soon, one fengalin emerged with a hungry stare, his flappy, fanged jowls smacking with drool. Though barely half the size of a geldtmare, this vicious creature was twice as voracious, sporting feline features mixed with the muscle and snout of a mongrel. Normally, the sound of Gustav's whistle was enough to keep most predators at bay, but this particular specimen seemed determined to stick around. Another handful or so were spotted waiting deathly still within the bushes.

"Buddy," muttered Laerzo while cautiously unsheathing a beautiful, cerulean-jeweled dagger with his left hand.

Gustav did not address his partner, nor did he wait for the fengalin to act before preparing his wrist bow. With the mere pull of a string, the contraption snapped into form, but in the same moment, the fengalin hastily charged from the brush. Still, he was already taking aim with remarkable calm. Gwyndolyn practically jumped when he masterfully unleashed a sharpened steel bolt through the eye of the leading beast, slowing the pack momentarily. Nodding to her, he blew his metallic whistle, evidently the same one from before, in swift retreat as the beasts chased him up a tree in the distance. Fortunately for him, fengalins weren't the best climbers, though their persistent leaping kept him scrambling from branch to branch with little opportunity to reload and strike again.

Gwyndolyn noticed a couple of the fengalin turn her way. She slinked behind Laerzo, who was already preparing to do battle with his dagger and a weathered steel guard strapped to his opposite forearm.

"I would grab something if I were you," he said in a stone-cold manner, pointing her toward a sturdy branch nearby.

Stripping its leaves in a hurry, she gripped the makeshift

weapon tight, just in time for their attack. Laerzo's heightened posture, flailing blade, and loud grunting slowed their advances briefly, but one of the fiends called his bluff with a fierce sprint. It managed to tackle Laerzo to the ground and pin him under its heft as it gnawed mindlessly on the metal of his guard.

Gwyndolyn shrieked, and before she could even think to intercede, the other was already charging her way. She swung her stick a few times in a fit of panic, startling the fengalin long enough to crack its head with a swing. It wasn't much phased though, countering with a snap of its fangs that caught her sleeve and grazed her arm in the process.

The sharp pain threw her off balance, causing her to collapse under the foe's weight. Even worse, her head struck against the grass. The world was a blur. Crying, she was now at the mercy of her attacker, which released her arm for the perfect opportunity to rip out her throat.

It would have succeeded too, if Laerzo hadn't intervened in the nick of time. Leaping onto the ravenous foe from behind, he stabbed it time and again with his silver dagger until it went still.

Shaking, Gwyndolyn squinted to where he'd been previously attacked, found the other fengalin sliced neck-down with most of its guts spilled to the ground. She assumed the threat had ceased as he helped free her from underneath the hulking corpse, but it let out a blood-curdling death cry, which promptly attracted the other fengalin. Still lost in a painful haze, Gwyndolyn could faintly make out their menacing approach, as well as Gustav's whistle, which failed this time to steal back their attention. Another bolt was loosed from his wrist bow but missed its mark by a hair.

Even if Gwyndolyn was able to stand on her own volition,

there was no way Laerzo could protect them both from the beasts. He might be able to best one, maybe two if he was lucky, but three in concert would surely tear them to ribbons in no time flat. Their bloodlust was truly frightening to behold, something she had never before witnessed, but Laerzo's refusal to back down gave her strength. Staggering upright, she steeled herself, knowing there was no other option but to fight.

This remnant of the pack had closed most of the gap when a fuming pouch suddenly landed a few feet in front of them. "Heads up!" shouted a gruff voice.

Heeding the call, Laerzo promptly fell to cover Gwyndolyn upon the ground. Just then, the pouch erupted into a cacophony of cascading colors, driving the fengalins back in fear. Gwyndolyn noticed something swing through the hazy aftermath like a glimmering rope, but she was too stupefied to make sense of anything. The soaring object sent one fengalin flying several feet away with a devastating blow, and coming back around, crushed the second one's head entirely from above. This sent the last fiend in a mad dash toward Laerzo and would've had him for supper if not for a swift bolt shooting through its neck at the last second.

Smiling stupidly, Laerzo jumped to his feet and met the husky figure stepping through the smoke. It was none other than Leopold in all his bombastic glory. "You smooth son of a—Hey, Gustav, get a load of this guy!"

Gustav checked to ensure every beast had been slain before responding with a stern nod, but Gwyndolyn still felt danger in the air. One look at Leopold's fiery scowl reminded her why.

"Girly, take another step and it'll be the last thing you ever do," grumbled Leopold, his hammer still swinging. She could tell the huffy, sweat-covered man hadn't run that hard in a while and wasn't looking to set a personal record any time soon.

"It's okay. All is well," said Laerzo, his brow lifting curiously. When Leopold stomped toward Gwyndolyn, Laerzo quickly blocked his path with both bloodied hands thrown up in surrender. "Good Dread, Leo! What's gotten into you?"

"This damn broad left my store the other day with a bunch of stolen goods!" raged Leopold, leering over Laerzo's shoulder. "So, I see her outside the shop today and she just blasts around the corner. I almost busted my gut trying to catch her."

"I only ran when you started after me like some maniac!" replied Gwyndolyn most indignantly. "Besides, I have stolen nothing from you. I don't even know you!"

"You can do better than that! You honestly thought you could lift an entire parcel of my wares without paying, did you?"

Such a foreign concept had never before crossed her mind. It took a long moment to even understand what he was saying. "But . . . I was not informed of any such payment!" She wondered how someone as meticulous as Madam Gebhardt could have forgotten such a vital detail. *How was I supposed to know?* she thought while awkwardly fielding stares from the others. "Look, I thought everything had been arranged, all right? Don't take me for some vagabond."

"But you'll take me for a fool! Lady, I don't claim to know you, but I know well enough that tins are the only 'arrangement' me and Momma accept as legal tender."

Unsure what to say, Gwyndolyn looked to the others for aid, though Gustav had wiped his hands of this trivial matter only to dirty them skinning one of fengalin nearby. The only one left to help was Laerzo, and judging by the look on his face, he planned to do just that.

"Hold on a second, Leo," he said calmly. "How much was the bill again?"

"Nearly twenty-five tins," grumbled Leopold.

Laerzo reached for his pouch. "All right, if I throw twenty-five your way, will you quit this?" Naturally, Gwyndolyn's attention perked.

"The due is hers to pay, not yours," answered Leopold, his ire beginning to subside.

"And pay she will. To me, another day," assured Laerzo with a smile, jingling his moneys around. "Let's put this misunderstanding behind us, yeah?"

Leopold thought it over while ironing the wrinkles from his stubby chin. "Fine, that'll have to do."

Laerzo gladly forked over the tin, making sure to wink over his shoulder to Gwyndolyn when he did. The smirk on his face quickly faded thereafter. "Right, you're hurt! Wait here, I'll be right back." He ran toward the cabin in the distance.

Gwyndolyn had forgotten all about her injuries. By now, most of the bleeding had stopped, but her other wounds were dirty, and the gash along her head needed dressing.

Soon, Laerzo returned with some supplies, mostly torn strips of cloth and a vial of clear liquid that smelled strongly of booze. Dabbing one strip with the vial's contents, he used it to clean the dried blood from her face before wrapping it around her forehead. The bandage stung, but it hid neatly under her bangs.

"Now, give me your arm," he said and wiped down the other scratches and lacerations with a separate piece of damp cloth. Finally, he dressed the wound with a quick tug over the knot, which sent sharp jolts of pain up her arm, though she didn't complain. "There we go. Much better."

"Thank you," said Gwyndolyn while staring into his gorgeous eyes. "So—Laerzo, was it? Do you ... live here alone?"

"Yep, just me for some time now. It's not paradise, but I get along just fine. Beats Common Ward, anyway."

"Wait, you lived there as well?"

"Yeah, since I was young, up until a few annums back." His eyes veered away uncomfortably.

"Why did you leave?"

The subject clearly made him uneasy. "It was just fine until the headmistress suddenly resigned and Gebhardt took over. Something about her always bothered me, but I could never figure out what. But everything changed after my friend—no, my ward-brother—disappeared."

Gwyndolyn assumed by Gustav's exaggerated sigh that Laerzo had told this story many times before.

"I don't understand it. He seemed fine to me, but one day, Gebhardt and some clinician started asking him questions and performing tests. The next few days, he said very little and then, just like that, he was gone. Not just him either. Some of the wards started disappearing as well, though at the time I just assumed they left to start lives outside Common Ward. Never saw a single one in Greneva again."

The notion hit Gwyndolyn a bit too close to the heart, and her eyes began to swell. "Do you mean he left the Institute too, or ..." She interrupted herself, too disturbed to finish her own thought.

"That's just it. I checked around if anybody had seen him, but nobody knew a thing, not even his bunkmate. After a while, one of the aides pulled me aside and told me to stop asking questions, or else." He had started pacing back and forth. "One day, I finally confronted Gebhardt in front of everybody during supper, and I demanded to know the real story. But I never got it, just the same nonsense. I called her a liar, plus a couple of other things, and stormed off. Before she even noticed, my bags were packed and I took off, never to return."

"I—was only trying for small talk," she explained awkwardly. "I mean, I didn't intend for you to—"

"No, it's okay." Still, Laerzo seemed all too eager to change the subject. "By the way, thanks for saving us, Leo. You showed up just in time."

Leopold puffed with conceit. "Well, I had all but returned home after looking for this one here when I heard Gustav's whistle. It was more shrill than usual, so I snuck my hammer out the back door and hurried over. Never expected to see those fengalin though. Don't they only hunt at night? And alone, for that matter?"

"That they do," said Laerzo while nodding to Gustav. "We've noticed some strange things in the forest as of late, but this definitely takes the cake. Guess it worked out in the end though, yeah?"

"Damn right!" cheered Leopold.

Gwyndolyn had had her fill of excitement. "Well, I really must be going. That is, unless there are other traps lying between here and Market?"

"Hold on a second," said Laerzo. "Can I see you again sometime?"

"What? I—I don't know."

"Come on, let's start fresh. At least give me a chance to make up for today."

Gwyndolyn paused for a long moment. "Perhaps, but you've already done so much."

"Well, we could, uh, go out. On . . . on a picnic!"

"A picnic?" replied Gwyndolyn and Leopold in unison. Gustav shook his head at the amateur while ripping fur from another fengalin.

"Sure! What do you say? I promise you won't be disappointed."

Leopold's thick brow shot up. "I suppose a nice meal couldn't hurt," he said, slapping his belly. Gustav also expressed some interest.

"I suppose," said Gwyndolyn. "But it will have to wait until after the midterm exams."

"All right, sounds good," said Laerzo with a hint of sadness. It appeared his plan to get the two of them alone had backfired. "Are you sure you don't want me to lead you back to Market?"

"No . . . no, I should be fine now. Really." She didn't believe that for a second but was too nervous to say otherwise. "It's this way, right? Right. Farewell for now."

"Take care not to get caught in any more traps, understand?" joked Laerzo, eliciting an incredulous stare from Gwyndolyn. "Kidding! Just kidding. You should be fine."

Gustav chuckled at the remark.

Waving goodbye, Gwyndolyn left them and headed back to town. By the time she returned, the day was late and the crowds had thinned. Scarlet and her posse were long gone. Gwyndolyn walked a couple of blocks before finding Maybel outside the boutique.

"Gwyndolyn, there you are! Where have you been?" she asked, picking up her bags from the ground. "My goodness, what happened? You look completely out of sorts!"

"It's a long story," replied Gwyndolyn, too embarrassed to tell her miserable tale. "I see the Enforcers let you go about your way. Did you find everything you needed?"

"Yeah, though the shop left its wares completely unattended. Not very smart, if you ask me. They're lucky someone didn't burgle the place." Gwyndolyn's eyes lifted slowly from the stuffed bag to Maybel's curious smile. "I left some change on the table, of course."

"Some *change*? That doesn't sound very academic."

"Well, there was probably enough to cover the bill, at least most of it," said Maybel with a wink. Just then, a scream blasted down the street that Gwyndolyn recognized as coming from Leopold. Maybel giggled most suspiciously before handing Gwyndolyn a separate bag. "By the way, I stopped by this here boutique as well. This is what you wanted, correct?"

A hairbrush, sewing kit, and some makeup were inside. "Why, yes it is," said Gwyndolyn. She was somewhat taken aback by the selfless gesture, assuming Maybel hadn't helped herself to a five-finger discount. Despite all that had happened today, everything turned out all right in the end. Thinking back to the forest, an idea suddenly struck her. "Say, Maybel. Do you like picnics?"

Later in the evening, Gwyndolyn returned to her quarters after supper. She'd received yet another act of kindness: an additional helping of stew, courtesy of the Madam. Considering all that had happened prior, she did have quite the appetite, though it possessed a certain odiousness and discoloration compared to the first bowl. Reluctantly accepting Gebhardt's good graces, Gwyndolyn finished the stew without much fuss, though it sat poorly in her belly, like she had just downed a bitter pill.

Currently, she struggled to concentrate over a mess of

parchment on her desk. Fatigue was already setting in, but the exams were quickly approaching, and she was still far behind schedule. It was difficult to tell what dragged her down more—the tumultuous day or the double meal. Probably both, she conceded, though in hindsight, that second portion of mush was definitely the bigger mistake. Her bloated gut left her feeling lethargic, yet she managed to get some more studying in before bed. Finally, with eyes drooping, her head lay down to rest.

Later still, she was jerked awake by a strange sensation. "What? Who's there?" she muttered, stumbling from her chair in a sleepy haze. Did it come from outside her door? Little could be seen in the dimly lit room, save for silhouettes moving to the lamp's flickering flame. At first, the shadows danced ever so slightly, but soon, the entire room began to sway as a strange malaise bore down on her, causing her to grip the chair for support.

It was then that a figure emerged in the mirror, wearing an exquisite white gown flowing against a wind that wasn't there. The woman's glowing amber hair was propped up mostly with several small daggers while the rest joined the dress's mysterious dance.

She looks so familiar, thought Gwyndolyn before again buckling against an onerous weight she couldn't describe. This time, she found herself cradled in the woman's arms despite the figure remaining but a reflection. She bathed in a warm light, though her touch froze against Gwyndolyn's skin.

My darling . . . Gwyndolyn.

It took a moment for her to realize the voice did not originate from the visage in the mirror, but rather from the depths of her mind. Gwyndolyn turned to confront the specter but found herself alone in the room. She wished to discount the experience as a mere dream, but the chill down her spine convinced her otherwise.

Don't you recognize me?

Upon further inspection, the lovely figure shared a striking resemblance to the woman framed on her desk.

"Mother?" whispered Gwyndolyn, unable to believe her eyes. "Oh, Mother, I have missed you so!"

You wound me, child. I have always been with you, in your thoughts, your dreams . . . always at your side. I am that which cradles you through the night, protects you from the wickedness of the world. Truly, you have not forgotten your very own beloved mother?

"No . . . no, I have not!" she cried out, quickly remembering the time of night. "I just cannot remember the last time we spoke . . . face to face."

Yes, you have been awfully preoccupied as of late. But who can blame you? Everyone flocks to you, my darling. Especially that boy in the forest. The woman's light faded slightly.

"There is something about him, Mother. He fascinates me. I yearn for him."

I yearn for you, darling. Leave that wastrel where you found him. He could never care for you like I do.

"I adore you, Mother. It's just that, the way he looks at me, I—"

No! There is no love in his affections. Pure selfishness belies his desire for you. He will remain by your side so long as he can exploit you, no longer. Then he will hate you just like the rest. Just like your father.

"I don't understand. What do you mean?" Gwyndolyn's gaze wandered from the mirror, only to be pulled back by a sudden force.

Their kindness is a mask, wrought of wicked wants. Same

with all the rest, even that mousy friend of yours. They simply covet your beauty and grace for themselves. Surely, you must see the envy gushing from their pores.

Gwyndolyn heeded her words, yet could not help but dwell upon the mention of her father. "Does Father truly hate me so?"

Without a doubt. From the moment you were born, he resented the bond you and I share, felt alienated by it. When he couldn't have it, you were sequestered away, and when he couldn't stop it, he disappeared. He abandoned you, child. Your abysmal fate is a direct consequence of his selfish nature.

She tried to deny it, but the words rang true in her heart. A terrible distress sent tears streaming down her cheeks. At this point, the voice had become hollow and ethereal. *My dear, please do not despair. It was for the best, after all. He never loved you. He couldn't. All men are slaves to petty egos and libido. They simply lack the capacity for love.*

"Mother?" uttered Gwyndolyn with shallow breath, her bones aching, and her skin all but numb.

The woman continued to speak as her glow slowly faded with the candlelight. *Trust no one. Every smile is a veiled sneer, every praise a curse in disguise. Show compassion, and they will only betray you in the end. They wish to victimize you at every twist and turn, but I will never leave your side! You are entitled only to the best, my dear. No one is more worthy of love than you! And I love you so. We must always be together . . . always, together.*

By then, all life had left Gwyndolyn's eyes. "Always, together . . . always." With a final flicker, the room fell to black.

CHAPTER

Gwyndolyn remained in bed minutes before her final day of exams, offended by the clocks ringing down the hall. *Did it strike seven or eight?* she pondered while drifting back to sleep. A fearful nag in her warned not to delay, but she'd lost too much sleep fretting over what had transpired that week.

Even despite the relentless cramming over the course of the past fortnight, taking the exams had become an exercise in futility. Maybel bombarded Gwyndolyn relentlessly, night after night, with questions about trivia, equations, historical timelines, literary plot points, written composition, the works, and still Gwyndolyn felt woefully unprepared. She persisted, believing she had a fighting chance in the days to come. Surely not in every subject, she reminded herself, but at least enough to keep decent marks overall and save face among her peers. She only needed to keep it all straight until week's end.

It was not enough. Gwyndolyn found the first few days of inquisition bearable, but rote memorization only took her so far. By midweek, she was in pretty bad shape.

So much material, she lamented. *So many words. So little time!* Strained temples one day led to beating headaches the next, which only forced sleep further into retreat. The night was not kind to her; neither was her finicky stomach. It left her in no condition to do much of anything, much less take an exam.

"Just a little longer," she murmured to herself, when out of nowhere, a familiar slap on the chalkboard woke her moments into class. She removed a spoon-like mirror from her pocket and ran her fingers through her tousled hair. She looked an absolute fright. She heard a familiar snickering from behind, but they tapered as Proctress Alberecht paced up and down the aisles. The instructor closely inspected each student while lining exams on the tables face down. There was a collective holding of breath as she stood up front, imparting one last scrutinizing glare. Only when the entire class had been thoroughly vetted did she give the signal to begin.

Gwyndolyn flipped her parchment over to a blank page, thinking it was a mistake or some extra precaution against cheating. Before long, it became all too clear that every page of the manuscript was completely bare. She saw no confusion or hesitation from her fellow classmates as they confidently scribbled away. Panic began to set in.

Surely this must be a joke, she thought, her pencil nervously tapping the desk. Soon her leg began to bounce, then both legs. Within minutes, she was a veritable wreck, so much as to annoy her peers.

Alberecht turned to Gwyndolyn in disgust. "Quit fidgeting and get to work."

Gwyndolyn tried to respond, but her moving lips uttered no words.

"All done," sang Scarlet as she strolled to the front desk.

"Me too," said Bethany, seconds later. "Any idiot could pass this, *obviously*."

One by one, each student joined Alberecht at the front of class until only Gwyndolyn remained seated. Nary a single word had been written, not even her name. She kept asking what to do, but in response, the others simply pointed and laughed. Maybel was there to join in from another class. Strangely, even people not enrolled in Academy, like Laerzo and his friends, shared a laugh. Pleas against their mockery fell deaf to Gwyndolyn's ears. They would not relent.

"Shut up!" screamed Gwyndolyn back in her bedroom as a vicious twist sent her crashing to the floor. She leaped from the cold, unforgiving woodboard to meet a fearful reflection still wrapped in sheets, as well as the rest of her messy abode.

It was just a dream, she assured herself while quickly ripping a brush through her damp hair. A newly tailored uniform hung on the door of her dresser, complete with a shortened white skirt and green jacket. Though she would always love her mother's old dress, it did nothing to help her fit in at the Academy. On the other hand, this new look popped without appearing too desperate. At least, that's what she told herself. After one final glimpse in the mirror, she quickly took her leave and slammed the door behind her.

The door slammed again later that day, this time from the inside. Gwyndolyn had already plunged face first into bed, marking the end to a most dismal week. She recalled the mounting grief from every blind guess and unanswered question before being forced to surrender her last exam. The affair was a complete wash, she concluded; no amount of time would have made it any better. She feared that her contemporaries would never let her live down such a disgrace, that the Academy might dispose of her altogether.

Muffled gossip emanated from behind the door, followed by a rapping on the door.

"Are you all right?" asked Maybel. Gwyndolyn gave no

intelligible response, only a spattering of muddled half words. Maybel continued knocking. "Come on, I know you're in there."

"Leave me be!" cried Gwyndolyn.

"Oh, it couldn't have been that bad."

"I hold you to bear for this," sniffled Gwyndolyn, her face smothered by a pillow. She heard a cautious jiggle at the doorknob, after which Maybel entered the darkened space, then came sounds of her tripping over a mess of books on the way toward the drapes.

Gwyndolyn whined and wiggled as the light drove her out of hiding, eventually tossing her pillow at Maybel in a pout. "It was as if each problem was proffered in a different tongue! Where was all the material we covered?"

"At least wait until the marks are posted before you get all heavy."

Gwyndolyn melted back into her covers. "Easy for you to say, Tenth Class. Sing that same tune when you're my age."

Maybel dawned a careful smile. "Will do. In the meantime, I know something that might cheer you up. You haven't forgotten, have you?"

"At the moment, I can hardly remember my name." Gwyndolyn winced at the stupid grin growing on her friend's face. "What's the matter with you?"

"Oh nothing. Say, wasn't there something we had planned after the midterms? You know, a fun outing of sorts?"

"An outing?" asked Gwyndolyn, pausing with a confused look.

"The picnic, of course!"

"Oh, that. I've not given it much thought since the other day. The others probably forgot all about it."

"I wouldn't be so sure if I were you," said Maybel, pointing toward the window. Gwyndolyn slumped over her bed to peer down at Gustav and Leopold, who were checking their inventories in the foreyard. Laerzo was nearby, leaning uncomfortably inside the gate. "We probably shouldn't keep them waiting."

"No, probably not. Go down and introduce yourself. I'll be available soon enough."

Nodding, Maybel took her leave. Gwyndolyn freshened up while watching them greet one another outside, though it didn't appear introductions were necessary. Leopold and Gustav waved kindly to the girl, who returned a fine curtsy. Laerzo kept his distance for the time being, but by the time Gwyndolyn joined them below, he had walked up to say hello.

"Good day, Gwyndolyn," he said, his mouth slightly agape. "I must say, you look great."

"Hello," responded Gwyndolyn with a bow that was slightly off-kilter. In short order, she had freshened her makeup and teased her hair, and had ditched her uniform for a light lavender jacket over Mother's dress and boots appropriate for gallivanting in the mountains. Though still aggrieved from before, she tried her best to keep up appearances. "We're all acquainted, yes?"

"That's right," answered Maybel in her usual upbeat manner. "I chat with these guys from time to time in Gotta's Grocer." She then turned to Laerzo and innocently cleared her throat. "Speaking of which, hello to *you*, stranger."

Laerzo took one long, pensive look at the girl with a hint of sadness in his eyes. "Glad to see you, Maybel. You've grown a bit since we last spoke."

"Thanks, you as well. It's funny what time will do."

"Gosh, it hasn't been more than a few moons, has it?" asked Laerzo, though he didn't seem too sure. Judging by the pouty look on Maybel's face, she could tell he had forgotten.

"Seven moons, one fortnight, three days, four aurams, and some change since you last paid your ward-sister a visit," answered Maybel with a slight pout. "But who's keeping track?" Despite her best efforts, she could not stay sour for long. "Oh, I've missed you, Brother!"

Laerzo gave her a big, long-overdue hug. "You're right, I'm sorry. Just got swept up with work, that's all." He quickly changed the subject before she had a chance to inquire. "But not today!"

"That's right!" cheered Maybel before remembering her manners. "Oh, thank you for letting me join, by the way!"

Leopold dropped his bag between them and resumed rummaging. "You bet! Somebody's gotta help me eat all this food! Got some real goodies in stock, let me tell you—"

"Anyway . . ." interrupted Laerzo. "How long have you and Gwyndolyn known each other?"

"Not long, though we've spent quite a while together this past fortnight or so. I was honestly surprised to be invited."

"The more the merrier," said Laerzo, his gaze returning to Gwyndolyn. She could tell he was easily taken in by her beauty. His staring came off a bit excessive, though she appreciated the attention more than she would care to admit.

It persisted long enough for Gustav to discretely elbow his friend from behind. "Ah! It's a great day out, yeah? This is gonna be . . . great." Laerzo cleared his throat. "You boys ready?"

"Better believe it," declared Leopold, eagerly flinging the stuffed, leather back sack over his shoulder. "Got everything we need, so let's head out!"

And so they trekked through the streets of Greneva, their destination a scenic alcove not far from the base of the Mount, where Gustav lived. Along the way, they entered Uptown, a fancy district for those with proper wallets and even more proper lifestyles. In addition to numerous guildsmen busy refurbishing the area, practically every block they passed brimmed with countless faces, most seldom seen in that part of town. Vendors busily cleaned their brick buildings and surrounding slab-stone streets while shouting their welcomes to passersby. The people were abuzz, and word on the street was that the mayor of Greneva would be appearing there within the auram to make an important announcement. The day was still young, and Maybel expressed great interest, so they decided to stop by on the way. Making sure to stick together, they inched toward a large stage swarming with droves of people.

"What's all this about?" asked Gwyndolyn, never a fan of big crowds.

"Bet it's something about Grenefest," replied Leopold. "The Mayor usually shows his ugly mug around this time to help plan the celebration, though according to Momma, it's more of a vanity project used to bolster his image. Personally, the past few have been a damn bore."

"Don't listen to him," said Laerzo while slapping his friend on the shoulder. "Leo had a good time last year, didn't you, pal? Remember how much tin, er—fun we had by night's end?" Leaning into one another, they laughed while rubbing thumbs to forefingers. "How about you, Gwyndolyn?"

"Pardon?" asked Gwyndolyn somewhat absentmindedly after a pause.

"What do you think about Grenefest?"

"Oh, I don't suppose I think much of it all. That is . . . I haven't been."

Maybel turned so fast her glasses practically fell off. "Really? Not even once?"

"Perhaps when we first arrived, when I was very young. My father was never available, you see, and being chaperoned by the help would've been no fun. Really, what little I know of it I likely glimpsed from my bedroom window."

"Like I said, not all it's cracked up to be!" assured Leopold after an awkward pause.

"Hush, you!" chided Maybel playfully. She turned to Gwyndolyn with an eager grin. "We're going to change that. It's a night where everybody gets to let loose for a change and celebrate another annum removed from the War with Gul'dan! I heard from Madam Gebhardt that the Mayor asked both Common Ward and the Academy for help with decorations. They must be planning something big this time around!"

"You don't say," said Laerzo. "Sounds like he's trying to push all the work onto others. Typical politicians!" To this, the three young men nodded in unison.

"Oh, he'll be plenty busy. I was thinking of pitching in myself. You all are welcome to join me if you wish."

"Sounds dreadful," replied Gwyndolyn under her breath just before a small band began to warm up ahead.

"Look, it's General Dietrich!" shouted Leopold, pointing toward a large stage in the distance. Dietrich was standing impatiently there with his deputy, Chief of Law Montgomery, as well as several public officials of the local Grenevan Polity. The General tirelessly scanned through the crowd with one hand on his blade's hilt, and the other running through his thick, wavy head of grayish-brown hair.

"Is it just me, or does he seem a bit on edge?" asked Laerzo.

Gwyndolyn watched his eyes follow Dietrich's scowl toward the Trust suddenly making way through the masses in their uniform gray trench coats. They took the stage, exchanged bows with the Polity, and then stood on the side opposite to Dietrich.

One of the council members raised his hands to the crowd in greeting. "Attention! Everyone, if you please! Thank you for joining us this fine day. With great privilege, I present to you our mayor, the honorable Quincy Rothbard!"

"Rothbard? Where have I heard that name before?" pondered Gwyndolyn while a short, plump, balding, redheaded man in cardinal threads stepped onto the platform, waving both hands generously. Gwyndolyn instantly recognized the young lady at his side, wearing similarly colored attire and an obnoxiously large crimson ribbon through her curly locks of red hair.

Ahh yes, the Mayor's daughter, echoed her mother's voice from within. *Look how she clings to her father, so desperate to be the center of all things. Be careful what you wish for. What a miserable wretch.*

Mayor Rothbard unwrapped a scroll of parchment and began to speak. "Why yes, thank you and welcome! As you well know, the harvest season is continuing apace, and I am happy to report our stocks are more plentiful than ever!" Once the modest spat of applause tapered, he continued reciting his prepared speech, one no doubt crafted by orators more eloquent than him. If he was good for one thing, it was reading aloud. "In celebration of our sustained vitality, and those working tirelessly to maintain it, I hope you will join me in attending the one and only Grenefest!"

The masses clapped again.

"This festival marks the twentieth anniversary of Greneva's reconstruction, yet I am happy to announce another spectacular reason to celebrate the occasion. We will commemorate our long-lost ally, the Trust, who was instrumental in Waldea's liberation now two decams ago. Since their triumphant return, not only have they helped revitalize our fields amid a terrible drought, but they've also graciously shared wealth of capital and knowledge from across the Great Chasm! As can plainly be seen, Uptown has been quite busy recently, with new electrified street posts, interior lighting, and devices that bring heat to home." He took a break from his speech momentarily to speak off the cuff, something his handlers absolutely seemed to hate. "I see some sour looks in the crowd, but fear not! These improvements will be afforded to all in due time."

This fielded him a smattering of skeptical applause, after which he returned to the parchment. "Of course, keeping our streets lit and our pantries full are but few of the many contributions the Trust has made since gracing this humble community with its presence. I must say, they have become quite a boon of innovation and trade between our peoples. And so, at this annum's Grenefest, they will be invited as guests of honor!"

With this, the Trust stepped forth to bow in unison before the cheering crowds. Dietrich reflexively tightened the grip on his blade.

"Those are the men we saw in Market," said Maybel. "They peddle all sorts of technalurgical wares, practically give them away. I've already taken a gander at some shops they set up around town."

"Kind of creepy, if you ask me," muttered Leopold with a hint of jealousy. Gustav hushed them both as the Mayor continued.

"Indeed, Greneva's progress has been splendid these past several moons! Day after day, our meager lives improve while the weight of each burden lessens. By the time our Alliance Commonwealths arrive at the festival, I dare say they will be hard-pressed to recognize our fare city at all. And surely, they will be most envious." Rothard paused for laughter, of which there was none. "But our gain will become theirs, and soon all of Waldea will shine as bright as the stars!"

With this, people expressed genuine excitement, though not quite as much as the Mayor had apparently hoped. Still, he threw his hands into the air to quiet them.

"And finally, in return for our support in the region, they have once again offered us their strength in times of need. It is thus with great pleasure that I, Quincy Rothbard, announce Greneva's official petition to include a *new* member into the Waldean Alliance." There were gasps in the crowd. "It is quite a wonderful development, one I have no doubt our allies will accept. We will join in earnest, and together, forge a new order for all posterity!"

To this, jubilation erupted as some began to chant "Rothbard!" with fire burning in their eyes. Everybody seemed elated with the news except for General Dietrich, who was asked to speak following the announcement. As it turned out, he would have nothing of it and stepped down in silent protest, leaving the Chief of Law to speak in his stead. Though a staple in Greneva, few seemed too elated to care about the General's sudden departure. The Mayor certainly didn't, as he was busy dancing to the band's fanfare. For the remainder of the presentation, various officials of the Polity took turns singing praises to their new ally while Laerzo, Gustav, and Leopold broke away to catch up with Dietrich. Curious, Gwyndolyn and Maybel followed behind, but not knowing their place, kept a short distance.

"General, wait!" shouted Leopold, rebuked by Dietrich's entourage, who quickly blocked the way.

"It's all right. Let them through," ordered Dietrich with a wave. "Mr. Gotta's family and I go way back. The others are acquaintances as well." He turned to his anxious, blonde-haired subordinate and placed a hand on his shoulder. "Connel, why don't you and your men take a load off at the Enforcer barracks? I'll be over shortly."

"Yessir!" he and the others shouted before taking their leave.

The General turned back toward his visitors. "Greetings, young men. I take it you're in good health?"

"Yessir!" answered Leopold with a suspicious amount of gusto, followed by a bow from Gustav. Laerzo gave both of them an odd look.

Nodding, Dietrich then addressed Laerzo with keen eyes. "It's been a while, Laerzo. Staying out of trouble?"

"I'm doing just fine," responded Laerzo a bit rudely before being nudged by his friends. "Er, thanks for asking."

"Glad to hear. You look well."

"General, what's all this about joining up with the Trust?" asked Leopold. "They're not even from Waldea."

Dietrich turned his head in disgust. "We're not joining anything. Between us, this is a takeover, plain and simple. Let the Mayor say what he will about our new 'ally,' but I have no intention of bleeding for them. My men feel the same way."

Leopold began to steam. "Damn it, why would Rothbard do such a thing?"

"Calm down." Dietrich scanned the area carefully before continuing. "I'm not sure why he did what he did. Politics, bribery, coercion, it doesn't matter. The point is that a new claim is being made on the Plateau."

"He doesn't hold that kind of sway, right?" asked Laerzo. "Does he speak for the Alliance?"

"That bit was for the mob, some meat for the moment. Once word has spread, he will bring his petition to the other Commonwealths, pressure them to consider. Probably over drinks at the festival. If he wins one over, it will be hard for the rest to resist."

"It's all happening a bit quick," growled Leopold.

"Indeed, and I must be quicker. Now go about your business, but keep your eyes peeled." With this, Dietrich took his leave.

Gwyndolyn and Maybel approached them soon after. "What, pray tell, was that about?" asked Gwyndolyn.

"Never you mind about that," answered Leopold simply.

"That sure was something!" said Maybel about the announcement, practically glowing with excitement, though no one seemed to share her sentiment.

Gwyndolyn was more agitated than usual. "Can we just go already? My head is throbbing again from all this racket."

"We shouldn't be too far from the boondocks," said Laerzo. "From there, it should be a short hike to the spot."

Continuing through the glamorous district, their trek became more of a climb, as each structure's foundation gradually skewed uphill. The simple wood buildings of Midtown were mostly gone, increasingly replaced with fairly uniform yet fancy stone-polished constructions scaling multiple stories tall. Farther along were even more impressive brick manors sporting similarly designed gates and spacious foreyards under balconies lined with colorful umbrellas. Maybel quite enjoyed the decadent display and made sure to wave at each well-to-do family lounging carefree. However, Gwyndolyn averted her gaze from the lavishness she so painfully yearned to regain.

Then, almost abruptly, Uptown ended as if some invisible demarcation insulated the posh district from its unsightly neighbors in the outskirts. They passed several sad residences throughout these rocky hills, the original homesteads before those fleeing war a generation ago founded Greneva. Some appeared abandoned or on the verge of collapse, while the less-ramshackle exteriors sported simple, unpainted wood fences enclosing modest gardens or gaggles of hen-cockel meandering the yard. The owners of these run-down shacks had little to their names, but what they did have was land and a bit of peace and quiet. Most of them, at least.

"What's happening over there?" asked Gwyndolyn, pointing to a distant pillar of smoke. "Did some lowly hovel catch flame?"

"Enforcers back on the prowl, no doubt," answered Laerzo in a grumble. "Those bastards are always sticking their noses where they don't belong."

"Come now," chided Maybel with a soft, familial tone. "They're just doing their job."

"To what end?" asked Gwyndolyn, interested only on account of the small detachment of soldiers making their way over. "They seem more concerned with us than the fire."

"You'll see soon enough," answered Laerzo before addressing the Enforcers still many paces away. "Look sharp, boys! The miserable bumpkins up here ain't going to dispose of themselves!"

"Easy, hotshot," murmured Leopold. "Good day, rightsmen! How can we help you?"

"You can start by stating your business," ordered one of the men in black.

"We're going on a picnic!" shouted Maybel quite enthusiastically.

"She's right," added Laerzo. "Not much else to do up here, wouldn't you say, fellas?"

"Except perhaps what ought not be done," responded another Enforcer. They were clearly not in a pleasant mood.

"We've been tracking a group of believers a full moon now. Received word they were gathering up here after dark. Just torched one of their spots."

"That'll show them," said Laerzo sarcastically. "What makes you think that was one of their spots?"

"If you must know, they've been leaving symbols drawn in dusty windowpanes. What's it to you?"

"Oh nothing. Just curious is all."

"A bit too curious," said yet another Enforcer. "Captain, I say we search them. For all we know, these kids are up to no good."

"Agreed," said the first man, pointing at Leopold and Gustav. "You two. Your bags, please."

Leopold relinquished his first, received it back about as quickly. It took a bit longer to search Gustav's things, and while rummaging through his parcel, the Enforcers flashed something to their superior with uneasy looks. He nodded for them to return the bag. "I think we've seen enough. Pardon the intrusion. We will be on our way. Don't stay out here too late, understood? Strange things have been happening after dark."

"Yessir!" answered Leopold with a slightly surprised stare.

And just like that, the Enforcers took their leave. Laerzo and the girls shot their friend an odd stare, but of course, Gustav did not say a word. He did return a sort of smug, satisfied expression, signifying to those in the know that no amount of prying would get anything else out of him. Still, all were happy to be on their way and resumed the trek through the outskirts.

Following the dirt road out of town, they avoided another patch of forest hugging the stream on the north side, instead climbing toward a nice precipice greeted by clear skies over their home. Gwyndolyn immediately recognized the view, albeit slightly off-kilter, and turned her stare upward toward the old manse farther east in the distance. On the other hand, Maybel's bulging eyes took in Mount Greneva's glory before eventually following the stream westward down the city, through the forests, and into sparkling Lake Tuley, just north of Thannick in the Heartland.

Meanwhile, Laerzo and Gustav anchored a large blue blanket under some rocks while Leopold struck a nearby flame to warm sourdough slices and creamy hamhern soup. Once Maybel and Gwyndolyn were seated on the blanket, Gustav removed a bounty of wildenberries and dried game caught a fortnight back, as well as some milk and stinky cheese that Laerzo had picked up from Leopold's shop earlier that day.

"It looks so wonderful!" exclaimed Maybel. "The food back home doesn't even come close. I hope it wasn't too much trouble."

"Not at all," replied Laerzo with a smile. "In our line of work, we pretty much eat like this every day."

His admission caused Maybel's cheer to dampen slightly. "Oh, how nice."

"Well, this is everything, right?" asked Leopold, his hungry eyes brimming with urgency. "Let's eat!" With this, he spared no time glutting on sandwiches as the girls sat by in a bout of shock. Gustav threw an elbow as if to say "slow down," but his friend was practically choking before long. The others casually laughed, yet the pace had been set, and so they made sure to indulge while there was plenty to share. The milk disappeared first, then the berries as Gwyndolyn's lips turned a vibrant red. The men fought over most of the jerkies as Maybel happily helped herself to the cheese, dipping some in her soup. Finally, Laerzo passed around a much-needed cantina of fresh water to wash up and help the food down. In short order, all swelled with plenty, letting waste not a single morsel of their brief, yet satisfying, meal.

After each had a moment of rest, Maybel showed her appreciation by cleaning while Laerzo and Gustav decided to practice juggling in preparation for Grenefest. They began tossing three weighted, wooden sticks back and forth before slowly introducing a fourth and fifth into the mix. Their act was somewhat clunky, though the two surprisingly managed to keep it together.

"Well done!" cheered Maybel, beating some crumbs from the blanket.

"Well enough maybe to earn some tin," replied Laerzo, trying to play it cool in front of Gwyndolyn. Her gaze had already returned to the Mount.

"How long have you two been at it?" asked Maybel, smiling after Gustav shot back two fingers between tosses. "Not bad for a couple of moons, huh, Gwyn?"

"Oh . . . I suppose," replied Gwyndolyn without paying much attention.

"You make it look effortless though," added Maybel. "I'm very impressed!"

Gwyndolyn glanced back toward the parlor trick. "Seems a bit too involved, if you ask me. Makes my head swim."

"Just wait until I light them on fire!" added Leopold, laying in the grass with a sinister smirk.

"The wood, you mean?"

Leopold laughed. "Of course!"

Gwyndolyn chuckled softly. "That . . . is going to end well."

"I'm sure it will be fine," said Maybel, eager to stick up for her brother. "Everyone likes to contribute in their own way.

Leopold and Momma Gotta are hosting the big bake sale, and I plan to help craft some streamers with others from Common Ward. What about you?"

The question caught Gwyndolyn off guard. "Who, me? I do plan to attend, if that's what you mean."

"Well, sure. But we could always use another helpful hand to decorate."

Gwyndolyn couldn't help but roll her eyes at the notion. "Probably not."

"You sure? Laerzo might pitch in too, won't you, Brother?"

Gwyndolyn chuckled when Laerzo shook his head subtly. "Sorry, don't think so."

"Come on, Gwyn! It'll be fun! It's a good way to meet new friends your age."

"I have plenty, thank you."

Maybel noticed the slight pinch in Gwyndolyn's face. "Don't worry. Folks just don't know you yet, that's all. I'm sure they'll come around in time, even Scarlet."

"Ha! That will be the day. I've never met someone so self-absorbed in my entire life. She and that lapdog of hers."

"Don't be so sure," muttered Leopold, his snipe at Gwyndolyn garnering a sneer. "Look, you're not all wrong about those sassy lassies, but so what? None of that matters in the real world, got it? You think I care about my old Academy days? What a bunch of rubbish!"

Gwyndolyn's saddened look quickly convinced him that his words of encouragement weren't very encouraging. Her silent brooding made him uneasy to boot. "What I'm *trying* to say is, you gotta lighten up a bit, that's all. Back me up here, fellas."

By now, his pals were completely locked in a battle of dexterity and rhythm, far too occupied to chime in. However, Laerzo's attention was stolen just long enough for a stick to strike the side of his head. He batted away the rest that flew his way, receiving shrugged shoulders and a smirk from Gustav as usual.

"Academy or not, little Ms. Rothbard is determined to make my time in Greneva miserable," brooded Gwyndolyn. "One day, I'm going to settle the score!"

Leopold slowly staggered upright with an awkward groan from his bloated belly. "Forget about her. We've got bigger things to deal with right now. I don't like what's going on with the Trust one bit. Bad news is brewing, something that could put the whole plateau in peril. I just know it!"

"Being a tad dramatic, don't you think?" asked Laerzo. "Those merchants weird me out too, but things have been on the uptick since they showed up. Honestly, how bad could it be?"

"Just ask General Dietrich. You saw the look on his face."

"That man you were speaking to?" asked Gwyndolyn. "I remember seeing him briefly at Common Ward. Yes, he did seem a bit cross earlier. Do you know him?"

Leopold paid her a sour stare. "He's only the Regent-General of Greneva, one of five leaders in the Waldean Alliance. Of course I know him! They call him the Good General, and not for nothing. He fought with my father in the War."

"That's right," said Maybel. "He has visited us at Common Ward ever since I can remember. He always makes a point to bring toys, sweets, and anything to spread a little joy. He even taught a few of us how to defend ourselves. Isn't that right, Laerzo?"

"Yeah, he's one of the good ones, I guess," answered Laerzo dryly, his response strangely somber.

Leopold nodded. "If Dietrich has enough sense to be on edge, then so do I."

"Well, until you know as much as he does, slow your role, yeah?"

"That's just it, Laerzo. This shady lot has been back for hardly an annum and thinks they own the place!"

"Oh, I wouldn't say that," responded Maybel, a bit put off. "They have caused a buzz in the city though. I've never seen anything like it! They're spectacular, if you ask me!"

"Oh yeah?" asked Leopold incredulously. "That's all fine and good, but how much do we know about them, really?"

"They helped us fight off Gul'dan," put Laerzo simply, Maybel nodding in agreement. "What's else is there to know?"

Neither Leopold nor Gustav seemed the least bit satisfied. "How about the name of their homeland, for starters?" asked Leopold. "It's weird that we just call them the Trust. And why is it that up until the War, we'd never come into contact with their people? Why did they help fight only to ditch us afterward? What have they been up to since? Why did they not send so much as a letter? And most of all, why return after all this time? None of it makes sense."

Laerzo threw his hands up. "All right already, I get it. We don't know much, but that doesn't mean anything. They've been bending over backward for us. It's no different from before. Besides, Greneva could use the help."

"If they are only here to help, then fine, but I won't take orders from damn strangers."

Laerzo's brow dipped cynically. "You'll gladly obey the Enforcers, though. We've seen some shady things happen on their watch too, today included. Just the other day, they dragged a bunch of elden folk out into the street just because one of them had a weird marking on their wall. Said they were Sh'tama fanatics, spies of the Mad Prophet Judecca, but I've known those geezers my whole life. They wouldn't hurt a flea. What does Dietrich have to say about that, huh?"

"Those folk know the rules as well as you and I!" shouted Leopold. "The Good General is just trying to keep that cultish claptrap off the streets."

"Oh, is that all?" asked Laerzo.

Leopold flared into a fluster. "What do you mean *is that all*? That stuff is dangerous!"

"And why exactly is that? They're just stories, Leo."

Maybel nervously looked around to ensure the coast was clear. "What kind of stories?" Her question made the others uncomfortable—everyone but Laerzo.

"Don't you worry about it, Maybel," answered Leopold quickly. "As I was saying—"

"Ancient stories," began Laerzo as if to put his friend on edge. "From what I can tell, there was some holy woman named Sancta spreading a message of—wait for it—*love* and *goodwill* across the land. Scary stuff, yeah?"

"*Laerzo . . .*" rebuked Leopold, but his friend seemed adamant on continuing.

"Avalon was King of Waldea at the time, and not a nice one. His vengeance swelled when Sancta refused to worship him over some goddess. The guy seduced her guardian and closest disciple, conspired with her to get even. I think Denestra was her name."

"Laerzo!"

"Oh, come off it, Leo! I'm not done. Long story short, Denestra betrayed Sancta and her friends for Avalon's hand in wedlock. He hurled them from the Mount on the day she became his queen."

Leopold paced, his face now red. "This is just great! You're one of *them*, aren't you?"

"I'm just me, no one else. Besides, I learned it from our pal Gustav here." Laerzo laughed while reflexively dodging another wooden stick hurled by his silent friend. "Don't get mad! We know you love hoarding all sorts of interesting reads in that dusty cavern you call a home."

"Get back to the story," said Gwyndolyn, now mildly interested herself.

"Yeah!" insisted Maybel. "Surely, that can't be how it ended."

"More like how it began," answered Laerzo. "Mount Greneva trembled so violently afterward that a chasm swallowed Avalon and Denestra, not to mention their castle perched high in the mountains."

Maybel's bright eyes widened. "So, that's why they call it the Great Chasm."

"I guess so. Anyway, the few surviving disciples proclaimed Sancta's prophecy had been fulfilled, that her sacrifice not only rid Waldea of its wicked king, but somehow made her a goddess in the process. The people didn't seem to take that very well, eventually exiled the Sh'tama across the sea."

"At least until a few generations ago," added Leopold on a sour note.

"How fascinating!" proclaimed Maybel suddenly, startling the others. "Perhaps that explains why we never had another king."

They all shared a long moment of reflection, after which Leopold finally broke the silence. "Well, good riddance! Better to be governed by Commonwealths than kings and queens."

Laerzo marched over to Leopold and poked a stick into his chest. "Speaking of which, you and Gustav seemed pretty chummy with those Enforcers back there. I'm dying to hear what all that was about."

Leopold shook his head. "Never mind that! The Enforcers should be the least of your concerns!"

"Why should I be concerned at all who runs this dump anyway? Those stooges in the Grenevan Polity, the Alliance, or the Trust—honestly makes no difference to me. You got that?"

"You can't be serious," replied Leopold, the brows on his reddened face again bristling. "For all we know, the Trust beat off Gul'dan just to take over themselves!"

"Sure waited a long time to do it then." Turning, Laerzo flipped the stick in his hand. "I'll take my chances with the Trust over those zealots any day. And if Judecca and his fanatics ever return? Our new alliance wouldn't seem so bad then, now would it?"

Lost for words, Leopold finally relented, if only for the moment. "Maybe you're right. I just wish we had more time to stand on our own feet again. What do you think, Gustav?"

Suddenly, he noticed his silent friend's eyes narrow at the southern sky, where a convoy of aero-freights approached from over the lesser mountains. Tight in formation, the ships flew closely overhead, a bit too close for comfort. In passing, the humming ascent toward Mount Greneva left behind a mighty gale, disrupting their picnic in the process. "Them again! What are they up to now?"

Gwyndolyn watched with utter disdain as they veered slightly eastward of the range, only to park in the courtyard of her old home. "That . . . couldn't be. What business have they at the manor?"

CHAPTER

Proctor Perdue's uncanny ability to lecture while asleep was truly a marvel to behold—for those still awake, at least. The crusty old man droned behind a short podium, eyes half closed, his mumbling a better lullaby than lecture. Gwyndolyn struggled through every unbearable moment of it, counting the minutes until marks from the midterms were said to be posted. It was no coincidence that the most fidgety among them were the widest awake, herself included. All the worse for it too, as each excruciating tick of the clock grew louder and more pronounced with a lagging rhythm, slowing time to mind-numbing proportions. Of course, Purdue and those who slept soundly were oblivious to this, but not Gwyndolyn. She withstood the power of his hypnotic voice until the bell finally rang.

The instant it did, she hurried out the door, toward a crowded bulletin board near the main entrance. There were inordinately lengthy sheets of parchment pinned, one for each class, designed so that the stellar students could hold their heads high and the rest would lower themselves accordingly. Some celebrated a job well done while others quietly withdrew, distraught by their mediocre showing. Some skimmed the list halfway and quit entirely, too afraid to follow it further. From a distance, Gwyndolyn made out marks for each subject tallied from left to right until reaching overall score, though it was difficult to see with several peers in the way.

She simply could not wait any longer. Shoving a few of the idle bodies aside, she started at the top of the rightmost list, labeled 12th Class, and began to scan. Her stare slowly sank in accordance with her spirits, and by the time she finally found her name, she had fallen on both knees. There it was, the name Gwyndolyn Carlyle, which hung low, not at the very bottom of the list but definitely in the lowest quintile. There, humbled upon the floor, she remained for one long, painful stretch of a moment, ignoring eager jostles from many others who nervously looked to reveal their own fates.

"Don't let it get you down," consoled Maybel from behind as she helped her devastated friend up from the ground. "Still plenty of term left."

Neither really knew what to expect of Gwyndolyn's marks. Modest written and mathematical proficiencies made up somewhat for piss-poor historical and geographical ineptitudes, but not much. Marks in sport were fine, though they could have been much higher. Other marks dragging from incomplete work could improve with extra effort. Overall, her performance was a blot on an already-sullied reputation, one which left her dismayed.

On the other hand, Maybel's marks must have been top-notch, for it took Gwyndolyn a simple glance at the Tenth Class list to locate her name in its lofty position. She wondered how the girl managed so effortlessly despite daily chores, homework, and tutoring, not to mention the multitude of errands she personally ran for Madam Gebhardt every day. Where did she find the time? Did she even sleep? Few would bother with such an unyielding burden, even fewer with a smile.

It was that smile—Maybel's defiant optimism—which festered like a wound inside Gwyndolyn. Her imagination may have been playing tricks, but she could almost feel Maybel's bulbous eyes burning sympathies through the side of her skull. That and the voice of her mother.

My dear, that girl rather enjoys lifting you up. Wastes no opportunity, in fact. Overachievers are the worst, are they not? Those under modesty's veil, most of all. Their desire is birthed not of betterment but creeping insecurity. They simply cannot help themselves. Her charity is a spit on your boot.

"That cannot be. Can it?" asked Gwyndolyn sadly to herself, but the thought persisted, causing her embitterment to swell. Disturbed, she slowly quit the crowd of jeering classmates and made for the door. To make matters worse, Scarlet crept up from behind, fresh from discovering her exemplary rank at the top of the list. As to be expected, she was very impressed with herself.

"Oh my, what a disappointment," she whispered derisively into Gwyndolyn's ear. "Saw your name on the board. Most unfortunate. Better luck next time!" Gwyndolyn was not in the mood, and turned to leave, but Scarlet quickly blocked her egress. "Where do you think you're going?"

Gwyndolyn kept walking. "None of your concern."

Scarlet flipped through a clipboard in hand with an almost morbid giddiness. "According to my roster, you're on festival duty."

Gwyndolyn paused a moment, her left eye twitching ever so slightly as she leered over her shoulder. "Excuse me?"

"That's right. Every day after class for the next moon, in fact. Don't act so surprised. You signed up, after all."

"I did no such thing," said Gwyndolyn, turning toward Maybel's nervous clearing of the throat. "What do you know of this?"

"Well, Madam Gebhardt assigned most of us wards festival duties," explained Maybel. "Didn't you check the board?"

Gwyndolyn was so sick to death of boards. The fingers of her right hand clinched tight. "Gebhardt." By now, she was utterly convinced the woman had nothing but contempt for her. She turned to them with a contrived calm, hoping to save face. "Perhaps, but what business is it to you?"

"Why, I have been made Chief Director of the Festival," exulted Scarlet. "The Mayor is an awfully busy man these days, and so I have graciously agreed to preside in his stead."

"How very kind of you."

Scarlet bloated with conceit. "I am kind, aren't I? And to prove it, I have handpicked some of the finest jobs just for you. At the Madam's discretion, of course." With an incredible smugness, she handed over a piece of parchment detailing increasingly daunting tasks, which caused Gwyndolyn to sweat. She found posting flyers easy enough but had no clue how to go about streaming decorations off poles and rooftops. Then there was the next charge, which stuck out like a sore toe: "*STAGE PREPARATION*" with the parenthetical "Complete Renewal" included for optimal effect. It went into great detail about deep cleaning, scraping, and thrice painting, the whole works. "That's just the beginning."

"And if I refuse?"

"Madam Gebhardt would certainly be disappointed, and I hear her least favorite children find themselves in a mess of trouble. My father would be cross as well, and we can't have that, now can we? Suffice it to say, I own you until opening ceremonies." Scarlet stared down Gwyndolyn one long moment before shooting her a painfully smug smile. "Bye for now!"

Visibly shaking, Gwyndolyn almost crushed the parchment in her hand, watching Scarlet depart with her friends in a fit of laughter. "How effortlessly she delegates her duties away. Like father, like daughter, I suppose."

Maybel tried to comfort her, but it was no use. Gwyndolyn let out a brief, muffled shriek into her sleeve and took her leave stomping.

Back at Common Ward, after a change of clothes and much-needed break, Gwyndolyn begrudgingly decided to get on with her new chores. There was a measly bag of tin waiting for her down at the front desk, as well as some premade, promotional Grenefest posters crafted by her fellow wards. She had little experience handling moneys, but something told her this pittance would not even begin to cover the daunting work ahead.

Scarlet intends for you to grovel, that much is certain. The Madam as well.

It was one thing to pester Gebhardt for additional funds, but the idea of prostrating before Scarlet was simply too much to bear.

"Wouldn't they just love that?" asked Gwyndolyn suddenly, much to the attendant's confusion.

"I beg your pardon?"

Gwyndolyn gave her head a quick shake while jotting her signature into the leather-bound ledger. "What? Anyway, I will be off now."

It made little difference to her either way. Even if she could afford every provision, hauling it around town at once would prove most difficult. To that point, she regretted leaving Maybel behind, despite being in no mood to chat.

Better for the girl's arms to snap than yours, said the voice in her head.

Shaking the dark, intrusive thought from her mind, Gwyndolyn realized she had lost herself in the bustle and rampant construction underway in Greneva. Workers could be found on every block, some under supervision of the Trust, constructing large metallic modules in alleyways. The men rushed to connect them to nearby buildings and rows of flashy light posts being installed throughout Midtown. Even some of the older brick ways were replaced with strange strips of incandescent sidewalks, which glowed white with each step. She found these advancements beautiful, if not a spectacle that, in concert with the projects cluttering the streets, made it needlessly difficult to get along. Even more than that, the look of it all was not completely foreign to her somehow, as if she had once glimpsed something similar long ago or in a dream.

A couple detours later, she did eventually find herself in Market, albeit with no clue as to where most of the items on her list could be procured. For a short while, she wandered aimlessly from shop to shop until heading to the only place she really knew to go, Gotta's Grocer. Inside, Leopold offered his welcome while turning to face the counter. He wore his same unusual attire, save for the orange band normally keeping his wild head of copper hair in check. "Good day, how can I help— Oh, it's you."

"Is that how you greet your customers?" asked Gwyndolyn dryly.

"Not those who pay for their goods, at least. You one of them?"

"Depends." Gwyndolyn threw down the list while jingling her bag of tin.

Leopold appeared as if it were music to his ears. "Now we're talking! Let's see here." He reviewed the parchment before shooting her a tired look. "You realize we're a grocer, right?"

"I know that!" shouted Gwyndolyn, quickly checking her tone. "I was wondering if you could point me in the right direction, that's all. I'll pay if I must."

"All right, no need to get all bent out of shape. My favors don't come cheap, though I might know somebody willing to help."

"Gwyndolyn?" asked a voice from behind. It was Laerzo. He and Gustav emerged from the shop's corner aisle, toting bags of salty treats and other assorted snacks. In a flash, Laerzo hoisted his goods onto Gustav before quickly approaching the counter. "Hey, it's great to see you again! How are you?"

"Well enough, I suppose," said Gwyndolyn, her faint smile slowly broadening. She suddenly snatched the list from Leopold and handed it to Laerzo. "Say, you wouldn't happen to know where I could find any of this, would you?"

Laerzo gave it a quick glimpse. "Sure thing! There are a couple of shops nearby that should have everything you need. The ladder might be a bit pricey, though. Hey, I thought you weren't pitching in for the festival?"

"I wasn't. It's a long story, really."

"No worries. Gebhardt put you up to it, no doubt." Laerzo returned the parchment. "Well, just let me know if you need a hand! I don't like to brag, but I can be pretty dependable when push comes to shove." His friends found this admission most amusing, but Laerzo was more than used to their guff. "Hey, Leo! Let me borrow your ladder for a bit."

"No way!" answered Leopold, his chuckle cut short. "It's not even mine to lend. What if I gotta reach something high up in the shop?"

"Just climb a box, or something. Come on, help a guy out!"

Protracted stares from both Laerzo and Gwyndolyn eventually guilted him into submission. "All right, but only if the boss says it's okay. Hey, Momma! Can Laerzo borrow the ladder?" The look on Leopold's face made it seem almost certain that his request would be denied.

"That's fine," answered Momma from the back room, much to his chagrin. "Just have him return it before close!"

Laerzo shot his friend a smug grin. "What's the matter? You almost seem surprised. That last batch of jerky Gustav and I hauled in made her a fortune, you know. We're practically family now!"

Both hunters shared a smiling nod as Leopold stomped into the back room and returned with the ladder. Grumbling, he practically flung it over the counter. "Appreciate it! I owe you one," said Laerzo with ladder in hand. He then turned to Gustav. "Sorry, duty calls. Mind covering my goods? I'll make it up later at O'Brien's Tavern." Gustav shared a subtle look of amazement with Leopold before nodding reluctantly. "Thanks, buddy." Laerzo finally turned to Gwyndolyn, who was failing to fight down a smile. "You ready? Good deal. Catch you two later!"

Without delay, Laerzo led Gwyndolyn a couple blocks over to the carpentry outlet, where she stood next to the ladder outside. A few minutes later, he rejoined her with a large bag full of green-flagged streamers and metal tacks, as well as some soap, scrapers, and scrubbers for the stage. They planned to stop by a paint shop next when they saw a group of Trust moving through the square with vibrant information streaming across the strange devices on their heads. She had become somewhat used to them toiling about in the city, but today, she saw a familiar face in their ranks.

"Hey, isn't that Maybel?" asked Laerzo. "What's she doing with the Trust?"

Gwyndolyn wasn't sure herself and had no real interest in finding out. "Gebhardt must've asked her to provide assistance, or something. She seems more than happy to oblige. Frankly, they are all she ever likes to talk about as of late. If she sees us, we won't hear the end of it. Let us procure the paint another time and head this way instead."

"I'd feel bad if we didn't at least say hello," said Laerzo with some discomfort, "but you're probably right. Let's go."

From there, they spent the next auram or so posting adverts throughout Midtown, working their way slowly to Market. When both ran out of posters to pin, Gwyndolyn suggested they head to the town square and hang streamers instead. It was easy for her to say; she simply stilled the ladder while Laerzo did all the work, securing each from post to post, though he didn't seem to mind in the slightest.

They had only begun to decorate, and yet some passersby were already taking note of the district's jovial appearance. When the day was done, Gwyndolyn swore she was actually enjoying herself, finding it refreshing that people were smiling her way for a change. Laerzo was smiling too. He gladly offered to return the ladder to Leo's shop, and suggested she check for him there tomorrow if more help was required.

She did just that, albeit a few days later when she felt up to it. Like a faithful hound, he had been loitering near the shop every day since, and when she finally strolled up, he was elated to see her. This time, she led him to Uptown with more flyers and tools to scrape old paint from the stage. Her fancy attire was in no way appropriate for the latter task, a deliberate trick she hoped would get her out of such an undesirable job. However, her plan backfired as he handed her a scraper and put her to work all the same. Still, she had no intention of dirtying herself. With a clever curtsy, she set the tool down and insisted she would accompany him after finishing with the adverts. She then took her sweet time while he scraped away most of the day.

Of course, his goodwill would only go so far. A couple days later, when she returned to the spot in similar dress, he wasted no time handing her a soapy rag and bucket brought from his cabin. And this time, as there were no more posters to post, she begrudgingly joined him on stage. Both tirelessly cleaned away as he recounted his early days with Maybel at Common Ward, or the time he bested Leopold at a melon-smashing contest where only using one's head was allowed. Though she frowned at the labor, his goofy antics and colorful storytelling made it noticeably less miserable all around.

Very gradually, she responded more favorably to the myriad of ways he tried lifting her spirits. A joke, a riddle, a playful jab, plain flattery—he employed anything at all to lower her steely guard. His confidence drew her in, suggesting he loved a good challenge if the prize was right. Even down and dirtied, she felt like the prize. Every time she smiled, his face lit with triumph, and on the rare occasion she laughed at one of his jokes, he was on top of the world. Neither seemed to mind that time became a fickle, fleeting thing. Even when Gwyndolyn realized the incessant toil had all but ruined her spare dress, she did not complain. It was a small price to pay for being together.

It somewhat saddened her then to miss Laerzo at Gotta's Grocer the next day. Despondent, she returned to Uptown by her lonesome, though she was met with quite the surprise.

The stage which caused her so much consternation had already been painted a beautiful white. Standing before it was Laerzo dressed in slacks and boots only, his tan, sinewy frame glistening despite being covered in paint. She strolled right over and planted a tender kiss right on his cheek, something he had eagerly anticipated since the day they'd met. The excitable lad proceeded to throw an extra coat of white on the stage himself while she watched his body under the shade of a nearby tree.

Day was beginning to retreat just as he finished. It was a job well done, and one she would not soon forget. She watched him wipe paint from his olive skin and collect his provisions to depart, but she wasn't ready to say farewell just yet. In a rare show of appreciation, she offered to carry some of his things back home, and he happily accepted despite not needing the help. Little was said along the way, perhaps due to nervousness of being alone in each other's company. For Gwyndolyn specifically, it had a lot to do with unpleasant memories of the forest. Still, she felt safe at his side and watched as he kept an eye peeled for trouble and pointed out every nearby trap.

The Solstar was setting when he opened the door to his home: a simple single room crowded with a table and chairs, some cabinets mounted by the window, an oaken dresser drawer, and his bed. The size of the place was not imminently impressive to her, but it did happen to offer a quiet comfort she'd forgotten since being cooped up with the other wards. Here, there was no one to govern them, and nothing at all to interfere or distract. They were left to do whatever one was supposed to do at a time like this, though neither really knew for sure.

"It's not much, but I hope you feel welcome," said Laerzo.

"Well, it's definitely secluded and . . . cozy."

"You almost make it sound like a bad thing. Sure beats living at the Institute!"

She couldn't argue with that. "True, but is this shack worth endlessly toiling with pelts and traps?"

"This *shack* is the humble abode of a free man. I toil every day to be sure, but I do what I want, when I want. That alone is worth a mountain of bloody pelts."

"Far be it for me to say otherwise. I was always taught that freedom was a curse, that without rigid structure, our very sense of self would unravel." Irked that she so effortlessly recited her father's Noetic nonsense, she began to mess with a lantern upon the drawer, her back turned from Laerzo. After a long pause, she asked, "But what exactly is it that you do . . . when you want?"

The question caught him somewhat off guard. "What do you mean?"

"It's not a riddle. You don't merely cherish this freedom for its own sake, do you?"

"Of course I do, and for other reasons that come and go. I don't think too much about it, you know?"

Slightly agitated, she twirled to face him. "No, I don't know. What else is there to do out here than kick rocks with those goofy friends of yours? What's so wonderful about being free?"

"Just knowing I can play by my own rules is enough for me."

"I'm sorry, but that's absurd. There are plenty of ways to get along without half the hassle. You just seem intent on making things more difficult for yourself." She began nervously twirling her hair. "For what, your loner ego? Some misguided sense of reputation?"

"You've got a lot of nerve saying that to me. Between the two of us, I'd guess you are much more preoccupied with keeping up appearances."

"Can you blame me? After all, I am heir to the Carlyle estate, whatever is left of it. People know me."

"So what?"

Turning away once more, she crossed both arms indignantly under her chest. Only, Laerzo twisted her back around and braced her unfurled arms closely against him, like their very first encounter. She resisted him at first, yet her defenses soon melted against him. He cupped both hands upon the back of her neck and shot a stern stare into her flittering, blue eyes.

"I'm sorry about your father," he unexpectedly stated after a long pause, much to her shock. Her eyes shut painfully from him. "I never knew mine. I can't imagine what it must feel like to lose someone you love." The notion caused her to pull away, but he would not let go. "It's okay if you don't want to talk about it. Just wanted to let you know, yeah?"

She could feel the back of his hand caressing her cheek, felt the way it made her body tremble. His warmth steadied her in time, brought much-needed warmth. "It's funny," she began, her eyes still closed. "The morning he vanished, I was surrounded by so many people, yet I felt so alone. It was no different at Common Ward. So many people, but really just me."

"How about now?" said Laerzo, his tender auburn eyes greeting her as she looked up at him once again. Then, in a flash, both locked into a long, passionate kiss that cast away all their pretenses, all the silly games they once played. She leaned to rest her head on his shoulder, at least long enough to catch a breath, but his balance suddenly shifted. In one smooth, seamless motion, her body had been swung into a graceful dip. The movement startled her, yet she adored being cradled in his strong arms.

He reversed the motion with a couple of extra spins,

humming a low, gentle tune, and before either realized, they were dancing.

How long has it been? she wondered, her face blushing as he warmed her heart. She had seldom ever danced with a man, much less without a proper tune; it bothered her not. His sudden coordination—perhaps intuition—the attentive counterbalance of her movement—whatever it was, she found herself impressed by his natural flow. Every step and sway he offered, she immediately followed as an unknowable song swelled between them. Who could really say how long the tune played?

Long had her eyes been blissfully closed in this seemingly endless moment when she heard the words bellow from deep inside: *He will only break your heart.* Whether real or imagined, the spell he cast upon her shattered at once, and she abruptly ripped herself from his arms and withdrew. Her face was twisted with anguish.

"What is it?" he asked sadly.

"It's nothing." Now far from his embrace, she leaned upon the window toward what little light there was left in the day. She glimpsed his pouting expression through the window's reflection, one which made it all the harder for her to admit their moment had passed.

"Do you intend to go?" he asked.

"It's getting late. I—"

"—have to return before curfew. That was what you were going to say, yeah?"

She glanced toward the door. "That's right. You might not care for Common Ward, but it's the only home I have."

"It doesn't have to be."

She turned to him hesitantly. "I don't follow your meaning."

"What would happen if you stayed here?"

"You know perfectly well. One simply cannot check in to Common Ward whenever she pleases."

"Then don't check in."

"What? I can't! What would Gebhardt say if—"

"Just forget about her for a second. Gebhardt, the Academy, everything. Just let it all go." The distress in his voice took her by surprise. "You could stay here with me."

She balked at the preposterous idea, practically laughed out loud. "Don't be silly. This is another one of your jokes, isn't it?"

"That woman has no claim over you."

The voice emerged from the hollow of her heart. *He wishes to claim you instead.*

The intensity in his eyes both moved and startled her. "You have no obligation to go back. That place is no good for you," he said.

"What would you know?" she snapped suddenly, causing him to recoil ever so slightly. Surprised by her reaction, she became increasingly uncomfortable, and eventually turned toward the door. "Sorry. I honestly don't know what's come over me lately. I must go for now."

Laerzo stepped after her. "Then I'll go with you."

"Don't worry, I will manage."

"Not good enough. You know the woods are not safe." He leaned over the bed and unclipped something from his bag on the floor. "If you must go alone, please take this."

It was the same jeweled dagger he'd used to aid her in the forest. Twilight caused the blue gem on the very tip of its ornate hilt to glow.

"You no longer . . . require its protection?" she asked softly, her eyes widening.

"I have others, though none quite like it," he said, presenting the dagger, silver sheath and all, with both hands. "It was given to me long ago by a man I once thought my father. At least, I hoped he would be."

"Oh, it must mean a lot to you then." Utterly baffled by its beauty, she knew without a doubt it had to be hers. *What's this? Fatima. I have not seen it in ages. How strange for it to find you. Yes, a fitting gift. Take it. You are entitled to much more.*

"Maybe. It would mean more in your hands."

Unsheathing the blade, she became lost in the reflection of its sheen for a strange moment. Then, without saying a thing, she clasped the weapon shut and turned again to leave.

"When will I see you again?" he asked.

She stopped at the door. "Soon enough. Thank you, Laerzo. Farewell for now."

Back home, Gwyndolyn returned to Common Ward, its lobby lit dimly by moonlight. She found the attendant snoring over the front desk, her thick binder now a pillow. Gwyndolyn approached, scanning the chamber before deciding to make her move. With utmost discretion, she carefully removed the binder from underneath the lady's pudgy arm and quietly flipped to the most recent entry, thankfully entered half an auram before curfew. She then slowly wrote her name on the next available line.

To appear truly authentic, however, a stamp of approval was still required. *The woman has it stored away*, she thought while scanning the room a second time. *The coast is clear, but for how long?* She hoped not to find out. Leaning over the desk, she reached down awkwardly toward its front compartment, but a shift of the attendant's belly soon barred entry. Flustered, Gwyndolyn studied its ebb and flow to access the drawer in short, sporadic peeks. Still, she was unable to snatch the prize inside.

Her time and patience running short, she risked a brazen yank of the drawer, which accidentally struck the bloating gut with inordinate force. Freezing, she watched the woman deflate enough to fully slip her hand into the compartment. The mark rested just beyond reach when the massive body came back down on the drawer, practically crushing Gwyndolyn's hand in the process. Each excruciating second drove the captive limb wriggling ever more desperately to grab the stamp's wooden handle. The moment it finally did, she threw all her weight against the attendant to pull free, her horrified gaze shifting between her swelling hand and the portly woman. Yet, despite all the commotion, the sleeping beauty did not miss a wink of rest.

Once the affair had been settled, Gwyndolyn headed up the left set of stairs to the main chamber's second floor while shaking some blood back into her pained appendage. This lower of two balconies beneath the muraled dome led into a side hall toward the staircase leading to the fourth floor. She was about to head up to her room when a sudden distant outburst caught her attention from an adjacent hall. The curious, late-night ruckus sent her tiptoeing past the stairs and around the next corner, where some of Common Ward's staff was apparently quartered. Quietly following a muffled conversation, she moved past several doors toward one at the end of the hall marked with a plaque which read *Headmistress Gebhardt.*

"Patience," Gebhardt could be heard saying through the door. "If we proceed recklessly, even your dolt of a father might grow suspicious."

"Unlikely," responded a dreadful voice Gwyndolyn would

recognize anywhere. "He was sold the moment those crowds began to chant his name. You know how single-minded he can be. I say we get this show on the road early."

"I am all too painfully aware of the Mayor's pathetic demeanor. He hasn't changed one bit since our initial . . . *encounter*. Nevertheless, more preparation is necessary between now and Grenefest. We will stick to the plan as it stands." There was a pause. "Scarlet, please don't look at me with that pout. Have I ever let you down before?"

What in Essa is Scarlet doing with Gebhardt, much less at so late an auram? thought Gwyndolyn before returning her attention to the conversation at hand.

"Are you sure it's going to work? We only have one shot if what you say is true. And I still don't understand what we plan to do about the Enforcers."

"Your understanding is irrelevant," spoke the tenor voice of a man vaguely familiar to Gwyndolyn, though not enough to identify. "When the time comes, they will do whatever we tell them to do. We have made perfectly sure of that. But the Madam is correct. Our dear . . . colleague needs more time on the Liminatum, just as we do to prepare the vessel. Speaking of which—"

"Worry not," interrupted Gebhardt. "She takes very well to the *medicine* we've been steadily administering, much more than the other candidates. They will be kept on standby just in case. However, the probability of needing them decreases by the day. I dare say she won't even require a vola to maintain *aspectral* compatibility, so long as her stress levels remain sufficiently piqued."

"To that end, I have dutifully played my part," began Scarlet with delight, "though I'm not sure what it has to do with anything."

"Without condescending, it's no different from tenderizing a flank of meat before the flame," said the man in a somewhat rude way.

"But never you mind about that," said Gebhardt. "Scarlet, how are rehearsals for your performance going?"

"Swimmingly. I'd say we've almost nailed it, haven't we, *Frater*?"

"Verily," responded the man. "Nothing more than simple rote memorization mixed with a bit of finesse. It will offer a striking impression to bring Greneva under our sway. I just hope it goes without a hitch."

"How many times must I tell you?" asked Gebhardt with cold indifference. "All endeavors carry with them a margin of error. We will make an example of those who do not *take*. The others will have no choice but fall in line."

"And afterward, I will be reunited with my family as promised?"

"Assuming all goes accordingly."

"Madam . . . we have a deal."

"My, my, young protégé, for someone so confident in his abilities, you sure do worry an awful lot."

"Forget about him," said Scarlet. "You and I will be granted our desire as well?"

"But of course," answered Gebhardt with a notable and most uncharacteristic sweetness. "*She* has never failed to deliver her promises so long as we keep ours. Rest assured, I will not fail her or you, for my scheme is most carefully planned, annums in the making. When this is all over, we will rule Greneva together, Scarlet, my one and true daughter."

This sudden admission drew a startled gasp from Gwyndolyn before she had the sense to clasp her mouth shut. Frozen in terror, she hoped it hadn't made her presence known. From what she could tell, the conversation continued without disruption. Still, fear caused her heart to pound so hard that she could no longer hear their words through the door. Even worse, each new breath was more strained and audible than the last. She knew it was past time for her to depart.

Turning, she glimpsed a strange gleam down the hall. It was tantamount to light from dual, ghastly orbs in the air, though they quickly retreated upon detection. Almost certain she had been discovered, Gwyndolyn quietly yet hastily took her leave back toward the staircase, only to find Maybel standing precariously around the corner.

"What are you doing up so late?" snapped Gwyndolyn in a whisper. "You scared the stuffing out of me!"

"I might ask you the same question," answered Maybel, her thick spectacles shimmering from the waxing moon peeking large through the drapes. "It's a bit late, don't you think?"

"Perhaps, but you won't believe what I just heard coming from—"

"We were supposed to meet tonight and study, Gwyndolyn."

"Never mind that! I'm trying to tell you something important."

Maybel returned a most frustrated expression. "Look, if you weren't up to it, you could've just told me."

"But I—" Gwyndolyn realized she would be hard-pressed to convince her friend, or anyone, what she had just heard. She decided to let it go for the moment. "I'm sorry. I got caught up with festival duties."

"After dark?"

"About that . . . I was on my way back from—"

"Uptown. I stopped by when you didn't show, but nobody was there."

Always watching you, remarked the voice within Gwyndolyn. *Didn't I tell you?*

"So, now you're keeping tabs on me?" asked Gwyndolyn.

"I suppose so. The stage looks splendid, by the way. I didn't know you were such a talented painter."

"Well, Laerzo did lend a hand."

"Yes, I'm aware you have been spending time together. It must be great to have people you can rely on."

Gwyndolyn did not take this slight well. "Oh, so that's how it's going to be? Remind me how my personal affairs are any of your concern."

"They are when you ditch me," answered Maybel with a wounded expression. "And of course I'm concerned! Your marks have continued to fall, and now you're skipping curfew too? What's gotten into you?"

"You seem to have all the answers, so let's hear it."

Maybel shook her crinkled face. "It's fine if you had a change of plans. Just maybe keep me in the loop next time."

"Yes, ma'am. Or, should I say, *Madam*?"

"Look, I don't want you to become distracted from what's important, okay?" There was a slight pain hidden in the back of Maybel's warbling voice.

See how she tries to control you? asked the voice.

Gwyndolyn shook her head. "By 'important,' I take it you mean yourself?" Just then, a cover of clouds over the moon darkened Gwyndolyn's already frightful expression. "Oh, how presumptuous. And pathetic!" Without thinking, she shoved Maybel to the rug.

"H-hey!" answered Maybel, just soft enough not to make a

scene. She rubbed her reddened elbow while slowly standing. "You are out of line!"

Gwyndolyn sneered down at her and pointed her finger at her. "This relationship has always been about you, though, has it not? Wherever I go, there you follow, forever a few steps behind. Tell me, Maybel. Does it ever get old as my shadow? It must be dreadful living vicariously through others."

"Just—just stop," winced Maybel. "I'm worried about you. If there's something bothering you, please tell me."

"What, so you can report back to Gebhardt?"

"It's not like that."

She's a horrible liar, said the voice within Gwyndolyn.

"Oh, spare me your pretense," said Gwyndolyn indignantly. "That woman has you tied around her finger. You were helping the Trust the other day, no doubt because of her. If she asked nicely enough, I'm sure you wouldn't hesitate to rat me out."

"How could you say that? All I've ever wanted was to be your friend! How can you just turn around and accuse me of betraying you?"

"It's true, and you know it!" snapped Gwyndolyn, her voice perhaps a bit too loud for the moment. "You look and act like her more by the day."

Maybel angrily raised the bridge of her drooping spectacles. "Big deal! Just what has she ever done to deserve your condemnation, anyway?"

"If what I just heard from her quarters is any indication, plenty. Maybe Laerzo was on to something after all. I do wonder how long she's been drugging kids at Common Ward."

"What? Not even he would make such a claim!"

"I just heard it from her lips, along with some other unbelievable claims. Did you know Scarlet is her daughter? No wonder they're both out to get me."

"Come on, Gwyndolyn. You can't be serious."

"As serious as Gebhardt's plot to take over Greneva?"

"Enough! I will not allow you to spread such lies." Maybel turned away in disbelief. "Look, it's late, and you've obviously had a long day. You should get to bed."

Just then, they heard a door creaking from down the hall.

"Now I've done it," said Maybel. "Somebody's coming." She went over to peek again when Madam Gebhardt suddenly turned the corner, giving the girl a scare.

"Oh, it is only you," greeted Gebhardt. "Who were you talking to?"

"Good evening, Madam. I was merely—" started Maybel while turning, only Gwyndolyn was nowhere to be found.

As Gwyndolyn quietly escaped up the stairs, she was intrigued to hear Gebhardt say, "It matters not. Come, child. I have been meaning to speak with you. We have much to discuss."

CHAPTER 10

The coming days brought sadness to Gwyndolyn's life. Since their falling out, she and Maybel had not shared a single word but perhaps shared a few sour glances passing in the halls. It soon became apparent how lost Gwyndolyn was without her, in more ways than one. The rigor of academics overwhelmed her, causing disorder in and out of the classroom. She skipped what she didn't understand, and struggled to complete the rest, but it all was too difficult to keep apace. The tasks she did submit were castigated as ill-understood, half-witted patchwork, and were graded accordingly. Some of the late work owed to Alberecht and the less-hospital proctors was rejected outright.

This left Gwyndolyn's marks at laughable lows across the board, a fact not lost on Scarlet. The star pupil wasted no time twisting her fellow classmates into a force of constant derision against "the dullard girl," as Gwyndolyn was so uncharitably named. Scarlet enjoyed every moment, fanning the flames. Even proctors got in a few cheap shots when they could, gradually singling Gwyndolyn out to set an example for other would-be failures. They all relished it, drinking in what became a ritual act of depravity on the daily. An incomplete task, an incorrect answer, a single moment of inattention—no failing of hers seemed to escape them now. Of course, Gwyndolyn's increasingly heated, unhinged temperament never helped matters, except maybe to fight back the tears.

Soon, the bullying spread outside of class as well. In the cafeterium, it became clear any traction she'd once made up the rungs of repute had been utterly squandered. Even Bethany, as generally unliked as she was, managed to score a couple of points in passing. Gwyndolyn agonized in her search for an open seat, struggled through waves of disgusted faces washing over her like a dreadful undertow. Swelling from table to table, they slowly pushed her back and away until she wound up coincidentally at the same smelly spot from her first day of Academy.

Only this time, there was no one to help Gwyndolyn defend against the mounting malignity. Her peripheral vision caught a glimpse of the staring and the plotting, but not the stale biscuit striking her head. She rubbed the crumbs away, only to endure a few more lumps of bread, some of which had been hurled soggy. All the while, that familiar cackle from Scarlet was joined by her contemptuous choir at the corner table. Gwyndolyn could only suffer the ridicule for so long before ultimately choosing exile.

The available alternatives weren't much better. Occasionally, she would find an empty classroom for some much-needed solace, though most were locked up when not in use. Then there was the lavatory, which quickly proved an intolerable place to eat, much less breathe. Storage closets were dark, damp, and nearly uninhabitable. She even tried camping out in less used hallways, only to be punished for loitering. In the end, a quiet nook behind the Academy became her only dependable eating spot, though by then, she didn't have much of an appetite.

She began to skip lectures here and there to brood in

seclusion. Every attempt to redeem herself had been stifled by a hatred previously thought impossible. *How could a person of my once-esteemed pedigree have fallen so far?* she lamented. *Did I truly leave that terrible an impression to deserve such condemnation?* Worst of all, she had managed to drive away the only people who seemed to care. Not just Maybel, but over time, Laerzo as well. With increasing frequency, Gwyndolyn found herself in his arms, cursing Scarlet, her contemporaries, Greneva at large, and even Father. Laerzo was always there to console her, though she came to loathe the way he doted on her, treating her like some wounded, defenseless creature. This growing resentment in her mind twisted his kindness into acts of condescension and manipulation. Nothing he did was ever good enough for her, and eventually, she spurned his affection altogether.

These were truly dark days for Gwyndolyn. Memories of each altercation, from friend or foe alike, lingered like leeches slowly sucking the joy she had selfishly taken for granted. During her most vulnerable moments, she had half a mind to make amends, only to double down, invent some new excuse to deflect the blame. And even if she did decide to swallow her pride, Laerzo was out west for days, hunting with Gustav per a note of absence on his cabin door. As for Maybel, she hadn't been seen for nearly a fortnight—not at Common Ward, Academy, or anywhere at all.

In her isolation, Gwyndolyn became increasingly paranoid that she was being watched at all times, perhaps not by her friends specifically, but definitely somebody. This creeping suspicion was strangely reminiscent to how she'd once felt during her arrested development at the manor. Time and again, she condemned the notion as preposterous, yet it remained all the same, following her between classes, in public, back home. She felt eyes upon her everywhere, suspected trouble lurking around each corner. Sometimes she even disguised herself in passing just to ease the eerie sensation. But it always seemed to follow a few steps behind. The most sudden movements or slight whispers now startled her, and the more she tried to ignore them, the more frightening they became.

Before long, endless worriment had all but consumed her. For days thereafter, she mindlessly waded through fragments of time punctuated by a ringing bell or a grumbling stomach. Currently, she found herself back in Proctor Perdue's lecture hall—for how long, she did not know.

How miserable you are, the voice within her swelled. *Will my words never sway you? We are entitled to so much more than this insufferably droll, meaningless existence. It keeps you from realizing the true nature of your birthright. You are of noble blood. Royalty in the flesh. Let us not fret another moment over such frivolity. We must quit this.*

"I will surely fail if I quit now," murmured Gwyndolyn aloud, her head resting face down on the desk.

And what, pray tell, would follow? Would you wither and die? Remaining here will accomplish as much. Do not allow these dregs the satisfaction of your undoing. Deny the children their silly games and leave them all behind. I will show you the way.

"But—"

Enough, my darling. Quit this miserable place.

Suddenly, Gwyndolyn awoke to an empty classroom. She sluggishly dragged herself out of her seat and into the hallway. There, her legs suddenly stopped without warning or reason, causing students to shove her aside or tease in passing. It mattered little now; she could no longer recognize any of their faces. Each had become blurred masks of gnashing teeth and crinkled sneers, which caused her face to twist accordingly. Soon, a crowd huddled around the sickly girl, who refused to move a single inch. Not that she noticed. To her, she was all that remained.

Quit this miserable place.

"Quit this . . . place," mumbled Gwyndolyn, turning with eyes glossed by a strange malaise. Clearly disturbed by this ghoulish demeanor, students made space as she staggered toward the exit with stiff, possessed strides, never blinking or acknowledging those around her.

She made it about halfway when a contemptuous voice blasted from down the hall. It was Scarlet.

"There you are! I've been looking everywhere for you. I'm starting to think a certain someone has been avoiding me as of late. Your early contributions to Grenefest seemed promising enough, but as usual, you have fallen woefully behind. We are days from the festival, and there is still plenty to be done. Know that I fully intend to work you to the bone."

The words did nothing to stop Gwyndolyn's departure. This apparent act of defiance riled up the crowd, as some of the bystanders began to hoot and holler. Most had never seen Scarlet's authority besmirched, and they were about to discover why.

"Don't walk away when I'm speaking to you!" roared a marching Scarlet. She grabbed Gwyndolyn's arm, only for Gwyndolyn to slap her across the face. "How dare you!" Scarlet's eyes were furious as Gwyndolyn once again turned to leave.

"She's gone and done it now!" shouted Bethany from behind, ever the brownnoser, and many around her agreed.

Their reactions only seemed to stoke Scarlet's ire. "Where do you think you're going? Face me at once—you insolent bitch!"

Gwyndolyn found herself dragged to the floor by a tuft of sandy-blonde hair and mounted in short order as wild locks of crimson enveloped her. She guarded against a persistent flurry of slaps from above until both hands were wrapped around her neck, causing a cascade of flaring colors. Garbled screams blasted from every direction, hurling ruthless mockery or cheering for blood. This whole affair was nothing but a game to them, a sick spectator sport she was tragically losing. It became difficult to see or breathe, and soon, every extremity of her body went numb.

"Get her!" screamed Bethany.

Enough. Rid yourself of this filth!

Suddenly, Gwyndolyn dug both thumbs into Scarlet's forearms and watched with pleasure the pain and fear take hold. Then, with frightening strength, Gwyndolyn launched her adversary aside in order to recover. Scarlet rebounded quickly as well to renew her attack, but this time, Gwyndolyn grabbed the incoming wrist, nearly snapping it as she flipped Scarlet over her shoulder. It was an effortless motion that caused an uproar from the crowd. They bitterly protested as Gwyndolyn yanked Scarlet upright by the hair like a rag doll and paid her a couple of brutal strikes to the face, one after another in slow succession. Try as her prey might to frantically shake free, she could not escape. Every bit of arrogance she once possessed, every bit of dignity, had been robbed with only horror left in its wake. The fight was over. All knew who now held the upper hand.

But the fight wasn't over. Harrowing screams filled the

halls as practically half the student body watched this menacing figure rip a chunk of red hair from her victim's scalp. Each onlooker was left utterly aghast by this vulgar display, paralyzed as their champion dripped crimson all over the polished black-and-white-checker-stoned floor. It was a most agonizing spectacle animated by Scarlet's pleas for mercy, which only caused Gwyndolyn's sinister smile to grow.

Ruthlessly pinning her prey up against a wall, Gwyndolyn noticed something pressing upon her thigh. The jeweled dagger had remained hidden beneath her skirt long enough for her to forget it was even there. For days, she'd contemplated using it on herself or another, waiting for somebody, anybody to cross the line. This was that time.

Go ahead, said the voice in her head. *Remove your Wicked Slight and rend her flesh.* Gwyndolyn did just that, slowly brandishing the blade for all to see.

"That's enough!" shouted Bethany as she bravely grabbed the arm holding the dagger, but Gwyndolyn easily flung her to the ground, nearly cutting her in the process. Bethany shrieked and began to cry. "Leave her alone!"

Smiling, Gwyndolyn turned back to her prey, placing the blade casually against Scarlet's cheek.

"Have ... have you gone mad?" garbled Scarlet as a drop of red trickled down its razor-sharp edge.

"We will show you madness," Gwyndolyn said alongside the disturbed dissonance of another dark voice. She basked in the mayhem surrounding her, so utterly exhilarated that both her pupils lifted into her skull. How terribly she desired this very moment.

A few students warily approached to intervene, but before

they could peel her away, she ripped the dagger downward, unleashing a ribbon of red from Scarlet's face. Gwyndolyn wanted nothing more than to watch the girl bleed out to the end, but a staggering clang of bells through the hall forced her to retreat in confusion. She escaped the crowd with a couple of parting swipes just as chaos began to unfold, taking her leave of the Academy once and for all.

The sprint back to Common Ward was a complete blur, but once there, her senses returned in waves of distress. Desperate to catch a breath, she leaned against the gates while listening to whistles from Enforcers in the distance. She wondered if hiding at the Institute would be wise, or if she even had time to change her bloodied uniform. Her panicked mind even suggested she jump in the river to escape, but she knew not how to swim.

It's no use, she bemoaned while counting down the moments to her capture. There was nothing she could do but strike her hands against the rails.

"Are you all right, miss?" said a violet-cloaked woman from behind. The tiny lady was accompanied by a young boy barely old enough to walk, yet their sudden presence caused Gwyndolyn to freeze. Gripping the rickety bars so tightly they were practically rattling, she hoped they would lose interest and go away. Her silence only made the mother more concerned. "Miss? You look an absolute fright."

Bracing for the inevitable, Gwyndolyn slowly turned to face them, still bloody and armed. "It wasn't my fault," she sobbed, shaking her head. "I had no choice." Both were frozen by the hysterical figure standing before them.

What are you waiting for?

"What?" asked Gwyndolyn with a gasp.

They will surely give you away.

"No," she whispered, glancing down at her dagger. "Please, Mother, no more!"

Kill them before it's too late!

Her stained blade rose of its own accord now, and before she realized what was happening, the woman had already been grabbed by the hood, sending a frightful shriek through the air. Gwyndolyn shook the cloth desperately to silence her, earning a moment of pause, but she knew peace would not follow. The woman screamed again while abruptly shaking free from her cloak, scooped up her child, and fled in terror.

With the once-distant whistling now growing in her direction, she knew it wouldn't be long before the Enforcers were upon her. A familiar heartbreak swept over her then, similar to the one suffered upon leaving the manor. It was happening all over again.

They would never allow me to stay here, she thought. *Not that I wanted to in the first place, but where else could I possibly go? Except maybe into the shadows. Yes, I must hide there in order to survive.*

Taking one last look through the gates, she threw the cloak around her back and hurried down the road toward nearby neighborhoods.

Blocks away from Uptown, she managed to elude a few passersby while looking for somewhere to hide. Her search led into a narrow avenue, where she dipped behind some crates to shrink from Enforcers marching through the streets. At one point, the sound of trampling boots grew exceptionally pronounced as several men stopped to stare down the darkened passage. Though almost sure they couldn't see her, she feared her pounding chest would tip them off. Thankfully, after a long pause, they turned their attention to something a couple of corners down and disappeared.

For a brief moment wading in darkness, she considered surrendering outright.

I was the one accosted, she protested silently.

She wondered if Madam Gebhardt might sort things out with the Enforcers, maybe speak directly with the Polity. Afterall, she was well-esteemed in the community, and very friendly to Greneva's council members. But she was also Scarlet's mother by her own admission. The Madam would never vouch for Gwyndolyn. It didn't matter who started the fight. Scarlet's mangled face would tell the tale.

Then there was the Mayor. He would certainly make sure Gwyndolyn was imprisoned, exiled, or worse.

No, she thought, *there is no turning back now*.

She did her best to wipe any blood from her dagger and skin upon her stained green overcoat before discarding it completely. Somehow her dress remained relatively untainted by the brawl. Then, for a long while, she remained in the shadows until it was clear all danger had passed.

Only after night began to set in did she dare to make her move. She would escape to the forest, that one place which might still grant her sanctuary, at least long enough to formulate a real plan.

Surely he will take me in! she told herself, hoping Laerzo had at the very least returned. If there was anyone able to help, it would be him. *He is no stranger to leaving everything behind. Perhaps he would even go with me.* More than ever, she yearned to be by his side, so much that her chest ached.

She peeked both ways from the alley and took a deep breath. *It's now or never*, she thought, mustering the will to act. It was a long-fought battle, but finally, her trembling body emerged from the darkness, taking quick yet cautious strides block by block, not without periodically hiding to check ahead. Some torch-toting men were still on the lookout, though their numbers were currently fewer. Most were apparently finished sweeping the area and headed back to Market, giving her a perfect opportunity to press on.

She continued into the classier part of the city, zigging and zagging through neighborhoods when necessary. It so happened that Uptown was much more illuminated now, what with new light fixtures courtesy of the Trust. Still, she experienced little resistance on her way other than occasional residents who were mostly oblivious to her presence. Gwyndolyn needed only turn her hooded face from them, and they would continue on all the same. Picking up the pace, she eventually reached the forest to escape under the cover of nearby trees.

By then, both weariness and wariness slowed her pace considerably. *All the better if I wish to avoid another trap*, she warned herself. That was the last thing she wanted. She would be a dead woman for sure. Pausing, she recalled the tricks Laerzo had taught her to detect them, even in the dark. Use the moon for bearing, follow brighter paths, avoid suspiciously thick piles of brush, spot any landmarks or contours previously encountered. Each helped a little in guiding her along, despite entering an unknown part of the wooded space. With a bit more luck, she would reach Laerzo's place undetected.

Unfortunately, her hope had run out the moment she set foot in that forest. She stopped abruptly to faint rustling above her, high in the forest, either her imagination or perhaps a fowl, before eventually continuing on. The sound seemed to follow her as if shifting silently from tree to tree, but every time she paused, there was only silence.

Just the leaves under my boot, she assured herself while making her way to a familiar grove.

At that exact moment, a sudden crack against a nearby tree sent her into full flight. It appeared any sense of direction, or discretion, had taken flight from her as well. She heard a loud rustle on her left, and after quickly dashing to escape, a giant thud to her right. Each brief sound struck aggressively close, yet never made contact, as if it meant only to guide her path.

She could barely make out anything in the shady blur but was almost positive nothing trailed her. Not on foot, anyway.

I must be losing it again, she assured herself during another frantic sprint. *Calm down and get your head straight!*

She stopped abruptly, listening for any commotion beyond the sound of catching her breath. From what she could make out, there was nothing pursuing her after all, not a creature in sight. That was until one last thud struck, this one pointy and inches from her feet, sending her straight into a mount of leaves, precisely where she was meant to go.

And before she realized, the world had again turned on its head.

I give up, she conceded in utter defeat, dangling once more. Her body had barely stopped swinging when a familiar metallic whistling jostled her terribly, sending shivers down her spine. Then came several Enforcers marching over the hill with torches in hand. She was soon surrounded by them, including one familiar to her, his pale features practically shimmering in the moonlight.

"Not again. Gustav, have me down at once, or so hel—"

She was met with a fierce blow to the head.

CHAPTER 11

For a long while, Gwyndolyn saw only black. Then came waves of violet, red, and amber, each pulsing color more pronounced than the last. The steady rhythm was joined by a beating heart, one that did not belong to her yet melted away her fear. Never once did she question the warmth it imparted. It was everything she knew, all she needed. How unfortunate it was then to feel this loving embrace weaken. She was no longer at peace.

Her eyes opened slowly. She was now a child in a small room slightly larger than the bed she lay in. A solitary window greeted her, as wide as a wall, its pane displaying a berry-ocher horizon along with the reflections of two bodies resting. One belonged to her, the other to her mother. Almalinda appeared as radiant as ever, but just as the Solstar waned, so, too, did her light slowly fade.

"I'm sorry, my darling. I didn't mean to startle you," Almalinda spoke gently, her voice guarding grief. "I am so glad we could watch the day fade once more before I go."

"Where are you going, Mommy?" asked Gwyndolyn, muffled into her mother's side, and nestled toward whatever warmth still remained.

"Well, that depends," began Almalinda in her usual academic manner. "It is said by some that I will traverse the starsky to meet many others in a celestial city. Others think I will scatter upon the vast soil of Essa and bathe in forever-light with the trees. Or that my being will sink to the center of all things, return to the All-Mother. Perhaps I will go nowhere at all, and my body will be reduced to nothing." With a forced smile, she lifted her daughter's chin. "Where do you suppose I shall be?"

There was great sorrow brewing in Gwyndolyn, yet she was headstrong, too stubborn to cry. The last thing she wanted was to make Mother sad. After a protracted moment of pinching her face, she responded, "Here with me, Mommy. Stay here with me."

Almalinda's voice darkened in tone and cadence. *Then that's where I'll be, whenever you desire.* The Solstar then vanished below the skyline, leaving coldness and death in its wake. For a while, the trembling child cradled a lifeless body until her loneliness became too great. No longer were there arms to comfort her, a pulse to guide her, and so she began to weep. But that was just a memory, one Gwyndolyn witnessed beside herself. No longer a child, yet the same stubborn girl as before.

"You faded so softly back then," said Gwyndolyn. "It was hard to believe you ever left."

It is a lie, said Almalinda, her words plain and cold.

"What is?" asked Gwyndolyn, trembling still. "What is . . . what . . . ?" Her bewildered words echoed through the room, ever more diluted and confusing.

You were there, after all.

"You mean here, before dayfall, when sickness stole your last breath."

Such a sweet sentiment, though a complete farce.

"What do you mean? I watched death claim you!" There was no response. "Tell me!"

My murder. It was most excruciating, I assure you.

"Murder?" The word was a revelation, one she denied outright.

Still refuse to face the truth? Allow me to edify.

Just then, terrible images draped over Gwyndolyn in layers. A child in the door. A woman strapped in bed. Figures in gray surrounding her, wands to hearts. Several of them. Tubes of indigo draining into her from a clear, hanging canister. Screams of utter madness. Gwyndolyn's eyes stung at each thought burning a miserable tapestry into consciousness, only it had always been there.

Sickened to the core, she fell on both knees, her arms wrapped around the back of her head. Try all she might to hide from the repulsive recollection, it was indefensible, irrefutable. Her mother had been warped irrevocably even after she no longer drew life from the world. The vision started anew, whirled in repetition several times before falling apart bit by bit. The room faded, then the Circle of Trust, then the woman. Finally, there was only her father and then nothing.

"Open up," spoke General Dietrich firmly through Laerzo's cabin door. He was accompanied by Leopold and Gustav on either side, plus several Enforcers, one of which carried a barely conscious Gwyndolyn over his shoulder. It was a night blackened by the cover of trees, strangely quiet for this part of the woods. "I know you're up, Laerzo. You've always been a lousy sleeper." Dietrich went to give the door a knock, but it swung open before he had the chance.

Laerzo emerged, sleepy-eyed and most irritated, with a wood bludgeon in his left hand. "It's going to be a long night," he said dejectedly. "Why have you come?" His brazen eyes shifted suspiciously toward the girl draped over one of the men's shoulders. "Gwyndolyn!"

"Good evening, Laerzo," said Dietrich, his face straight and unassuming. "It's late, so I won't waste your time. We need to talk."

Laerzo gave him and the others a sour stare of disbelief, as if he was dreaming. With the slightest movement, his bludgeon slowly nudged the door closed.

"Better come with us," insisted Leopold, his thick, meaty hand forcing it back open. "The General has questions about you and the girl. We've got other things to discuss too."

Laerzo matched the deathly expressions strewn across their faces. "I knew the Enforcers were a bunch of brutes, but I never expected them low enough to batter a lady! So help me, if Gwyn is—" A distressed look from Leopold stopped Laerzo before he said something he would later regret. "What's the matter? Got something to say to me? You already woke me up, so let's hear it."

Dietrich stepped forward. "Not here. Laerzo, please understand that our meeting now is not made casually. If it were feasible, I would have waited until the morrow. I humbly ask that you cooperate."

Laerzo did not appear at all happy to hear those words. "Wait here." He slammed the door, then joined them outside a short time later in his usual leather jacket over a burgundy jersey and locked the cabin. Torches in hand, they traveled through the dark for some time, delving deep into the forest before settling down under a short cliff. Some of the men established a perimeter while others collected kindling for the fire. Of course, Leopold sprinkled some unidentified powder from his pouch, struck flint, and proudly watched the flame rise.

Meanwhile, Gwyndolyn felt herself set against a tree, awake, though still in a stupor. Through the flames, she saw Laerzo watching her, bound and injured. The shifting expression on his face suggested he was waiting for the Enforcer's might to turn on him next. She shifted accordingly as well.

Dietrich approached with a large, stern man. "Laerzo, I believe you've already met Regent-General Bruno Maddock of Stolgrum."

Laerzo stood at once and clasped hands with the hulking beast of a man. "Yes, we spoke briefly at the last festival." If there was one thing self-evident about Maddock, it was that he would not be trifled with. Though about the same age as Dietrich, he sported more gray through his wild head of short black hair. He appeared the way one might expect a man to look after tearing through a Holy War, scarred and grizzled from head to toe. Upon impressively broad shoulders rested a steel-mesh jersey under the same obsidian mail as the others. Unlike them, however, the blade he carried on his back was so large it practically dragged along the ground. For this reason, and a few others, he never sat while on duty, which was pretty much always. Too uptight, ever on guard. His disgruntled disposition made it clear something particular was troubling him.

"Charmed," said Maddock in a gruff, unpleasant manner, his voice as dark as the night.

"I'm sure you're wondering why we have gathered here tonight," began Dietrich. "For the time being, we have been ordered to conduct our duties apart from typical Enforcer regimen."

Laerzo shot him a queer look. "You mean . . ."

"That's right. This company is under official business of the Waldean Alliance, not the Enforcers. I hope you understand the implication." By that, Dietrich meant they were on a war footing. He waited for Laerzo to nod before continuing. "Our orders are directly from Lord Lionel. We are tasked with investigating all things related to the Trust. Details are few, but my local deputy, the Chief of Law, believes their influence is spreading further and faster than originally thought. Mr. Maddock here agrees."

"Yes," said Maddock coldly. "Those creeps recently paid our headquarters a visit in Stolgrum. That man, Rothbard? He was there too with an invitation to attend Grenefest. Not just for us dignitaries. Every single member of the Alliance. This alone is highly suspect. Lionel agreed. My men were pissed that I was sent alone instead. No holiday for them? Too bad."

Dietrich nodded. "Furthermore, in a written correspondence, Chief Montgomery delved into strangely unsubstantiated claims that the local barracks have been compromised in some fashion. There was no clear mention of whether the building itself was infiltrated or simply surveilled from outside, but needless to say, tensions are running high between the Enforcers. As a result, our attempts at discerning the Trust's activity thus far have been abysmal to say the least. This elusive technalurgy of theirs, as well as the swift nature of their aerocraft, keeps them one step ahead of our men at all times. If not for Mr. Grimstad here, we would've remained clueless to the recent string of disappearances, most notably that of Dr. Lawrence Carlyle."

"Hold on a second," interrupted Laerzo, his face pinching.

"Are you trying to say that Gustav has been working with the Alliance?"

"For quite some time. He's our Special Reconnaissance Officer."

"Don't play games with me! I've known him for too long now. He's never been known to converse with anybody, much less the Alliance. He doesn't care one bit for the likes of you."

"Easy now," warned Leopold, taking a cautious step forward with his hands raised.

"How can you be so sure?" asked Dietrich. "Has he *said* as much, or did you come to that conclusion yourself? Perhaps you are simply projecting your own misgivings onto him."

Laerzo bristled at the thought. "What is that supposed to mean? No, he hasn't said—well, he doesn't really say anything—but I can tell. We have an understanding."

"As it turns out, so do we. Of course, it wasn't always the case. When we first encountered him in the mountains many annums ago, Gustav proved a most difficult individual. His unwillingness or inability to communicate with us almost suggested he was feral in nature, though after some deliberation, we found him to be quite astute. Perfectly literate, in fact. Given pen and parchment, he told a tale of his abandonment in early childhood, which he managed to survive by himself for all this time. Because of this, he possessed an uncanny knowledge of the terrain, so much as to draw maps of the surrounding area with incredible accuracy."

"Get to the point, General."

With a slightly disgruntled look, Dietrich cleared his throat. "Long story short, we struck a deal. Gustav would be given free rein of our Grenevan wilds in exchange for his talents."

Laerzo was not impressed, though clearly frustrated how

much Dietrich claimed to know about Gustav. Perhaps even more than he did. "Great. Anything else?"

"Yes, a couple more things, actually." The General then turned to Leopold. "Mr. Gotta."

"Sir!" barked Leopold, increasingly apprehensive by Laerzo's newfound fixation of the obsidian mail under his fiery cape and chained hammer.

"Oh, not you too, Leo!" shouted Laerzo in dismay. "I knew there was something shady going on with you both lately, but nothing like this."

"Come on now. Why did you think you and I have been training so hard lately? For the thrill of it?"

The look of betrayal on Laerzo's face intensified. "You told me you were trying to work off that belly of yours! I would've never lifted a finger had I known it was for them. Dietrich must've buttered you up real good!"

"Don't start with that again, you hear me?" Leopold paced a few times, searching for the best way to explain, but he was never one to mince words. "All right, fine! You're damn right he did! Didn't anybody ever teach you that when somebody makes you a good deal, you take it? You strike while the iron is hot. And wouldn't you believe it? He offered me iron to strike!"

Leaning back, Laerzo burst into laughter until a nasty glare from Maddock shut him up. "You've got to be kidding me. Just wait until Momma hears about this. She's gonna kill you!"

"She don't gotta hear about nothing! Besides, I've done this on my own time, not hers. Think about it, man! This is an opportunity to follow in my father's footsteps! She'll understand once she sees what I can really do."

Laerzo shook his head with both arms crossed. "So, how long has it been, then?"

"Four or five moons now. I've been casting gear for the local regimen, making some good tin on the side too!" Leopold's face winced with guilt. "Don't give me that look! How else am I gonna open my own shop one of these days, huh? Besides, I'm taking orders one way or the other. Better they come from General Dietrich!"

Laerzo lowered despondently in front of the fire and tossed in a few twigs. "This is too much."

"There's more, I'm afraid," continued Dietrich. "We would like you to join as well, effective immediately." He carefully watched the young man's face twist through the flickering flame.

"I refuse," declared Laerzo, jumping upright. His answer was almost immediate.

"Don't be so quick to decide—"

"What's to decide? I don't much care for your Enforcers, or the Alliance for that matter. Too violent, if you ask me." To this, he deliberately stared over to Gwyndolyn, who gazed silently into the fire.

Dietrich rounded the flame to address Laerzo more personally. "That violence helped end the War. Otherwise, you would be living a completely different life."

"Right, and what about after that? How do you justify turning your ire against the people you swore to protect?"

"Sorry, I don't follow—"

"Like dreadfire you don't! The Enforcers snuff out people's faith and drown their spirits in the name of the law."

Dietrich took an ominous step closer, his eyes narrowing, probing. "Tell me, Laerzo, what do you know of faith?"

Knowing he had treaded into dangerous territory, Laerzo's bold stance shrank ever so slightly. "Nothing, and I may never know." This response pained him for reasons he did not quite understand. A bout of anger eventually drove his gaze from

Dietrich, muddled by something like disappointment or deep-seated shame.

"Then why claim to care? Does it really matter?" It was clear Dietrich tried to give the boy some slack, though to Laerzo his cold dismissal was a slap to the face.

"I don't care how crazy those Gul'dani zealots were, or what they believed! We aren't them! You have no right to take away our hope! And you surely don't send us a bill for the trouble!"

"Ah, the crux of the matter," chuckled Maddock.

"What's funny?" Another look from the menacing man quickly reminded Laerzo who he was addressing.

"We did what had to be done," said Dietrich firmly. "There was no telling if the remnants of Waldea's faithful were friend or foe. We could not risk another conflict with the Sh'tama; it's as simple as that. And as for the bill, moneys are, in fact, required to offer protection. Even you know that much."

"Yes, and every tin comes from the tip of your blade."

"Yours as well."

"Don't try to act the fool. You extort people, use fear to maintain power. Don't seem that different from Gul'dan, if you ask me. I won't deny that people need protection, but who will protect them from you?"

Dietrich donned a curious smile, definitely not the reaction Laerzo expected. "It must be great for you to live such an isolated life in the forest. Have you ever wondered who makes that possible?"

"I do just fine by myself, thanks," insisted Laerzo, confidently tugging straight the flaps of his leather jacket.

"That is where you are mistaken. You aren't just by yourself. In fact, the land on which that cabin was built does not even belong to you."

"What? It's mine because I made it mine!"

Dietrich shot him a disappointed stare. "That's not how it works, I'm afraid. Did you honestly think you could just bunk up somewhere without consequence?"

"I'm not burdening anybody! What difference does it make?"

"All the difference. What you don't seem to realize is that your entire livelihood is secured through us. For your information, we've long since known about your humble dwelling. In fact, I originally intended to demolish it, return you to Common Ward, but Gustav here appealed in your favor. We eventually agreed that your peaceful existence there would be honored. At a price."

"What *price*?" asked Laerzo, turning angrily to Gustav. His friend simply crossed his arms, signaled with a tilted head to return attention to Dietrich.

"Your cooperation. That is, when you were old enough to understand your place in the world, when your service would be required. Long have I watched over you, patiently upholding my end of the bargain, but no longer. At last, the bill has come due, and you will pay it."

Laerzo seemed defeated. "So, then I have no choice in the matter?"

"You thick-headed whelp!" blasted Maddock from behind. "What do you think we're offering now? There's always a choice." This declaration startled Gwyndolyn, as did Laerzo's nervous laugh.

"That's funny, huh?" asked Maddock. "We could always throw you behind bars."

"How much?" answered Laerzo simply.

"Beg your pardon?" Dietrich interjected, his patience also running short.

"How much do you want? If I'm going to be extorted, might as well just give me a number."

"I assure you that amount is beyond your ability to pay, with tin at least. No, what we need now are allies that can be trusted." Dietrich calmly approached Laerzo, rested a hand on his shoulder. "Listen. We've known each other your whole life. Despite an upbringing that was less than ideal, and perhaps this poor showing tonight, I know you're a good man. Your friends are lucky to have you, and the Alliance would be as well. It may seem like you're under attack now. Well, you are. Indeed, every one of us is under threat, and so we must take up arms once again and fight for right. Laerzo, the time has come for you to look beyond yourself and serve others. Please join our cause."

"Come on, Laerzo!" grumbled Leopold. "You know the Trust is up to no good! They've been everywhere lately, act like they already own the place. Are you just gonna stand there and let them walk all over us?"

Laerzo honestly did not know what to do. "Are you two sure this is the right path?"

Both Leopold and Gustav nodded to each other in kind. "It's not a bad gig. You can at least count on us, right?"

"I guess so." After a moment of pause, Laerzo turned to Dietrich. "Fine. You have my cooperation, but if I see you so much as try screwing over me or my friends, I'll bring the whole lot of you to justice myself."

Dietrich was refreshed by the young man's righteous spirit. "Very well. I will take that into consideration."

"Enough of this," interrupted Maddock. "What of Thannick and Ogden? Rothbard's convoy no doubt approached them as well. Think they'll accept?"

"It's difficult to say. Cael would be hard-pressed to refuse after the Trust pumped half of Lake Tuley through her fields. As for Tybal in Ogden, you know how stubborn the man can be. Back then, he only fought alongside us to purge Gul'dan from his waters. Otherwise, he does not tend to play nice with anyone. I doubt the Trust will have his ear for long."

"I don't know, Sigurd. They did help liberate Ogden after all."

"Even still, the War has left him incredibly hostile to outsiders."

"Or anybody at all." Snarling, Maddock spit into the fire. "Some things never change. That bastard had better not buckle now. Same with Cael. The last thing we need is for the band to split just in time for the Mad Prophet's return."

Fear swelled in Dietrich's men at the mere mention of that moniker.

"Any sign of that has yet to be seen. Gul'dan is likely still licking their wounds from the last foray."

"With all due respect, General, so are we," responded Leopold.

"Your concern is noted, but let's stay focused on the matter at hand. Currently, we lack enough information to fully gauge the Trust as a threat. That needs to change before any definitive action can be taken."

"So, what did you have in mind?" asked Maddock.

"As we all know, Grenefest is only days away, at which time everyone will be busy celebrating, our guests of honor included. Depending on how many of them show up to the festival, we may have an opportunity to investigate their new embassy at the old Carlyle estate." The suggestion gripped Gwyndolyn's attention, catching her off guard, though she said nothing.

"Sounds dangerous," said Laerzo. "You don't mean for all of us to sneak into this place, yeah?"

"Of course not," said Dietrich. "Hear me out. If a small number is deployed, maybe two or three men, we should be able to surveil their compound without incident. For this task, I have chosen you, Leopold, and Gustav."

"You don't waste time, do you?" asked Laerzo somewhat sardonically.

"Sounds good to me," answered Leopold with forced excitement. To Gwyndolyn, his lack of confidence was warranted, given his extra baggage and colorful, eccentric flare. On the other hand, she didn't find him noticeably noisy tonight, or even back when he'd ambushed those fengalin in the forest. Upon closer inspection, she noticed the chain snugly wrapped around his armor over his gut.

"What about you, General?" asked Laerzo.

"What about us?" growled Maddock with a sneer. "Learn to mind your business and keep that trap of yours shut, Cadet."

"Laerzo, General Maddock and I will be taking part in the festivities," answered Dietrich casually, downplaying his friend's predictably short temper. "After all, we dignitaries of the Alliance must keep up appearances. What would the Mayor, or the Trust, think if none of Waldea's regents showed up?"

Leopold stroked his scruffy, bronze chin. "Fair enough, but are you sure it's wise? What's the plan?"

"I'll go," volunteered Gwyndolyn suddenly, leaning against the tree. Her eyes gazed upon the fire.

"You're all right!" exclaimed Laerzo, perhaps a bit too emphatically, considering the circumstance.

"Not an option," declared Dietrich. "You will be lucky to survive the next fortnight after what you did."

Laerzo scratched his head. "What exactly did she do, Dietri—erm, General?"

"She got into a nasty brawl with the Mayor's daughter at the Academy. Ended up cutting her pretty badly." Dietrich reached low behind his back and removed a jeweled dagger from the belt underneath his green cape. "Speaking of which, recognize this?"

Laerzo's face turned white.

"Now wait just a minute," interrupted Gwyndolyn. "Scarlet was the one who started the fight, almost strangled me to death! My actions admittedly crossed the line, but I was simply trying to defend myself!" She wouldn't admit it to them then, but she did feel a sliver of remorse for Scarlet, no matter what umbrage they shared.

Leopold did not seem convinced. "Gwyn, do you really expect us to believe Scarlet Rothbard was to blame? After all, you were the one bringing weapons to class. And this isn't the first time you've broken the law!"

Gwyndolyn defiantly shook her messy head of hair. "Forget about that. I can be of use to you!"

"Don't think you can bargain so easily for your freedom!" shouted Maddock.

"Look, I overheard you mention my father. It didn't occur to me at the time, but he was involved with the Trust somehow, even used to host them from time to time at the manor. Their residence in my home is no doubt connected to his disappearance. It simply cannot be coincidence."

"Interesting theory, but I'm still waiting for your point," said Dietrich flatly.

"Simply put, no one here knows my estate better than me. I also happen to know where Father kept his research and other records locked away. There should be some mention of whatever business he had with the Trust written therein. If you spare my life, you'll have them, assuming they haven't already been taken."

Dietrich mulled over the idea for a short while before slowly approaching her. "And just how do you intend to gain entry?"

Gwyndolyn paused for one long moment. "There is a wine cellar in the garden on the manor's north side, one with an underground path leading inside. We can slip in through there, get what we want, and leave all the same."

Dietrich paused a long while, his eyes piercing the fire. "As much as I hate to admit, our options are few and time is running short. I will allow this—"

Maddock let out a tired grumble. "You can't be serious."

"Quite, though there are conditions which must be met. First off, cause trouble in Greneva again and I will have your head. Next, as the barracks are currently off-limits, you will be placed under our watch at all times up to and during the operation. And last, in the event you are taken into custody by the Enforcers or the Trust, you will not repeat a word of what has been shared tonight, understood?"

"And my condition is that of simple mercy," responded Gwyndolyn out of turn.

"If you think this will wipe the slate clean, think again. However, I will consider a more lenient punishment if warranted. Do you understand?"

Gwyndolyn simply nodded. Much like Laerzo, she didn't like to be ordered around, but there was no other recourse than to accept his terms. Still, she welcomed this chance to uncover her father's plight, or at least lessen her own. If helping could possibly lead her to him, she would play their game.

Dietrich cut her binding with the jeweled dagger before handing it to Laerzo. "This was my gift to you, and you alone. Did she steal it?"

"Sir, it was entrusted for her protection, but I will reclaim it and guard her myself from now on."

"I'm not sure that's wise. You seem more than acquainted with the girl. A bit too invested, if I say so myself. Why should I leave her to you?"

Laerzo looked deep into Gwyndolyn's eyes. "Because I understand how she thinks, and she trusts me enough to obey. Please allow this opportunity to prove myself, General."

Dietrich took a deep breath and exhaled slowly. "Very well, but I hold you directly responsible for her conduct." With a glance and a flick of his wrists, he summoned forth two soldiers, one producing an obsidian mail, the other a sheathed sword. Dietrich watched Laerzo's eyes widen. "Take these. Both are standard issue, but they should serve you well. Welcome to the Alliance."

CHAPTER

A new day had risen, yet Gwyndolyn remained trapped within the throes of a horrible dream. The brutal confrontation at the Academy, the subsequent escape, and not to mention her dark encounter with the Alliance, all felt distant and hazy, too dreadful to have happened. She insisted each recollection was but a fabrication of her subconscious, a throwaway line often uttered by her father during Noetic sessions. Try as she did to dismiss them, they nonetheless flipped her reality on its head, haunted her, and left her exhausted, irritable, and disoriented. She didn't recall much of that sleepless night, save for the embers of the campfire that still smoldered in her mind.

Equally surreal was departing with Laerzo from camp that morn, especially the way he donned the Alliance's black armor over his burgundy shirt. It was a look she found both strange and alluring, similar to how she felt wearing his oversized, dark-leather jacket under her stolen violet hood. None could see her expression, but she sneered at Dietrich and his company as Laerzo bid them an early farewell. She was baffled by how the same lot who had so recently coerced them both were suddenly their allies. It was yet another inexplicable development that only added to her confusion.

This sense of disillusionment proved quite persistent. While walking back to Laerzo's cabin, she felt at once imprisoned and free, condemned yet acquitted. Sure, she was still bound by the wrists, but at least she wasn't currently rotting in a dungeon somewhere. And without having to worry about class or chores, her responsibilities were much fewer, unlike Laerzo currently. The more she thought about it, the more her fear diminished. Unfortunately, so did her ability to truly appreciate the gravity of the situation, that the future of her meager existence was uncertain, and what remained of it was on now on lease.

Still, between the two of them, Laerzo appeared more highstrung by the strange turn of events. After all, he had been made a Cadet of the Waldean Alliance, given his first order by the Regent-General himself. Such a development was something far removed from his personal ambitions, as far as she could tell. The order was at least an effortless one, to lay low with her until further notice. It was obvious he was not happy about it in the slightest. She could tell he didn't like to be ordered around, assumed he was searching for some reason, any justification at all to disobey.

And she happened to be absolutely right. Upon reaching their destination, she saw him give an odd stare while opening the door to his place.

"What's the matter?" asked Gwyndolyn, matching his expression. However kind enough he was to remove her bindings, she instinctively refrained from entering the cabin.

"I need you to stay here," he responded gravely. "There's something I need to attend to."

"What? I'm not about to let you play hooky on your first assignment."

"It's no big deal, yeah? Just stay here, and I'll be back soon enough."

"The look on your face says otherwise. You're supposed to stay with me at all times, remember?"

"I know that!" Laerzo shook his head, exhaling heavily through the nostrils. "Listen, last night got me thinking about Maybel. We saw her spending time with *them* the other day, and if what Dietrich says is true, she might be in trouble. I need to check up on her, make sure everything is okay, or else I won't be able to focus on the task ahead."

Gwyndolyn shared his concern, as she hadn't seen Maybel in some time herself. "She's probably already left for the Academy."

"It's still early enough. I should be able to catch her at Common Ward if I leave now."

"Well, if you're so intent on going," she began as he turned to leave. "I'll just have to join you then."

Laerzo turned back abruptly, his wide auburn eyes guarding against frustration. "No, that's not an option. Please, just cooperate."

"I refuse! If you're going there, then so am I. Everyone will be checked out anyway. I might as well grab my things."

"And if somebody sees you?"

Gwyndolyn shook her covered head incredulously. "You're a Man of the Law now. Just lie to them. Say you're escorting me to the Enforcer barracks, or something. Besides, I can keep a low profile in this, at least long enough to change into something less conspicuous."

They spent one long moment defiantly staring each other down.

"Do you want to see Maybel or not?" she said. "Stop wasting time. I'm coming with you, unless, of course, you want me to tell Dietrich you defied his command."

Laerzo pinched the bridge of his nose. She knew he didn't have the strength to argue. "Fine, but don't make things any worse for us, yeah? Dietrich will kill me if he finds out. We get in and out of there with a quickness. No messing around."

"What's the matter? Afraid you'll run into the Madam?" asked Gwyndolyn antagonistically.

With a sour glance, Laerzo went inside to grab the rest of his things, leaving the door ajar. "I mean it, Gwyndolyn."

"Yes, sir!" she answered impudently, her flippant attitude a cheap deception to save face. In fact, it was she who wished to avoid Gebhardt if at all possible, or pretty much anyone at the moment.

They left soon after, following a northern path up through the woods, which eventually led into some of Greneva's more convenient back streets. It was a roundabout route to their destination, but at least one without anybody searching for the girl with a bloody dagger. Gwyndolyn wouldn't have noticed anyway, being mostly hidden beneath her veil. She trailed closely behind the narrow sight of Laerzo's boots, gaze lowered, only occasionally daring to peek beyond. Being obscured from the world, however, did little to calm her fears. She felt utterly exposed, surrounded by shame and ridicule at all times. It didn't matter that most were asleep this early, and that the rest were far too exhausted to wonder at the figure in the hood. Still, she was consumed by her dismal happenstance, increasingly possessed by the fear of eyes gazing upon her. Angry, fearful, shame-filled eyes.

The day was still young by time they saw Common Ward in the distance with its bridge glistening over the stream. Laerzo suddenly slowed his pace and turned into an alleyway with Gwyndolyn. "When we get there, do me a favor. Keep a low profile and let me do the talking, yeah?"

"Easy for you to say," mumbled Gwyndolyn while yanking down her hood. "No doubt, I've become the talk of the town once again."

Laerzo suddenly grabbed both of her wrists. "That's right. I almost forgot to tie you back up before we left."

"I'm not wearing that rope again. It hurt my wrists."

"We don't want anyone to see you walking around freely, remember? At least keep both hands hidden behind your back."

"All right, fine," snapped Gwyndolyn and pulled away.

Laerzo's worries were finally starting to surface. "It's bad enough that I was ripped from bed in the middle of the night, plus all the rest, but to see you there, I—"

"You still don't believe me, do you?"

"I honestly don't know what to think. You know, there's always been a fire about you, ever since we met. Honestly, it was part of what drew me in. But lately, when I look at you . . ." Laerzo paused to brush a tear pooling at the corner of her eye. "There is somebody else, somebody who scares the piss out of me. Then I hear what happened yesterday and—"

"And what?"

"I just hope to never meet that person."

Gwyndolyn twirled away from him. "I don't know what came over me. I didn't mean to. Everything was a blur that day. Scarlet tackled me in front of everyone, beat on me mercilessly. The others could have stopped her, but they didn't. They loved every moment of it. "

Laerzo stopped briefly to check behind his shoulder. "Hey, I'm sorry that happened, but—"

Suddenly, her shameful countenance lowered, disappearing under the hood. "At least until I cut down their idol. You should've seen their faces then."

Yes, my darling, affirmed the voice from within. *You were spectacular.*

Eyes bulging, Laerzo shook her wildly. "Gwyndolyn, stop! Do you even hear yourself? What's gotten into you?"

Tears streamed down her chin. "I don't understand. Any of it. Ever since I left home, this life of mine has gone terribly wrong. It's like my mind has been split in two. I feel like I'm going insane." Gywndolyn grabbed both sides of her hood and began to shake. "I should have stayed cooped up on the Mount. Coming here was a mistake. This was never supposed to happen. It's all wrong!"

"You're wrong," protested Laerzo, his hands tightly gripping her shoulders. "It wasn't a mistake. Not everything has been wrong, not everything. I'm still here."

Her head turned from him. "Duty-bound."

Laerzo gently lifted her chin, donning a sour stare. "Look, I'm no happier to be in this predicament than you. I get it, though. Things are really messed up, but we can still figure something out."

"You can't mean that. What's done is done. There's no changing it."

"I'll protect you if need be. That's my job now, remember?"

Gwyndolyn looked up to him, stared carefully into his eyes before nodding sadly. "If you say so."

Slightly relieved, she shook the hilt of his broadsword in a somewhat playful manner.

"How hard could it be?" he joked while snapping loose the scabbard's buckle. Then, in false reverence, he brandished the blade and raised it to the Solstar peeking between the buildings. The weapon was nothing exceptional, though it seemed sharp enough, and the size and weight fit him well. "My fellow Enforcers have set the bar awfully low—"

"So, you finally admit to being one of them?" she asked, her amusement mixed with a hint of suspicion. Like him, she was never on good footing with figures of authority, and now that he was one, a part of her feared he might treat her like the others did.

Laerzo secured the sword in its sheath. "I'll play one for now."

"And if we run into an actual Enforcer?"

"You just leave that to me. Now come on. We're almost there. And remember, the less time we spend, the better."

Upon approaching Common Ward, the usual image of bustling activity in the foreyard—of children laughing, playing, and running—was nowhere to be found. This was fortunate for them both, yet Gwyndolyn couldn't help but feel strangely put off by the empty space. It wasn't completely empty, however. They found members of the Trust tinkering with some large device along the stone structure's outer wall, a metallic canister of sorts. She had never before seen them on the premises, and their presence gave her great pause, enough that she almost fled right then and there. Still, resisting the urge, she kept her stride a couple of paces behind Laerzo as they approached the entrance and made their way inside.

Neither fully prepared themselves for what was waiting therein. Scores of wards dwelled in the lobby and beyond, dressed casually despite that time of day.

Where are their uniforms? wondered Gwyndolyn in a panic. *Has the Academy been canceled?* Given what had transpired the day before, she supposed it was fairly likely, and also very unfortunate.

Nonetheless, Laerzo proceeded to the front desk, while she remained close to the entrance, hood draped low, occasionally peeking out at her growing audience. She noticed some of the elden siblings actually more interested in their prodigal brother's return, but they were few in number. As for the ones staring her way, they appeared strangely dull and unalarmed despite seeing right through her disguise. Her heart pounding, she considered waiting outside instead, but her legs would not budge.

"Good day," said Laerzo to the usual attendant on staff. "I have come to see Maybel. She hasn't already left for Academy, has she?"

"Hello, sir. You have, in fact, missed her," the attendant replied, her recollection of him slowly returning. She hardly even noticed Gwyndolyn standing idle at the doors. "What is the reason for your visit today?"

"I wish to speak with Maybel. Can you leave a message?"

The attendant's nose began to crinkle. "Well, that depends. What is your business with her?"

"Ma'am, kindly mind yours. Since when do I need a reason to see my sister?"

"*Sister*?" The woman leaned forward with a suspicious squint. "That's right, I thought you looked familiar. You have some gall referring to her in such a manner. Like I said previously, she's not in right now, but I wouldn't tell you even if she was."

Laerzo leaned forward with an interrogative stare. "Is that so? Then you're lying to me now?"

The attendant did not respond, though she was obviously flustered by the accusation.

"Fine. Have it your way. Though if I were to, say, *commandeer* your records, her signature for this morning would be found, correct?" He watched the attendant lean back, as if the signet engraved into his armor had caused her to shrink by some sort of spell. Hesitating, she tilted the binder into her lap as if to guard its contents, opened it, and flipped to the most recent page. "That's correct."

"When did she sign out?" asked Laerzo. There was no response. "Answer me, or I'll haul you away right now."

"How dare you!" she huffed indignantly. "We do not make public the goings-on of our wards, even when threatened by the likes of you. Rest assured, your superiors will hear about this most unprofessional display!"

As they continued to bicker, Gwyndolyn suddenly noticed more of the Trust working in various parts of her periphery, each wearing flickering pairs of goggles under gray hoods. One was near a window, another next to the right set of stairs. The third working beyond the lobby bore a strange resemblance to the young lad who left Common Ward moons ago.

Henery, was it? she asked herself. Couldn't be.

There were others strewn about as well. *How long have they been standing there?* she wondered as a drop of sweat fell from her brow. Even more disturbing was the fact that none of the wards seemed the least bit concerned by their presence, or even remotely aware. On the other hand, the Trust became increasingly preoccupied with *her* presence and conferred with one another in a most suspicious manner. No longer able to stand by, she hastily marched up to the desk and snatched the binder.

"I beg your pardon?" shouted the attendant. "Miss, you are out of line!"

Ignoring the woman's protestations, Gwyndolyn thumbed feverishly through the thick pages before crashing the binder upon the desk. "What manner of sick game are you playing? Maybel hasn't been here for days!"

"And just who do you think you are?" sassed the woman as she peeked under the veil. A few moments later, she recoiled in fear for her life.

"By the look on your face, I'm sure you're perfectly aware." Gwyndolyn slammed the tome shut and shoved it into Laerzo's arms for future reference. "Now, if you'll excuse us, we will be retrieving a few things from my quarters."

Laerzo followed quickly behind as she stomped to the left staircase. "That was not part of the plan," he scolded in hushed tones.

"There's no time. Let's just hurry and get out of here."

Just as they began to climb, a voice booming from above immediately brought both to a halt.

"Not another step!"

It was Madam Gebhardt at the top of the stairs, accompanied by the conductor from Market. Whether out of fear or force of habit—maybe both—every nearby child and staff member of Common Ward lined into rows in front of the entrance, their rigid faces now filled with trepidation. A simple snap of Gebhardt's fingers sent Laerzo and Gwyndolyn's traitorous legs reversing slowly back down the stairs to the center of the lobby. Neither dared turn their backs to the woman, even in retreat.

"Miss Carlyle, you've really done it this time."

Gwyndolyn rudely averted her gaze. "Not sure I take your meaning."

"Do not play me for a fool," warned Gebhardt as she descended. The conductor followed behind, his pitchfork ringing ominously with every step. Other members of the Trust took note, but otherwise continued working. "I spoke with the Mayor yesterday, and he's absolutely incensed. Given the nature of your heinous crime, I'm frankly shocked you've been released from your cage. But as it happens, the Mayor, in his great wisdom, has granted you a temporary clemency. He wishes to avoid any untimely controversy by postponing your trial until after Grenefest. You should be thankful, though I highly doubt you are. If it were left to me, you would have been immediately locked away forever to rot."

"Better there than here."

"Gwyn!" whispered Laerzo fiercely in her ear. His left hand twitched against the hilt of his blade.

"I'm surprised to see you here as well, *young man*," said Gebhardt, staring him up and down. "Your new look practically speaks for itself, but I must insist you state your business at once."

Laerzo awkwardly lifted his belt as if to muster the courage to speak. "I am here under business of the Alliance, officially, part of a . . . special investigation." Despite his best effort to wax professional, the words came across somewhat clunky and contrived. "Where is Maybel?"

"She is not here. Curious, what exactly does that girl have to do with the incident at the Academy?"

"I will be asking the questions, if you don't mind." Laerzo paused, somewhat impressed by his resolve, before continuing the interrogation. "These records show she has been gone for some time now. I ask again, where is she?"

"Why, Maybel is off pursuing a promising future with some of our friends here."

"Madam, I ask that you speak plainly."

"You would. To be utterly clear, she has quit her stay at Common Ward."

This response struck Laerzo like a brick to the head. "What? You've given her up, just like that? But she's only a child!"

"I did not give up anything. You see, in lieu of helping the

Trust prepare for the upcoming celebration, she became increasingly intrigued by the machinations underpinning their technalurgical prowess. It did not take long for them to acknowledge her potential and offer an apprenticeship. Laerzo, you should've seen her face brighten when she spoke to me! Naturally, I insisted she first complete her time at the Academy, but both parties made quite a compelling case to the contrary. How could I refuse such ambition? In the end, I was more than happy to oblige. Proud, in fact!"

"An interesting story, but this isn't the first time somebody suddenly disappeared from these halls."

Gebhardt smiled angrily, her nose flaring. "Oh, I see now why you don this shaky veneer of officialdom. It is not Miss Carlyle's crime you are investigating at all. Now I will ask *you* to speak plainly. Say what you mean, boy."

"You delivered her to them, didn't you?" Laerzo's accusation was bold enough for the Trust's hands to idle. "I know her. She wouldn't just pick up and leave everything behind."

"Rich, coming from you. How many did you leave behind? Far more than the ones in this room, I'd wager. They looked up to their big ward-brother, and Maybel adored you most, yet you abandoned them all the same. It should come as no surprise that she followed in your footsteps, the only difference being you left to live for yourself while she departed for a nobler cause."

"Noble cause? What on Essa are you babbling about?"

"My, how truly dense. Even you must've recognized Maybel's notable intellect. She's as bright as they come! It was only a matter of time before she grew bored of rudimentary studies. And, as much as she loves her siblings, she would only stagnate in a place meant to guide *common* wards." Gwyndolyn sneered at the rude insinuation. "Besides, is it not the destiny of every child to one day quit these walls? To pursue some great calling in the world?"

This much Laerzo could not deny. "Not this quickly, you don't. Not with these— strangers!"

"Are we really so strange?" asked the conductor suddenly from Gebhardt's left side. Golden bangs peeked from under his white hood, partially covering his tinted VISI goggles flittering with symbols and color. His smile widened with amusement as he stepped forward.

"Is that an honest question?" asked Gwyndolyn derisively.

Laerzo gave her a stern stare before continuing. "Tell us why you're here."

"At Common Ward?" asked the conductor.

"In Greneva," answered Laerzo flatly.

"Just lending aid to those in need. Isn't that what friends are for, Laerzo?"

"How do you know my name?" asked Laerzo, his voice strained.

"Never the brightest bulb, was he, Madam?"

Laerzo gripped his blade. "Excuse me?" He watched the mysterious figure step closer still and remove the hood from over his handsome head of golden hair. His eyes, however, were still obscured by the VISI.

"Are you sure that's wise?" asked Gebhardt. "Some things are better left unspoken."

"At this point, what does it matter?" answered the conductor, his response garnering an apathetic shrug. He then returned his attention to Laerzo. "Don't you recognize your own ward-brother?"

It took a long moment for Laerzo to respond. "It can't be. Algus, is it really you?"

"In the flesh."

"But that's not right. My brother could not see—"

"This visor makes it so."

"Forget about that!" interjected Gwyndolyn. "Boy, tell me at once why have you taken residence in the Carlyle estate!"

"Insolent brat, don't interrupt!" snapped Gebhardt.

"It's perfectly all right, Madam," responded Algus while adjusting a dial on his VISI. "Ah, there we are. How good to see you again, Gwyndolyn. We met during one of those wonderful banquets your father used to throw, yes?"

"And in Market. Now answer the question! What business have you at my manor?"

"I do believe you mean *our* manor. You and your father simply occupied it for a time. Did you know he worked for the Trust? Of course, you must have at least suspected. But something you may not have known is just how valuable an asset he was. For that reason, we funded his research, each member of his staff—my apologies—*our* staff. Every accommodation imaginable was provided to obtain what we required."

"Which is?"

Algus ignored her question and continued without pause. "Only his feet began to drag, and our members grew impatient. By the time of his sudden disappearance, his work had still not been completed. Ultimately, we were forced to intervene and take matters into our own hands. So, to answer your question, unlike you, we have *all* the business there to finish what he started."

Gwyndolyn crossed her arms, revisiting those dour days in a new, terrifying light. The late-night galas, the constant sense of surveillance, her father's endlessly long aurams of work, and each servant's clumsy, duplicitous explanations for keeping them apart. All those annums—she could never fully understand any of it until now. The whole thing was a conspiracy, she lamented, assuming what he'd said was true. She had no reason to doubt him. Though his words did not fully explain what had become of her father, she had been far too frightened to find out.

"Algus," Laerzo began. "Tell me what has become of our sister."

"Calm yourself. Maybel is simply taking part in one of our *other* projects. I must say, the Madam really knows how to pick them. Like me, she has already proven herself invaluable toward our endeavors."

"If you harm one hair on her head—"

Algus let out a condescending laugh. "Though I don't appreciate the accusation, you have my word that no harm will become of her. After all, we have taken every precaution—"

"Enough," interrupted Gebhardt with a grimace. "Our business here has concluded. I would ask that you leave at once."

"There is still the matter of Gwyndolyn's belongings," said Laerzo.

"Belongings? Why, they remain right where she left them." It only took a moment for Gebhardt to understand his implication. "Surely, you weren't planning on taking her with you?"

Laerzo was somewhat confused by the response. "With all due respect, she is in custody of the Enforcers—"

"As I am solely responsible for her well-being, Mayor Rothbard has permitted me to keep her under my direct supervision. I thought you were here to return her! She is to remain on house arrest up to the day of trial."

"Perhaps you would rather look after your daughter, Scarlet," said Gwyndolyn without so much as a thought. The entire room filled with murmurs. Even Laerzo stared incredulously in her direction.

Gebhardt simply laughed in turn, though Gwyndolyn could see the proverbial wheels churning behind the Madam's spectacles. "Child, I have absolutely no clue what you're talking about."

Laerzo then put the interruption behind them and continued to argue his case. "Madam, General Dietrich himself has entrusted her to me, and until he issues new orders, that will not change."

Gwyndolyn could hardly believe those words left his mouth.

"*Well*! Aren't we in charge?" sneered Gebhardt with animus. "I suppose I have no choice then but to cooperate for now. Still, you will go no farther. I'm sure she won't be needing much in gaol anyway."

"As you wish." Laerzo extended his hand back toward the entrance, where the line of wards had yet to budge. "Gwyn, Miss Carlyle. This way."

"One more thing. If you truly insist to leave here an Enforcer, it is imperative you act like one. I see Gwyndolyn is not currently bound. Restrain her."

"Pardon?" asked Laerzo before realizing Gwyndolyn's hands had been exposed for some time. Still, he did not heed her command and continued walking.

"I'm sorry, perhaps I haven't made myself clear. This monster has been charged with barbarously ravaging and disfiguring the sole heir to the Rothbard Estate, our mayor's own progeny. If permitted to leave here unbound, Gwyndolyn could very well commit another act of carnage. One on your watch, I might add." At this point, Gebhardt was almost seething with hatred. "So, I say again, restrain her. Immediately!"

Laerzo was in a difficult position. "I'm sorry," he spoke softly, trying to shrug off Gwyndolyn's injured stare. Though clearly moments away from tears, she refused to give Gebhardt the satisfaction of seeing her weep. Remaining silent, she felt the hood flip over her head as Laerzo gently pulled both her hands behind her back and bound them with rope.

Right before both guests took their leave, however, Gebhardt made one final pronouncement. "Child, I disavow you. You are not wanted. Not here, not in Greneva, not anywhere. May the sadness of solitude find you for your wicked ways."

By the time they cleared the premises, Gwyndolyn ached for a fight, but fearing any more unwanted attention, she held her tongue while Laerzo led her back through the side streets. Not that it did her any good. Morning was now in full swing, and with it came the crowds and the onlookers. People whispered and jeered all around her, their pity and condemnation bombarding her from every angle. Someone hurled a few objects at her, though nothing hard enough to hurt. Her only hope then was that the onlookers could not see her sorrow, nor the tears streaming down her face.

It is just as I foretold, said the voice from within. *Did I not say he would betray you? That they would all turn against you? Have you nothing to say to him?*

It was a long, grueling ordeal, but eventually, they made it back to the forest. By then, Gwyndolyn was fuming. She whipped toward him. "I can't believe you would humiliate me like that."

"What did you want me to do?" asked Laerzo.

"You could've just walked away. Or least untied me afterward. Since when do you care what she thinks, anyway?"

Laerzo averted his gaze. "As much as I hate to admit it, she had a point. If I'm going to conduct myself as a man, I can't just play fast and loose with the rules anymore."
A fool like him could never protect you.

Gwyndolyn kicked clumsily at him. "All you proved back

there was how cowardly you really are. She treated you like a scared little boy, and you buckled. It's disgusting to even think about how quickly she had *your* hands tied."

With a quick jostle, Laerzo turned her about-face and shoved them both forward. "Watch it, Gwyn. I've given you a lot of slack, in more ways than one, but that is quickly about to change."

See how quickly he turns on you? You must be incensed!

Gwyndolyn let out a goading laugh. "Well, go on then!" He did not respond, however determined she was to provoke him.

"Enough, already."

What a lousy pushover, the voice continued. *You see his weakness? Makes me sick!*

"Whatever you say, Rookie."

She finally got her wish. Laerzo grabbed her by the neck of her jacket—or rather his jacket—and pulled her dangerously close, practically dragging her toward his cabin. "I've had enough of you. Since when did you become so damn rotten?"

A part of Gwyndolyn was aware of how irate she had become, yet strangely unable to regain her senses. It was as if she had become a spectator in her own life, intoxicated from intense hatred brewing deep inside her. The feeling was as terrible as it was thrilling, regrettable yet captivating. So much so that she didn't realize they had reached Laerzo's cabin until she heard him angrily fumbling his keys.

After opening the door, Laerzo violently tossed her body like a rag doll to the ground.

"How dare—"

"Shut up," he interrupted, his face furiously twisted. "I can't believe I ever felt something for you. Don't let me hear another peep out of you, or so help me, I'll—"

"You'll what? Big talk from such a small man. You won't do

a thing!" She was angered to see him smirk for the first time that day. "What's so funny?"

He did not respond but instead grabbed some spare rope from his wall, threw her onto the bed, and looped her hands to its left post.

She was livid. "Untie me at once! Hey! Where do you think you're—" but by the time she could finish, he had already slammed the door behind him and locked it tight.

CHAPTER 13

Laerzo could tell the Enforcer life was not for him. His first day on the job, he had already skirted protocol, abused his authority, and acted foolhardy before Gebhardt and the others. It pained him to know his conduct was no different from that of his contemporaries, that in short order he had become the self-serving brute he'd always resented. It made him wonder if he fit in just fine with the Enforcers after all, if it was really the kind of man he was inside. Unfortunately, the only one to blame for Laerzo falling short of his lofty expectations was himself.

Even worse, despite engaging in a blatant conflict of interest for Gwyndolyn, he still somehow managed to earn nothing but her scorn. Their nasty falling out looped endlessly in his head, winding him up a little more each time. It honestly surprised him how long he'd put up with her, how much his wounded ego would allow. It was not like much of what she said could be denied. Most of all, he had no business wearing the uniform. Still, like any man, he could only take so much abuse.

Currently, the sad sap found himself several pints deep while sulking at his usual spot, O'Brien's Tavern. Though regarded favorably among its regulars, the place was considered by most to be an over-glorified hole dug under the local butcher house in Midtown. Decorating its otherwise drab, cobblestone walls were trophies and memorabilia from the War, as well as strange knickknacks like the mounted head of a hamhern, or the painting of a scantily clad woman from ages past. What little light there was came from candles strewn about. Its few windows were always shuttered, causing the passage of time to flow in odd and unexpected ways. Though not a place for many, those frequenting this meager establishment liked it plenty and often. In fact, a certain few liked it even better after dark, congregating to give thanks to Sancta, a secret very closely kept.

At the heart of it all was a mighty hearth cooking the butcher's daily scraps into stews and other tasty staples by none other than the tavern master himself. O'Brien was the king of his castle, surrounded by a square of bar space not unlike any four-sided rampart guarding its fort. He was tall, bald, large, and in charge. His formidable demeanor was betrayed by humble attire, a somewhat dingy apron over leather slacks and a simple black shirt. Consumed by all things culinary, he really knew his way around a delicious morsel, and took great pleasure in it too, even if half ended up in his fiery beard. At times, some would characterize him as rough around the edges, though the man was just aggressively hospitable to a fault. Those who entered his domain would be hard-pressed to leave on an empty stomach, even if they wanted to. He'd gladly give away the shirt on his back to make a patron happy.

"How you holdin' up, Laerzo?" asked O'Brien with a steamed rag draping over one shoulder. "You haven't eaten anything all day. I've got just the thing—My world-renowned hamhern stew, slow-cooked in white amaranth and gillie herbs, not to mention my special blend of spices picked just the other day. Made sure to marinate the ham in some of my best wine too. I see that look on your face. No, it won't get you boozed up any more than you already are, though it does pack a mean punch! Great for hangovers. Everything made fresh or your moneys back. I'll get you a bowl—"

"Jus'nother mead, thanks," murmured Laerzo, his head wobbling on both forearms. O'Brien filled his mug while pushing over some stew. He didn't take no for an answer.

The tavern's entrance suddenly blew open. "There you are!" shouted Leopold with Gustav, descending the stairs and making his way over. He jostled Laerzo from behind while Gustav grabbed a seat nearby and waited for a drink. O'Brien knew the drill. He served Gustav a shot of something dark, the usual, which Gustav tossed back in one go, bottoms up. By the time his cup hit the bar, it was already being refilled. Leopold gave both of them a grumpy look before continuing. "You never checked in with the General. He's been asking about you."

"Good for him."

"What's the deal? Looks like you're sinking in shallow water."

"Let the lad alone," said O'Brien while pouring another drink farther down the bar. "From what I gather, he's had a rough one. Been here practically all day grousing about."

Leopold watched Gustav slam his second drink like it was water, though he was more concerned with Laerzo. "Damn it, you know how much of a lush he can be. Can't hold hooch to save his life."

"Of course I do," answered O'Brien with a guffaw. "At the moment, he's my new favorite customer—er, begging your pardons, gentlemen. He's the most generous one today. Aye, a generous customer for an even more generous proprietor! If he wants to forget his lady, I say let him!"

"Lady? Oh, you must mean Gwyndolyn. Say, Laerzo, where exactly is she? Supposed to be watching her, aren't you?"

"Pfft. Don't wanna think about tha' honeydoo right now!" answered Laerzo with a slight slur. "Putter und'arrest, locked 'er up, threw away the key."

Leopold shook his head. "You gotta be kidding."

"'S fine. She's back at my place. Tied up where she belongs. Am I right, fellas?" Laughing, Laerzo slapped Gustav's back, only to receive a strange stare in return.

"All right, buddy," started Leopold as he rested both hands on Laerzo's shoulders. "You're clearly out of your mind. Time to take you home."

"You two just got here!" shouted O'Brien. "Stay and take a load off. Have a drink!"

"No thanks, but go ahead. Sure looks like you could use one."

To this, O'Brien almost looked a fright, gazing over toward the gnarly set of old obsidian armor hanging off the far wall. "Oh no, I haven't downed a single drop since I fought in the War. Booze does strange things to me, brother, and then I do strange things, if you get my drift." Then, without skipping a beat, his demeanor quickly returned to normal as he shamelessly placed a wooden spoon in Laerzo's right hand. "At least stick around until Laerzo finishes my world-famous stew!"

"No dice!" answered Leopold, glancing from the untouched bowl back to O'Brien. "You know perfectly well he never ordered it." Tossing the spoon on the counter, he tried to help Laerzo to stand, but his friend shrugged him away.

"Don't baby me! I can walk jus' fine," said Laerzo before spilling over the floor like a tipped pitcher. "See?"

Leopold shot an insistent expression at Gustav. "Come on. Help me out, would you?"

Before lending a hand, Gustav finished his third drink and gave the tavern master a farewell salute.

"All right, you jokers, but I have to make a living somehow," said O'Brien with guarded disappointment. "Don't forget your tabs are overdue!"

"With a few extra items included, I'm sure," teased Leopold on their way to the door. "Sometimes I don't know why we even come here."

"You know exactly why, tubby. I got you by the horns! You'll be back. Just don't forget to bring your tin when you do."

And with that, Laerzo climbed the steps out into the early night, with some assistance from the others. He was surprised to meet the moon so soon, though his heavy head quickly lowered to the cobbled road hazily glistening in the streets. Both friends practically had to drag him through Market, thankfully not that far from the forest. From there, they followed the usual route clear of their snares, stopping once or twice to let him retch behind nearby bushes. His stench lingered as they continued on, yet farther ahead, they picked up another scent in the air.

"Did we set up camp?" asked Leopold, testing the wind with his finger. "Smells like kindling from the east. The others should be farther south of here."

Laerzo wriggled free, picking up hints of sweet oak and tar, which soon led him from the beaten path. His eyes burning, he staggered carelessly through brush and thicket toward the growing smell. Thankfully, the others were close behind. If not for their swift intervention, he would have plummeted down a steep hill overlooking his neck of the woods. They held him at the precipice, all staring curiously at an orange flickering in the distance.

It was ominous indeed, and quite unexpected, but so was their drunkard friend, who suddenly slid down the path. His friends were left in the dust, and by the time they caught up with him, he had collapsed face first in the dirt, one jaunt short of his residence.

"No!" he roared, watching a massive inferno burn beyond the foreyard. The others tried to restrain him from staggering upright and doing something brash, but he shoved both aside and approached what remained of his home. However, it was too far gone. In the end, all he could do was watch every plank of charred wood crackle and pop as the wanton destruction brought him to his knees.

Soon after, another bout of sickness left him short of breath, heavy and rigid like a stone. His body faltered, but before fading completely, he caught the blurred image of a figure accompanying him in the grass nearby.

CHAPTER 14

For how little there was to burn, Gwyndolyn thought Laerzo's home had endured much longer than it had any right. In the hazy darkness, she recalled earlier that night when she'd been locked inside, busying herself by counting his possessions, big and small, on fingers and toes. Like her other makeshift distractions, it was a quick affair, which proved dull and disappointing. She tried checking for other provisions, perhaps hidden beneath floorboards or tucked within a secret panel behind his bed, but the constraints did not let her go far. She had grown tired from staring at the same meager space, tired of struggling to wriggle free from it, and eventually fell asleep.

Not long afterward, terrible creaking sounds and smoking brimstone roused her. She abruptly awoke to the side dresser tipped over, its drawer agape, and a rolling candlestick setting the floor ablaze. A wild, persistent gust from the nearby open window had quickly spread the flame over practically half the interior. Something danced beyond the flame, possibly drapes in the wind, or perhaps not. She would have watched its hypnotic sway to the very end if something else hadn't caught her attention.

It was the dagger—her Wicked Slight. It had spilled from the dresser, its silver laying feet from the bed, the blue gem gleaming purple against the flame. It captivated her even as she coughed and gasped for air. She was amazed by how absent-minded Laerzo was to leave it in such an unguarded place. A good thing, too, for it ultimately granted her freedom from the flaming death trap.

Unfortunately, she now found herself in another cage, this one at the local Grenevan gaolhouse buried beneath the barracks. The place was like any other dungeon: damp, cold, bereft of natural light, and much less hospitable than her previous confines. The cell provided had none of the furnishings she could clearly see in others: a bed, chair, bucket of water, scraps of sheet upon which to lay. Even worse, both hands were still bound behind her back in the most uncomfortable manner, pulled extra tight. Any attempt to lean against the wall caused pain, and so the floor alone welcomed her. All in all, it was quite miserable, though she supposed that was the point.

The passage of time therein was difficult enough to track without restless bouts of slumber pulling her in and out of consciousness. None could really be considered sleep, though each managed to drudge up the same stark images gripping her like some fever dream. She was at once cold from the stone floor, sweating from memories of raging heat. The longer she was forced to recount those moments, the more frightening and disjointed they became. And the flame inexorably grew every time. Soon she stood before a pyre as tall as the sky. It had a life of its own, seemingly amused by what it had done.

Even when able to forfeit rest, she had no choice but to return to that harrowing night. She silently interrogated herself before anyone else had the chance, if only to jog her memory.

How did the fire start? she began. A gust of wind must have blown over the candle. *And the dresser too?* Perhaps not, but who would know if it had or hadn't? It was naught but ash now. What was causing a commotion in the flame? Some one was there, she swore it. It wasn't just a figment of her imagination. It was the source of the blame, not her. Surely, it couldn't have been, yet each answer felt increasingly suspect. She couldn't remember much else really, not even how long it was before the Enforcers hauled her away into the night.

Everything had become but a blur, with only the reek of soot on her clothes to remind her that what had happened was not a dream. It had since mixed with some odious vomit, maybe something she rolled over in her sleep. With the scant light available, she checked her boots for dung before following the source of the stench to the front of her cell. Just as she sniffed along the bars, a raspy throat cleared from the adjacent cage.

"Who's there?" Laerzo's coarse voice suddenly asked.

She immediately recognized him, though surprisingly, his presence brought her great distress, so much that she waited a long while before finally answering. "Laerzo, is that you?"

"As far as I can remember." His soft chuckle quickly devolved into a coughing fit. "I see they finally locked you up in some place proper, but why am I here? One nightmare into another, it seems."

"Laerzo, I—"

"Why did you do it, Gwyn?"

The accusation was like a punch to the gut. She waited a long while before responding. "How could you ask such a question? You know perfectly well I wouldn't—"

"Save it. I knew you were upset, but to do something like this? I didn't think anyone could be so petty."

"It wasn't me. I awoke in your bed surrounded by flames. They almost consumed me! I saw—"

"You saw what?" he interrupted, his patience already spent. "This had better be good."

"There was—" She paused, almost afraid to say it aloud.

"Someone at the window. I saw the most frightful being in the night."

"Right, you saw somebody. Just standing there, in the flame."

"I swear to you."

"Don't mock me. You honestly expect me, or anyone, to believe that?"

"You must! I know what I saw. It desired my very life, I just know it. Perhaps it was Scarlet, or even—"

"Oh, let me guess. Gebhardt stalks in heels, torch in hand. Give me a break!"

Her body began to tremble. "Would you just listen? For all you know, it could have been General Dietrich! We both heard how he practically threatened to tear down your home."

"That makes no sense. I've given him what he wants."

"They've always hated us, Laerzo. Gebhardt, Dietrich, and the rest. They see us as nothing more than a—"

"Enough!" His outburst rattled the entire chamber. "Just—stop talking. I've got nothing left, Gwyndolyn, nothing but the smothering husk of a life. At least I still have that much. Let's see how long you hold on to yours." Both shared another painful pause. "I hope you hang for what you did."

The venom dripping from those words ripped a sob from her chest as she fell on her side. "You . . . you don't mean that."

"I hope you hang."

There were no words she could offer to undo his contempt. More than ever, her body yearned to comfort him, to win back his good graces, yet a space between them now existed, one much stronger than the wall they currently shared. Never had she felt so close to someone, yet somehow worlds apart. His sorrow had been tempered into an ironclad hatred he would not soon forget. All that was left for her to do was weep, hoping something, anything would clear the heavy anguish in the air.

A few aurams later, the long-standing silence was finally dispelled by footsteps descending in the distance.

"How you holding up?" asked Leopold, who stood with Gustav, both completely clad in black. Leopold packed away his orange cape, something he seldom did, probably to appear less conspicuous. His fat fingers fumbled through a ring of keys while Gustav chucked a pouch into his friend's cell.

"Hard to say," answered Laerzo. Gwyndolyn heard him uncork the pouch and chug down its contents while Leopold continued rattling the keys. "Could you hurry up with those? You're giving me a damn headache." He tossed the pouch back to Gustav. "By the way, why am I wasting away in this heap? I thought the barracks were off-limits."

"You don't remember?" Leopold shared an odd glance with Gustav. "Probably better that way. Some Enforcers not under Dietrich's command showed up and hauled you and Gwyndolyn away. Don't worry, though. The General got your charges dropped. Most of those on duty aren't even here, so no worries, I guess." With some determination and a good many tries, Leopold finally threw open the door. "Now, let's get going. Tonight's the night."

Laerzo proceeded slowly from his cell. "I must've been in here a while. Is it already time to infiltrate the manor?"

The mention of her home drove Gwyndolyn upright to the bars.

"For you?" asked Leopold. "Afraid not. New orders. Dietrich wants you to gear up and report to the festival for patrol duty."

Laerzo shook his head so fast he almost lost balance. "Just hold on! What about the mission?"

"*Easy*, pal. You've had a rough night, remember? Take a load off and enjoy yourself when you can. We'll handle the rest."

"Oh, I see. He needs to keep a close eye in case I screw up again."

"Don't give me a hard time, got it? I don't make the decisions around here. And since when do you care about the 'mission' anyway?" Laerzo bumped Leopold's shoulder on the way toward the stairs. "Sorry, man. Cheer up! Let's have some fun later, all right?"

Nodding, Laerzo carefully climbed the shabby stone stairs and left his friends alone with Gwyndolyn. "Rise and shine," said Leopold, opening her cell. "Let's get one thing straight. You'd be stuck in this pit if we didn't need your help. Not a damn peep until we get outside, understand? I'm not above putting you out if need be."

Before she could respond, he gagged her with a strip of cloth while Gustav enveloped her body with a black, burlap sack.

Grenefest was already well underway by the time Laerzo arrived on the scene. The massive turnout was to be expected, but in his disheveled state, he was not at all prepared to deal with so many people glutting the streets. From the looks of it, those in attendance from across the Plateau easily rivaled Greneva's entire population, though he had no way of knowing how many thousands had actually shown up. This annum, most of their otherwise-modest attire had been accentuated with flashy neon trinkets and faux-flower necklaces complementary of the Trust, as promised by Mayor Rothbard, who, in rare form, had more than delivered.

Laerzo was in no rush to report for duty and so decided to take in some of the sights while he still could. First he had to pass by booths filled with spirits and ale, the thought of which made him ill. Soon after, savory smells led his nose toward a couple of familiar faces. Momma Gotta was sporting baked goods next to O'Brien's usual rotisserie meats and stew. Both were chummy enough, though rivals in competition. They greeted Laerzo happily, yet found his lack of appetite most disappointing.

He left them with the only thing his embattled stomach would allow, a cold flagon of water. While chugging it down, he watched some of the younger folk in the street with vibrant ribbons. Some formed rings, while others let loose flowing rivers in a lovely dance of lagging light. A few blocks later, he saw a different crowd watching goggled participants shooting projected images with pointed fingers at one of the Trust's VISI-game booths, something he found interesting if not a little over his head.

Even more impressive, though oppressive to his throbbing skull, was the sheer amount of light and hue flowing through and above the city. It was all so much at times that night appeared as day. When possible, he avoided near-constant streams of bright banners glistening between light posts by focusing his gaze upon the distant multitude of colorful paper lanterns gently floating in the sky. Even then, a fleet of festively decorated aero-freights would occasionally blind him with projections of luminescent fireworks or shifting shapes midair over Greneva. The sheer spectacle of it all was quite impressive, though more than enough to make his head spin.

Eventually, he ran into a recognizable Enforcer, who escorted him to his post in a more subdued space just beyond Market. Though it gave Laerzo the opportunity to recover, he found patrolling over a few measly blocks immediately dull and arguably a complete waste of time. He spent most of that time brooding over the mission, intensely curious how the others were faring without him. He truly hated being left behind, which was understandable for any ward abandoned at the door of Common Ward, but the fact that a criminal like Gwyndolyn was still allowed to go made it especially loathsome.

I should be there with them, he told himself, though on second thought, he would likely wring Gwyndolyn's neck if given the opportunity. Nevertheless, as far as he was concerned, this was yet another of the many injustices perpetuated by the Enforcers.

Moments slowly stretched into aurams with little to show for it. Laerzo's assignment, if it could even be considered one, felt more like punishment than an honest day's work, though he didn't fault Dietrich for it. After all, in short order, Laerzo had blown his chance at a good first impression. On the other hand, keeping his job despite drinking himself stupid on the clock must have meant his goodwill with the General hadn't all been squandered. Laerzo just hoped he could make it up to him somehow, at least enough to save face.

Still, he hated how pathetic the idleness made him feel. *There's still time to ditch this place and catch up with them*, he insisted before his frazzled body made it clear he was going nowhere. With dead eyes, he fumbled his thumbs a while longer until a group of bothersome drunkards loitering nearby caught his attention. Unwittingly, their joy embittered him, and he found it incredibly irksome. But it wasn't just them. There was something strange in the air that night. Even the distant music was too much for his liking. *Must they all be so loud and carefree? I wish they would shut their traps and leave!*

Just then, a deep voice within suggested he make them

do just that. *Why not make them? That's right, I do have that power. After all, they are disturbing the peace. This is my purpose now, yeah?*

Suddenly, his posture became more adversarial, his grip upon the blade tight. He caught himself staring them down, though they were too elated to notice. It would be so easy to push them around in their lowly state. The notion swelled dangerously within him, and for one long moment, he imagined the things he would do to them. Terrible, violent things. Without thinking, he proceeded toward the nearest rabble-rousers, drawing his weapon ever so slowly. Its blade beautifully mirrored every color in the sky, but he cared not. There was only one thing on his mind now. *They know nothing of decency. I will teach them.*

"Yoo-hoo!" a shrill voice suddenly chirped in his direction, and just like that, whatever strangeness came over him fled.

What was I thinking? he thought with a mean slap to the head. He could only assume the last drops of booze were still creeping through his veins. Still, the seamless twisting of his emotions felt like some heinous preamble of things to come if he left his heart unguarded.

Turning from the loiterers, he was surprised to see a figure so garishly dolled up she did not appear real. Half her face was powdered white with reddened cheeks and lips while the other half hid behind a strange porcelain mask. Heavy, intricate knots of braided copper hair sat twisted atop her head like a crown held together with a giant red ribbon. Below a fluffy white shawl made of fur, her chest was bursting from a burgundy bustier with a matching skirt and boots. Her glossy, almost unnatural exuberance gave him the impression she was either drunk or under some other chemical influence.

"Well! Look at you!" greeted the creature, though he said

nothing in return. "Silly me. Of course you don't recognize Scarlet Rothbard in such decadent decorum. I forgive you!"

"Ah, yes. How do you do, Miss Rothbard?" he asked, somewhat amazed to see the Mayor's daughter out and about so soon. Her theatrical look started to make more sense, especially the mask along her right cheek. Though upon closer inspection, it seemed no amount of makeup would be able to fully cover some of the bruising she'd incurred from days before.

"Much better now that you're here. Be a gentle sir and kindly escort me from Market. I have some business with my father Uptown and wish to be rid of this . . . riffraff."

The request wasn't overly appealing to him, though by now, he would use nearly any excuse to quit his post. "Very well."

"Excellent!" She wrapped both her hands around his left arm, and they were off. "How long has it been, uh . . .? Your name—wait! Don't tell me. I couldn't forget such a handsome face if I tried. Laerzo, was it?"

He could tell she hadn't actually forgotten at all. "Yes, Miss."

"Now, there's no need for any of that. You may call me Scarlet if you wish, but only for tonight." The odd, flirtatious pitch in her voice made him feel uncomfortable, cheapened. "You are quite the curious one. Has anyone ever told you that?"

"Not to my face."

"Well, it's true. One day, just like any other, you up and quit the Academy, never to return. See what I mean? Surely, you must've imagined how your peers took something so terribly curious."

"To be honest, I never gave it much thought."

"Really? All for the best, I suppose. Most assumed you had gone and died in the wilderness like some sort of hermit boy, myself included. That was what they called you, I'm afraid. In fact, it was only recently when I noticed you were alive and well, with a certain someone."

He snatched his arm back while continuing apace. "What's your point?"

"My *point* is that you have once again gained my attention."

"Is that so?" he asked, his tone casually dismissive. "It's the uniform, isn't it?

"Hardly. Well, maybe now that you mention it. I never thought much of you back then, but after seeing you with *her* the other day, I decided that I must have you for myself. How does that sound?"

"Not interested."

She giggled defiantly. "My, so quick to answer! Surely there's something I can do to change your mind." With an arm now over his shoulder, she leaned heavily upon him while groping up and down his obsidian mail.

"Miss, please, I'm on official business."

"Then give me the business! I'm entitled to as much. Don't tell me you're deaf to the swooning of young ladies. Like I said, I already know better, you absolute stud!"

When her uninvited hands tried to rouse his appetite in other ways, he broke away with a sad contempt in his eyes.

"Who do you think are you to deny *me*?" Scarlet demanded. He dismissed her outright and began to walk away. "The gall! Perhaps the others were right. You are a bit simple after all."

"Don't mistake simple for easy," he responded without turning.

She rushed ahead to stand in his way. "You will be mine at once, understand?" Her conceit disgusted him, reminded him of another spoiled brat.

"No one is entitled to another. Didn't the Academy at least teach you that much?"

"Oh, I understand," she scoffed before not so discretely removing a small glass decanter filled with a strange, odorous wine from underneath her dress. As she took a dainty chug or two, the dark contents shot new life into her otherwise dead stare. She then promptly stashed it away without offering any to him. "That woman still has your pair of pride pursed away. How pathetic!"

"I assure you, my *pride* is intact." He defiantly grabbed the crotch of his trousers, much to her delight.

"Well, the next time you see my dear Gwyndolyn, please let her know I want there to be no hard feelings between us pretty ladies. After all, I will survive, but *she* on the other hand—"

"Feel free to tell her yourself. I do not wish to see her."

"Hmm. Lover's quarrel?"

"Let's just say she means as much to me as you do: Nothing at all. Let her croak, for all I care."

A forced smile tightened the stitches in Scarlet's face. "*That* I will make absolutely sure. Now, if you will excuse me, I must be off. Something special has been prepared for tonight, and I simply cannot be late. I do hope you enjoy the show. Till we meet again, Laerzo."

With this, she threw her powdered nose into the air and marched right through a nearby crowd on her way to join the Mayor on stage in the distance.

It took him a moment to recognize the banquet area he'd helped Gwyndolyn spruce up days before. It was much nicer than he remembered leaving it, what with many luminous ornaments now dangling from the rooftops and a quartet of stringers plucking sweet sounds nearby. Those in attendance brought a certain magic to the plaza as well, their proper attire shimmering fabulously under the moonlight. Some danced the night away, while others flagged down dapper servants offering complimentary refreshments and appetizers. These ladies and gentlemen were many fewer than the droves found in Midtown, yet they were protected by a sizable contingent of the Enforcers standing along the perimeter, the Chief of Law included.

Laerzo had just downed a fancy cake of some sort when he was suddenly waved over by General Dietrich in the distance. Parties weren't really Laerzo's thing, yet he had no choice but to oblige. The closer he approached, the more peculiar he found the General's company. Dietrich was chatting up one gorgeous brunette, which was not unusual, though she sported an impressive spear strapped to the back of her sleek, sleeveless bronze dress. Both watched casually off to the side as General Maddock locked proverbial hooves and horns with some surly, black-bearded brute wearing a regal blue velvet jacket with golden trim. This intense standoff did not make Dietrich uneasy in the slightest. Rather, he and the woman found it somewhat entertaining despite their status as dignitaries.

Laerzo snapped to attention a few paces away, bracing himself for some formal reprimand. Much to his surprise, Dietrich greeted him with a smile and slap on the shoulder.

"Glad to see you're feeling better," said Dietrich before turning to the lovely lady. "Laerzo, may I present the Regent-General of Thannick, Cael Tannenbaum."

"Nice to meet you, ma'am," greeted Laerzo with an eager handshake. He admired how she effortlessly balanced her rough, calloused stature as a warrior with the sterling grace of a lady.

"Pleasure," responded Cael with a slight twang in her tone, mildly amused that their hands were still locked. "Sigurd, this the new recruit you've been telling me about?"

Dietrich cleared his throat until Laerzo awkwardly withdrew. "This is the one."

Laerzo didn't like the sound of that at all. "Sir, about yesterday—"

"Say no more, Cadet. You're in good company tonight." Dietrich stared over at Maddock and his opponent. "Well, for the most part. *Lady* Tannenbaum here is in rare form. I can't remember the last I saw her in anything other than overalls, a scarf, and a plate of mail. Isn't that right, Cael?"

"Keep it up, and it'll be the last thing yah ever see," responded Cael with a smile. "I very much dislike these formal affairs. Just not my style."

"You don't say," remarked Laerzo. "Could have fooled me. You look great, by the way."

Blushing, her gaze veered off ever so slightly. "Easy, lover boy. I'm already taken. It was Siggy's idea that I play dress-up for a change."

Laerzo gave her and Dietrich an odd stare. *Siggy?* he thought while trying to repress a chuckle. "Oh, I didn't realize you and the General were a thing."

Cael burst into laughter. "Are yah kidding? No, I would never . . ." She received a pouty glance from Dietrich, cleared her throat. "Pardon. That's to say that I belong to another. My husband is mingling somewhere nearby with the kids. Now, where did he go? Ah, there they are." She then waved lovingly to her sizable family in the distance. "That there in the tan suit is my husband, Trevor. He's chatting with my sons, Cecil, Nicollo, Petro, Ramus, Simon, Zeb, and my daughters, Carla, Marta, and Shella."

"I don't see your youngest," mentioned Dietrich. "How's young Gabbie doing? You had her a few moons ago, yes?"

With every bit of grace Cael could muster, she turned from him, her eyes lowering gently. "She didn't make it."

"I'm so sorry, Cael. I didn't mean to—"

"It's all right. These things just happen sometimes. Sweet Gabbie wasn't the first to go." Facing him again, she raised her glass. "Here's to hoping she's the last." Clinking glasses, both then returned their attention to the men still grappling nearby. "Would yah two give it a rest already? We all know this long-standing feud of yours ain't gonna be resolved tonight!"

"Are they okay?" asked Laerzo. "Perhaps they had a few too many—"

"Shut it, whelp!" snapped Maddock, his forehead still pressed firmly against that of his rival. Their wild, unflinching eyes never strayed from one another, not even to acknowledge Laerzo's company. "What do you say, *Lord* Tybal? Do you yield?"

Tybal Thorne brazenly snarled as if to showcase one of many shimmering treasures scattered within his gilded smile. "Not a chance, you drunken, mangy, no-good son of a—"

Just then, the downward swing of Cael's spear caused both men to part hands in a flash. The blade quickly rebounded in case either cared to take umbrage with her interference. "There, neither of yah is victor or loser. Just like in the good ol' days. Happy now?"

"How could I be?" grumbled Maddock with a sneer. His ire quickly shifted back to Tybal's frilly frock, which parted like a waterfall down and around the man's boulder of a belly. Maddock rudely flicked the tacky, makeshift medals and accolades conferred by Tybal's sycophants down south. "Our score remains unsettled."

"No surprises there," said Tybal while slicking back his

greasy head of hair so jet-black it appeared to be dipped in ink. He was slightly shorter than Maddock, though a bit rounder and arguably just as mighty. "As always, I remain undefeated as Lord of the Vanguard, whereas you are nothing but Lionel's lapdog."

"Scoundrel, come at me!"

"Enough!" protested Dietrich. "Bruno, you know he's just messing with your head. As for you, Tybal, we do not accept self-imposed ranks among those in our order. Like it or not, you are Regent-General, no more, no less. Take it up with Lord Lionel if this is no longer suitable. I'm sure he'll lend an ear."

"Aye, like he did when Gul'dan stormed my beaches, no doubt. If I remember, and I most certainly do, Ogden's pleas were cast aside as crazed puffery until it was too late. Every single one of you would've been slaughtered if not for us. Our sacrifice gave you the time to mount a defense, though by then, it did us Southerners little good. To this very day, nothing has been offered to address this, our disgrace, not even a single tin to strengthen our glorious seawall. No matter. As usual, I will protect Waldea myself, even if none are brave enough to acknowledge or appreciate it."

With this, he turned to leave.

"I've never seen yah quit a party so soon," said Cael playfully. "And what of your vote? Decided whether to support the so-called Greater Alliance?"

Tybal looked back over his shoulder with a scornful stare. "I abstain. My attendance was meant only to oppose Lionel, but he didn't even have the clams to show. With leadership like his, maybe we should welcome the Trust after all. A matter for another time. For now, I bid you farewell: Cael, Sigurd, *Bruno*." With this, Tybal strode arrogantly into the night with his counsel flocking to rejoin him.

Cael lowered the butt of her spear through its harness. "Some things never change. Is it just me, or does he bring another moronic moniker with him every time we meet?"

"At least he has withdrawn his claim as King of Ogden," said Maddock. "I'm surprised his men haven't cast him into the Waters Emeralda by now."

"Yah got that right. I do agree with one thing he said though. Rothbard's proposal won't be taken up tonight, not without every vote present. About time for me to say goodbye as well."

"Already?" asked Dietrich, almost sad to see her go.

"Afraid so. Yah know us Heartlanders are early risers. Besides, if we don't reap our harvest, who will keep yah city boys nice and fed?"

"You have a good point there," chuckled Dietrich before hugging her tightly. "Take care of yourself, all right? Let me know if you need anything."

"You too. I'll be seeing yah." She joined her family and departed soon after, leaving only Dietrich, Maddock, and Laerzo behind.

"That was something else," declared Laerzo, still somewhat smitten with Cael. "You all seem to go way back."

"That's right," said Dietrich mid-drink. "We met around your age, fought Gul'dan together. Granted, we were just runts back then."

Nodding, Laerzo placed his hand on Dietrich's shoulder. "By the way, sorry about earlier. I didn't mean to embarrass you. I could have sworn there was something going on between you and Cael."

"It's fine. We have history, to be sure, just nothing quite like that."

"That's because he was hounding over Cael's sister," said Maddock with a jerkish smile.

Dietrich shot him a contemptuous look before quickly changing the subject. "Anyway, do you have anything to report?"

"I don't," said Laerzo. "Everything seems by the books to me. Any word from the others?"

"Not yet, but they should be fine. From what I can tell, most of the Trust seem to be gathered here in Uptown." Dietrich waved away a servant trying to refill his drink. "You're probably in no mood to drink, Laerzo. Fill me up, Bruno."

"Fine," grumbled Maddock before revealing a large canteen full of something strong and taking a swig. "Bring your own hooch next time."

Just then, they turned toward the stage where Mayor Rothbard, Scarlet, and members of the Polity were clinking glasses in a bid for attention. The stringers were first to notice, their plucks shifting to carry the new tune. Then, one by one, others joined in, some gently tapping glasses with rings or cutlery, others flicking with fingers. Soon the whole crowd was in concert. They seemed quite satisfied with themselves, though Laerzo couldn't guess why. Finally, once focus had been paid in full, their chiming ceased to graciously allow Rothbard his prized moment. He accepted it happily, removing another piece of parchment, no doubt one prepared by his handlers, to recite a few words.

"Well met, and thank you. How very honored we are to have you on this fine occasion! I do not wish to take up much of your time, but my daughter, Scarlet, has gone above and beyond to make tonight possible. Ladies and gentle sirs, please do a father proud and give her a warm round of applause!"

The crowd eagerly obliged as Rothbard put Scarlet front and center. She gave a kind curtsy in return before whispering something into her father's ear.

"Oh!" he said aloud. "I've just been informed that a . . . light show will begin shortly on behalf of—who again?" Her eyes rolled, and she repeated the message. "That's right! Our guests of honor . . . who must have suddenly excused themselves. Now, where did they go off to? Oh well. Upstanding, those folks! Please enjoy!"

Soon after, a salvo of dazzling explosions bloomed like a bouquet over Mount Greneva. There were golds and reds, pinks and purples, blues and greens as far as the eye could see. The display was so bright that it turned night into day, so tremendous that most, if not all, of Waldea could revel in the spectacle. Some sky gazers in the plaza found it almost too much to look way, even if they tried. Many were rendered utterly mesmerized, if not momentarily captivated, by the grand display—that is, except for Maddock, who seemed preoccupied with something lower, closer to Mount Greneva. He took another protracted chug of swill from his personal flask, the cheap stuff like he preferred.

"Easy, friend," insisted Dietrich, eyes still affixed to the swelling bursts of arched light overhead. His friend's gaze, however, grew menacing as it focused toward something else in the backdrop. Laerzo followed Maddock's stare to the Mount's jagged outline, which had begun to glow a faint indigo. Nobody else seemed to notice, or if they did, they didn't seem to care. To them, it was simply another effort by the Trust to impress its allies, but to Laerzo, it was ominous. He turned back to Maddock, watched him down every last drop of his flask, and belch spectacularly to the stars.

"Not a chance," answered Maddock defiantly. "I like to drink before a good fight."

CHAPTER

15

"You . . . gotta . . . slow down," huffed Leopold, lagging behind the others in a dark, stuffy path made mostly of wooden planks and dirt. Gwyndolyn and Gustav were about as exhausted but ignored his plea nonetheless, keeping a steady click through the underground with torches in hand. Their earlier hike up Mount Greneva's base was brutal, as was scaling the compound's walled perimeter from the north, something they did to avoid detection despite the front gates being wide open. This did them no favors though, as they encountered a trio of Trust patrolling the courtyard therein. Each was promptly bested, bound, and hidden away, yet Gwyndolyn could not help but feel their cover had already been blown. She did not intend to stick around and find out.

Their plan had gotten off to a rough start, though not without its upside. After dispatching the Trust, Leopold and Gustav took the liberty of stripping down their foes and taking the uniforms for themselves in the hopes of continuing undetected. The pitchforks were left behind to avoid causing an undue commotion, but they otherwise wasted no time donning the strange attire, gray coats and visors alike. Serendipity did have its limits, however; Leopold's disguise was two sizes tighter than appreciated, and Gwyndolyn's was too tall. Still, it was quite a welcome turn of events, without which they were almost sure to fail.

It also appeared, so far at least, that Gwyndolyn had not led them astray. The wine cellar was exactly where she'd promised it was, on the north side of the courtyard, as well as the path that presumably led into the Carlyle estate. Of course, this was all subject to change. They continued through the dark, each hoping the other would not pull any untimely tricks when things got tough. Gwyndolyn had no clear intention of double-crossing them, but she reserved the right if it suited her purposes. After all, they more or less told her she would be abandoned if need be.

When they reached a short set of stairs leading upward, Leopold hunched over with hands on his hips for composure. Thus far, he had managed to keep quiet his chained hammer hidden underneath the coat, though the weapon's lopsided weight was starting to cramp his left leg. "Can barely . . . walk in this thing . . . without the buttons . . . popping off."

"Then . . . mug a fatter . . . guard next time," whispered Gwyndolyn before catching her breath. Noticing a gesture from Gustav, she handed over her torch and watched him extinguish both. "Breaking in was the easy part. Don't start complaining now."

"I will complain . . . thank you kindly," said Leopold. "This lousy getup . . . doesn't breathe well over my . . . armor. Don't even get me started . . . over these bulky headsets. What a bunch of . . . gibberish."

Gwyndolyn shared his disdain for the VISI. It rested heavily upon the bridge of her nose, and the colorfully crowded layers of information it presented only served to confuse her. She did happen to recognize schematics of the surrounding area on her display, a shifting map of sorts. Not that she needed directions traversing her former home.

Reaching the end of the passage, Gwyndolyn signed to stay

behind while climbing the steps to a door aglow with cracks of light. She opened it and peeked beyond.

"There are a few people around, but it should be fine if we act casual. Now, come on. My father's wing is still a ways off, fourth floor on the opposite side of the manor."

Nodding, they joined her into one of the manor's many corridors, a part of the service wing tucked in the back of the main floor. Several maids and cooks used to run food between the nearby kitchen and dining hall, but no longer. The appearance was similar to most other parts of the interior, white-walled with dark-stained molding, rosewood floors, sometimes with vaulted awnings, and currently, nothing else.

Seems the Trust studies little in the ways of decor, she thought, noting the absence of artwork, flower-filled vases, clocks, or center-carpet rugs. Also gone were the thick white drapes, replaced with thick-sheeted polymer blinds, very out of style. The manor's nakedness filled her with grief, as did seeing strangers now dwelling about. Had her angry eyes not been shielded, she might have raised suspicion to those in passing. Fortunately for her, they were largely preoccupied by the images strewn across their visors.

Reaching the south end of the floor, Gwyndolyn led them into a stone stairwell multiple stories tall and perhaps wider than it needed to be. Leopold groaned at the long, twisting, polished wooden steps, and recoiled as the sound bounced up the chamber. Both the others froze, their bewildered gazes shooting from the stairs to their careless companion. With wide eyes, they waited well after the echo died before daring to proceed. There were two full revolutions per story, and by the time they reached the top, they were spun dizzy.

"Please . . . just a . . . moment," pleaded Leopold, his stout frame rattling.

"Very well," gasped Gwyndolyn, hands over knees, her flimsy legs like noodles. Gustav shook his head at both of them before taking the lead, peeking through the entrance into Dr. Carlyle's wing, the master suite. He waved his hand at the north, then flashed two fingers leftward, indicating a pair of trench coats loitering halfway down. Gwyndolyn leaned her head to the left, beckoning for them to join her, and they entered casually into the hall, making sure to nod at the Trust in passing.

Turning the corner, Gwyndolyn sighed in relief, as did Gustav, though a bit premature when they realized Leopold didn't follow. Both leaned back into the hall, aghast, for he had just managed to catch his breath before crossing the hall with a sucked gut, chest pumping. They were almost certain the jig was up, yet somehow, Leopold managed to reach them without incident.

"These disguises sure did the trick," he whispered after rejoining Gwyndolyn and Gustav, greeting him with an exasperated stare. They all turned to find a beautifully polished dark-cherrywood door with a silver lock staring back at the end of a shorter hall. It was the same door Gwyndolyn used to steal into all those annums past, the one guarding her father's private den.

"We're here," she announced as they approached the door. "Do you have the tiny metal prongs I requested?"

Leopold unfastened a couple of buttons to rummage through his belt pouches hidden under his graycoat. Soon enough, he produced some thin steel wires cast by his very hammer earlier that day. "Might be able to pick it myself, if you can't remember how."

"We'll see. There should be two locks total." Gwyndolyn

worked both wires into the door, shifting each at different angles while her hands slowly danced around the lock's periphery. It took a minute, but she eventually heard a satisfying clunk and entered without delay. A sizable yet barren antechamber was found within, unique in shape and height. At its end was another locked door, which she picked open as well.

This time, she paused briefly before plunging into the darkened threshold toward a lantern upon the wall. It filled the room with a familiar hue, one which both warmed and pained her heart. Unlike the other emptied spaces, this one appeared uniquely beautiful, still fully furnished, untouched as if frozen in time. More pristine was the molding, which crowned the dazzling chandelier and hugged the stained wood floor under an intricate black, green, and gray rug. To the left, a plum-colored couch was flanked by two busy bookcases, and to the right was an old, smelly chalkboard. Perhaps the most memorable, however, took center stage over the large oaken desk, a brilliantly commissioned portrait of her dearly departed mother. How Gwyndolyn used to love gazing upon it whenever her father would leave on business! She hated how he'd kept all this to himself, not just the decadence, but Almalinda too. Even now, the painting served as a mirror through which she quickly lost herself, both a sad reminder of the past and a hopeful glimpse into future days.

Only after she properly paid her respects did the others think it acceptable to enter. Leopold promptly crashed on the couch with a clang, while Gustav perused rows of literature nearby. Many were academic and referential tomes, some advanced in nature, but none specific or eye-opening enough to be useful. He eagerly stashed away some for his own purposes, upset he couldn't take the whole library with him. A particularly thick book flew at Leopold, persuading him to help search the cabinets.

Meanwhile, Gwyndolyn ran a few fingers across the dusty surface of the desk on her way toward its compartments. Each one she opened was empty, and little by little, her worry intensified. Soon, all were drooping open with nothing to show.

There has to be something he left behind, she insisted while removing each drawer from its socket and twisting them every which way. Nothing. She stared carefully deep into and around the hollowed sockets of the desk. Nothing. Not even a secret letter stuck underneath. There was simply nothing left.

She was about to have a fit when a soft, lovely sound suddenly echoed from the large, gold-painted frame looming above: *Come hither, my darling.*

The familiarity of those words shook Gwyndolyn, instantly pulling a tear down her cheek. Then, seemingly with no agency or forethought whatsoever, her body slowly turned to the wall, gripped the painting at its base, and swung it along a hinge to reveal a mysterious steel door within.

"My golly, that's a beaut," began Leopold with Gustav nodding in kind. "Not a single crease or crack on the whole thing. Excellent craftwork. I bet there's something real special in there."

Gwyndolyn agreed, though the secret door struck her somewhat disheartening. There was no knob or lock to be found, no recesses to prod at all. Both arms caressed the edges of the door to spring some hidden latch, but all attempts were in vain. The side of her head pressed eagerly to the cold exterior in wait for further instructions, or at least to be graced by that voice again. "I know you're here somewhere, so please—"

"Tell me you know how to open that thing," said Leopold as hope slowly drained from his face. "You don't, do you? So, we came for nothing then."

She turned to him with a frustrated stare, though it only proved him right. She was clearly at a loss, though whether out of sheer pride or desperation, her resolve persevered. Gently resting her forehead upon the door, she closed her eyes with both hands clasped tight. The words from before were still echoing in her heart, and though the painting was turned from sight, she could swear Almalinda was smiling upon her all the same. "If it's really you," said Gwyndolyn, "please help me."

There was no response at first, but then, through some strange providence, the steel container unexpectedly clicked. At once, Leopold and Gustav dropped their books with heads cocked.

Gwyndolyn took another moment of reflection. "Thank you, Mother," she whispered with a deep breath. Approaching the metallic interior, she reached in toward two thick-stitched pads of parchment laying by their lonesome without a speck of dust on either. She handed one to Gustav, who passed it on to Leopold after a quick glance. "*Quartzcore & Other Aspecteral Phenomena* by Dr. Lawrence P. Carlyle," recited Leopold with some difficulty. "Seems pretty dense, if you ask me. Look, that one reads "*Liminatum: Theoretical . . . Impressionality Matrix.*" The words came off as utter gibberish, but he tried his best not to sound like a complete dullard. "Any idea what this is about?"

Gwyndolyn shook her head. "I haven't the slightest. It sounds important enough."

"Is that really all? Maybe you missed something further back."

"No, that's all. Let's get out of here. Something tells me

we've got what we came for. I think. Besides, all warmth has suddenly left this place."

As they began to depart, she carefully returned the painting to its rightful position as the vault door sealed with a satisfying click. Finally, after a deep breath, Gwyndolyn bid Mother a fond farewell and took her leave with the others.

Back outside the antechamber, Gustav scouted ahead before shooting his thumb into the air. They trailed back through the now-empty hall and downstairs from whence they came. Leopold seemed much happier on the decline, perhaps too much so, for every eager step downward caused his chains to shake. Thankfully, the coast was still clear, allowing them to descend without too much worry.

Just shy of the main floor, however, Gustav suddenly halted with one hand protruding, the other tapping his ear. He twisted down and around the entrance to the rear hall, where his keen eye spotted the same men from before. This pair had joined with a few pitchfork-wielding Trust, also known as pitchforks themselves, partly down the way, completely blocking the path to their escape in the cellar. The other path was occupied as well, guarded by men who seemed to be on alert. Gustav quickly flashed three fingers, then four, then only his thumb, which turned disappointingly to the ground.

"This way," said Gwyndolyn, signaling them to retreat upstairs. They found her frantic look somewhat off-putting, but they followed regardless, as neither would fare better wandering on their own. She took them back to the second floor, and after a quick scan, swiftly up the hall past the library and guest rooms. An unsettling noise considerably slowed her pace, something like a distant whimper emanating up ahead. She intended to continue forth, but upon reaching the crossing, she abruptly chose the perpendicular path leftward instead.

Their ears followed the muffled utterances ever closer to what used to be the old nursing ward. With each turn taken, the signs of distress continued to grow until they arrived at the infirmary's central door. Gustav kept a lookout while the others noticed something moving beyond its opaque window. Gwyndolyn curiously marched over for a closer look, and practically stuck her face up to the blurry glass when Leopold suddenly tackled her to the ground.

"What are you doing? Trying to get us caught?"

She stared back, more vexed than concerned, counting with four fingers before resting an ear against the lower half of the door. Much of the chatter inside remained indiscernible.

". . . the vola won't keep . . ."

". . . dose is the limit . . ."

". . . need to settle her . . ."

Gwyndolyn could hear faint sobbing all the while, and it didn't take long to figure out whose. Her heart was racing, her resolve burning. There was no time to waste. She brandished her dagger that was hidden beneath two layers of garment.

"Where did you . . .?" started Leopold, backing away from the weapon that had somehow returned to her possession. His eyes locked briefly with hers, but before he could react, she had already thrown open the door.

On the other side, they met poor Maybel, her eyes teary and dismayed, her mouth frothing. She was wearing a simple white gown, strapped to a metal table with indigo tubes jabbed into both arms. A few trench coats surrounding her watched on with a startling lack of concern, them and the pitchfork lazily lounging with his rod against the wall. It was all completely unexpected, yet so terribly familiar to Gwyndolyn.

Do you remember? a voice inside suddenly asked. She didn't want to, but the nightmare played out once more, nearly slowing time to a halt as past converged with present. The painful screaming, dispassionate figures in gray, the violet pouch of chemicals dangling like a hangman, all reminiscent of her mother's last moments. It was too similar to be a coincidence.

"Stop it!" screamed Gwyndolyn suddenly as the Trust stared back, bewildered. Leopold tugged on her to retreat but quickly ceased after witnessing his friend writhe in agony. Maybel let out a painful cry as the nearest man adjusted one of the needles already scraping within her arm. This distracted her captors, but the pitchfork had already retrieved his rod, ready to attack.

It's now or never, thought Gwyndolyn, her muscles clinching tight.

What will you do? asked the voice. *Watch the same tragic fate begin anew?*

No, she answered, *I will watch them bleed.*

Just then, as if granting a wish, Gwyndolyn's Wicked Slight inexplicably flew from her hand into the pitchfork's neck. It happened so suddenly that none could believe their eyes, and equally unimaginable, it returned to her hand just as quickly. She might have guessed it had never left if not for the fresh red dripping down its edge, or the pitchfork gurgling to death.

The man soon keeled over, the clang of his weapon upon the marble floor, filling the room with violent dissonance, which brought everyone to their knees.

Thankfully, Leopold managed to recover before his foes. Throwing off his overcoat, he quickly unraveled his chains and deftly dispatched them with one fell swing of his hammer. Still shaking, he watched Gwyndolyn stare up at him while cleaning the bloodied blade on her victim's garbs. "Not even gonna ask."

They then rushed to release the belts constraining Maybel's arms. Though addled, she was clearly happy to see them, cognizant enough to slowly remove the painful tubes from her skin. Leopold helped her stand, only for Gwyndolyn to shake her hysterically.

"You dolt! What are you doing in a place like this?"

"You came for me," responded Maybel happily, still somewhat squeamish.

Leopold shoved Gwyndolyn back before leading Maybel to the boots and spectacles atop a folded green uniform dress and white blouse on a nearby metallic cart. "I'll carry you if I gotta, but we're leaving right now!"

"No . . . I can still walk. Just tired, that's all."

Gwyndolyn nodded. "Good, now let's go!"

They had just rejoined Gustav when deafening sirens began to blast every which way. "What in the...?" asked Leopold, turning back toward one of the Trust from the infirmary. With the last bit of energy available, the crippled man had apparently dragged himself to a flashing device on the wall and flipped a couple of switches before passing out. "Must'a rigged some sort of warning. A battle cry. Damn it!" Heeding the four flailing fingers from his silent friend, Leopold readied a pouch from his belt, lit its fuse, and lobbed it around the left corner and down the hall. His fingers closed one by one, marking the countdown. "Plug your noses and follow me!"

He was off by a long second, but the explosion came soon enough. It sent him in a mad dash the opposite direction, his chains jingling. The others were close behind, their nostrils pinched as they ran. Maybel twisted back briefly to watch their pursuers collapsing in a noxious cloud of smoke. "What was that?" she asked in a comically nasal manner. "Smells like rotten hen-cockel eggs, or burning hide!"

Another pitchfork surprised them at the next crossing, resonance brimming from his forked rod. Fortunately, he was no match for Gustav, who lodged a bolt into the man's chest before even realizing it. This opened their path clear to the corner proceeding the foyer down into the main floor. Taking a quick peek, Gwyndolyn witnessed several Trust standing before its double doors leading into the forecourt. The number was disheartening enough without her recognizing some of her former servants standing in the ranks. They never left, she concluded, jerking her head back to avoid the teeth-clenching vibration bouncing off the corner wall.

"It seems they have the exit locked down. What now?"

"Of course they do!" griped Leopold, checking his belt of powders. "I thought we were headed back out the side!"

"That was the plan, at least. We'll just have to force our way through."

"Watch out!" shouted Maybel as another strong blast from down the stairs painfully shook every bone in their bodies. "Apparently, the resonance of their pitchforks can be amplified in concert. They mean business!"

"Is that so?" responded Leopold sardonically, mixing a few bags together. Yet another wave nearly brought them to their knees. "Well, I'm all about the business!"

"Surely not more stink?" asked Gwyndolyn despondently, a hand returning to her face.

"I would cover your ears this time. Fire in the hole!"

Sparking another fuse, he chucked the bloated concoction around the corner, fingers counting again, but this guess was even worse than the last. They all stared at him quizzically. "Huh. Must've been a dud. Let me try anoth—"

Suddenly, a much more destructive blast ricocheted from the walls, practically blowing out their eardrums. Leopold was unsurprisingly used to deafening noises and flew into the foyer to take stock of the impact. The entire chamber was filled with smoke and bodies groaning, some charred, others barely moving. He signaled the others to join him toward the exit, kicking a couple of stragglers on his way.

"It's locked," said Gwyndolyn after yanking at the doors.

"Then unlock it! We don't have much time."

Gwyndolyn removed her metal prongs and got to work, but just as she was starting to make progress, one of them snapped in half. "Quick, hand me another!"

"What do you mean *another*? Those were the only two!"

"Stingy as always. I think your craft needs a little work."

"Why, you—" started Leopold when some of the Trust began to rebound. "Damn it, I'll handle the door then. Just keep those creeps occupied until I do!" In an act of complete desperation, he started whacking his hammer upon the right door's metal casing in hopes of smashing the lock.

Gustav jumped into action, kicking a rising foe across the face on his way toward another striking his pitchfork near the stairs. Thankfully, Gustav was able to close the gap and wrestle over control of the rod before being blasted.

"Heads up!" shouted Maybel, pointing to two additional pitchforks emerging from the other end of the staircases. "Gwyn, do that trick from before. You know, with the dagger!" Gwyndolyn might have obliged if she knew how, but Gustav was forced to fend for himself. Just as he clocked the foe over the head with his own weapon, the newcomers sent him crashing up against the wall with terrible resonance, sent the pitchfork sliding over to Maybel. She was too weak to wield it.

"Quick, help me with this!" shouted Maybel.

Gwyndolyn grabbed the wayward rod and struck it to the ground. Despite its overwhelming pulse in her hands, she managed to lift the trembling prongs against the Trust before they could strike again. Her attack drove them away for a moment, at least long enough for Gustav to recover and for Leopold to finally swing open the doors. The guards returned soon after with even more reinforcements, but by then, Gwyndolyn had escaped with the others into the night.

Just beyond the gates, each one of them suddenly stopped dead in their tracks. The gate, the stone road leading down the path into the forest, every blade of grass, the night sky—all was tainted by an otherworldly hue. It was very disorienting, yet Maybel was the first to follow the strange light to its source, shrieking when she found it. The entirety of Mount Greneva was glowing indigo as solid as the moon was white. The sight was terrifying in its beauty.

For a time, they were so stupefied that Gwyndolyn alone noticed the Trust were still giving chase, and in greater number. She struck the pitchfork in her hands as hard as she could. Its vibration broke the spell over her friends and normalized the surrounding space. "Quick, you must flee! I'll give you some time, but hurry!"

"Oh, no you don't!" shouted Leopold.

"What do you mean?" asked Maybel as narrow bands of resonance flew their direction. "You're coming with us, aren't you?"

Gwyndolyn laid a couple of pursuers low before striking the ground once more. "There's too many of them. You'll be captured again before long. Do you want that?"

"No, but—"

"So, just forget about me and leave before it's too late!"

A most curious thing happened when Gwyndolyn spoke these words. The others abruptly acquiesced to her command, saying nothing more as they sprinted down the hill, not even so much as a goodbye. It came as quite a shock to her, maybe even a slap to the face, but they did do as she asked. Her gaze returned to Mount Greneva, an undeniable presence almost demanding she behold its majesty. She obliged, after which a terrible warbling humbled her, brought her body low and curled prostrate as if in worship. It was the pitchforks approaching. Now numb, she could only faintly sense the grass between her fingers, the scrambling of boots around her, and then nothing at all.

PART II

CHAPTER 16

Hardly an auram had passed since Mount Greneva's unwavering transformation captivated its children below. At first, many supposed it was yet another spectacle prepared in lieu of this momentous night, yet the Mount's expansive glow was far too intense to be merely for show. All-encompassing, it covered every inch of the night, bringing all levity and celebration to a halt. Though eerily breathtaking, it quickly proved overwhelming for the meek and unassuming, who fled to their homes or behind buildings for some respite. Still, none could fully escape its intensity, which seemed to saturate the air. The people became tainted by it, haunted even, falling into despair.

Soon, hysteria swept through the city as festival-goers indulged in their worst vices and fears, even many of the Enforcers. Those who were already drunk and belligerent became violent marauders who preyed upon those who stood in their way. The duplicitous and conniving engaged in thievery to a startling degree, swindling neighbors, or breaking into shops and homes to pillage whatever they pleased. The lustful sought lust by any means, and the perverse as well, and there was great debauchery in the streets.

Those attending the banquet in Uptown reacted somewhat differently and found it all more of a fabulous tribute, even as it drove them mad. The stringers were forced to play until their fingers were bloody stumps, then their toes. Meanwhile, some danced the night away, and after their bodies collapsed, they rolled and writhed gleefully in the streets. Others clamored for servants to bring every last morsel and drop of drink upon which to dine. They glutted until they became sick to their stomachs, and even after retching, they would not stop. When the servants could no longer accommodate, they were chased and flogged for fun.

Laerzo, too, was utterly gobsmacked, though he was thankfully dragged into an alleyway by Generals Dietrich and Maddock before mania could fully grip them. A few other Enforcers followed, watched Laerzo pace back and forth before lowering to retch.

"What in dreadfire is this?" the cadet screamed at his betters while taking in their unhinged stares. His stomach was still churning. "The people have flat-out lost it, and I don't blame them. Not one bit. It completely beggars belief. It defies all reason! I can't—"

In a sudden fit of anger, Maddock violently yanked Laerzo upright and pinned him to the cobblestone-slab wall. This made the others somewhat frantic as well, though none dared intervene. "Be silent, whelp, or so help me, I'll—"

"Gentlemen!" exclaimed Dietrich with such striking authority that their frantic natures were belayed at once. "In times of chaos, it is incumbent for Men of the Law to keep their wits intact. Our calm must be unwavering, stone-cold. If not, we will only add to the madness in these streets."

"But General," began Laerzo with fresh hints of hysteria.

"I need you to *relax*, Cadet," interrupted Dietrich while motioning for Maddock to follow suit. He then led his men in taking long, deep breaths, speaking again once the others had regained enough composure. "This impulse in the air is palpable to be sure, yet no different from how a soldier feels in the heat of battle. Wouldn't you say, Bruno?"

"Aye," answered Maddock flatly with dark, steely resolve. A tinge of exuberance remained in his indigo eyes.

"So, let this be a battle of another sort. Never lose yourself to the passions of the moment. Let us fight for sanity, stand for order, focus on the task at hand, and nothing else. Leave all doubts behind. Do you understand?" Dietrich was not satisfied with their silent acquiescence. "I said, *do you understand?*"

"Yessir!" they all shouted in unison, even Maddock.

"Good. Now let us do our duty. March!"

Returning to the streets, they found their compatriots had backed the base of the stage, trying their best to guard the fearful Polity from the masses. Those not completely taken by the calamitous sight had flocked to Uptown, seeking guidance and protection from the perilous turn of events.

"You gotta do something, Mayor!" cried Momma Gotta from the crowd. "My stand has been trampled, and who knows what has become of my shop. I thought Greneva was a place of order. What say you?"

Rothbard nervously watched the crowds cheer her on. "Everyone, please remain calm. It appears some of our fellow Waldeans have had a bit too much frivolity for one night. Fear not! Our Enforcers are already working to quell the overindulgent."

"What a load of cripe!" shouted O'Brien from farther back with a bloody cloth wrapped around his head. "Even some of the Men of the Law have lost the plot. I caught a couple rummaging through my tavern for spirits and got this nasty gash for my trouble!"

"That's quite the accusation, tavern master!" answered Montgomery, the Chief of Law, from onstage. "We Enforcers serve to protect, not plunder. Do you have any witnesses to this alleged misconduct? You'd surely better, or—"

"Or what? You'll give me another rap over the head? I'd like to see you try!"

This caused discontent in the crowds to fester.

"This doesn't look good, General," said Laerzo while trying to ignore the mountain glowing in the corner of his eye.

Dietrich gazed back with a stiff, frigid stare. "Steady on, Cadet. That goes double for you, Bruno!"

"*Yessir!*" griped Maddock, cocked and ready to pummel the first person foolish enough to start trouble.

"I hear your words," assured Mayor Rothbard. "You are right to cry for justice! But please, do not add to the unrest of this momentous evening!"

"This is all your fault!" screamed a frantic man from the masses.

"What do you intend to do?" shouted another to the Polity, who could only cower before their constituents. Suddenly, a scuffle broke out in the rear section, causing all sorts of terror to ripple through the crowd. The Chief of Law dispatched some of his Enforcers with a point of his finger, but things were too far out of hand.

"This is madness!" proclaimed an older gentleman riddled with bruises. His voice was strained to its limit. "Sancta, save us!" he began to chant over and again, drawing some hisses in the crowd.

"None of that!" squealed the Mayor, a chill running down his spine. "We voted long ago not to speak those words!"

When some of the mob tried to silence the man, Momma Gotta met them with a couple of stiff fists. "He's right! This is what happens when we bury her name deep within our hearts. How shameful we are to discard her! We must return to righteousness. We must call forth Sancta at once, and purge this wickedness from the land!"

Scarlet suddenly stepped forward, somewhat amused by the outburst. "*Sancta*? You're right that her absence is to blame. That's because she abandoned you long ago! In fact, the Sh'tama had it all backward. It was actually *Denestra* who sacrificed everything to save you."

"My dear girl, what are you saying?" cried Rothbard, now clearly terrified for his daughter. He could already see Enforcers begin to swell around her. "Stop this at once!"

"Blasphemous girl!" rebuked Momma Gotta. "Denestra is the Usurper! She sold out Sancta and her disciples to win King Avalon's favor in the ancient days. Lest you get it twisted."

"Don't you see?" asked Scarlet, her smile curling deviously. "Denestra is calling to us from above! She's the true Avatar, the forgotten Queen of Waldea." As she continued this peculiar manner of speaking, the Enforcers finally moved to restrain her by the arms, though she didn't seem at all concerned. "Bless the Holy Mother, Denestra! Bless those who invoke her name! I call upon you, most hallowed Queen! Please save me from the scourges of man! Make me a disciple of your will!"

The entire lot of them stared dumbfounded at the flagrant display, but nothing could prepare them for what transpired next. Deafening song rang out from above as if to herald a ring of white light growing around the Mount. Then, from its peak, emerged a concert of luminous beings clad in shining white robes. Uniform in splendor, each descended with wings spanning twice their height, each face like a star.

Save for one, brighter and more beautiful than the rest. It appeared before them with wings numbering seven: two from its feet, four in flight, and one draped over its face. It held a golden staff topped with a gem of pure cerulean floating between two prongs. Whereas the concert circled high above, singing harmonies to the crowd, this exceptional figure hovered but several feet over the stage to make a thunderous announcement.

"Release the girl, for she has called my god by name. I say to you, girl, repeat it and receive her favor, now and forever."

Scarlet broke free of the Enforcers and summarily fell to her knees. "Yes, the Trust has taught me about you! You have come in the name of Denestra, the one True Mother of all! The Bringer of Light! I submit myself to her!"

Laerzo found the awesome being's voice strangely familiar, though it did not become apparent why until the seventh wing lifted from its brow. "Algus?" Laerzo cried in wonderment before the startled throngs. "What on Essa happened to you?"

"You dare claim to know his name?" shouted Scarlet. "He has come from on high!"

The being stared down at them and smiled faintly. "Yea, I say to unto you. I am the one who hath spoken to the Holy Mother. I alone know her decrees! She calls us blessed creatures heralds, yet you may call me Frater." Spreading his likeness wide, he doth proclaimed, "Hear me! Our True Mother, Denestra, commands you give her praise!"

"How shall we praise her?" asked Scarlet.

"From her holy Hypha Tree, a wine will be made. Accept its sacrament in her name lest ye become ashen in body and soul! Give tithings of blood and toil, erect a bastion high upon the summit in her honor. Those who defy her will shall be cast into the bowels of the Mount. Only then will they be made to know the truth!"

"*Daimon!*" shouted Momma Gotta. She was utterly disgusted by the thought. "We keepers of the Sh'tama faith would never pay tribute to the Usurper! It is Sancta that warrants our praise! Come, faithful, let us pray in *her* name!" At once, she joined hands with O'Brien and her congregation in a circle, and chanted Sancta's praises in sweet, reverent tones. This, of course, was an affront, not only to the Enforcers surrounding them, but also the Polity, Rothbard included. The resplendent being—Frater, it was called—simply stared on and allowed the altercation to take place.

"They have violated the peace," announced the Chief of Law. "In the name of Waldea, I order them to be restrained and taken into Enforcer custody."

"Yes, haul them away!" repeated the Mayor, sweat dripping over his fat, pinched face.

"This is terrible," said Laerzo, utterly petrified by the revelation unfolding before his eyes. "Sir, you have to stop this at once. The chief is your deputy, yeah?"

"Monty is simply observing the law as it stands," answered Dietrich, much to his cadet's consternation. "As long as he keeps the peace, I will not interfere. Besides, I must admit that I am quite beside myself at the moment. I cannot deal with the Enforcers any more than I can these beings in the sky."

A struggle briefly ensued between the prayerful and the Enforcers, but wishing not to cause undue bloodshed, Momma Gotta and the others eventually offered themselves willingly in the name of peace. Still, the Enforcers had quite a task on their hands, for the crowds clamored for the faithful to be struck down then and there. When these Men of the Law would not oblige, the growing mob eagerly took matters into their own hands.

This outburst finally snapped Laerzo and the generals swiftly into action. Moving in, they guarded the accused from flagons, plates, and other objects flying in their direction. Momma Gotta cried out as a sharp piece of cutlery struck her in the shoulder. "Sancta, I am yours! Please do with me as you will!"

"Leave them alone!" one voice suddenly erupted right before a massive star fire exploded overhead. It was Leopold with another concoction, followed closely behind by Gustav and Maybel. "Harm a single hair on Momma's head, and I'm coming for you!" shouted Leopold with pouch in hand.

The crowds staggered in confusion, but only for a moment.

"You're back!" shouted Laerzo, though he noticed one person missing among them. "Hey, where's Gwyndolyn?"

"Who?" asked Maybel plainly as Leopold rushed to his mother, who was being hauled on stage with the others.

"What do you mean, *who*? She was with you earlier, wasn't she?"

After a moment of reflection, something seemed to click in Maybel's head. "Oh, that's right. Well, she told us to forget about her and flee, so . . . I guess we did? Very strange, now that you mention it."

"I can't believe you right now. What about you, Gustav?" Just then, Laerzo noticed a strange aura wash over his friend in waves. One moment, it was indigo just like the Mount, and the next, it was completely bereft of any taint at all.

Algus noticed this as well, appeared most displeased by the sight, but Scarlet approached him, pointing to the criminals with one arm and her holy messenger with the other. "Frater, your devout followers wish to rebuke these wicked souls. How shall they be judged?"

"They have turned ashen, their features gray. And so, these cursed will spend the rest of their days deep within the Mount." The moment Frater spoke these words, the appearance of Momma Gotta and the others became emaciated and pale. This sudden revelation caused gasps in the crowd. Then the heralds descended in pairs to snatch each ashen person away.

"Hold on, Momma!" roared Leopold, jumping onstage. He tugged with all his might to keep her steady, and Gustav even shot a bolt into one of the herald's legs, but sadly, Momma Gotta was stolen into the night. "Momma! Damnit!"

Laerzo noticed another winged creature point toward his ghastly, glowing friend. "Gustav, watch out!"

But it was too late. While the creature hauled Gustav away, the aura around him stole some of the heralds' light in pulses.

"Oh no," Scarlet began disingenuously. "My dear father has also turned ashen! I will miss you dearly. Repent, and you may still be saved!"

"What are you . . .?" asked Rothbard when his daughter ripped a red hair from his head and handed it to him white as snow. "This cannot be! No, don't take me away! Scarlet, tell them I'm with you. Please, I beg you!" His protestations did nothing to save him from being snatched up like the others.

By then, Scarlet was beaming with excitement. She shot a wicked glance to the cowering polity before turning to face the Chief of Law and his Enforcers. "My dear Montgomery, who do you serve?"

"We . . . serve the law," he answered reluctantly.

"*Denestra* is the new law, understand?" She proclaimed her words loud enough for all to hear, and both crowd and Polity bowed, one by one. She waited for the chief to capitulate as well before continuing. "Good. Now gather your men and bring me every last disbeliever and ashen you find. We will sort them out in due time."

Once the Enforcers descended upon the people, all chaos broke loose. Dietrich and Maddock tried to quell some of the unrest, but things were clearly beyond their control. Suddenly,

Dietrich turned to Laerzo. "You must take the others and flee to Stolgrum! Tell Lord Lionel what has happened!"

"What?" asked Laerzo as Maybel clung to his side. "But what about you? Leopold and I will stay here to help!"

"No, nothing good will come of that. The Enforcers have been compromised, and you are no Enforcer. Besides, can you not see the condition Maybel is in? She needs her brother right now." With a quick pat, Dietrich rustled her bangs before waving Leopold over. "General Maddock and I will stick around for a while yet, but don't worry. When the time is right, we'll take leave of this place with haste. If you do not see us in Thannick after three days, continue on to Stolgrum without us, understood?"

"But—"

"That's an order! Now get moving!"

CHAPTER 17

Laerzo thought the night would last forever, that the indigo would never fade. He and Leopold led Maybel as fast they could under slivers of tainted light drifting through cracks in the forest's canopy. Arms at the ready, the fledgling cadets were practically at their wits' end, desperate to keep all fears in check, impressed their friend had done the same, at least thus far. It was no easy feat for any of them, for every bleeding tree they passed became sickly with rotten bark covered in leeches, leaves blazing with cursed embers. A persistent squall kicked up dust, turned flashes of this eerie light into lanterns or spirits floating in the haze. It thickened the air, made it foul, heavy on his already-weary lungs.

Whenever their bodies floundered, they took a moment to rest under the cover of brush, yet never remained for long. A disturbance would always send them scrambling, something like fowl mistaken for heralds overhead, or the sound of crunching foliage nearby. At one time, Maybel insisted she could hear delirious pleas for mercy filling the haunted space, nowhere in particular, yet near enough to fill her heart with sorrow. It was unclear to whom they might have belonged, perhaps unfortunate souls overwhelmed by the awful light or ensnared by zealous Enforcers in pursuit of their ashen. One particularly shrill set of screams could only be imagined as vicious creatures driven rabid in the night, whether they be beast, man, or prey.

Regardless, the three of them continued toward what they assumed was the west. It was difficult to figure how far they'd come, as the moon was a lousy guide, obscured by trees and the persistent eerie light. They were truly desperate to quit those woods, yet their legs would only deliver them so far in one night, definitely not to the outskirts of Thannick. Laerzo pointed toward a comfy ditch tucked away from the relentless glare of Mount Greneva, suggesting they give in to their aching limbs. When his friends protested, he insisted despite his own judgment it was mostly fatigue playing tricks on them. Neither believed him but gave in to his sweet lies so long as he promised to keep first watch.

Once they had settled into the crevice, he perched along the high ground and watched their eyes quickly drop. His weren't too far behind, though he kept his word for a time, scanning his surroundings the best he could. When his alertness faded, he stood upright, and when that failed, he leaned against a nearby tree for support. He even tried pinching himself once or twice to keep his eyes from falling.

It was the bramble rustling farther down the ditch that brought him back to full attention.

"Who goes there?" he called out, but there was no response.

Must have imagined it just like before, he thought.

Those two would have woken up otherwise, but then again, both were deep sleepers, something he always envied in them. Wiping his eyes, he squinted to check for varmints or other creatures scurrying about, but all was still. He was just about to nod off when the noise returned, this time in a shape clearly emerging from the shadows. It was a man, his ghastly face partially illuminated by rays of indigo. It was General Maddock.

"Boy, am I glad to see you," greeted Laerzo with a soft, tired tone. "What happened? I thought you were going to stick around Greneva."

Maddock put a finger to his lips while brandishing the greatsword from his back. Strangely, neither Dietrich nor any others joined his company. He was still far away, but Laerzo could see the intensity in his eyes, the sweat gleaming from his scarred brow. He seemed hurt, run-down.

There was another rustle, this one behind Laerzo. Drawing his blade, he spun around the tree, only nothing was lying in wait—nothing in front of him, at least. As he twisted back around, Maddock was suddenly standing before him with his mighty weapon poised to swing. Laerzo fell backward and hit his head on the tree, though still positioned to deflect the incoming strike. Just as he tried, however, both their blades completely disappeared, much to his shock.

That was only the beginning of Laerzo's misfortune. A pair of thick, calloused hands took hold of his neck and seized the life from his throat. He grasped both hands tightly, already too exhausted to peel even one away. Before long, his body was lifted with uncanny strength and propped against the tree. Kicks from his dangling boots only angered Maddock, who slammed the cadet's head.

Laerzo could swear somebody was calling out to him then, but the words seemed worlds away, and he was too preoccupied by tiny rivers of red sliding down the General's hulking, sleeveless arms. The blood mortified him, even more so when he discovered it was gurgling from his own throat. His only hope was that it would help him slink through Maddock's grasp, though no amount of blood could loosen such a murderous grip. His vision now a blur, Laerzo was at his limit. All he could do was stare into Maddock's wild, indigo eyes and wait for the rest of his life to fade.

"Would you wake up already?" boomed Leopold while shaking his friend by the shoulders.

Shooting upright, Laerzo sent Leopold tumbling down the ditch before quickly brandishing his blade. "Stay back!" Laerzo's free hand felt the back of his head, found nothing but a bug bite. "Oh, it's just you, Leo. What's going on?"

Leopold brushed himself off while shooting a nasty leer up the hill. "You told me to wake you when it was my turn to stand guard, remember? Sorry I even bothered."

Laerzo slowly sheathed his weapon. "I thought you were . . . out to get me."

"Not yet anyway. Don't tempt me with a good time." Leopold took a long, deep breath, his wide nostrils flaring. "I don't know what happened last night, and honestly, I don't want to know. But look! The light is gone, and dawn is on its way."

Laerzo was more suspicious than relieved. "Apparently, and who knows for how long?"

"No kidding. Best not stick around to find out. Besides, I want to fall asleep in a proper bed tonight. My back is killing me, no thanks to you."

Laerzo looked around for Maybel. He found her rolled into a ball nearby, still fast asleep. "Maybe we should let her rest some more first."

"No can do," said Leopold while dawning his orange cape and headband from a nearby pack. Wearing both seemed to put a pep in his step. "You heard the General. He needs us to report back to Headquarters. Why don't you carry her for now?

If you ask nicely, I might help out later. Now, come on. Dietrich wouldn't want us to dawdle."

Once every provision had been gathered, they gently saddled Maybel onto Laerzo's back and soldiered onward. There was, indeed, a welcome shift in the atmosphere, a quiet calm replacing the horrible curse with its stalking shadows and creeping noises. There was no telling exactly when or why the eerie tinge from the east had vanished, though it mattered little then. So long as the new day continued to dispel their fears, they were more than happy to resume the journey ahead.

Still, there was a palpable tension in the air like a faint buzzing, which neither could seem to shake. At first, they assumed it was just their heads swimming from lack of sleep, but even the wildlife nearby seemed to act in strange, unpredictable ways. Pesky bugs that usually filled the air now covered entire tree trunks like flittering blankets. Then there were the brown-furred squrats, normally meek, fearful forest varmints now aggressively dropping from branches, their hungry stares watching the travelers pass. Conversely, the more irritable and territorial hamhern, with their black, narrow eyes and tusked snouts, were now all too quick to flee at the faintest of noises, including affectionate snorts from their own kind. Even fowls of various sorts would occasionally swoop down with talons drawn, mistaking the hair on their heads for overgrown grubs.

They seemed especially hungry, as did Leopold, whose gut was grumbling louder than usual. While rummaging through his things, he suggested they rustle something up, perhaps snag some quick game on the way. Of course, he had plenty of snacks to spare, though perhaps not enough to last the trip for three. Laerzo shook his head softly as not to disturb Maybel.

He hadn't come prepared with traps or much else to hunt with, and questioned how quickly they could score without the aid of a certain someone.

This led to thoughts of Gustav and the others still painfully present in Laerzo's addled mind. He wondered whether Dietrich and Maddock had fled, more the former of the two for obvious reasons. Gwyndolyn's absence was noted and appreciated, though he was curious where she went off to as well. Even O'Brien crossed his mind a couple of times, enough to make him guilty for never paying his hefty tab. There was plenty he wanted to discuss, almost too much, yet both spent much of the morn taking turns carrying Maybel in silence, attempting to determine what had happened to their people, to their home.

Occasionally, he glanced over to the anxious, angry look on Leopold's face, no doubt on account of Momma. Laerzo knew she was a tough, resilient woman like most Waldeans who survived the War, but like Leopold, he wondered if they would ever see her again. The thought of those winged creatures spiriting her away haunted him even then, that and the fact that his kid brother was among them.

The Algus I knew would never do something so horrible, he thought, hoping he wouldn't be forced to confront him.

Around high dawn, they agreed to settle down and take a break. Leopold left to gather some food, while Laerzo stayed behind with Maybel, who was still fast asleep. Her face was pale in the daylight. He rested his hand under her bangs and noticed she was running slightly hot. Until now, it hadn't even occurred to him to ask what had happened in the Carlyle estate. Given recent events, a part of him didn't want to know.

Leopold eventually returned with some herbs and truffles for a quick stew, as well as a pouch filled with jiccam berries for Maybel whenever she decided to wake. They ate mostly in silence, keeping an eye peeled in case their meal happened to attract any undesirable company. Strangely, they were left completely at ease, or rather unease. The forest was almost completely bereft of sound, which struck them quite nervously. They quickly finished their meal and hit the trail once more.

It was sometime later in the day when Maybel began to stir. Even before rousing from her slumber, her cute button nose lifted from Leopold's shoulder and crinkled against his pungent scent. It was stale and unpleasant like sour milk, though faint enough not to completely offend her senses. She awoke with a squeaky yawn, slightly displeased to find Leopold carrying her, yet thankful the odious smell did not emanate from her brother. "The morn has come already?"

Laerzo was happy to finally see her coming around. "And passed. You slept right through it, not that I'm at all surprised. How are you feeling?"

"Well enough, I guess." Her eyes were drawn upward to the light peeking through the leaves.

"What's the matter?"

"Nothing. Well, it's strange. For a moment, I thought we were going the wrong way."

"We've been heading west the whole time," said Leopold, his voice somewhat restricted by her arms crossed around his neck. "Can you walk? I could use a load off."

"Oh, sure. Thank you, and sorry for the trouble." Her dismount was fairly clumsy, but she was happy enough to be on her feet again. Greeted by the Solstar through a parting in the canopy, she gazed longingly upon it until tripping over the root of a tree.

"Ouch!"

"Careful! Are you sure you're all right?" asked Laerzo,

turning to help her up. "I can carry you a bit farther, if you'd like." She said nothing in response and only stared blankly upward. "Maybel, I'm talking to you."

"Yes, I'm fine. It's just . . . this stretch of forest is supposed to be narrow, correct? Yet we still haven't cleared it. Isn't that odd?"

"Not necessarily. Our pace has been somewhat sluggish. Don't worry, we'll get to Thannick sooner or later."

"Westward, right?"

"Yes, Maybel, to the west." Laerzo didn't like the way her attention was meandering, how she appeared increasingly scatterbrained. Following her line of sight, he suddenly stopped to give her bony shoulders a shake. "Didn't anybody teach you not to stare into the Solstar? You're going to go blind!"

"Well, blinder than she already is," joked Leopold.

"That's just the thing," began Maybel. "I have been for some time now, yet it's almost like I'm not staring at anything at all."

Leopold tried to block her path, but the mousy girl quickly eluded him. "Are you crazy? Look away, you silly girl!"

"It doesn't matter. Don't you get it?"

"She's right," muttered Laerzo, now leering upward himself. "I could stare all day, and it wouldn't bother me. What does this mean?"

"It can really only mean one thing. That isn't the Solstar."

Leopold scratched his head of rusty hair. "I don't follow. Care to explain?"

Only Maybel couldn't, at least not right away. Scanning the surrounding area, she turned around again and again, slowly at first. However, completely out of the ordinary, her movements seemed deliberate enough.

Laerzo stopped her in fear she would become dizzy and stumble again. "Enough. You're scaring me."

"Just then, I felt the warmth at my back," said Maybel, much to his confusion. Then she broke away and ran several feet ahead before pointing up through another clearing in the forest. Her other hand raised as if guarding against something. "There!"

"Where? I don't see anything," replied Leopold, only he soon shielded his eyes as well. "So bright—wait! You don't mean—"

"Exactly. There's no mistaking it now."

It took Laerzo another look at both points to understand. "But if this one's a fake, that means—"

"We've been heading north this whole time!" shouted Leopold. "Damnit, what in dreadfire is going on here?"

"It seems somebody has been playing tricks on us," responded Maybel with a hand cupping the back of her head. "It was the same way last night. Every time we made some progress, something spooked us in another direction. Almost as if we were being prevented from leaving Greneva. That's the impression I get, at least."

"So, then what are we supposed to do?"

"Well, if the real Solstar is here, then we should move this way instead," declared Maybel with some certitude. "What do you say? Shall we give it a try?"

Laerzo could not think of a better suggestion. He just wished they had noticed it sooner. "All right, let's give it a shot."

Changing course, they made way along a new path, hoping it would deliver them into the Heartland sooner or later. About an auram or so afterward, they could see the beginnings of a clearing up ahead. Giggling, Maybel was pleased she could return their kindness, albeit in a small sort of way. Laerzo and Leopold were just happy to have her along. Their spirits lifting, they picked up the pace, eager to leave the forest and find a road leading into Thannick. Once they finally did, however, their smiles began to fade.

The detour had taken them farther than they'd originally thought—so far that Lake Tuley now greeted them but a couple of clicks north. From the humble fishing town hugging its northwestern tip to the tributary on the opposite end, this expanse of majestic reservoir was quite breathtaking to behold. They traced its gracious stream eastward all the way back to Mount Greneva, which, as far as they could tell, had returned to its original state. Also, the Solstar's impostor had mostly faded with distance, a strange sight to behold. Each stared upon the mountain town for a long moment in silence, wondering when, if ever, they would be able to return.

Laerzo then shifted back north-westward to the town upon the lakeside. Tuley was its name. He wondered if they should seek out a place to stay there, but he saw no ferries to carry them across the waters. And reaching Tuley on foot would take too much time that would be better spent heading back south. They weren't going to reach the small stretch of hospitality in Thannick properly before dark, either, and that meant every door in town would likely be shut. Those in the Heartland were simple people, early to bed and even earlier to rise. If lodging wasn't booked ahead of time, last-minute travelers would simply be out of luck until the next day.

Maybel suggested that if the fields would be their sleeping grounds tonight, they might as well take a moment and enjoy the view. Laerzo and Leopold agreed. After finding a nice spot of grass upon a hill in the clearing, each basked in the cool evening breeze while watching the Solstar gaze upon itself in Tuley's glistening waters. The oranges and reds in its reflection were occasionally interrupted by ripples of fishing boats passing. And as more returned to harbor, the fowls circled overhead the flopping fish.

Leopold noticed one such man along the south side of the lake, with a long, limber strip of wood more akin to a walking staff than a reeling rod, though it seemed to serve as both. He leaned upon the rail of his wagon, one strangely without any geldtmare to pull. Much of its metallic frame appeared dirty, or perhaps rusted, for it refused to shine. The man loaded his catch for the day, perched upon a high seat, with the staff he secured vertically into a slot on his right. A couple of tugs at his lever sent the large contraption popping and sputtering steam or smoke, or perhaps both. Laerzo and Maybel were delighted to see it propel itself back toward the road, surprised to see Leopold scoffing. The look on his face suggested he recognized the man, and that a part of him wished he hadn't.

"Fantastic!" cheered Maybel with a smile and an idea. "We have to go see how that works! Think we can get a ride?"

"I don't know if we can. Reach it in time, I mean."

Laerzo jumped upright. "Only if we don't act. Let's get a move on!"

"Wait a—" But before Leopold could say no, the others sent him dashing after them down the hill.

CHAPTER

"This ol' wagon's in rough shape, Gibbs," griped Leopold, leaning uncomfortably upon the carriage railing. He and the others were surrounded by hay, baskets filled with spuds, greens, and fruits; and a bucket of smelly fish. His nose hated the way each scent mixed with the trail of smoke in the air. "Can't you pick up the pace?"

"'Fraid I can't hear yah up here," answered Gibbs over the chugging of the engine, though his playful tone suggested otherwise.

"You might if the rickety screws on that core were tightened. Can barely keep that rotten crop you call fuel from leaking!"

"Anything else, sonny?"

"Nothing you haven't heard before, old man! If you just took my advice for a change, this hunk of junk would operate a lot smoother!"

The man twisted in his seat and stared back in a tan bucket cap with small, beady eyes hiding under gray brows like whiskers. The matching mustache curled on each end of his wide, bumpy nose. He wore a white long-sleeved shirt tucked into dirty mustard overalls and waxy brown water boots practically tied around the knees. "You ungrateful porker! This *hunk o' junk* usually purrs without yer heft on board."

"Is that so?"

"Darn right! Don't believe me? Let's have a good ol' fashioned race. I reckon she's smoke yah plain and simple!"

A sudden bump interrupted their argument and roused Laerzo as well. He stared dully at the same patchwork of land that had put him to sleep. Now much of its vibrance had retreated with the day. He looked over to Maybel at the opposite corner, her legs hanging off the back of the wagon, then to the Solstar poking from the horizon like an egg yolk upon the road. In the distance, the Reapers had finished storing their barrels of red amaranth, white coriander, and chili beans in nearby barns before turning in for the night. Now he had only the incessant bickering to keep him entertained, at least long enough to fall asleep.

"Youngsters these days got a weird way of showin' thanks," continued Gibbs. "Didn't the Alliance teach yah any manners?"

"Don't worry," replied Leopold with a dismissive tone. "Told you I'd get this thing spruced up for the trouble!"

"Yah know full well *this thing* has a name! Show some respect to ol' Bessie here."

Leopold rolled his eyes. "Oh, how could I forget? Tell me, Gibbs, when's the last time you gave Bessie a nice cleaning?"

"Beg yer pardon? That's awful personal to ask."

"No, it's not. There's smoke in the exhaust pipe. You know damn well you gotta flush the chamber every now and again. And would it kill you to scrape off some of this rust? It's the first time I've seen her in such bad shape."

"Keep yammerin' and we'll see who's in bad shape, sonny!"

"Listen here, you—"

"All right already," interrupted Laerzo, wiping the drowsiness from his eyes. "Mr. Gibbs, we are—"

"Gibbs is fine, thank yah kindly."

"Sure, Gibbs. We're grateful for the ride, really. Where'd you find a gadget like this, anyway?"

"Oh, here 'n there. Every bit of her was scrap left by the Trust in the old war. You'd be surprised how much our farmhands trip over on the daily. I've been tinkerin' quite a bit since then, yah see?"

"You and Leo both, I take it."

"Yah got that right! Met him ages back, stubbing his fat toe on some junk while I was tradin' stock with Momma. Told 'im I'd pay for any he hauled to my yard. Boy, was he all about it! Anytime they was in town, she'd drop him off and we'd spend all day gatherin' scrap. Before yah knew it, he was tinkerin' around, even meltin' spares when he needed 'em. He's a sucker for that manner of thing now, I'm sure yah know!"

"Better to make new than due, old man," quipped Leopold.

"Yessir. Only a matter of time till we got the rest pieced together. It was gettin' Bessie to move that got me really guessin'."

"How did you?" asked Laerzo, his interest slightly piqued. He was surprised Maybel hadn't jumped at the chance to ask herself.

She doesn't seem very talkative at the moment, he thought.

"Well, you see," started Leopold, somewhat uncomfortable by the question. "We stewed some fermented lavabeans in various vats of hooch. Took some effort to find the right mix, but we were in business before long."

Gibbs let out a high-pitched cackle, one Leopold didn't appreciate in the slightest. "That's one way of puttin' it! A couple of times he lit 'imself up good tryin' to make a sweet treat for my girl. But would yah know? That son'bitch came through in the end! Me and Bessie been back together ever since."

Leopold shook his head. "What a name, Bessie. She an old flame? Ball and chain?" He chuckled when Gibbs wouldn't answer. "Sounds more like some loud, brick-house of a woman who put you through the ringer in your younger days."

"No clue what yer yappin' about."

"You gotta hit the town more often, Gibbs. Find yourself a real catch."

"No need. This big gal here is my one and only! 'Sides, yer one to talk! Never seen a fine lady 'round yah m'whole life! Don't keep 'er or yer Momma waiting too long, yah hear?"

As they started another go-round, Laerzo stared back to Maybel, who still faced the dimly lit road. She was snacking from a small pouch, occasionally tossing something like large seeds left and right into the fields. Gone was her usual pep, which had carried them through the day, replaced with a pouty gaze lifting toward nothing particular in the starry sky. This air of loneliness around her saddened him, took him back to the very day they'd first met at Common Ward.

Back then, he watched from afar as his siblings found Maybel shivering alone in the cold after a violent knock at the door. She couldn't have been more than four, and he'd been ten. He remembered her being surrounded in the lobby, petrified and emotionless while draped in blankets. She gave no answer to their questions, not even a name, for over a fortnight. Most wards quickly found her to be a chore and eventually ignored her altogether. Laerzo, on the other hand, saw a part of himself in her, the recluse. For many days, he watched over her from a distance until he finally found the right time to say hello. She opened up to him with some hesitation, but from then on, the two became inseparable. She always followed him with a smile.

Not at the moment, it seemed. *So much time has passed,*

he thought in disbelief, though filled with a warm reminiscence. He plopped down alongside his old friend. "I see you're finally getting your appetite back. How are those jiccam berries?"

From the pouch, Maybel lifted one of the orange orbs half the size of her palm, placed it in her mouth, and sucked out the juice with a pinched face. "Perhaps a bit too sweet," she said, her mouth still full. "Or sour? I don't know. My stomach has been off lately."

He watched her remove the withered husk, partially unconsumed, and toss it to the roadside. "They got seeds in those?"

"Pits, I suppose," she replied, eating another.

He didn't recall jiccam berries having pits. "Mind if I try one?"

"Sorry, haven't had much to eat lately." She seemed fairly squeamish.

"You hanging in there? Still look under the weather." He placed his arm around her shoulder, after which she leaned on him reluctantly, still eating away. "Homesick?"

She discarded another pit. "Of course. Greneva is all I've ever known. I hope everyone is okay."

"They'll be fine. It's you I'm worried about. What were you doing up in those mountains anyway? With *them*." Staring down, he watched her pop another berry in her mouth. "Was it really your idea or Gebhardt's?"

"What?"

"Did she put you up to it? Come on, you can tell me. You don't always have to do what she says."

"I know that."

"If she's hurting you—"

"That's enough."

"You don't have to stick around, is all I'm saying."

She shrugged him off. "I'm not like you, okay? I can't just leave my brothers and sisters behind."

"That's not fair. It's not like we never saw each other." Leaning forward, he turned toward her, but she wouldn't meet his gaze. "Look, I'm sorry, but I couldn't keep living under that roof."

"I don't want to talk about it."

Laerzo said nothing for a time before continuing. "I wish things didn't have to change, but they did. Ever since that day—"

"Not this again."

"There's just something about her, I know it!"

"Drop it for now, please?"

"How can I? After what she did—"

Maybel finally faced him, looked him dead in the eye. "What did she do? Give us a home? Clothes? Food to eat? You act like she killed Algus or something, just so you'd feel better after he died. She didn't, okay?"

"I know that now. He's alive, Maybel!" He watched her startled stare return to that same spot in the sky. "Didn't you recognize him? That winged figure from Grenefest. Tell me I didn't imagine it. It was him!" His outburst caused the others to go silent.

"What're you two on about?" asked Gibbs, still minding the road. "Hold on a tick." He reached for a lantern at his feet, hung it on his staff, and lit the wick, imparting them all with a slight golden glow. "That's better. I like a little gossip now 'n again. Do proceed!"

"The festival," said Laerzo. "I take it you weren't there last night?"

"No, sir. Had to be up at the crack'a dawn. What of it?"

"People really lost their cool," said Leopold. "There was this strange light coming from the Mount."

"I saw the show from down here, boys. So much color in the sky! Those works must'a cost an arm and a leg!"

"Not the fireworks, Gibbs, the mountain! It was glowing like a poker in the flame."

Gibbs scratched his head. "'Fraid I don't follow. Sure yah didn't tie over one too many?"

Leopold stamped his boot on the creaky floorboards. "Gibbs, not even your eyes are that bad! It covered the whole city, and then some! You seriously didn't see it?"

"No need to get worked up. Must'a just turned in early, that's all."

"Needless to say," interjected Laerzo, "things got really dicey. There were these shiny winged figures flying around, and they started hauling people through the air!" To this declaration, Gibbs simply shook his head as Laerzo continued. "General Dietrich eventually ordered us to flee and head toward Stolgrum."

"The Good General, yah say? That explains the armor."

"That's right. We have no idea what's happened in Greneva since."

Gibbs didn't know what to make of it. "Well, shoot! Sounds pretty rough, I guess. Of course, I hung up my armor a *long* time ago." He suddenly turned to face Leopold. "Speakin' of which, yer momma know yer a military man now? Don't think she'd take kindly to that, not one bit."

"She'll get over it," answered Leopold dryly, shaking his head. "It doesn't matter now."

Gibbs could tell by his friend's glum expression something had happened to her. "Don't you worry. I've known 'er a long time. That Momma's a tough one. She'll be just fine."

"Thanks, Gibbs."

Maybel grabbed her stomach with one hand and her mouth with the other. It seemed the jiccam berries weren't sitting well. Laerzo turned and patted her back until her twitching body began to settle. He put the back of his hand on her forehead. "You're burning up! Leo, toss me some water, yeah?" He caught a pouch and handed it to Maybel, who drank in small sips. "We need to get you some place to rest."

Maybel returned the pouch with a slight frown, her face heavy and pale, her body trembling. Moments later, she covered her mouth again, only this time could not stop from retching. Most of it fell through her fingers to the roadside, except for one of the pits she must've swallowed from before. The thing repulsed both of them to look at. It seemed rotten, hollow, almost wiggling in her palm. After a brief moment of bewilderment, she tossed it away while Laerzo poured some water to rinse the filth from her hand.

"How embarrassing," she said, rubbing the hand dry, her voice beginning to quiver. "I—I'm sorry."

"Don't be," said Laerzo. "It happens to the best of us. Promise!"

"I've been nothing but a burden since we left." She began to whimper. "I just wish that darn buzzing would go away!"

Laerzo shot her a confused look. "What do you mean?"

"You don't feel it? It's like last night in the forest. Causes pressure in my head. I feel . . ." Maybel suddenly drifted off, her stare returning upward.

"Like what?" When she wouldn't answer, Laerzo helped her fully into Bessie's carriage before laying her down. "It's okay. Just rest for now."

"This whole time, I feel . . . like we're being followed. It's silly, I know, but I can't shake it!"

"This run-down wagon is giving you a hard time," said Leopold as Gibbs's mustache bristled.

"He's right," assured Laerzo. "There's nothing following us."

Tears ran down her face. "You're wrong. Something is above us."

Laerzo stared with her into the dusk, saw only a cloud faintly highlighted by the burgeoning moonlight. "I don't see anything."

Maybel propped herself up. "Look closer! It's like a faint warble. It's right there. You must see it!"

"Just take a deep breath."

She became quite upset when they wouldn't believe her. "It's there! Ooh, I'll prove it to you!" Looking around, she plucked a sourfruit from one of the baskets nearby and chucked it from the wagon, surprisingly far. They were even more stunned to hear a thud in the sky before the fruit plummeted straight to the ground. The impact sent a ripple around an outline of indigo looming overhead, traces of some shape growing, or perhaps simply getting closer. Before they could figure out which, a white light suddenly illuminated them completely as the ghostly form reacted to Bessie's chattering. An ominous hum accompanied this ethereal mass as it descended gradually into a howl. Its shape solidified. It was an aero-freight.

"What in the . . . ?" asked Gibbs, so mesmerized that his drooping hand accidentally sent them veering off-road. He quickly jerked back the controls.

"Pay attention!" grumbled Leopold while throwing a spud at the old man's head.

Laerzo's eyes widened at the vessel's front latch opening. "We have to go. Now!"

Suddenly, Maybel shrieked as a giant four-fingered claw

dangling from a thick cord came crashing down. It missed them by only a few feet and promptly retracted moments later.

"Watch out!" she shrieked.

"You gotta be kidding me!" shouted Leopold, stumbling over bales and buckets on his way to Gibbs. He feverishly glanced at the remainders of each pouch on his belt before mixing nearly all of them together with a wild stare. One quick smell check later, and he was ready to roll. "There. This should do it."

Raising his staff, Gibbs tried to knock the concoction out of his hand, accidentally tossing his lantern onto the gravel road. "Dag-nabbit, boy! No gittin' any ideas now! Yah know what happened last time!"

"You said she could take it, so I'm giving her all I got!"

"Sonny, don't yah dare!"

It was too late. Leopold lifted the lid on a blackened canister running down the core and dumped the pouch's contents. "Gibbs, I'm sorry! It's Bessie or us!"

With a tremendous growl, Bessie exploded forward just in time to avoid another plummet from the menacing steel hand. Her sudden burst practically threw Maybel and Laerzo overboard. Grabbing one another, they kept from spilling off the back. Meanwhile, the aero-freight sped up to try again, only this time, the claw clipped Bessie through her wood planking and snagged part of the rear axle. They would have surely crashed then and there if not for Gibbs's quick correction.

As the claw attempted to retract, it shook the wagon and sent Maybel tumbling off the busted frame. Laerzo caught her left hand just in time, though she was still dangling. His footing began to slip.

"Keep her steady, Gibbs!"

The claw tried to lift them, but in doing so, lost grip of the axle and tumbled briefly along the dirt road before rebounding.

"Left!" cried Leopold just as the vessel unleashed another attack. Despite a prompt course correction from Gibbs, its pincers ripped into the wagon's rear right corner and somewhat slowed its speed. This at least allowed Laerzo to pull Maybel back on board, though both twisted back toward a sudden smashing sound.

Standing defiantly behind them was Leopold with his feet secured under thick bales of hay, the full slack of his chain unleashed and spinning. A couple of solid strikes hit the claw as it started lifting, and he was only getting started. His hammer wailed on the defective limb time and again with powerful yet precise swings, which caused the mangled mess to shake frantically. The aero-freight was about to cut its losses and disengage when one final blow came down and severed its claw entirely.

The instant it did, however, Bessie hit the road hard and went flying off into the fields. For a long chaotic moment, they barreled crooked through the unknown, smoke everywhere, their screams muffled by roaring engine and whipping stalks alike. Fortunately, her tank ran dry, and she puttered out somewhere surrounded by tall rows of unharvested crop.

Each shaken passenger stared at the destruction wrought in their wake while disembarking. There were no more lights overhead, no signs of the aero-freight humming. Outside of leaves occasionally bristling in the wind, they could not hear a single thing. For some time, they walked blind under thick cover of crop, guided only by the sound of each other's movement, until a clearing finally came into sight.

"You were a good girl, Bessie!" mourned Gibbs with a tear in his eye, though she was no longer visible in the fields. He faced Leopold with a painful yet triumphant stare. "Whaddaya have to say fer yerself now, Sonny?"

CHAPTER

Vast was the void of slumber where Gwyndolyn dwelled, adrift in a stagnant sea. Her existence was but a glimmer without voice or dimension or context, the beginnings of something resembling her. But who could really say how she came to be, where, or for how long? Every moment was restless, arrested, like an eternity. There was no rhyme or reason to her, other than one vital sentiment. She was not at peace.

But maybe there was more to her after all. She sensed a light pulse, faint and seldom at first, then with greater frequency. It very gradually caused her solitary point of being to broaden, and with it, her perception expanded in all directions. Shallow notions of form extended, split, and localized into distinct parts wrapped in the same vague numbness. She now felt at once part of and adjacent to the pulsing at her core. Steady lifting and lowering implied movement, a concept all but forgotten. An occasional twitch or tingle would remind her over time. Eventually, her disparate components budged one by one.

"Look, faithful sisters, she stirs."

What were these sounds? They did not seem to come from her. There were various gradations of shadow looming as well. She was frightened by the notion of something existing beyond herself, that she could even perceive such a thing. It was revolutionary, yet within her rigid confines was the blank slate of a mind, one desperately yearning to be impressed upon by something, anything.

Just then, she recognized a softness resting over her. It was bunched lightly in places, heavily in others, offered her warmth. Perhaps too much. Her waking form shifted gradually from within, becoming chafed and irritated by some sort of shroud. The more her parts squirmed, the more distressed they became. Some seized while others struggled to be free.

"I knew she would finally wake! Rise and shine, Lord Daughter."

These familiar utterances resonated in her troubled body, tightened into a dull pain as other sensations followed. The ceaseless friction around her created an overabundance of heat, then perspiration, which only continued to tangle. Small, individual digits of the limbs—yes, they were limbs—curled and cramped against what felt like a smothering cocoon. Her pulsing core hastened, became more aberrant. Her patience thinned, her muscles weakened, her breath shortened.

That's right. Breathe! she thought. A painful bellow soon leaped from her lips.

"The Dew still lingers heavy upon her. Come, sisters! Let us usher her unto this blessed day."

By now, a jumble of additional voices murmured nearby. Their words were hard to pull apart. Some seemed inviting, some inquisitive, a few demanding. All called to the one named Lady, or Blessed Daughter. The commotion drew nearer, and just as Gwyndolyn's eyes finally ascertained the nature of this prison-like veil, a hand suddenly fell upon her shoulder, causing her captive self to quake. Another hand tightly gripped her flailing ankle. A shriek drove some of them back and emboldened others. Her left foot was now exposed, kicked its oppressive yoke, and with one final twist, her body unraveled unceremoniously to the floor.

The strange onlookers winced at the less-than-graceful rebirth of a girl now sprawled at their feet. Gwyndolyn looked incredulously at the bed looming above her—from that soft, fluffy mattress down to the thick fur rug, which had caught her fall—then around the room. All was cast in a gentle amber light tinted through beautiful, translucent drapes not yet drawn. This strange glow covered the entire space in a reverence shared by its occupants, some of whom were already kneeling low before Gwyndolyn. She took in their long white tunics over dark-violet dresses as they carefully lifted her upright and tied a sheet around her naked body like a gown. Her gaze met faces obscured by white silk veils secured by purple ribbons tied as bows around each neck. Looking through one of the veils, she couldn't help but recognize the lady underneath, was surprised by the fact, then pondered, *Why shouldn't I recognize one of my servants?*

"Blessed day to you," said the veiled woman.

"Blessed d—" Gwyndolyn began to recite. "Wait, what is this?"

The woman went to open the drapes. "Not sure I follow, my lady. This is your room."

"My room..." Gwyndolyn's response was almost a question. Of course it was. As the amber glow lifted from the space, she found every piece of furniture where it had always been. Yet it was somehow more lavish than she remembered. From the golden posts of her feather bed to the elaborate design carved into the armoire, each item felt simultaneously familiar and foreign, just like her servants.

"Are you feeling well?" asked another veiled woman.

"I suppose so. Could have done without you all in my quarters."

"Our apologies," started the first attendant, her elder voice both stern and fair. This woman seemed to speak on behalf of the others. "Hypha is not always kind to those who partake of her holy waters. We didn't expect it to subdue you for more than a day."

Gwyndolyn couldn't think of the last time she'd slept that long. She wasn't sick, or at least didn't recall falling ill. In fact, she felt quite refreshed, if not slightly disoriented.

"It seems the Dew still hangs heavy. Fear not. Everything will make sense soon enough." Clapping both hands together, the woman rested her fingers upon the veil at her chin. "This sacrament has surely left you parched. Sisters, bring her something to drink."

"Yes, Matron!" replied the other servants.

Matron, that's right, thought Gwyndolyn while watching the others scramble out the door. She slowly made her way to the window, expecting for some reason to see children playing down below. Instead, she was greeted by mountains looming just beyond a gated courtyard. It was a sight she had seen thousands of times, yet she was surprised by it and bewildered by her own surprise. She silently sorted through each aspect of the vista: Greneva surrounded by trees farther down the mountain, a river climbing the base, the tall spikes of the metal gate wrapping around the manor. All to be expected, as was the stable of geldtmares stationed inside the courtyard next to a large, circular stone path with rows of tiny trees and bushes planted along the circumference. And then there was the massive golden sculpture erected in its center.

"What?" murmured Gwyndolyn just as her attention was stolen by two servants entering the room. One held the door while the other carefully carried in an ornate silver tray, upon which was a matching pitcher next to a crystal goblet. Before Gwyndolyn could regain her earlier thought, this shimmering vessel mesmerized her, caused it to evaporate like mist vanquished by the dawn.

"Oh, thank the Holy Mother!" another voice boomed through the open door. "She's alive!"

Gwyndolyn froze, her teeth reflexively clenching for no particular reason. Like most everything today, the voice was familiar, but the way it uniquely grated on her senses confused her. With fingers pulling tightly into fists, she twisted about-face with a quickness, but it was too late.

"You had me so worried, Lord Sister!" the girl cried into Gwyndolyn's chest after practically tackling her to the ground. For a moment, they both shared a tender moment, and those around them all cooed with joy at the embrace. It was only when Gwyndolyn lifted the girl's freckled cheek did she recoil in shock.

"Scarlet!" shouted Gwyndolyn, her addled disposition now brought into clear focus. Resisting some strange urge to strike, she gazed upon this kindly girl in the same attire as the others, only with a burgundy under-dress and no veil. Similarly colored ribbons were neatly tied around her neck and a single braid of curly red hair streamed down her back. Scarlet's face was as smooth as the day they met, but wet with tears flowing from her light-blue eyes.

"You slept for so long, I began to think the worst! Don't you worry me so, not ever again. Understood?" Scarlet turned to the others. "Don't just stand there. Bring her some refreshment!" She then turned back to Gwyndolyn with a sullen look. "You look dreadful, Lord Sister. Is everything okay? I told Frater Algus to pick me instead, but he wouldn't listen!"

"Lord . . . Sister?"

"I know you would rather have me call you by name, but I'm afraid that time has come and gone. Sanctified, you have awoken as Blessed Daughter, chosen to walk a most righteous path. Your success was expected but not certain. I was beginning to worry, despite Frater's assurances. Had you remained asleep for much longer, it would've been forever, a sign you were refused her favor."

"I beg your pardon. Whose favor?"

"Surely you haven't forgotten. Why, none other than our Holy Mother!"

Not even if I tried, thought Gwyndolyn as Almalinda's beauteous form was fresh in her mind. "Of course not. But what do you know of—"

"*Denestra*, blessed be her name!" they all declared while falling prostrate.

Their gesture left Gwyndolyn utterly flabbergasted. Soon the space between her eyes began to throb.

Why would they worship my mother, Denestra? How did they even know her name?

Her mind was a muddled blur. Perhaps it was best not to think about it too much. As the pain subsided, she quickly grew impatient at the others still lowered in reverence.

"Stand now," she said. They all obliged.

"Lord Sister," began Scarlet. "You do not look well. Pray tell, what manner of nightmare had you in such a fright?"

Gwyndolyn thought long and hard about the question, but before she could respond, Matron interjected: "Child, you know it is taboo to ask such things. The visions gleaned in Hypha's sacrament should be left for Frater to divine."

"You are correct, Matron. My apologies," responded Scarlet humbly. "Perhaps it is better to dwell on the big day ahead."

She noticed Gwyndolyn still at a loss. "Come now, Lord Sister, you have been too single-minded these last moons to forget now."

"Her mind is still mending from the long slumber. It is no wonder she forgets such things. Perhaps she will return to rights after a nice cleanse." Matron clapped again. "Sisters!"

At once, the servants lowered a separate piece of fabric not unlike their veils over Gwyndolyn's head and wrapped body. Soon after, she was led from the room down the hall to a nearby tub room already brimming with warmth as they entered. There was nothing much to the white chamber other than a beautiful marble cistern just large enough to fit one person comfortably. At first, both elbows pinched the bedsheet around her to resist the prying hands underneath the veil, but she eventually allowed them to remove it. Additional hands then helped her carefully step into the bath while two lifted the sliding veil away from the steaming waters, folded it into a neat square, and set it aside.

Lowering slowly, Gwyndolyn disappeared a moment under the cover of bubbles. The water's temperature was exactly how she liked—just hot enough to thaw. Any more, and her delicate skin would quickly begin to shrivel. Fragrant oils were poured over her hair and skin, massaged intensely into her scalp, face, neck, and shoulders. Other servants massaged her back and arms thoroughly, working out every knot. Occasionally, they would dip her below the water. Her brief bliss within the soothing cistern was interrupted, however, as they extracted her at the first sign of wrinkling. Unfolding the veil, they covered her once again and used it to help pat her dry before leading her back to her chambers.

Gwyndolyn was then offered a light petticoat, which she donned as an undergarment before the veil was discarded for good. She suddenly found herself in front of a large golden armoire where there was a gorgeous gown laid out, which immediately captivated her. She gazed upon the sheer whiteness of the dress, followed its intricate stitching like flowering vines up the sleeveless bust. It elicited warm memories of what her dear mother used to wear while impressing a beauty more ancient than anything she'd ever seen. She watched the gown lower over her raised arms, felt its softness settle like a cloud upon her skin. By the time the servants yanked to straighten its fabric, the hemming fell just below her knees.

Next, lifting her feet one at a time, they raised long white stockings fastened with purple ribbons just below the hemming. Both she and her servants alike were delighted by a quick spin of the dress. Scarlet then approached from behind with a dark-violet cape and placed it over Gwyndolyn while crossing its long silken cords a few times diagonally down her chest. Both were wrapped at the waist like a belt and tied at the front into another bow. Gwyndolyn loved the way it modestly accentuated her form, yet she couldn't help but feel it belonged to someone else.

"What do you think?" asked Scarlet while grooming each lock of Gwyndolyn's blonde hair.

"This is . . . is it really me though?"

"Who else could wear such a thing? You look radiant."

Gwyndolyn felt the compliment land a tad hollow. "And yet, something seems off."

"No need to be modest," beamed Matron as she and the others briefly backed away to admire their work.

"Shall we pin your hair up today?" asked Scarlet.

Gwyndolyn nodded and closed her eyes while the handlers braided her bangs into each side of her head. She hated the way they tugged every stray hair tight, even if the work was proper. Once finished, they wrapped her long braids into a neat bun atop her head like a crown. Such a style was needlessly extravagant but seemed fitting, given her attire and the occasion.

Strangely, she felt one of the braids unravel. Peeking through the mirror, she noticed a queer look on Scarlet's face. "Having a rough time, Sister?" asked Gwyndolyn jokingly, her eyes lowering again.

There was no response, only the feeling of slight trembling through the tuft of hair. Gwyndolyn became agitated as each individual strand was sorted and examined. "Where has your mind wandered?"

The toiling only intensified. Carefully honing through the mirror, Gwyndolyn quickly snatched a strand between her fingers, causing Scarlet to freeze.

Was it just a trick of the light? Gwyndolyn asked herself while examining what appeared to be a white hair.

Before she could decide, Scarlet's thumb and forefinger suddenly plucked it like a serpent striking.

"The nerve!" boomed Gwyndolyn as she whirled in a tempest of violet and slapped down the girl. "Have you gone mad?"

Scarlet fell to her knees, welling with tears. "I'm sorry, dear sister! Please forgive me!" She bowed repeatedly until she was snatched up by her contemporaries. Two of the others quickly restored the loose tuft of hair to its previous arrangement.

Just then, a snap of Matron's fingers sent them all flying from the room. "You know how excited your sister can get at times," Matron said, kneeling low to fit and buckle tall, beautiful leather boots to Gwyndolyn's feet. "I have a special gift for you today. May you cherish it always." From the armoire she removed a thin golden circlet embossed in the center with a sparkling violet gem and rested it upon Gwyndolyn's forehead.

"It's wonderful," said Gwyndolyn simply.

After giving the girl one final spin, Matron simply waved to the door with a smile.

Scarlet waited quietly outside to join them in traversing the multitude of corridors in Gwyndolyn's hallowed home. From glossy floor to silken ceiling, each one was carved of pure marble as white as snow. Walls were segmented by pillars installed with torches, positioned between sagging arches of violet, gold, and white cloth. Above every other dip of drapery hung beautiful wreaths of flowers imparting the same aroma Gwyndolyn fondly recalled from the gardens beyond these walls. In passing, she watched some of her servants bow to a strange symbol etched into one of the walls, a modest line piercing two moons fashioned into the shape of an eye. She could not speak to its meaning but assumed it was important all the same.

Torches burned dimmer as they continued, yet both great light and music was brimming ahead in the main hall. They entered into the upper level of a large vestibule near two grand staircases moving down and around an enchanting silver tree. It was nearly as tall as the chamber and a fourth of its size, with branches glowing solid white. Choirs were positioned on opposite ends of the stairs, singing hallowed hymns, facing several curved rows of marble benches split by a central path toward steel double doors at the opposite end.

Slowly descending the left staircase, Gwyndolyn could see someone kneeling before the shining tree. He was a pale man in a long, thin, white-hooded coat with stitching that burned gold like his hair. There was an aura around him not unlike the tree, though it was more subtle. Strewn at his feet were both a crystalline flask and metal staff, the former containing a liquid glowing indigo and the latter carrying the symbol she'd passed before. While some of the congregation in the chamber stopped to acknowledge her presence, he kept still, his head bowing low. She wondered why he wouldn't turn and face her like the others.

Perhaps he was simply lost in the music's splendor, she thought while admiring the robed men and women's beatific hymn. The tune sounded of sadness, but its melancholic progression was but a prelude to hope sweetly swelling. The servants joined the concert while Matron and Scarlet brought Gwyndolyn before the kneeling man. The three waited for the hymn's blissful resolution, and for the choir to quietly be seated among the rows of marble, but even then, the reverent man would not stir. It would be one protracted moment before he stood with his staff, and another still before finally turning from the tree.

"Verily I say in the name of Denestra, welcome to you, oh Blessed Daughter!" proclaimed the man, his arms lifted out in adoration. There was another eye symbol engraved on the heart of his robe. Gwyndolyn found his intense emerald eyes absolutely thrilling. "I am Chief Herald and Prophet of the Holy Mother, yet before you, I am but a humble messenger and disciple, Frater Algus. In her name, I have been sent with revelations of dark days and bright beginnings alike. Halae! I say unto you: Just as the fruit of Hypha did miraculously grow this past moon, and did its wine cast you into slumber, and did you toil day and night, so too did you awaken purified, forgiven, and sanctified! Those who emerge from this hallowed sacrament have transcended a deluge of wicked dreams molded from a once sinful heart. Blessed Gwyndolyn, how did you escape the terrors? Please impart unto me your dreams."

"I—I'm not sure," said Gwyndolyn, somewhat captive by the white of the Hypha Tree. "That is to say, I don't remember much. I was taken from home and cast down the mountain to live a meager life. The people there reviled me. That's all, really."

"Those fleeting shadows were deceptions drawn from Hypha's Dew to test your resolve. You have done well to survive them."

"There was something so real about all of it, Frater. I—"

"Please, my lady, call me Algus. Dreams are like that, but which strikes truer now? All that misfortune? Or this singular moment?"

"This moment, breathtaking to be sure. But what if it's only the beginning of a greater nightmare?"

Algus bowed with a smile. "Hear me, Blessed Daughter. The time spent in that illusion may have seemed endless, but an illusion it was, nonetheless. Nothing it imparted can compare with what stands before you now. You wonder if this is but another? Could your mind conjure beauty as brilliant as this? Could your heart hope to possess it? Where would one even begin to imagine such resplendence? You cannot, however much you may try. There is nothing wrong in admitting it. If providence could be found within, I dare say none would ever seek out the Holy Mother."

"But I still feel as if I'm dreaming."

"That will pass in time."

"And I don't recognize these people, or this chamber."

"This is your home, Gwyndolyn. We are your servants."

"What about everything else?"

"As I have already said, let it burden you no further."

"But why suffer at all? Why was I given Dew from the Hypha Tree?"

Algus lowered his head for a long moment before responding. "It is foretold that Hypha will bear fruit in times of great upheaval, when wickedness spreads like a miasma across the land. The once humble people below are stricken with a fever of selfish overindulgence, and some have begun to fall ashen. As each mind sours, both eyes begin to fade, and eventually, so too will their hair run gray. The same drink which had tested and transformed you will be offered up for the salvation of the masses. You alone have been chosen to give them what has been given!"

Gwyndolyn shook her head. "I don't understand. Was that drink not like a poison? Was it not some miracle that I awoke at all?"

"Ah, but there lies the crux. In waking, you have been sanctified, and through you, so too has the drink. That which you will bear from this holy place, it will no longer pull those who drink into darkness but heal! With it, their indulgence will be tamed toward more righteous ends."

"And they know of such a thing? That I will offer this gift to them?"

"Seeing is believing, Blessed Daughter. Seek out those suffering below and lift the cloud from them. Only then will word of the Holy Mother's second coming spread. Only then might you one day return to dwell with her."

Gwyndolyn's brow raised at those last words. "You are saying I might meet with my mother?"

"Ye, I say unto you: Those who do her bidding will surely gain favor, but you alone are fated to walk with, and eventually, embrace the Holy Mother! You have been chosen for this great purpose!"

There was hardly anything in the world she wanted more. Just the thought of being reunited with her long-lost mother brought a tear to her eye. Clasping both hands to her heart, she began to see what appeared to be her mother's visage floating before the shining tree. The crowds cried out in joy, as did she. She could hardly believe her eyes.

"Halae! What wondrousness, this gift given!" proclaimed Algus, his staff uplifted. "You humble disciples are party to this testament. Go now and spread word of her coming salvation. Blessed Daughter, you will soon follow in their wake, descending unto the people to heal in the name of the Holy Mother!"

"Halae! Al'Haleia!" the crowd behind Gwyndolyn chanted as they marched out from the chamber. "Halae! Al'Haleia!"

After most had quit that hallowed space, Algus addressed Scarlet and Matron directly. "You both remain the most devout among us. Though Hypha's Dew was offered up to Gwyndolyn, I have no doubt that you have been granted divine favor as well. Walk with her. Help her fulfill the prophecy as revealed here this day."

"Halae! Al'Haleia!" They both proclaimed in unison.

Matron then faced Gwyndolyn. "The first of many trials may be complete, Blessed Daughter, but the days ahead bring new tribulations. Come with me, and I will help you prepare, least of all with a proper meal."

CHAPTER

What little sleep Laerzo managed since reaching Thannick was tragically cut short by another flash of light in the fields. Like before, its brilliance enveloped him, causing him to clamp his eyes shut, and with it, came the Trust's return. He could already begin to make out traces of the aero-freight looming overhead once more, knowing this time, without Bessie to carry them, they would surely be snatched away. Unable to see the others, he feared they'd already been taken. Either that or they had scattered through the fields to save themselves. The ward in him feared this most of all.

Then came the sound of boots on the march. They grew with each step, moved with purpose. Still, his body refused to stir.

Why can I not escape? Where are my friends?

With great effort, his head eventually jerked from side to side as if looking for them. It did little good while trapped by the blinding light. Every breath was a struggle. He heard deep, muffled voices approaching, none of their words discernible, followed strangely by the creak of a door. His eyelids fluttered as a silhouette eclipsed the light, hovered near, and reached closer.

"Steady, Cadet," spoke a stern yet gentle voice, and just like that, Laerzo was at ease. He awoke to his left hand firmly secured upon the hilt of his sword, which lay on the table aside his bed. The fields no longer surrounded him as he'd imagined. Rather, he was in the infirmary at the local Enforcer station in Thannick, where he and the others had been resting. He saw General Dietrich's formidable frame block the light peeking through the window, with Gibbs standing at the door with his fisherstaff. Leopold was against the left wall of that door, snoring, his armor in a corner pile.

There was something damp hanging in Laerzo's other hand; it was the rag he'd used to cool Maybel's head throughout the night.

"Maybel!" he uttered before turning to her bedside. She was resting quietly to the right of him, her pale feverishness somewhat improved.

Dietrich could see the worry strewn across the lad's face. "Mr. Gibbs tells me you've all had quite a night. Be sure to thank him for his service."

That's right, thought Laerzo. Not only had Gibbs saved them, he even called in a favor with some of Thannick's finest. They were surprised just how willing the Enforcers were to offer accommodation at such a late auram. It suggested the old man had more than a favorable reputation around these parts. Laerzo watched him close the door. "Thank you, Gibbs. I don't know where we would've ended up without you."

"Ah, shucks!" he answered while approaching. "Yer very welcome. 'Sides, it was all Bessie at the end of the day."

"How is she doing?"

"Well, the old girl's pretty banged up, but she'll make it. No thanks to him!" To this, Gibbs jabbed Leopold in the gut with his staff.

This sent Leopold leaping to his feet, with one fist pounding his chest and the other striking the sky, the standard salute of the Waldean Alliance. "Reporting for duty!" he shouted before regaining his bearings. His eyes narrowed at the first sign of his attacker. "What was that for?"

"Keep it down, tubby," answered Gibbs. "Yah know dang well what that was fer."

"I don't wanna hear it. It was me that got us outta that bind, you know! You should be grateful."

"Oh sure, *real* grateful. Next time yah stick anything fishy in my Bessie, I'll be the one stickin'. Get my drift?" He was offered no response other than a sour stare. That was more than enough for him. He turned to Dietrich. "Anyway, I let the boys downstairs know what happened. Can't say they believed me. Definitely some strangeness goin' round these parts."

"You don't know the half of it," replied Dietrich.

"We didn't expect you so soon," said Laerzo. "What happened back there?"

Dietrich took a deep breath. "Too much, but I will say this: Many in Greneva, my company included, have been compromised by a group professing the return of their goddess, Denestra. Apparently for some time now, too. Even Chief Montgomery was answering to new masters behind my back. We were forced to as well, or at least play the part until it was time to go. When we finally did, it was quick and quiet. We rode most of the night to get here."

"So, General Maddock is with you then?"

"Yes, he's waiting outside with our . . . *guest*."

"Who's that, sir?" asked Leopold while sitting up.

"A subordinate of mine. Connel is his name."

"Think I remember him. Tall, lanky fellow. Never really said much." Half of Leopold's brow lowered curiously. "You don't seem happy he's tagging along."

"I'm not. Connel is a traitor. He tried outing us when we finally made our move, and he almost blew our cover. Maddock promptly took him into custody upon retreat. He has a lot of explaining to do once we return to Headquarters, that's for sure. Speaking of which, we're heading out."

"Already?" asked Laerzo as he reached for his armor hanging off a nearby chair. "You just got here. And what about Maybel? She needs more time."

"We're taking her with us, of course."

Laerzo glanced pensively back at his sister. "Are you sure that's a good idea?"

Gibbs slapped him on the shoulder. "Yer kind to look after the girl, but don't cha worry. I fixed up a nice carriage to Stolgrum. I doubt she'll miss a single wink the whole way!"

"He's right," added Dietrich. "She'll be fine. Now suit up, both of you."

After getting ready, Laerzo lifted Maybel by the knees and shoulders, and carried her out the door. They walked along plain, white-walled halls past a few stained doors on each side, down one flight of stairs, and into the back offices, where several Enforcers were about to start another dull day. Most had already kicked up their boots, as there was never much ado in the Heartland. The men did make sure to stand and salute—not only Dietrich, but also Gibbs in passing. Another at the secured partition released them into an empty lobby, where they took their leave.

Outside, they found themselves on a cool, cloudy corner of town square. There really wasn't much to the place, mostly matted dirt roads split five ways over several blocks. Each one was lined with tight strips of wooden buildings one or two stories tall. They were more or less uniform save for various tints of window trim or colorful business signs and banners. Laerzo scrutinized the skies while slowly heading a half block down the road toward a simple yet sturdy black wooden cart.

There, Maddock tended to both geldtmares, one of which was burdened by a gangly man over its haunches. The man was bound behind his back, wearing the Trust's signature gray trench coat as well as a gag and a giant bump bulging from his black head of hair. Judging from the bags under his closed eyes, he'd hardly slept during their trip. It didn't appear Maddock had either.

Leopold opened the carriage door for Laerzo to carefully hoist his sister inside. Leopold then turned to Gibbs, still leering his way nearby. "I'll be seeing you, Gibbs! Don't croak before then."

"Yeah, all right," he responded with an agitated smile. "And don't yah git too comfy in Stolgrum, yah hear? Y'all be back before yah know it! I've made sure of that." His last remark was mostly uttered under his breath.

"Whatever you say, old man!" Leopold waved and hopped in the carriage. As for Laerzo, he took a much-needed moment to stretch while watching Dietrich pull Gibbs aside.

"What do you think?" asked Dietrich. "Those two Alliance material?"

Gibbs returned a hearty giggle. "I suppose 'bout as much as you fellas were back in the day. I 'member whippin' y'all real good for a while there!"

"Funny, I remember Cael doing most of that work. " Dietrich's eyes fell a bit sullen. "She was really something, wasn't she?"

"No doubt. Still is too. That's why I passed her the reigns, after all." Gibbs gave Dietrich a long stare before continuing. "You two gettin' along these days?"

"More or less. She insists what happened between me and Shella is water under the bridge, but sometimes I'm not too sure." Laerzo noticed Dietrich stare directly at him when speaking that name, though he hadn't the slightest clue why. After a brief pause, the General continued. "You know Cael likes to keep her cards close. I didn't even realize her youngest had passed until the other day."

"Yeah, well, she's got a lot on 'er shoulders. She's a tough one, always has been. So are yer boys. Lookin' forward to seein' yah whip 'em into shape!"

"And I as well!"

"It's about that time," barked Maddock, already upon his geldtmare. "Sir, it's been good catching up, but we don't have time to chat."

"He's right," said Dietrich while mounting the other mare. "Take care of yourself. We'll be in touch soon. Oh, and whatever you do, be wary of anyone traveling westward. Even if you've known them your whole life."

On that harrowing note, Laerzo entered the carriage with the others and felt it snap into action shortly after. They started on a steady, courteous clop through the center of town, their heavy eyes to the road. This first leg of the trip proved rough for the tired riders, yet if weather remained fair and geldtmare steeds swift, they expected to hit their pillows hard that night in Stolgrum. Neither rider paid much attention to the sleepy town itself, other than to greet occasional residents happily waving on foot, from benches or carriages of their own. It surprised Laerzo just how many had gathered from the small town to celebrate them, given his personal feelings about the Alliance. Still, he could not help but feel some pride swell in his chest.

The geldtmares picked up the pace once reaching a span of homesteads on the western side. Some covered the land in a quilt of colorful crop like the vibrant red and blue tellia weed used in dyes, white amaranth dried and pounded into flour, or golden chuteseed, Waldea's tallest and most plentiful staple. Orchards occasionally graced these fields with tight rows of dark chokeberry and sour palms used mainly for tinctures, or star fruit and light lemelon cultivated as sweet treats. Some crops were less noticeable, like rooted spuds or spicy lavabeans; in a few moons, when the climes begin to cool, these would be replaced by equally shy chillybeans for a hearty winter yield. Every acre was lovingly maintained by humble, hardworking families as well as their geldtmares, which were more than happy to till and tamp in exchange for some crop.

Other verdant clearings were dedicated to the husbanding of these noble creatures, as well as various other livestock. For instance, buckmule provided an excellent source of wool, milk, and cheese—that is, if you knew how to herd them safely. Then there were the droves of hen-cockel laying eggs for their allowance of chuteseed. Even hamherns were domesticated for meat and fertilizer, though these specimen were much smaller and more docile than their wilden counterparts. Some farmers would alternate between crop and cattle every other annum to renew the soil, while others stuck to what they knew. Other plots yielded nothing at all, though these usually belonged to moneyed families who simply enjoyed the size and splendor of the Heartland.

Most of this beautiful scenery, however, was lost on those inside the carriage. Laerzo did enjoy watching the fields pass, but when combined with the rhythm of the road, it practically put him to sleep. As for Leopold, he was no stranger to Thannick, as his wares were traded there on occasion, and so had little desire to sightsee. Both would rather catch up on much-needed shut-eye. Unfortunately for Laerzo, he was a terrible sleeper, unlike Maybel, who rested soundly the entire time. He had always envied her uncanny ability to sleep through just about anything. In fact, as Gibbs predicted, she did not miss a single wink.

It took much of the day for them to finish crossing Thannick, but once they managed to swap their exhausted geldtmares at a border outpost, the near boundless expanse of farmland was quickly traded for a noticeably rockier terrain. The Steppes of Stolgrum were mostly that, a steady incline of hillside surrounded by clay and crag protruding from the ground between a sprawling of trees. By and large, travel toward the Plateau's west end was more of a chore and less hospitable to life. As a result, few farms graced these parts, save for maybe a vineyard here and there. The ramparts of the city could already be seen up the hill in the distance; however, it would be some time before their weary steeds cleared the increasingly winding roads on the way up.

Day was hanging low by the time they finally made it to Stolgrum, and even then, it would be another auram or so before reaching their destination near the cliffside. On the way, they passed through some slums peculiarly clustered on the outside of the main wall, stopping briefly at the gate until entry was granted into the city.

Laerzo and Leopold had never seen this part of Waldea before and quickly came to admire the simple yet elegant brick architecture, which dwarfed their dismal mountain town in every respect. The commercial district formed a sort of triangular core with two common residential areas both north and south along the eastward front, as well as a more moneyed district to the west preceding Fort Lionel. The northeast commons they crossed appeared as blocks of interconnected buildings that looked more like barracks than homes. They were not gaudy or plain, but rather exhibited a uniform practicality that distinguished itself from what they were used to at home. Of course, the further they traveled, the more beautiful and distinct the various properties became. Their fingers rubbed reflexively as both gawked through the carriage windows at these wealthy, gated estates not unlike those in Uptown.

By that time, Maybel had been up long enough to take in the sights. Though still weary, the bustle in the streets filled her with excitement. "I've never seen the capital of Waldea before, aside from some sketches in a textbook. Though equal to the other Commonwealths, it is easily the wealthiest and most powerful."

"Tell us something we don't know," said Laerzo with a chuckle.

"Okay, mister smarty! Did you know about the Radiant Cliffs?"

Laerzo remembered hearing those words between naps during his old academy days. "Yeah, I've heard. What about them?"

"What about them? We're talking about the Radiant Cliffs of Stolgrum, here! The entire western tip of the cliffside is covered with beautiful blue gems, which shine so bright you can only gaze upon it later in the day."

"Lucram ore," added Leopold. "Very versatile material. Doesn't come cheap either. It's mostly used in chandeliers and other high-end fixtures to brighten homes, but I've heard it can be very durable if properly tempered."

"And also very beautiful, like the jewel on your dagger." Maybel paused upon noticing Laerzo's frazzled stare. "Oh, sorry. Anyway, we should go see the cliffs sometime."

"That's not why we're here," reminded Laerzo bluntly. "You're sick, remember?"

"Ooh, you're no fun." Maybel crossed her arms in a frumpy yet playful manner while a smile slowly returned to her face. "Promise me you'll take me there after I get better?"

Laerzo nodded happily. "You got it."

The Solstar was once again setting in the north by the time they finally arrived at the grand walls of Fort Lionel, Headquarters of the Waldean Alliance. Laerzo and the others could hardly believe the sheer girth of the fortress walls, which spread in such a way as to insulate itself effectively along the contours of the cliff. Flying high from the ramparts were large black flags with the Alliance's gilded signet of a cradled mountain, symbol of the Plateau. Inside the outer perimeter, they could see a grand structure the size of a castle, but with the same practical aesthetic found in most of the residential districts. An even bigger flag was posted at the top, which could be seen from many blocks away. They had never seen such a colossal banner in all their lives.

Dietrich and Maddock waited impatiently for their soldiers to draw the bridge through the gates. Soon enough, a few emerged at both base and crest of the mighty walls, though they mostly stared while muttering back and forth among themselves.

"Open the gates!" roared Maddock at his men. They seemed strangely noncompliant, which only agitated him further. "What are you waiting for?"

"All parties must pass a close inspection to enter," announced one of the soldiers upon the rampart. "No exceptions."

"Inspection? Do you not recognize your own general? I command you grant us entry immediately!"

"Sir, with apologies, these are orders straight from the top. Surely you would know that." Nodding, the soldiers nervously noted his confused response in their records.

"Why, you dithering—"

"Bruno," interrupted Dietrich. "Our lord has every reason to be suspicious, as do we. Let's just cooperate and see what comes of this."

Maddock shot back a nasty sneer. "Not a chance. Let me show you how I do things in Stolgrum. You, up there!" He received no response from either of the gatemen above. "Henrik, is it? How is your son, Olly? He is a few annums elden, yes?"

"Ah, yes! He's doing well," one of the guards eventually responded. He seemed unprepared for the personal line of questioning from his normally impersonal superior.

"That's real good. Hey, Henrik? Do you want your boy to grow up without a father? Because if you don't open this wretched gate at once, I will climb up that wall, snap your skinny little neck, and dangle your riddled corpse in front of dear Olly! Do you get me, soldier?"

The guards stared wide-eyed at one another only for a brief moment before Henrik cried, "Open the gate!"

"Very subtle approach, my friend," remarked Dietrich a tad blithely. "I suppose the Madman has to keep up his appearances somehow."

"Damn right, Siggy. Onward!"

With a snap of the reigns, they proceeded through the gates into the bailey with Headquarters looming even larger behind the inner walls. At once, it gazed down upon them while they started across this vast, spacious clearing, one filled with multiple companies of men duking their hearts out. Training had apparently concluded for the day, as most eagerly went to stuff their bellies in the barracks stationed on the bailey's northern end. Some guards were around to wave their guests toward the stables on the opposite end. Just in time, too, for the geldtmares had been pushed to their limit. Laerzo and the others poked their heads from the window as Dietrich thanked both creatures with a hearty pat before turning them over to the stable hands.

"Lock this traitor away," ordered Maddock as he chucked Connel from the back of his steed into the arms of a couple nearby guards. "I will deal with him later." He then pounded on the carriage to its passengers, visibly perturbed while watching them exit one by one. "Don't we look well rested."

"Much better now, thank you," answered Maybel, still a bit drowsy. Her earnest response dispelled some of Maddock's derision, at least until he interrupted a chuckle from the others with a simple glance of his vicious eyes.

Dietrich called them to attention. "If you're all ready, we must speak with Lord Lionel at once."

"Shouldn't we get Maybel somewhere to rest?" asked Laerzo.

"Oh, I feel a bit better now," answered Maybel stubbornly. "Please don't delay on my account."

"I'm glad to hear that," said Dietrich. "but Laerzo is right. Don't worry, the infirmary is on the way, after which I would ask that both cadets join us."

"What?" asked Maddock somewhat agitated by the suggestion. "What business do grunts like them have with Lionel? We don't need them to report!"

"With respect, they witnessed the chaos at the festival, not to mention whatever happened at the Trust's compound."

His forehead twitching, Maddock exhaled deeply as he

turned to leave. "Fine, but do not speak unless spoken to. Not a word. Understand? Follow me, and be quick about it."

They crossed the bailey west to another checkpoint before Fort Lionel's inner walls. Maddock needed only leer at the guards for them to grant him and the others passage. From there, they crossed into another expanse, this one a stone-paved garden with lush trees and shrubbery not seen anywhere else in Stolgrum. Laerzo glanced at squads patrolling these parts, frowned when he imagined himself among them.

Beats patrolling Greneva or Thannick at least, he thought in passing.

As gorgeous as it was, this paled in comparison to the fort itself, a true fortress to be told. It was only then did the newcomers realize how massive it really was. Save for some of the archwork, each identically carved slab of powder-white stone was practically half their size. Judging by its scale and the number of windows visible in the front, Maybel predicted the compound to be a hundred rooms big. She wasn't far off. The grand entrance humbled their approach, made each feel tiny while entering the equally impressive main hall. Like most of the building, its introductory chamber was wide, built of beautifully polished white stone. They made their way down a stretch of black rugs hinted with gold, passed Alliance banners of matching colors hanging along each lengthy, vaulted wall. Several halls were found along each side, many impressively long, given how tiny some guards appeared in the distance.

There was a vertical opening at the far end of the space with additional banners hanging and a circular climb of stairs wrapped as wide as the walls. Every step, sneeze, and sniffle echoed through this space, including those from the guards greeting them with a salute. Maddock took them up and around the chamber three or so times before pausing in front of one of its connecting passages, pointing toward the nearest pair of guards.

"You, take this girl to the infirmary."

Dietrich nodded, noting a sense of guilt coming from his sickly guest. "Don't worry, Maybel. They'll take care of you. We'll check in after our business is finished."

"Very well," said Maybel with a courteous bow. "Thank you for inviting me to this remarkable establishment. I hope to speak with you all again soon." With a curtsy, she greeted the soldiers, who kindly took her away.

"Are you sure I shouldn't go with her, General?" asked Laerzo.

"She'll be fine. We must report in with the Lord General." Dietrich turned to Leopold. "Speaking of which, I take it you're prepared to give yours, Mr. Gotta?"

Leopold forgot he had anything to report. Quickly tossing his bag to the ground, he rummaged for something before straightening with a sigh of relief. "Yes sir, but this late? I didn't expect to give it until tomorrow."

"He insisted we speak with him the moment we returned. I've already sent someone ahead to announce our arrival. Let's not keep him waiting, shall we?"

From there, they wound up another couple of stories, then followed a new strip of black velvet down a noticeably wider corridor. These walls so happened to have not only Stolgrum's black banner, but those of the other Commonwealths as well. There was Greneva with the Mount's silver signet atop dark green, Ogden with its golden anchor awash in vibrant blue, and that of Thannick's vermilion tree planted over a nice copper. They passed each on their way toward another pair of soldiers who were already saluting them before a large stone arch that housed tall wooden doors. Nodding insistently, Maddock bade for both to make way, pushing them and the doors aside when done too slow for his liking.

Unlike most of the fort, this chamber wasn't particularly large or grandiose. It included the same stretch of carpeting between four wide pillars, each again with the organization's various banners, up to a handful of stairs preceding a wide oaken table with many chairs. Another especially large black banner was draped upon the far wall behind the table. Standing in front of it were two figures, one a tall, stout, bald, white-bearded man in exquisite armor of ivory ore, matching scabbard, and a black cape with golden trim. This was none other than Lord Lionel, High Commander of the Waldean Alliance. In addition to his regalia, the man's exceptional poise and aura matched every bit of his station, commanded the utmost respect.

The other was a man whom Dietrich and Maddock seemed surprised to see. The figure was a bit mysterious, clad in a long, hooded mustard cape over matching tunic and golden mail adorned with etchings not common to those parts. His face was darker than most in Waldea, even the day-worn Reapers in Thannick, though rich, smooth skin blessed the man, hiding his age well. Several pepper-brown braids peeked from under his cover, some sewn with shiny ornaments, and one woven in gold draped along his face. The end of this solitary braid was affixed with symbol neither cadet had seen, namely two moons, the smaller of which laying upon the other, both pierced vertically by a spear. Laerzo also noticed a stunning scabbard partially hidden on the man's right side, mostly ornate silver woven with a crisscrossing of gold.

"You again! My Lord, what is he doing here?" asked Maddock without any attempt at decorum. The man in question simply smiled.

"Bruno," chided Dietrich gently under his breath.

"Good to see you as well, Mr. Maddock," answered Lionel, more than used to his subordinate's unruly demeanor. Laerzo rightfully suspected that Lionel didn't enlist Maddock for his diplomatic aptitude. "That's hardly any way to speak of our esteemed guest."

"Esteemed? I know this man as well as you. He's a professor of . . . *faith*, one of the Sh'tama!"

"Perhaps so."

"His kind are not welcome in Waldea! You should know this better than any, my lord."

"It is the practice of that which we forbid, not necessarily the people themselves. Today, we are joined simply by a messenger from across the Waters Emeralda."

Maddock was having none of it. "What would the people think if they saw you two together?"

"I don't know. What do you think?"

"I think they would be outraged! We have long since shunned—"

"Gul'dan's treachery from our land, yes. Not those who have suffered it. Surely, not those who helped us resist it. As you well know, the Sh'tama of Egress Island, as we call it, are strictly at odds with Judecca's heretical faction currently ruling over Gul'dan. And as such, whether openly or in secret, they are our allies, important ones at that. Please conduct yourself accordingly in his presence."

"It's been a long time, Azacca," greeted Dietrich, after which the smiling man bowed, his attention shifting to Laerzo. With wide, curious eyes, Azacca whispered something brief into Lionel's ear while Dietrich continued. "My Lord, I bring you my newest cadets, Leopold Gotta and Laerzo of Greneva."

"It's a pleasure, gentlemen, but you didn't come here for introductions. What of Greneva?"

At once, Maddock and Dietrich told him all about the Mount's transformation, the heralds and their Goddess Denestra, the subsequent acquiescence of both Enforcers and Waldeans alike. All the while, Lionel stood with cold, unflinching posture, taking in every word without question or comment. Once they'd finished, he and Azacca briefly glanced at one another. "Denestra, is it? A name recently brought to my attention."

"By this man, no doubt," grumbled Maddock.

"Accursed be whose light blinds," spoke Azacca with great ardor, his strange countenance like a song. "We call her Deceiver, Usurper, venomous thorn. Lest you be mistaken! It is she who hath forsaken Sancta, and given her just reward, remains trapped low in *Qua'cana*, or Quartzcore in your tongue. There be she among the lowest. Woe to all who speak her name."

Dietrich had not heard Sh'tama scripture uttered for some time. It rang true enough in his heart, yet felt improper to hear. "That's right. Some in the crowd called her Usurper. The Mayor's daughter claimed she was the true savior. Once the heralds descended praising her name, the crowds were all too willing to agree. You should have seen it, my lord. Their fervor was not unlike the zealots of Gul'dan. By the time we retreated, they were already amassing a righteous mob."

"More like an army," said Maddock.

"So it begins anew," conceded Lionel, his silver brow pinched. "Azacca, it is just as your leader has foretold. But when you delivered word of his vision to me, I assumed it

Judecca's return that was imminent. Are you sure it's this other force?"

"Master Dural tells no lies," said Azacca assuredly. "Denestra or no, the Mad Prophet will come in time. Mayhaps not straight away. His host belongs to none other than Denestra's beloved king, Avalon the Wicked, Slayer of Sancta. Let us pray word of her return never reaches him."

"Indeed. Still, to hear this coming from inside our borders is most unexpected."

"With all respect, sir," interjected Laerzo, "it isn't, not really. Ever since the Trust arrived in Waldea, strange things have been happening. Disappearances, shifts in the Polity, illusions, the whole lot of it. I think they're responsible."

"Save your conjecture, Cadet," responded Maddock most unpleasantly.

"Let's hear him out," insisted Dietrich. "Laerzo, what makes you so sure?"

"My brother, Algus, for starters. He vanished annums ago, only to reappear as a member of the Trust. He was among the ones we saw that night in Grenefest. They are responsible for this, I just know it."

"I do recall you claiming to recognize the Chief Herald." Dietrich turned to Leopold. "What say you, Mr. Gotta? What did you see in their manor on Mount Greneva?"

"Well, I'm not sure about all that, but they were up to no good! Some strapped poor Maybel to a table. They were hurting her! When we came to the rescue, the whole place went crazy, and we barely made it outta there alive."

"Hurt her in what way?" asked Lionel gravely.

"I don't know, they were stickin' tubes in her arms, pumping some purple liquid. She hasn't been right since."

Lionel stroked his white beard inquisitively. "And what is her relation to the Trust? Were they tracking her?"

"Sir?" asked Laerzo. "She's my sister, just a girl from Common Ward who got mixed up with them. That's all."

"I see. She is here, yes? I would very much like to speak with her when she's able."

"Her, and one of Dietrich's turncoats, Connel," added Maddock. "I've already sent him to the brig for questioning. He should be able to tell us a thing or two about them. That is, if he knows what's good for him."

"Why don't you leave that to me, Bruno?" asked Dietrich with some worry, implying he would be more soft-handed in his interrogations. Maddock stubbornly paid him no mind, after which Dietrich continued, "Anything else, Mr. Gotta?"

Leopold paused for a moment before his face brightened. "Oh, that's right! We found some of Dr. Carlyle's research, though I can't say I understand any of it. We think it might have to do with what's going on." He removed the parchment from his bag and handed it to Dietrich. After skimming it briefly, Dietrich presented the documents to Lionel.

"Liminatum?" recited Lionel with some interest. Though a great fighter in his time, he was a renowned academic. "A word I have not once heard in my many years of scholarship. We will take these under review. Mr. Maddock, please keep me apprised of the prisoner's testimony. Also, I need you and your team to keep a lookout for anything unusual about our men. If this Connel turned on us, we must assume more are waiting in the midst. Be sure to warn the other Commonwealths as well."

"One step ahead of you, my lord," replied Maddock. "Thankfully, the other Regents-General didn't appear to get caught up with whatever happened in Greneva. We left a message for Cael on our way back, suggested she alert her militiamen. As for Tybal, *His Highness* usually bars my messengers from his gaudy tower in Ogden, but I'll see what I can do."

"Very well," said Lionel with a nod. "Good work, gentleman. If there's nothing else, you are dismissed."

"Sir, a question if I may," said Laerzo. "We're not going to war with our own people, are we? I mean, Waldea barely survived the last one."

"That has yet to be determined, Cadet. Something tells me this question has more to do about your brother than anything. Am I correct?"

Laerzo was impressed with Lionel's intuition. "I guess so, sir. It's not clear why he or the others are acting this way, but I know Algus; he's not a bad person. We just have to snap them out of it. That's all."

"Do not underestimate the Usurper!" commanded Azacca. "She lays claim over all she crosses. Always coveting power. By any means will she obtain it."

"But we don't even know if she's real!" shouted Leopold somewhat out of turn.

"The Sh'tama do. We hath seen her in visions! She resides bound in the World's Blood, *Lutzrat*. Trapped in *Qua'cana*, center of all things. I say unto you, if Waldea will endure, Denestra be bled from this land like poison from a vein."

CHAPTER 21

For Laerzo, life in the Alliance was an exercise in futility. Only a handful of days had passed since arriving at Fort Lionel, and his bags were packed already. He found the thankless hustle a complete waste of time, toil for its own sake. Training day in and day out was one thing, but waking up at the crack of dawn to do it? That was a bridge too far. And for what? Three meals and a bed? They didn't even give him a couple of tins to enjoy an occasional night out on the town. If this was what it meant to be a soldier, he wanted no part in it.

Still, duty called, this time in the form of a letter sent to his barracks. It instructed him to meet General Dietrich for reasons that were painfully predictable. A lecture about duty would likely be waiting for him; that, or some other such nonsense.

Dietrich is soft, he thought. *He wouldn't go above and beyond to discipline somebody as green as me. Now, if Maddock had anything to do with it, that would be a different matter entirely.*

On his way, Laerzo strangely reminisced patrolling Grenefest with a modicum of fondness. At least then he was left to his own devices. What he would've given to go back to the days before all this.

Not so promptly, he arrived at Dietrich's door on the first floor of the north wing. He glanced once more at his letter before knocking.

"Come in," shouted Dietrich. Once Laerzo entered, the General pointed to a chair sitting opposite his desk without so much as looking up from his parchment. "Please, have a seat." As always, his tone sounded more disappointed than angry.

Laerzo obeyed, glad enough to skip whatever it was he was supposed to be doing at the moment. Leaning back with a yawn, he clasped both hands behind his head while Dietrich continued to jot something with an ink-tipped feather pen. "So, you wanted to see me?"

"Yes. How has life in Stolgrum been treating you? Everything to your liking?"

"Well, food in the barracks is a little bland, and they won't let me leave to find a good ale. Maybe we can do a little sightseeing soon. Find a nice go-to spot."

"You're not here to see the sights. You're here to train for war." Dietrich looked Laerzo dead in the eyes. "I've been informed of your delinquency over the past few days. Twice now, you've strolled into training an auram late. You didn't even bother to show up this morning. What do you have to say for yourself?"

"Just can't seem to get enough sleep, you know? I'm sure my body will adjust sooner or later."

"Sleep is a luxury some soldiers are forced to do without in hard times."

"Guess I'm not much of a soldier then, am I?"

"You are, just not one who is willing. Regardless, if Waldea is to prevail, we need young men like you to step up and give your all, from dawn to dusk, every day. There's no telling when things will take a nasty turn."

"Yeah, well, things are pretty nasty now, if you ask me." Turning his chair to the left, Laerzo crossed both boots over the corner of the desk. He was feeling pretty bold at the moment.

"But you know what? While I was busting my ass the other day, I got to thinking. Why even bother?"

Dietrich was clearly displeased, though not about to let his cadet get a rise out of him. His reaction remained one of strict indifference. "Come now, Laerzo. You already know the answer to that question."

"Do I? I mean, you've threatened to take away my home before, but Gwyndolyn already did that. As far as I'm concerned, there's nothing really keeping me here, is there?"

"Not even Maybel? Leopold?"

Laerzo shot a clever smile. "Leo made his own bed with the Alliance. And Maybel would follow me anywhere. I'm sure we could find some place to stay and scrape by until something better came along."

"I'm afraid this city works a bit differently than you expect. Stolgrum didn't raise the largest company of soldiers in the land by accident. Without some connection to the Alliance, personal or familial, not much in the way of opportunity will be afforded you here. Think I'm kidding? You both would end up in the slums by next moon. Now, that might be suitable to your ends, but not Maybel's. You wouldn't want that for her, would you?"

Laerzo's smirk settled into a grimace. "Maybe we take our chances back in the forests of Greneva then. When necessary, I can be awfully resourceful."

"No doubt, but you'd just end up a thrall to those zealots like the others. Wouldn't be very free then. And I know you wouldn't want that." Dietrich shifted his glance toward the boots until Laerzo removed them. "Look, nobody said this was going to be easy, but a little discipline will do you good. It's liberating in its own way. Give me some time to bring out your potential. I'll make a soldier out of you yet."

"Isn't that Maddock's job?"

"That's *General* Maddock, cadet. If you were one of his men, sure, but being from Greneva, you answer to me. Be thankful for that." Standing, Dietrich began to pace behind his desk. "Still, he has been quite vocal about your provisional admittance into the Alliance. Lord Lionel has his concerns as well."

"Provisional . . . admittance?" asked Laerzo, unsure of the term's meaning or implication.

"Put simply, you have not yet proven yourself willing or worthy to wear that uniform. You see, we have a certain standard to uphold, and it would not look good for either of us if you failed to meet it. I have vouched for you, after all. Now, Command has called for your initiation in order to discern whether my decision was warranted."

Laerzo ran a hand through his tussled black hair. "Well, no pressure there. What kind of initiation?"

There was a sudden rap at the door. Dietrich moved to answer it, but before granting his new visitors entry, turned back with a grave stare. "It seems you will find out soon enough. Laerzo, you must steel yourself for what happens next."

Standing, Laerzo made little of the foreboding words until two rank and file soldiers escorted Azacca, the Sh'tama figure from the other day, into the chamber. The strange man's countenance gave both Dietrich and Laerzo pause for reasons they could not explain.

"Blessings to you," greeted Azacca with a bow, his smile wide.

"So, Lord Lionel has decided then," said Dietrich. "Azacca, are you sure?"

"Have faith, *Generale*! Everything comes in its time. This be no different from our first crossing, yes? You remember it well.

Both then and now, great revelation be given. So hath Azacca, the Godsend, come to be your guide. Sancta be praised!"

Relishing the disquiet caused by these words, he watched Dietrich leave his desk, nod solemnly, and exit without another word, though the two soldiers remained. Azacca snapped his fingers, prompting one of them to hand over a thin chain attached to a small, ornate cage inside which a tiny ember was lit. Azacca then gently bobbed and flicked the vessel toward Laerzo, releasing tufts of a pleasant, musty smoke. Everyone found the combination of scent and dance of the chain slightly intoxicating, Laerzo most of all. With great interest, he watched Azacca extinguish the flame and return the relic, somewhat oblivious to the other soldier stepping forward with a dark pouch like a mask held overhead.

Laerzo retreated behind his chair with an addled expression. "Stay back! What are you up to?"

Azacca raised his right arm to stall the guard before he himself approached. His large brown eyes matched Laerzo's auburn stare all the while, sharing impressions both stark and subtle. After one final bobbing glance, Azacca tilted his head with a slight frown. "Misgiving hangs heavy, I see."

Laerzo did not blink or break his gaze. "I'm not afraid, if you mean to scare me."

"No need to fight. Save your strength and follow me."

"What will you do? No harm will come to me?"

"That will be of your own choosing. Fear not." With one hand, Azacca moved the chair between them aside, and with the other, raised thumb, middle, and index fingers. Laerzo did not flinch even as his body swayed from the incense. "Good. A few words before we begin." Most expectedly, his somber face swelled with almost boundless joy. "Light upon the rock be blinding! May it show you the way."

"Huh? That's it?" asked Laerzo, disarmed by the strange man's nonsense. And just as his guard lowered, so too did the veil over his head. He was slow to resist, and by the time he did, both arms had already been seized from behind. Little could be seen from beneath the veil, though light had not been completely shielded from his vision. A hand lay gently upon his left shoulder, followed by the wind of a fierce whisper.

"Neither fret nor fear be of service this day. I say unto you, *galante*, peace now." The voice floated lightly on the air, much like the hazy aroma all around them, causing Laerzo's every muscle to unwind. Despite his apparent mistreatment, there was a sincerity in those words he could not help but trust. Not that he had much of a choice.

With a hesitant nod, he allowed Azacca and the soldiers to lead him from the room. They marched through several halls, taking the occasional turn or flight of stairs downward, until stopping abruptly. Nothing was said, though the clanging of armor suggested that salutes had been exchanged between his escorts and at least one other soldier. This was followed by what sounded like heavy stone grinding as a deeper darkness opened up before him.

He was then taken into a descending path, whereby all remaining light and heat gradually vanished. Like before, he did not hear a single word spoken, only echoes of boot steps falling upon uneven rock. Judging by their number and rhythm, he determined one of the men must have stayed behind. The manner they continued down the cold, winding way made it seem like they were taking him in circles, deliberately trying to confuse his sense of bearing.

Just as he had grown tired of stumbling in the dark, traces of light once again began glimmering beyond the cloth. A refreshing gust of wind met him soon after, flavored by the salt of the sea. Both gave him hope that they would soon clear the narrow tunnel, and that hope came true, though it fell quickly to the feeling of wood shifting under his feet. He suddenly became more disoriented than ever, his gut sinking similar to how one loses balance on a ladder. This he dismissed as some effect of the savory smoke, but it was gravely unsettling to say the least.

They stopped again, only this time he could feel hands removing his binds, as well as affixing something to the back of his armor, which the men tightened with a big tug.

"Hurry up, soldier!" ordered one of the men. "I don't want to spend another moment here, understood?"

"You don't have to tell me twice!" answered the other. This, of course, meant Azacca was the one who had excused himself earlier. "Everything is ready."

"What's this all about?" asked Laerzo after a brief silence. "Come on, don't leave me hanging here."

He then realized both the men had already departed. Another moment passed, then another, and again until he was finally fed up. *No more games*, he thought while reaching for the thread to loosen his mask when suddenly a horn above him blasted.

He had no clue what transpired next, not at first, but his body knew in an instant. There was that jolt in his stomach again, like startling from a dream, followed by his whole self brutally whipping in a whirl of black, but not for long. Something scraggy and impenetrable, like a wall of tiny, scraping nails, struck him, causing his body to lurch violently. Fortunately for him, the spinning slowed dramatically as he repeatedly met with the roughened contours, after which he simply floated there for a time, all direction ripped away, gravity heavy on his bones.

Turning, he rested his back on the jagged surface, waiting for the shock to pass. As it did, pain began diffusing into a more broad, persistent ache throughout his limbs. Only then did his mind pull together some semblance of bearing. It wasn't helpful just to guess, but he did not dare remove the mask, as the forms and forces beyond him had proven themselves cruel. In the moment, that was really all he cared to know.

Still, the strain from being suspended would not allow him to delay for long. Tilting his head upward, he lifted the veil just enough to recoil from a flash of intense light slightly hinted blue. It took time for the color emblazoned upon his eyes to dwindle, and even longer for him to try again. When he did, his gaze was sent downward, though he struggled to make sense of the distant green waxing and waning beyond his boots. It was the Waters Emeralda crashing against the rocks below. That could mean only one thing, though he was too horrified to admit it: He had been left to dangle upon the Radiant Cliffs of Stolgrum.

The terrible sight caused his body to shake like a hooked fish in the water. "What have you done?" he roared, his lungs heaving in the stuffy bag. A vain attempt to gain some foothold left him spinning once again, and he resisted the urge to retch while his body eventually returned to stillness.

Pushing thoughts of the drop from his mind like the light from his gaze, he wondered about the upside of his predicament, deciding after some hesitation to brave another look. The veil was lifted again, this time fully above the brow, and for a while, he allowed the intense blue light to permeate the closed lids of his guarded eyes. This he did in preparation to catch a singular glimpse at the space above. He forced his red, tear-filled eyes open, struggling to make sense of the image burning into sight. Lids quickly clenched, he pulled back under cover in pain, filled with despair by the gap between him and the cliff's edge.

They intend to kill me, he thought. *Some initiation!* There was no way Leopold had been subjected to the same impossible task. Even if Laerzo possessed the strength to reach the top, the distance was still not entirely clear to him, and he had little clue where to begin. The only thing sheltering him from this ridiculous trial was at once what prevented him from besting it. Should he remove the veil or not?

It was quite the conundrum, one which eventually caused resignation to wash over him. But in the midst of this hopelessness came a newfound calm followed by a strange idea, one he swore was not his own. It was the last thing he wanted to do in such a situation, and oddly enough, the only thing yet to do. The compulsion became so obvious he wondered why it had taken so long to cross his mind.

At once, his defiant eyes stared upward once again, this time through the veil. To his surprise, a sea of glimmering stars shone, in the middle of the day no less! He quickly lost himself in the myriad of shining specs, nearly as many as could be found in the night sky, but something akin to a constellation gradually shifted into focus. Soon he saw a great serpent staring down at him, startling him to his core.

Then came an even stranger idea, that some of these points of light were much nearer than they seemed. His right hand left the comfort of its rock for the nearest star and grabbed it tightly.

He could hardly believe it.

This is the way, he declared graciously while securing another step, then another. Each successful movement slightly loosened the rope at his back, giving his lungs room to breath.

Soon he reached what previously appeared to be the

serpent's tongue and took a quick moment to rest while fixating boldly upon its piercing gaze. Such a striking sight seemed to dare Laerzo to continue on, and continue he did, scaling the great snake's winding form with a newfound fearlessness. His body was clearly exhausted, yet filled with strength he never knew existed, strength which gave him hope.

How proud he was to finally surpass the great viper! However, a new trial had taken its place. The slack upon his harness was increasing, and with it, the rope's weight, retarding his pace and conviction. It hadn't really bothered him up until that point, but now it was all he could think about. That or the sudden realization that one fall from this height would likely cause the whip of his slack to snap him in two.

Even worse, there was nothing gleaming nearby to show him the way. His hand reached slowly up and around for the next move up the cliff, but he felt only shallow cavities that would likely not support him for long. It was then that his fatigue truly set in, leaving him to pause a few moments and regain his strength. Breathing heavily, he searched again for anything to aid him, but given how closely he clung to the rock, seeing beyond his immediate position was almost impossible.

There has to be something left to climb, he thought. Suddenly, his attention shifted from the light to his rope. Though the heft of it was daunting, he hoped it might still prove useful. Steadying himself, his left leg lifted part of the rope over the right knee long enough to pinch the rope between both legs.

Good. Now for the noose Gustav taught me.

His right hand left its support, managed to wrap the slack in concert with both aching knees, but only one time before returning to the rock. Moments later, his second attempt wrapped it twice more. His failing strength would only allow one more go. In one fell swoop, he pulled a loop through the twists of rope, released it from his knees, and placed his left boot through the opening.

Thankfully, the knot was up to snuff. Shifting his weight, he gripped the rope and left the cold comfort of the rock entirely, spinning there until his body was able to rest. But now the weight was taxing his leg, causing it to cramp. He was running out of time, though thankfully, he was far enough from the rock to surveil the remaining climb. He found traces of a new path. To his right, a bright vein of lucram trailed upward to the top. It wasn't close, but with the right amount of swinging, he might be able to reach it and finish this mad climb.

Turning, he yanked the rope back while his foot pushed the loop forward. Then the opposite, back and forth. His careful movements built momentum as the bright strand of stars pulsed closer with every swing. However, a gradual warbling grew from that momentum, sending a frightful friction buzzing down the thick fibers of the rope.

Just a little more, he thought, his aggressive pushing and pulling becoming all the more desperate. As he prepared to make his move, the rope snapped with a deafening crack.

He could feel his gut sink watching the slack give way completely, and for a moment, everything was chaos. His fingers clawed frantically at empty air as he fell against the rock face several feet lower. His heart pounded as he fought to secure his grip. He managed barely, only due to the jolt of terror through his body, which gave him the strength to carry on.

"Now you've done it!" he could faintly hear somebody scream through the sound of his panting, thought it might have just been his imagination. Still, hearing it gave him hope that the end of his perilous climb was near. He scaled the remainder of the cliff with surprising haste, even more so after hearing another voice, one less worried than the one before.

"Peace be with you. I hath done only that which Sancta commands. Why not take a look? Just a peek. Go on then!"

"Azacca," snarled Laerzo just as his bloodied right hand met the strange sensation of flat dirt. Pulling himself up to the edge of the cliffside, he was met by someone who yanked him by both arms onto solid ground and ripped off his mask.

"Unbelievable," said Dietrich, gaping back at the others.

"*Now* you speak of belief," answered Azacca smugly.

Lionel was thoroughly impressed. "Azacca, please forgive our doubt. It seems the truth of your words endures another day."

"Let his fate endure longer still!" shouted Azacca, pointing to the hobbled figure before them. "Halae! She delivers you!"

The man's words did not reach Laerzo, however, his heavy head inches from the ground, seizing with bits of breath. His hands desperately plunged into chunks of grass as if the dirt beneath his nails were a blessing. He heard himself give thanks in the silent underpinning of his rattled mind; to whom, he did not know. Pleasant wind across the cliffside also received his gratitude as he propped himself up on rattled knees. He was visibly trembling—expected, given his recent plight, though the wild, furious look in his eyes suggested it had nothing to do with fatigue.

"You've done well, Laerzo," said Dietrich with some surprise. Laerzo refused to acknowledge him or meet his gaze, though the subtle swaying of his body told Dietrich that Azacca's incense still had its hold over him, just like last time.

"This much I expect of my apprentices," answered Azacca.

"Good *Generale*, t'was once you, the scared boy, dangling from these cliffs. Remember?"

"All too well. Every now and again, I still awake tormented in the night. I'll never understand the point of it. If the worthy are already known to Sancta as you claim, why subject them to such perilous feats?"

"My teachings elude you, do they? How she places a fire deep within us? Danger only helps stoke it, and burns the soul lest it forgets." Azacca stared back to Laerzo, whose animus of the old man was brimming. "Yea, I see fire in you, fearless *galante*."

"You dangled me from a cliff," declared Laerzo in disbelief. Rising slowly, his fierce gaze wiped everything from sight except for Azacca's smile.

The silent standoff continued for some time before Azacca slowly unsheathed the sword along his belt, the ornate, silver one from before. For one protracted moment, its humming blade rang beautifully through the air like a bell. After it had quieted, he inexplicably rested the tip of its blade upon his own chest, offered the hilt to Laerzo. "Now we will see how bright."

"Careful, soldier," warned Dietrich.

Taking the hilt in his hand, Laerzo would've swung right then and there if not quickly captivated by the sword's impressive craftwork. The finely honed, pale-blue edge seamlessly blended into its silver base, exhibiting impeccable balance and light weight. Though apparently an antique of indeterminate age, its caliber far exceeded anything he had yet seen in the Alliance. He was too in love with it then to realize, but the lucram blade shone a hue reminiscent of the light that had guided him up the cliffside.

"Make Rudra sing, and she will be yours," declared Azacca,

his words a challenge that Laerzo eagerly accepted. At once, he thrusted at Azacca's throat, then spun wildly to cleave his head clean off, but the sluggish maneuvers were in vain. In return, Azacca simply shot back a conceited smirk, which only goaded the next clumsy attack, then another, and another. Laerzo's efforts time and again washed off the man with little effect. There was a trick woven into the man's myriad of braids, namely the shiny, metallic ornaments that distracted his foes and deceptively signaled movements that never manifested. Laerzo could not help but focus on what appeared to be a mess of snakes whipping about instead of the man's frame, irritating to no end. How he wished to sever just one if only to prove he could.

Of course, Azacca wasn't there just to show off. His ring-heavy fingers rapped Laerzo's jaw with such speed and fluidity that it took a moment for any to notice, Laerzo included. By the time he did, Azacca had already slid a few paces backward into an irreverent bow with both hands wide, chest slightly angled forward, face lowered dismissively. Laerzo quickly redoubled his approach, this time with a bit more humility. However, every swing and slash proved equally useless at besting Azacca's quick footing and clever feints.

"An aimless blade finds no home. Focus unto me! Do not hold back."

"Only if you draw your weapon!"

"You would rather wield pity over a blade? Foolish! As for mine, spin me again if you wish to see!"

Azacca continued to bob and weave while occasionally teasing a hand for Laerzo to strike. One would wave, then the other, sometimes both or neither. Every so often, his mane would play its part, causing the cadet to focus again on the glimmering trinkets swinging from his chaotic threads. When he did, Azacca struck him across the face a second time. "Again!" After another similar bout, he slapped him once more. "Boy, some light does not guide. Keep your eyes to mine!"

Laerzo did just that, and soon began to match his opponent's flow. For a while, they danced well together, but this too was a trick designed to breed complacency. Before long, Laerzo even started to believe he'd gained the upper hand, or at least until he realized Azacca was purposefully slowing his pace. This caused him great anger, drove him to push recklessly. His frustration only intensified when Azacca shifted his gaze from the battle toward Dietrich and Lionel, sometimes for seconds at a time, clearly meant as an insult. Even worse, he did this with both arms nonchalantly joined at his back.

"Smug bastard!" shouted Laerzo. "If you want me to strike you down so badly, then so be it!"

He waited for the next time Azacca dropped his guard and slashed downward, almost certain he would draw blood. Instead, not only was he disarmed with a quick twist of the wrist but cut at the chest with a dagger dangling from one of Azacca's hindmost braids, one loosened while his hands were hidden. This took Laerzo completely by surprise, and before he could counter, Rudra was already humming a dulcet tone at his throat, wielded again by its original owner.

"But a glimmer of the man I hath met," said Azacca without pride or malice. "Long be the road between him and this *galante*."

"I am called Laerzo, you treacherous fiend! At least remember that much before you finish me off."

Azacca laughed while withdrawing the blade, its song silenced inside the scabbard. "I fear you mistake my intent."

"Oh, please! Why would anyone drug, drag, and dangle another from a cliff?"

"Why, indeed. To test his mettle! Yours be strong enough, though not too sharp! That will change in time."

"No thanks to you," griped Laerzo as Dietrich and Lionel approached him with uplifted spirits.

"Come now," said Azacca lightly. "One sorely defeated hath lost twice. You take a step toward glory! I will help you take another, and one day, you will make this lucram blade sing! Until that time, Rudra remains mine to hold."

"You never cease to amaze!" exclaimed Lionel. "Waldea is blessed to have an ally such as you. Perhaps one day, she will be free to realize it."

Laerzo was shocked to hear such an utterance of praise. His eyes eagerly fell upon Rudra like his one true love had been snatched away. Winning her back was suddenly paramount in his mind, other than maybe using her to run Azacca through. He decided then and there to humor the man, at least long enough to get his revenge and claim the blade. With arms crossed, he turned his head to spit. "Don't act high and mighty! You couldn't teach a fish to drink."

"I wouldn't be so quick to judge," said Dietrich. "I was much like you in my youth. This man taught me quite a bit back then. You would do well to follow him."

"And follow me he shall!" proclaimed Azacca boldly. "Rejoice, Laerzo, for today joins a propitious boy with his master!"

CHAPTER 22

Journal of Gustav Grimstad

—Date Unknown—

Woke up at home. It's dark. Writing between bouts of delusion. Will try to mark dates later. Waves of indigo with every breath. Lips are parched, stomach churning, body battered. Fever is running high. Don't dare to stand. Couldn't if I tried.

Must have blacked out again. Don't know how long has passed, still dark. Possibly night of Grenefest, maybe not. Can't be sure. Remember little after leaving the manor. Chaos everywhere, the forest trailing beneath my feet. A bolt lodged in one snatcher's neck. Everything was spinning. Maybe just me. Woke up briefly in a ditch, then on the run again, closer to home. Most of it was a blur. Must have crawled back, trousers ripped, legs scratched and bloody. This cave reeks of filth. Maybe just me. More sickness incoming.

Finally woke to hints of the morn after many failed attempts at a proper night's sleep. Still running a fever. Threw my damp, retch-covered clothes as far as I could manage. Wasn't very far. Unwrapped the bandages at my neck as well. Doing so only seemed to worsen this pulsing sensation. Makes it hard to keep balance or move around, but I'm starting to adjust. Wasn't nearly as bad compared to the original onset that night, though the delirium became noticeably milder in town. I have no idea what's causing it. Once enough strength returns, I will try to retrieve some food stocks from across the room. At least get some water in me. I doubt my body will keep either down for long.

Seems later. Judging by the light shining into my cavernous abode, it's probably some time after high dawn. Had a dream, the first in a long time. It wasn't a good one. I remember lying on a table under a bright light. My father, a renowned clinician, was there to inform me of an accident I had suffered to my windpipe. He was operating, had my throat split wide open. I remember how unsettling it felt to feel nothing as he worked. Said I would never speak again, kept repeating it over and over under that light. Told me never to try or it would cause more damage down the line. Wrapped my neck up tight.

It's so strange. I never knew what had happened to me back then, why I had ended up on that table. Just woke up there one day, couldn't remember a thing beforehand. And every time I pondered it, this intense panic set in like a switch inside me had suddenly flipped. I did try to speak a couple of times, but the words never came. I learned quickly not to think about it. Didn't matter much at that point, anyway. What's done is done. Anyway, fatigue is beginning to set in again.

It's much later now. Must have slept all day, but at least I slept. Managed to get some sustenance in me. So far, so good. I don't have much left though. Will have to hold out until I can leave my bedside. Who knows when that will be.

Had another bad dream, if you can even call it that. More like a memory I hoped to forget. It started out pleasant enough. I was flying with my family from Archeim to Greneva. Just the three of us. My brother and I were very excited, as we didn't realize at the time anything existed beyond the Great Chasm. We were on our way to visit Uncle Larry, as Father called him. I don't know if he was actually our uncle though. Probably just a colleague of his, or a close family friend. I remember the sense of urgency on my father's face as he flew us in his personal shuttle, a very tiny vessel.

We were almost there when a violent shaking brought us down fast. Things went black for a while, but the thing I remember next was waking in a smoldering pile of rubble in a forest next to Father's corpse. It was grotesque—I'll never forget it. As for my brother, he was presumably hurled to his death somewhere nearby, but I never did find him. At least until annums later when I briefly spotted him in town, before he disappeared on me once more. Even that fateful night at the festival, could have sworn I saw his face again, but delusion may have just gotten the best of me.

Anyway, despite all attempts to stay awake, my body drags me back into the void. Let's hope for a better dream. With any luck, this strange feeling will quit washing over me by the morrow.

Day 28 by the 9th Moon, 1212

Today was a little more productive than expected. Still experiencing that pulsing indigo, though my body has more or less gotten used to it by now. Occasional bouts of hallucination, mostly distant, nothing severe. From what I can tell so far, it seems related to my breathing. For instance, whenever I hold wind within my gut, the color almost completely fades. Conversely, the heavier I breathe, the more the color intensifies. There has to be something going on in my head, but I haven't the faintest clue what. The sensation still gives me an occasional headache, but that might have more to do with illness and lack of food as of late. I will continue to document this phenomenon whenever new information becomes evident.

Finally made it out from under my rock, so to say, at least long enough to replenish some provisions. Nothing too substantial, mostly some sour cabbage from my go-to patch, various shrooms, and wildenberries for now. The local flora seems different, slightly tinged in hue and taste. Maybe just me. Filled my gourds at the stream, had a quick rinse, caught a fish for later. Good thing, since my usual traps were mostly ignored or curiously triggered with little to show for it. One was covered in blood, which trailed into the bushes. A few might have been stripped by other hunters in my absence. Out of caution, I reset the ones closest to home in case unwelcome guests get any ideas and come looking for me. If they do not trap, it might be a few days still before I can muster the strength to hunt.

Speaking of days, I checked the moon rising tonight, realized four days had, in fact, passed since Grenefest. That means I had fallen in and out of consciousness for practically two days straight. I will update my entries accordingly.

Day 2 by the 10th Moon, 1212

I'm feeling much better today. Cleaned my home in the morning before hauling sheets and garments to the stream for a good scrub. Did not take long to notice a gleam overhead amid clear skies. I scaled a particularly tall tree for a better view and was surprised to find convoys of luminous arcs flying as a ship would sail upon the waters. Never before have they been seen in these parts. Not even back on the main continent. The bulk of them were massive boats with masts glowing an intense white as well as wide, feathery wings guiding their golden hulls. When in motion, trails of prismatic light were left in their wake. One was larger and more pronounced than the rest with many more wings protruding from each side. It seemed to glow like me, though I'm not sure why. There were also men in white armor seated upon winged geldtmares, flying around the vessels. At least, I think they were men. Quite beautiful to behold, as splendid as they were terrifying. Where did they come from?

I'm starting to think they have been among us all along, hiding on the mountains' hindside, or perhaps within. That is where the craft seemed to appear during the festival, after all. Something about them seems so surreal, much like those creatures I had the displeasure of meeting up close that night. Heralds, I believe they were called. It might've just been the delirium setting in, but they seemed to exhibit dual forms. One moment, they were bright and otherworldly, and another, they were reduced to men in cold, metallic cores, their wings actually wheels within spinning wheels. It is not easily describable, even now. Each likeness overlapped the other, both seemingly legitimate, though I got the impression that the dimmer of the two was the real deal.

The countless folks ushered up from Greneva were utterly fixated by these supernal, shining forces. They feared and revered them, even worshipped them at times. Looking from afar, they almost seemed like an army being amassed. Everyone was clad in simple white garb—at least, white at first, anyway—and were given picks and other crude implements to carry up the mountainside. Spotted camps along the path leading into a large site, whereby a foundation is being carved into the Mount. Incidentally, not far from the old Carlyle estate. So many strange happenings I've seen there as of late. As for Greneva itself, not much is happening other than the steady movement of people between city and Mount. The streets seem eerily empty most aurams of the day. Would investigate further if not for my current state. For now, it's best to observe from afar.

Day 4 by the 10th Moon, 1212

Visited a waterfall today for a much-needed wash. This space, tucked into the forest, is easily my favorite spot, with little in the way of visitors. It was nice to go somewhere secluded where my current condition would not cause alarm. There I observed something interesting: the indigo emanating from me was noticeably dampened in the waters. It also could not penetrate the water, or if it did, was quickly dispersed within it. I spent a fair deal of time there reflecting upon the nature of these forces. Both were of similar kind, yet constantly competing with one another. It brought me calm to witness their respective waves waxing and waning, crashing and dissipating in a predictable flow.

That was not all I observed. While still bathing, I retreated just behind the falling stream upon spotting a procession of the Trust chasing a few frantic residents up along the riverside. I was startled by the way these fearful figures bellowed as they scrambled, sometimes on all fours. From what I could tell, their features were mangy, the color about them muted. At times, they didn't even seem like people at all, something more base, fearful yet sinister. They were afraid of the white-robed men pursuing with pitchforks in hand, but most noticeably, they were utterly terrified, or perhaps repulsed, by the water. They didn't dare enter it even if it would have helped them escape.

These creatures were eventually cornered at the edge of the basin not too far from where I remained hidden. I was surprised to see more Trust trailing behind, accompanied by none other than Gwyndolyn. Quite curiously, she did not seem captive in any way that I could tell. Quite the contrary, she was escorted by several attendants and warriors, treated with the utmost care as she gracefully approached the runaways. Her appearance and demeanor were nothing short of radiant, and I mean that in the actual sense. Just as I have been cursed with this strange aura, she too appeared to emit a faint white light, though not in waves like me.

She held a crystalline carafe filled with what seemed like wine that she soon opened and poured into a bowl held by one of her servants. Then, dipping a branch of laurels into the wine, she made some declaration, almost like an incantation, and sprinkled it onto the deranged figures. What happened next was nothing short of extraordinary. Their depraved forms were lessened, at least long enough for her to offer them the wine. They accepted, and upon drinking, were fully restored. I recognized one of them then. Bethany, I think her name was. She was utterly jubilant—so obnoxiously, in fact, that some of the guards kept her at a safe distance. Gwyndolyn seemed slightly surprised at what she'd done, but as everyone continued to sing her praises, she swelled with confidence and conceit.

They left shortly after, and when it seemed safe enough, I did so as well. I must confess that I haven't been able to think of much else since. Though never particularly smitten with Gwyndolyn, I currently cannot get her out of my head. Hopefully, a good night's rest will help set me straight.

Woke in the middle of the night to lights flashing just outside my abode. Did somebody see me earlier after all? Perhaps not, though it got me thinking whether this was the first time such a thing has happened. Might've been too tired to notice before. At any rate, I do not like the sudden increase of traffic this close to home. If they were to find me, I would have little choice but to fight. Will have to keep an eye out and plan accordingly.

Day 7 by the 10th Moon, 1212

After taking some time to cover the entry to my abode with vines and brush, I stayed indoors for the next few days to catch up on reading. I will forever be grateful to my father for instilling in me his ardent love of reading. I must say, my avid page turning has garnered me quite the humble collection of texts over the annums, including my most recent additions.

I took my time attempting to discern some of those tomes from the manor. Despite my best efforts, they are largely beyond comprehension, much pertaining to the composition and effects of particles and waves—of "resonance," as it is called. Reminded me of being in the waters. To my surprise, one was signed by my father, Dr. Gustano Grimstad. Judging by the note he left within to Dr. Carlyle, they must have been close. Uncle Larry, indeed. Had I known it was him we were supposed to meet, I would've made a better effort to contact the man. His disappearance is all the more unfortunate, though it suddenly makes more sense. Whatever it was he and my father were working to achieve, somebody wished to interfere with most deathly intent. I very much hope that he is still alive.

Day 9 by the 10th Moon, 1212

My time is short. Just before solset, while hunting from my usual spot in a tree, a murder of fowl suddenly beset me completely contrary to their nature. I lost my balance and tumbled, though thankfully, the bush below mostly broke my fall. Still, the impact ripped a cry from me that briefly caused an entire strip of the forest to light up with indigo. I did not think myself capable of unleashing such vociferous force. It was tantamount to an arrow parting the waters. Notably, the space within was not tainted like what surrounded it, as if I had torn through some unseen fabric in the aether. Even more strangely, the indigo flooded back into the empty space soon after, mended it in a sense, and eventually, disappeared altogether.

It frightened me to see it. I was not the only one. Some loggers finishing up nearby spotted me on the move, started screaming "ashen" until I fled. I do not know why. Soon, heralds were visible just beyond the canopy. How many, I do not know. So long as I held my breath, they could apparently not see me, but doing so too often proved quite taxing. I did not feel safe hiding back home, yet managed to stop by for some of my things. I write now on the run, able to elude them so far.

I fear it's only a matter of time before they find me. If by some chance they don't, I will perhaps take my chances in another nook deeper into the rock and hope for the best. If they do, they'll snatch me up the Mount like before. That is, if I let them. I'd rather die than let them. Father, please watch over me.

CHAPTER 23

"Bruno, we've been at this all day," said Dietrich in a sparsely furnished room overlooking the dark, dreadfully cramped space a couple of stories below. It had been over a fortnight since arriving at Stolgrum, yet the turncoat Connel had still not divulged anything significant. Dietrich could tell by the way Maddock stared down into the chamber that he was running out of steam, or more importantly, patience. Of course, the stubborn man would never admit it. It was no wonder, considering how exhausted Dietrich himself felt lingering auram after auram in that stuffy room. Aside from a couple of creaking chairs tucked under a rickety wooden table and a lantern running noticeably low on lavabean oil, it lacked any furnishing that might have dulled this painfully prolonged process.

"I swear he's staring at me," growled Maddock, his gaze never leaving the cell below. If not for the solitary window carved high into its northern wall, no light or life would be found dwelling below at all.

"You know this chamber allows us to observe in complete secrecy. No eyes can see beyond these walls."

"Then why have our eyes been locked through the pane's tint this whole time?"

Dietrich knew his partner was about ready for another round with the prisoner below. "Because one naturally stares up in a pit. Come take a load off, would you? You're making me nervous."

"He's gotten smug as of late. Just let me beat something out of him already!"

"That would not be wise. I know Connel; he won't keep a tight lip forever. If you lose your cool now, it may be days before we get anything out of him."

"It may be days either way, Sigurd. This whole thing has been a bust."

"Granted, we've learned little of the Trust, but maybe we can at least determine why the other gaolmates at Lionel have roused since his arrival." Dietrich watched Maddock make for the door. "Don't give him the upper hand, all right?"

Maddock turned partially, his left nostril flaring in accordance with his scowl. "I don't need you to tell me how interrogation works. Have fun pouring through Carlyle's tome though." He slammed the door on his way back to business.

Dietrich was actually impressed by the restraint shown thus far by his grumpy friend. Any poor soul unfortunate enough to cross Maddock during the War would assuredly be buried soon after. It pretty much explained the man's unflattering title outright. By contrast, Dietrich, a particularly cold, calculating man, received the less formidable title, the Good General; it was a forgone conclusion, considering the contrast of company he kept back then, Maddock included. Dietrich wagered it would not be much longer for the Madman to rear his ugly head. Until then, he threw his weatherworn boots up on the table, staring pensively at the thick stack of parchment laying within reach.

Though he always considered himself a competent academic, Dr. Carlyle's work put him to shame quickly and often. Try as he did, none of the nearly endless litany of enigmatic equations scribbled therein could be deciphered into anything remotely actionable. The word "Liminatum" did flash before his eyes occasionally, but it meant little to him then. Even Lord Lionel, another notable scholar in his own right, was completely baffled by the voluminous text.

It was only after Dietrich poured through journal entries in the second bit of research that some semblance of understanding came into focus. Surprisingly, these pertained to conversations with Dr. Carlyle's daughter, Gwyndolyn. Most of their early Noetic sessions covered her general well-being and emotional progression following the death of her mother, but those dating only two annums back became much more interesting. He happened upon some phenomenon by which the girl's behavior began to change in unexpected ways. She would occasionally fall into a trance of sorts and become unresponsive for minutes at a time. Discussion would eventually resume, but with a marked contrast in her tone and temperament. Dr. Carlyle likened this individual to an older woman, and not a particularly pleasant one at that. It was as if she assumed a different personality entirely.

He originally happened upon the strange encounter by chance, though in time, he learned to induce it with the sound of a bell. Some sense of lucid continuity persisted between subsequent sessions; however, it was highly emphasized that Gwyndolyn retained no memory of these conversations. Judging by the writings, they were never openly discussed after the fact. Dr. Carlyle insisted the keen intellect, vast knowledge, and way with words simply could not belong to his daughter. The woman mentioned being "rooted" to the girl through some shared desire, most notably to be free from her lowly existence. Dietrich's eyes lit up when he learned this aberrant persona called herself Denestra.

Just then, a crash pulled his attention toward the lower

chamber. It seemed his wager was well bet. "Damn it, man." Abandoning his post and papers, he dashed out the door down a coiled path of stone stairs, barging into the adjacent room where Maddock could be seen looming over a newly bloodied face. "At ease, General!"

Connel cleared his throat with a wad of crimson spit. "And here I thought we had become chummy. We are brothers in arms, aren't we?"

"Don't play stupid with me, Two Coats. We know you've been compromised by the Trust. What I want to know is for how long and why. Out with it!"

"Perhaps I was a man on the inside."

"Sure, just not the way you claim. Tell me, how come your Enforcer uniform faded that night as we rode into Thannick? Why were you wearing that gray trench coat?"

"Not sure what you mean. Perhaps you simply had too much to drink that night."

Maddock erupted with a solid kick to the man's chest, watched the wretched husk squirming to sit up before pressing a boot firmly upon his neck. "I'm done playing with you. Tell me why you betrayed us, or I'll beat it out of you."

"Easy does it," said Dietrich while taking a slow, cautious step forward.

Connel shot back a defiant smirk. "These few days have left me a bit famished. Be a gent and bring me something, would you?"

"You don't deserve a single scrap!" growled Maddock, his boot growing heavier by the moment.

"We'll send for food," began Dietrich. "But perhaps you would be willing to speak to something else in the meantime. I hear your fellow inmates have been awfully noisy as of late. What sort of impression do you get from them?"

"*Impression*, you say?" replied Connel oddly. "Doesn't take much to rile up caged animals, General. They always throw parties for new friends. Made me feel *real* welcome."

"And what if some have confessed stories of one such as yourself trying to make his escape? Know anything about that?" To this, Dietrich received no response.

"What? No witty comeback?" Maddock guffawed. "Tell me a good one, and I might make your meal worthwhile."

"Sorry, the taste of blood has suddenly ruined my appetite." Connel took a hook straight to the face.

"That's enough!" ordered Dietrich, but Maddock did not pay him any mind.

Connel began to giggle. "Is that the best you can do?" His voice seemed deeper than before.

"Don't tempt me with a good time, maggot!" boomed Maddock, his voice now echoing many times over through the chamber. Dietrich pulled him back just before his boot proceeded to smash the captive's thin, stubbled jaw. The two generals scuffled for a brief moment thereafter. "Let me go, damn it!" screamed Maddock before throwing Dietrich clear back to the door.

Suddenly, the sullied man began to stir, and though shackled, he managed to stand against the wall with surprisingly little effort. There was a different air around him, his posture, his exuberant gaze, the long, balmy smile now strewn across his mangled face. Blood bubbled in a slow, deranged chortle from the depths of his throat.

"Want some more?" asked Maddock, half acknowledging Dietrich's admonishing stare a couple of paces away. "You're just begging for pain."

"No doubt," replied Connel menacingly, his voice now split, as if somebody shared his words in a lower tone. "It is what brought me here, after all. I have forgotten just how fickle flesh can be, but it matters not. I would gladly suffer much more. Anything to be rid of that place."

"What's the matter? Those scumbags giving you a hard time in the dungeons?"

Connel's brief flash of amused bewilderment implied he was referring to something else. "I know not of whom you speak, but judging by this magnificent agony and the taint on your knuckles, that title better suits you."

Maddock was again ready to pounce, but Dietrich stepped forth with an arm extended between them. "What is your name?"

"Why, General, you already know that much."

"Do I? Why don't you tell me again?"

"I cannot fathom how one would suddenly forget all about his subordinate."

"You're correct, I wouldn't. But it isn't him I'm speaking to now, is it?"

"Sigurd?" asked Maddock, completely baffled by this new line of questioning.

Dietrich's eyes narrowed. "Just who would *you* be exactly?"

"Not sure I follow your meaning," replied Connel, his devilish smile slightly broadening.

"I think you might." Dietrich took another step forward, pausing briefly before he continued. "Denestra, is it?"

Connel's eyes shot wide open, after which he laughed so hard the blood in his throat almost caused him to choke. After regaining his composure, his head tilted strangely. "How utterly fascinating to hear that name come from someone like you. Even if it causes every hair on this body to stand in venomous disgust. Still, that is not me."

"Neither is *that* body, as you have so put it. From where have you come? How is it that we are speaking?"

"Very perceptive, though I'm not sure such a thing can be fully expressed. Let's give it a shot, shall we? Imagine being—how to say, a twinkle of light—weightless in a sense, yet perpetually grounded at the center of all things. There you remain, pulled downward almost in perpetuity. It is quite wearisome. Yet sometimes if you struggle to lift yourself, you may see another light farther away, one greater than you, beautiful, captivating. You are drawn to it. And if there was a connection strong enough between you and that light, even for a moment, you would feel inclined to extend there, to explore, yes? See, it feels natural for one such as I to extend as the opportunity presents, no less than for you to breathe."

"I think I understand somewhat. What is it you want, then?"

"Don't be obtuse, General. To extend, of course. I'm not certain what has caused me to root within this body, or even how long I will stay. It just so happens this is not the first time I have lifted into various cavities of this dungeon. There is a lot of pain here, you see. I think that's what calls us."

"Us? Then there are others."

"Well, sort of. Other Aspects, at least."

Dietrich recounted this term being mentioned a few times in Dr. Carlyle's work. "Aspects? How many?"

"Who can really say? I'm sure there are parts of yourself not yet known or recognized. An Aspect tends to attract toward what it knows best. In my case, through bliss of pain and sorrow."

Maddock's face became increasingly troubled. This dark conversation was completely beyond him. "What in dreadfire?"

Dietrich continued. "But pain and sorrow are casual affairs

in a gaol. Surely, whatever this is would be commonplace there, correct? Then why here and now? Or has this always been so?"

Connel's brow lifted. "Yes, at least since the last conflagration. It was quite spectacular, almost drew our light to the surface of your world, though it sadly lulled too soon. However long ago this occurred in your time, I know not. For us, it was but a single moment."

"War of the Faith," whispered Dietrich. "The pain wrought by such a conflagration . . ." The being's hold over Connel began to fade. "Why tell us this now? How can we know any of it is true?"

"Something tells me you already do, *Sigurd*." The man's body shook with painful laughter. "You wanted to know my name? In times past, I was once called Ichabod. I suppose that will have to do. It was nice chatting with you. Something tells me we will meet again, very soon."

His laughter continued for another maniacal moment before falling completely silent, and then the turncoat Connel fell and stirred no longer.

"Keep it up, Leo!" cheered Laerzo, surrounded by fifty or so pairs of soldiers sparring in Fort Lionel's outer bailey. He gripped Rudra firmly in both hands, his focus again drifting even as he was locked in a brutal scrap with Azacca, their third so far that day.

"I think I'm . . . gonna . . . piss myself!" panted Leopold, sidelined a short distance away. Though not fighting himself, he was given a special type of trauma to whip him into shape. Over and over again, he would unwrap his ten-score chain while keeping the hammer elevated, strike a distant target on the ground, perform a quick push-up, then rewrap the chain. He managed well enough at first, though his gut presently struggled to pull wind. "Can't . . . take much . . . more!"

"You've got this!"

"Eyes to mine!" warned Azacca, pressing against Laerzo with another blade. Both light and thin, it paled in comparison to Rudra's exquisite construction, yet Azacca wielded it with remarkable force all the same. He had been stalking Laerzo for nearly an auram with no indication of slowing. "Will falls where minds wander. Clearly can you fend and drag. Now strike!"

Laerzo responded with a couple of lackluster swings, followed by a needless spin attack, which Azacca countered with a kick to the ass. Laerzo then rebounded with a flurry of swipes, all of which were easily dismissed.

Azacca cleverly withdrew his steel on the last attempt, which caused Laerzo to stagger and fall. "Again!"

"Hyah!" screamed Laerzo with a rising slash, but this left him wide open, and soon the tip of the opposing blade was hovering beneath his chin. Jumping back, he tried again, his clumsy rejoinder resulting in a trip that returned him to the ground.

"Again!"

Hopping upright, Laerzo noticed the long battle had finally caused his foe to break a sweat.

The man just might be mortal after all, he joked to himself. *Let's just see how well he keeps his focus now!*

Cracking a smile, he disrespectfully stabbed his lucral blade into the dirt and turned completely to check on his friend. Leopold had since discarded most of his armor, but even without the extra heft, he appeared moments away from passing out. His stout frame seemed a bit less rotund these days, more solid now, bordering on barrel-chested. It was also steaming red.

"Give this guy a break already, would you, *Master*?"

Azacca did not hesitate to strike. "I told you, eyes to—" but his blade quickly lowered in defense of a surprise attack, a fairly well-executed one at that, though not quite fast enough. Still, Azacca was amused by the slight, slowly backing away from Laerzo's dirty blade out of respect.

"Not bad, but beware!" said Azacca. "A trick learned can be turned, yes? Good. Now again, and spare not!"

As they both closed the gap, a bell from one of the towers announced mealtime. Azacca lowered his blade. "Halae! All things in its time!"

Laerzo was not about to let this opening go to waste. He launched into a leaping strike, but by the time he noticed a smile curl upon his master's face, it was already too late. In a flash, Azacca's feint and counter sent the young man crashing.

The Godsend picked up Rudra to clean and return to his scabbard before lifting his student from the ground. He smirked at Laerzo's displeasure. "Brightly does the fire burn, but not enough to make this fair blade sing! Perhaps another time. For now, we rest." He extended the branch to Leopold as well. "Enough, Young Gotta!"

Leopold promptly collapsed. "Sweet . . . surrender!"

"You look like a simmering lump of coal," joked Laerzo as he approached to help his friend stand. Perhaps it wasn't the best time to gibe the poor fellow, but he could never seem to help himself. "Last one to the mess hall cleans the table!"

Some minutes later, both cadets plopped down with a tray full of food and stuffed their faces. Laerzo was halfway into his second hearty bowl of biscuit stew when he noticed Leopold was already finishing his fourth. The speed by which his friend could down food was no surprise to those who knew him, but this disgusting display was on another level entirely. The husky lad could have given a geldtmare a run for his money! Leopold let out a satisfied moan as he scraped the dish clean and beckoned to the busy server for another. His thrice-filled glass of salt water was already half empty again.

"Easy, pal!" said Laerzo with a laugh. "This gruel won't taste any better on the way up." He reached over to grab another bland biscuit between them, the last on the table, but without looking, Leopold snatched and devoured it, washing down the dry knot of bread with the rest of his water. "My meals only travel one way, and it ain't up."

"Come on, at least leave me some scraps."

"In your dreams! I saw you slacking out there. Gotta hustle, in battle and the kitchen. If you ask me, I earned every bit of meal in this hall. Sancta knows I need it more."

Realizing what he'd uttered aloud, Leopold looked around nervously, but nobody seemed to have heard, and Laerzo didn't care. Leopold eventually shrugged and moved on.

"Besides, those who can't grow up must grow out, if you catch my meaning." To this, he lifted both arms in a cocky flex.

"In more ways than one," joked Laerzo. He caught a glimpse of a familiar face in a black skirt-dress, cute apron, and modest hairnet pushing a cart full of food nearby.

"Over here, Maybel!" Seeing his sister returned to her cheerful self was about as refreshing as the cold pitcher of water she eagerly brought to share. "You look well. Had me worried for a while."

Maybel took a lovely bow before unloading another round of food and drink from her cart onto the table. "Thanks. I've been feeling much better. Everyone has been so kind to me these past few days that I thought I'd put myself to work. You know, to show my gratitude." She gleefully watched Leopold pounce on his fifth bowl and let out a silly, high-pitched giggle, the first they'd heard in some time. "It turns out they're always looking for more help in the kitchen, so here I am."

"Ain't that the truth," replied Laerzo, his eyes turning to Leopold. "I bet you're all working double-time right now."

"Thank you for your service," replied Leopold with a barely discernible mush-mouth, ignoring his friend's latest jab. "Got any cream for these biscuits?"

"I don't think so, but let me check in the back."

Leopold let out a fearsome belch before muttering, "You're the best, Maybel!"

"Don't mention it. I'll be right back." As Maybel turned, both Azacca and General Maddock approached from her left. "Oh, hello Mister Azacca, General. How can I help you today?"

"No formalities, Maybel-girl," Azacca kindly replied before offering the others a slight bow. "Your company suits us well enough, thanks be given. Come with me, if you will."

Laerzo quickly choked down the rest his grub. "Come on, at least let our meal settle before you drag us back out there."

Azacca let out a wholehearted laugh. "Our blades will meet again in time, but I speak of the girl."

"Who, me?" asked Maybel, somewhat surprised. "I still have some cleaning to do but would be happy to go with you shortly. In the meantime, is there anything I can get you two? Mister Maddock, er, sir?"

"Nothing for me," grumbled Maddock, never one for formalities. He seemed a bit more strung out today than usual, not at all pleased to accompany Azacca. "Leave that to the others. Lord Lionel wishes to speak with you."

"Oh, is that so?" The sudden request caught Maybel off

guard. "Sounds important. Then we shouldn't keep them waiting. If you'd allow me to return this cart first—"

"No worries," replied Azacca, his arm extending toward the swinging double doors into the kitchen. Maybel gave another quick curtsy to them all before taking her leave.

Laerzo didn't know whether to be upset or relieved. "Wait, what about our training?"

"Quit your complaining, soldier!" snapped Maddock. "You two are off to work the quarries deep within Stolgrum until the final bell tolls."

Leopold banged his fist on the table. "Now we're talking! I've been meaning to check out the forge down there, maybe catch a gander at those old steam-powered gunners the Trust abandoned after the War. I hear you've got all sorts of crazy things down there just waiting to be tinkered with."

"Like they'd let you anywhere near their arsenal," chided Laerzo, recalling what Leopold had done to Bessie during their harrowing escape. His attention turned to the swinging double doors, where Maybel returned, holding her tummy with one hand and a napkin to her mouth with the other. Something else caught his glance as it emerged from the back room, presumably some varmint feeding in the kitchen, though by the time he gave a second look, it had already scampered away. "You doing okay, Maybel?"

"Yes, no problem," replied Maybel as she stored the napkin in her pocket and turned to Azacca. "Ready when you are, sir."

CHAPTER

24

There was a knock at the door. "Enter!" responded General Dietrich. He and Lord Lionel were soon joined by Azacca and Maybel, who stood at the end of a long, oaken conference table with many similarly fashioned chairs. This room was much smaller than the pillared chamber past the main hall. It didn't show much in the way of flare other than a crossing of spears mounted along the far wall and even more darkly stained molding that crowned the ceiling. A couple of stacks of parchment were spread out in front of Dietrich.

"Thank you both for meeting on short notice," greeted Lionel with both arms extended. "Please, come and sit with us." After the two had become situated in adjacent chairs on the opposite side of the table, he nodded for Dietrich to begin.

"How are you feeling, Maybel?" asked Dietrich.

Maybel promptly stood again, lowered into a prolonged bow. "I'm well now, thank you. My Lord, it is hard to express how much I appreciate your men rushing me into the care of this great fort."

"You're very kind, but there is no need for formalities here," responded Lionel, his hand again extending for Maybel to be seated. She gave another quick bow before returning to her chair.

"Well met, Maybel," said Dietrich plainly. "We simply

wished to speak with you, our guest, regarding your recent journey. I hear you've been busy working in the kitchen."

"Yes sir. It's nothing I wouldn't do back at Common Ward, anyway. I hope I haven't been an imposition."

"Not at all. We're humbled to have you in our service. Tell me, what caused someone your age to leave Common Ward?"

"Why, I simply went with Laerzo when you ordered him to take me and flee. Considering what happened that night, I didn't think it was an unreasonable request."

"Apologies, I didn't mean during Grenefest. Your brother informed me that you up and quit the Institute some time before. Doesn't seem like the Maybel I know."

Maybel let out a slight frown. "Perhaps it was a bit unlike me. I do love my siblings very much, but one cannot stay under that roof forever. Besides, I knew Madam Gebhardt would take good care of them in my absence."

Dietrich casually pulled his inked quill and parchment close. "I see. When did you first decide to join the Trust?"

"Oh, I don't know. Maybe a few moons ago. I saw them at Market and thought they were amazing." She noticed him jot something down.

"So, you did wish to join them?"

Maybel found his phrasing somewhat odd. "Yes, after the Madam arranged an introduction with some of them. I was a little nervous at first, but she insisted and assured me that leaving home was all part of growing up. They said I could visit home whenever I wanted, that I should at least give it a try."

"So, you went with them willingly?" asked Lionel.

"She insisted, and it was all right."

"What can you tell me about them?" asked Dietrich, continuing to take notes.

"Well, they are very smart, driven persons. I sometimes

tagged along as they conducted research. It was all a little over my head, I'll admit. All were very eager to bring about their vision. They seemed very single-minded to that effect."

"By research, you mean the Liminatum?"

"I have heard that term before."

"As have I. Is it some sort of object? A tool, perhaps?"

"I'm not sure exactly. Technalurgy plays a role, but I get the impression the Liminatum itself is not something you can touch."

"If you had to guess, what might it be?"

"Apologies, General. The few times I've heard it mentioned, its meaning always eluded me."

"This is important, Maybel. Please describe it to the best of your ability."

Maybel paused thoughtfully before answering. "Well, they seemed to imply it helped regulate how a person felt. For instance, if someone was in pain, it might alleviate that pain. Or if one lacked self-control, it might help build discipline. Almost as if it offers an open mind, changes the way they see the world. Does that make sense?"

Dietrich exchanged a brief glance with Lionel. "Yes, I think it does. Thank you. Anything else?"

"Nothing that comes to mind. It's all very advanced, you see."

"So it seems. And what of this vision?"

"Simply put, they wish to share their knowledge and impress plenty upon the masses. To right the wrongs of abandoning us after the War."

"Perhaps too simple, young lady," interjected Lionel. "I take it you approve and support their cause?"

"It's a fine cause, my lord." She didn't sound very convincing.

"Do they not also seek to impress their will upon the land?"

"Well, I don't really know. I suppose they might." Maybel shifted somewhat anxiously in her seat before continuing. "But if that was their intent, they sure waited a long time. As far as I can tell, they've really helped better people's lives."

"Based on reports out of Greneva, I'm not too sure. Assuming their activity is benevolent, what do they truly seek to gain?"

There was a hint of agitation in her voice. "What do you mean? As I've said—"

"Alas, but to what end?" interrupted Azacca, after which the girl remained silent and somewhat perplexed.

Lionel stroked his white beard. "Is this sentiment of theirs echoed in private?"

"It was expressed plainly by the Madam and Trust alike, yes," answered Maybel.

"That all seems well enough, but how did they treat each other?" asked Dietrich, staring down at his papers. "You were with them for nearly a fortnight, correct?"

"That's correct. To be honest, they mostly ignored each other entirely, me included. Their work was very fascinating, after all. It was easy to get lost in the work."

"And when they didn't ignore you?"

Maybel was beginning to drag. "W-well, we ate together most days and sometimes played VISI games with one another." She could tell they had no clue what that meant. "That is to say, games viewable within special goggles. They taught me how to use the VISI. I quite liked it."

Azacca's eyes lifted in curiosity. "Oh? What sorts of games?"

"Well, there was this fun one where everyone hauls like a pie or some paint at each other. We all chose different ways to look before starting, and we played for some time. Only, when we stopped, none of us knew who the others were within the game." She paused with a sad smile before continuing. "There was another where we donned beautiful armor that glowed any color we liked, battled with steel and spell. It made some of the others kind of scary, and I didn't play long, but it was very pretty."

"Ah, stunning. Full of treasure, no doubt. A shame none of it is real."

There was a long, uncomfortable moment of pause, and Maybel could sense they were all dancing around something.

Dietrich put down his pen. "Maybel, you know you can tell me anything, correct?"

The sudden question struck her like she'd done something wrong. "Sure, what would you like to know?"

"What happened, Maybel?"

"Are you referring to something specific?"

"Speak true," pleaded Azacca. "Young Gotta told us, understand?"

Her face began to pinch. "I don't know what you mean."

"Leopold said you were in a lot of pain when they found you," said Dietrich. "You were bedridden."

"Y-yes, that. That is, I felt dizzy one day, and then sick the next. They took care of me."

"They were standing around while you screamed in pain—"

"They were trying to help me, all right?" Maybel's eyes began to tear. "They—they gave me medicine, and I fell asleep."

The others took another deep pause before Dietrich pressed on. "Maybel . . ."

"My chest began to hurt, and then . . . then, I don't know."

"It's okay, Maybel."

"It hurt, and I don't know, okay? I don't know! And then Gwyndolyn was just—there with Leopold, and we got out of there." A few sobs escaped her then, but she wouldn't look away from them.

"No tears now, Maybel-girl," said Azacca with sadness more through eyes than words. "Let no pain find you here."

Dietrich nodded solemnly. "None of us quite know how to deal with whatever has been happening lately. I surely don't. All I know is that you were the closest among them. Believe me when I say it can be hard to speak about painful things, but we want to protect you. Before we can do that, we need to know as much about them, and you, as possible. Please know we're on your side. Can you help us, Maybel?"

After taking a moment to recompose herself, she meekly responded, her voice still shaking, "Yes, I understand."

"Another subject, please," Azacca insisted, pointing to the heap of parchment. "Tell me of purple skies in the mountains." He seemed both tickled and intrigued by such a concept.

"That's right," said Dietrich. "What did you make of the indigo coming from the Mount?"

Maybel tilted her head slightly. "It was beautiful, though we were all pretty focused in the opposite direction. At least until returning to the festival."

"And how did it make you feel?"

"How do you mean, exactly? I remember feeling ill, and a bit scared, but that had more to do with what was happening around us."

"You mean the heralds?"

"Mostly the crowds, actually."

"Are you saying those winged figures didn't startle you?"

"I suppose so. Their beauty was terrifying in a way, but also captivating. I had never seen anything quite like it."

"Not even in one of your VISI games?" asked Lionel.

"Sir? I'm not sure what they have to do with—"

"And what of the skies of Thannick?" asked Dietrich, his questions again becoming more direct. There was no response, so he continued. "When did you seem to notice the Trust was following you?"

"Well, I saw a shadow trailing our wagon at first. It was faint under the moonlight. Then there was some outline of warbling in the air."

"And you didn't see this back in Greneva?"

"What? No, I don't think so. But it was hard to see beyond the forests then."

"Are you sure?"

Maybel was confused by Dietrich's line of questioning. "I don't know. Maybe? What are you trying to say?" She appeared attacked by their serious, silent stares.

"Why was the Trust trailing you?"

"I don't know that they were. Maybe they were out helping the farmers."

"Come now," insisted Lionel, his patience running thin. "Why then would they feel the need to hide themselves? How is such a thing even possible? You don't find it the least bit suspect?"

"Now that you mention it, but some people don't take too kindly to—"

"We don't either!" shouted Dietrich, his voice startling the lot of them. "How could we? You have all but admitted to being groomed into a cult, experimented on, hurt, almost killed. And despite all that, you still defend them! Why, Maybel?"

"What do you—?" started Maybel, her eyes most aggrieved.

Dietrich's eyes welled. "I've known you since you were but a child. Never once have I seen you like this. Please tell us what's wrong." He watched powerlessly as the girl's body shook and shrank from them, watched the hands over her troubled face fail to contain the tears.

"I . . . I'm not—I don't . . ." she started, her mind seemingly coming apart. She removed her thick spectacles, rubbed her dampened eyes. "Their vision . . ."

"Maybel, please." Dietrich could hardly stand how she continued to resist. "They tried to kill you!"

"At ease, *galante*!" defended Azacca. "Clearly, she suffers at their hand even now."

Now curled over the edge of the table, she wept openly for some time while the men tried to keep their composure. Each had said their piece, forced the issue despite the pain obviously inflicted upon her. Among them, Dietrich was the worst for it. All he could do now was hope that their pointed words had reached her even for a moment, long enough for her to come around, return to rights.

Finally, she managed to lift herself and face them, however unsightly and disheveled. "Y-you're right. They aren't what they claim. At least, not some of them." She took another moment, her sadness turning to anger—the first any had ever sensed from the young lady. "They hurt me and tried to hurt my friends. They drove me away from . . . everything I loved."

"Most truth rings bittersweet," said Azacca.

"I—I did find them fascinating, that much is true, but I didn't join them. Rather, I didn't want to until—" She looked directly at Dietrich now with wide, slightly panicked eyes. "Surely, we were all deceived! Madam Gebhardt couldn't have known, I swear it! She would never—"

"Don't worry about that now," responded Dietrich softly, even as he suspected Gebhardt all along. The woman always rubbed him the wrong way, exhibited a slight hostility every time they interacted. He had long questioned the mysterious happenings around her institute, how her influence had so quickly spread throughout Greneva. He knew surprisingly little about her, only that she didn't seem native to those parts. "It's all right."

Maybel then turned to the troubled Lord Lionel, who hadn't spoken for some time. "I'm not with them! That's what all this is about, right? I wanted to help others, not hurt them!"

"Thank you, Maybel," Lionel replied with a calming gesture. "We just needed to hear you say it, that's all."

"Yes, well met," added Dietrich. "We know you meant well." He reached for a large binding of parchment, the same he'd studied for many days now. "Perhaps you can better help us understand."

PART III

CHAPTER

25

"We have returned," announced Gwyndolyn into the pocket of shade beneath a large bridge bending across Greneva's stream. She was as beautiful as the day was fair, the Solstar's brilliance imbuing her white dress and geldtmare. So much that her approach lit the surrounding space, subdued only by the dark-violet cape that draped over them both. She was joined by Scarlet and a modest cadre of saintly pitchforks who, per Frater Algus's command, spent most of the morn confronting the balmy dregs that stalked the streets.

"Welcome back, my children," greeted Matron from the underpass. Lifting her dress, she modestly stepped down from her carriage, which was parked near the waters, where a makeshift camp had been established. Her own sect of adherents followed closely behind. "Radiant as always. I pray that light aided you in delivering the wayward masses from their lowly state."

"Yes, but of course," answered Gwyndolyn haughtily as two servants carefully helped her down from the geldtmare.

As if there was any doubt, she thought, somewhat put off by the woman's insinuation. Gwyndolyn was the Blessed Daughter, after all. Her will be done. And as such, triumph became a forgone conclusion in her mind. Whatever she desired to have, or wished to do, it became so, by her hand or that of another. Unfortunately, her holy station required her to serve a goddess she neither knew nor cared about, let alone the people she was meant to save. This tedious task brought her no joy, only fostering feelings of spite and indignation.

Still, she forced an exuberant smile even while waving one of her servants away for fussing over some dust upon the hem of her dress. "It was quite effortless, really. My mere presence was a command to fall prostrate before me, and they obeyed at once—that is, except the few who had fully turned, but they were quickly surrounded long enough for the heralds to spirit them away. You should have seen these creatures, Matron. They were so twisted that their features sharpened, and frightfully so. Eyes, ears, teeth, and all the rest. They were almost daimonic in appearance. As for them, I simply sprinkled the wine over them, making sure to evoke the Holy Mother's rites, just as you taught me."

"And?"

"What else?" interrupted Scarlet as she dismounted from her own steed unaided. Landing a bit awkwardly, she dusted herself off before approaching. "They shed their ghastly forms in an instant, dropped in adoration. I have seen Gwyndolyn perform this sacrament many times over, yet even now, it is truly shocking to behold."

"What exactly is shocking?" asked Gwyndolyn, turning just enough to cast a glare from the corner of her eye. "This is what my goddess has called me to do. I, and I alone, have such a power."

"Yes, of course," said Scarlet, bowing as she took a step backward.

"Very good," said Matron with a cheerful clap of her hands. Her eyes briefly shifted away from Gwyndolyn. "Did you send those newly saved to the gated temple near the Academy to receive further succor?"

Gwyndolyn's smile returned. "Oh yes, and to sing my praises on their way to any who would listen."

"Some must not have listened well enough." Matron pointed over Gwyndolyn's shoulder. "Do you not see the crowd nipping at your heels?"

Gwyndolyn and Scarlet turned toward a large group of ardent onlookers in the distance, their gathering in no way hidden.

"What can I say? They absolutely love me," answered Gwyndolyn, her arms spreading wide. This conceited gesture lifted her cloak, revealing the tall, glass carafe hanging heavily on a belt she stole from one of her servants, still partially filled.

With a guarded sigh, Matron asked, "And did Frater not tell you to return only when the carafe had been emptied of its sacrament?"

"He did, Matron," said Scarlet, quick to interject. "Lord Sister was reminded of this, but she became tired and demanded I take it from her. Oh, how I wished I could help her administer its blessing, but we all know only she can possess it, lest the sacrament spoil. She alone can spread its nectar unto the people. Isn't that right?"

"You are correct," said Matron. "Gwyndolyn, Frater was very explicit in his plea. Given by any other, Hypha's Dew will not bestow the blessing of the anointed, but rather, will plunge all who accept it into the same nightmarish torment you once barely escaped. I know the burden can be heavy at times, but you must be the one to carry it, and with great care. Do you understand?"

"If I must," answered Gwyndolyn belligerently. "Still, I see no reason why it cannot be dragged in a carriage such as this when I wish to rest, and I do."

"The people are humbled to see you bear it among them."

"But it's heavy! And according to you, I must lower from my steed every time before brandishing it. Could Denestra not have bestowed a less burdensome vessel for this purpose?"

"If only," murmured Scarlet, a slight which Gwyndolyn heard but was too preoccupied to pay any mind.

"It is right and just," said Matron. "You wouldn't want to risk dropping it or wasting its contents, would you?"

"But why should the chosen one even suffer moving about on foot when the ground itself is not worthy?"

Matron paused. "That you bless the very dirt is a testament to your glory."

Gwyndolyn did not appreciate the hint of frustration coming from the woman's words. "Nonsense! It is a needless waste of my blessing. I am like a goddess, yes? The people will be all the more humbled to receive my gift from on high. And if by happenstance it is lost, we will simply procure more from Frater."

Matron lowered her head and took a deep breath. "If you wish. This caravan is yours to do as you will, but doesn't it seem a bit unbecoming of your divinity?"

"Of course, only a gilded carriage would even begin to do me justice, and so that is what I shall have!" When Gwyndolyn spoke these words, the already handsome cart began to glisten gold despite being cast in the shade. Near and far, all who stood before her, even Scarlet and Matron, fell prostrate at the sight and gave thanks. Gwyndolyn swelled even more while trying to hide her own surprise at the transformation. "Yes, this will have to do for now."

"Blessed be she who turns timber to treasure!" shouted Matron, after which the others chanted, "Halae! Al'Haleia!" However, she still expressed a slight hesitance when asking,

"This is a fine tribute indeed, but will it not hide you from the people?"

Her arrogance lowering into a thoughtful scowl, Gwyndolyn paused before responding. "Your point is taken. If I must, my gift will be administered atop a geldtmare leading the march. No, a parade! We shall sweep through Greneva, driving the wicked into the streets, and those I sanctify will gladly follow wherever I take them."

"What a splendid idea, Lord Sister!" praised Scarlet. "I, your lowly disciple, will of course join to serve at your side."

"No, my child," said Matron in casual protest. "You have done much this day. Let another serve while you rest in the carriage with me." Scarlet nodded in quiet acquiescence as the veiled woman continued. "Blessed Daughter, upon your command, let us take leave of this place. We shall rally the righteous on our way to the temple, where Frater has asked us to join him. You will recognize it by the golden gates. There, we will pay homage to Denestra, praise be upon her."

"Yes, I command it," said Gwyndolyn glibly as her disciples quickly packed up the caravan and returned their godhand to her glistening steed. Soon, the radiant carriage parted the reverent crowd as it emerged from under the bridge in all its splendor. Taking the carafe in both hands, she declared, "Onward!"

"Are we there yet?" asked Scarlet, gazing disappointingly at the jubilant crowds outside her carriage window. Being kept hidden from the grandeur on display was bad enough without Gwyndolyn heaping all the praise. Scarlet could hardly stand seeing Gwyndolyn celebrated so whole-heartedly. "We're back in Uptown. She's taking us in circles!"

"Temperance, please," said Matron simply.

Scarlet snatched the curtains shut. "I still don't know why you dragged me in here. And don't tell me I'm tired. We'd only been gone for a few aurams!"

"If you had agreed to wear a veil like the others, I would've allowed it."

"I will not! How is anyone supposed to see me if my face is covered?"

"That freckled face wouldn't last another moment under the Solstar. I can already see it begin to peel. You wouldn't want that, would you?"

Scarlet's flushed face deepened another shade of red. "You're a liar. It's like you're trying to keep me from the people. I was supposed to be the one out there, not her!"

"Not so loud," Matron chided in a hushed whisper. "We have both sworn to serve Gwyndolyn, but please don't think me unsympathetic to your part in this. I know you would make a fine Blessed Daughter. Still, it was no mistake that she was called to bear the Holy Mother's light. At least for now."

"Matron?" asked Scarlet curiously.

"Let us see how long she can rightfully wield it. Perhaps she will only burn bright for a time. Then another would need to be chosen, yes?" Matron and Scarlet both nodded slowly in agreement. "In the meanwhile, why not serve comfortably in her shadow?"

"There's nothing comfortable about it," whined Scarlet, her pouty stare turning to Matron. "Waking her, feeding her, cleaning and dressing her, obliging every haughty tantrum, gripe, and desire. Yielding to her will! You see how she flaunts her station, sucking the very air from our chests. It makes me ill! When will it be my turn to shine?"

"Patience, child. If what you claim Frater spoke to you

is true, it will come soon enough. Have you no faith? He is Denestra's mouthpiece; his words are sacrosanct."

"Yes, I have heard his promises, but I still don't understand his plan. Just how will the people flock to me when I beckon? Compared to her, will they even know who I am?"

"You are Scarlet Rothbard, daughter to the *former* mayor, heir to the land, the true chosen. They *do* know you. If not, then soon. Do not concern yourself with what has yet to come. The machinations of the plan are between Frater and the Holy Mother. Follow it faithfully, and I believe all you seek will be yours."

This encouragement was intended to calm and uplift, but it only served to enervate the disgruntled girl. Every moment Gwyndolyn was allowed to live was one too many for Scarlet, who wanted nothing more than revenge for the scar currently hidden upon her cheek. Still, she offered no further complaint. With both eyes now shut, her smoldering silence was the only prayer she could give, and even that was asking too much in the moment.

After saying a prayer of her own, Matron suddenly began, "Speaking of the Rothbards, I don't believe I know much of your mother."

"There isn't much to know about *Lady Rothbard*," responded Scarlet despondently. "She was a distant, callous, selfish, nagging lush. No redeemable qualities of any type."

"None at all?"

"None. She wasn't even particularly beautiful, though she was always gallivanting around to that effect. I lost her when I was younger. Even before, *Mummy* could never be bothered to raise her only child. This was why Father hired Madam Gebhardt as my governess, at least for a time. She was there to take care of me, tutor me. Everything I ever learned about becoming a woman came from her. She was more of a mother than that harlot ever was!"

"Well, you turned out quite the woman. I'm sure when the time comes, you will truly make her and Denestra proud." Matron peered out her window as the carriage began to slow. "Look, we are not far from the temple. When we arrive, make sure not to let Gwyndolyn or Frater see you sulking, or they will send you away."

Gwyndolyn and her caravan took their sweet time trotting through the streets, much more than it should've taken to reach the temple. She led them up and down every avenue on the way just to reap the praise from passersby. Their sweet exultations were like music to her ears, becoming more pronounced as they joined those who already followed behind.

She was so filled with joy that every building she passed began to shine brighter than day, an intense white that only increased the revelry in the streets. She simply could not get enough, though short of turning around altogether, she knew her destination would greet her sooner or later.

She might have guessed all this splendor would cause the wicked to shrivel and hide, but it drove out all sorts of abnormal figures from their homes. Each malification, as Frater Algus called it, was a reflection and amplification of the sinner's vice, a pale precursor toward becoming fully ashen. Some took inordinately sweaty, distended, long-tongued forms, while others were simply more sharp-toothed and brutish in their appearance. The egotistical inflated, the meek shriveled, the salacious profaned, and most importantly, the violent lashed out.

It was not long before a pack of barbarous fiends attacked the parade, hoping to extinguish the source of its light. Of course, pitchforks were there to lay them low, their resonance momentarily peeling back each foe's devilish features until they abated. Gwyndolyn dipped the bough in a shiny dish held by one servant from an adjacent steed and sprinkled the dumbstruck while proclaiming the words practiced many times with Matron, "I cast away your sin in the Holy Mother's name! Serve her now and forever!"

Eventually, Gwyndolyn and her disciples arrived at the temple, where Frater was said to dwell. It didn't take long to locate the golden gates or the throngs of anxious people who were not yet permitted to enter. Some were twisted to various degrees, some not, and others were already saved, but all were humbled by the luminous temple before them.

Gwyndolyn was amazed by how many had gathered in hope of being spared from the throes of wickedness, happy for the contingent of pitchforks keeping them in check. As her caravan approached, the masses parted as if repelled by her light, at least long enough for her and the others to clear the gilded gates.

Gwyndolyn squinted for some time at the temple. It was vaguely familiar to her, attached to some distant memory from her dream.

What did they call this place? she asked herself, finally remembering the name Common Ward. Gone were the dirty clothes hangers and obnoxious children playing about. Wishing to enter, she twisted her head back and forth, waiting impatiently atop her geldtmare for attendance. Scarlet came rushing over, toppling a fellow servant, to help Gwyndolyn down from her mount.

"Beautifully done, Lord Sister," she greeted, yet to her chagrin, Gwyndolyn ignored her, remaining largely focused on the tall temple looming overhead.

Matron approached with the gilded saucer and passed it to Scarlet. "Let's not keep Frater waiting any longer. This way, please."

As they approached the archway, Gwyndolyn paused to gaze upon two colorful depictions in tall, rectangular stained-glass windows above the entrance. To the left was Holy Mother Denestra clad in a flowing violet gown, an exquisite beauty both strong and tall, with black hair pinned neatly under a blossoming diadem. The other was of her husband, King Avalon, an austere, formidable man of similar complexion and elegance, his crown solid gold. Gwyndolyn paid them homage as if she'd known this her entire life.

From there, she entered into the temple's vestibule, where another group of devotees bowed in greeting. They ushered her and the others up the middle of the temple, their collection of quiet steps upon the dark, glossy floor becoming quite clamorous in the emptiness of this space. Gwyndolyn again stared upward, this time at the domed compartment of the chamber with its multitude of paned windows decorated in familiar illustrations. Propped in the center of the far wall was a large depiction of Denestra and Avalon standing with hands joined on a mountaintop as three shrouded women fell tragically to their deaths. This imagery struck Gwyndolyn as strangely out of place, though she could give no reason to justify this reaction.

Their procession stopped a few paces short of the altar, where Frater Algus knelt in front of what appeared to be a large, crystalline bowl. At this time, several guards at the entrance were letting some of the people slowly into the vestibule. Those graciously granted entry had sworn upon pain of death to pay this place and all those within it due reverence. And pay they did, quietly filling out rows in the main hall as well as balconies on both sides of the upper floors. Word of mouth must have spread through Greneva like a wildfire that day, for some of the guards were forced to push the crowd's excesses back through the entrance before securing the doors behind them.

Watching this unfold, Matron placed a gentle hand upon Gwyndolyn's right shoulder and whispered, "Behold all the people who have followed you into this hallowed space."

"It may have been hallowed before, but no longer," responded Gwyndolyn with a similar softness. "Must they shuffle and grouse about so needlessly?"

"Ignore them. They have become fearful of this broken world, thirsty for guidance. Know that within these walls, this duty belongs to Frater, and Frater alone. His words ring loudest, for they are spoken through him by the Holy Mother. Therefore, let us servants allow him the courtesy to edify uninterrupted."

Gwyndolyn sneered at being called a servant but held her ego in abeyance for now. It was about time for graces to begin, and so they all joined Algus upon the altar, flanked on both sides by candelabra. Ornate pillows sat off to the side. The crossing of double crescents loomed like a single large eye at the rear of the altar for all to see. Everyone made sure to bow in greeting, except for Gwyndolyn, who stared curiously at the crystal cauldron positioned at the center of the space. It rested upon three wooden legs apparently constructed from branches of the Hypha Tree. Steeping within the vessel were chunks of pulp, which tinted the surrounding liquid a lovely lavender. The subtle stream of bubbles emerging from the pulp was assumed to be juices escaping, though she could not help but liken it to the last gasps of something drowning.

Her captivation was suddenly interrupted by greetings from Algus, who was now positioned behind the cauldron facing the crowd. Raising his hands, he loudly proclaimed: "Holy Mother, today and always, we come to offer you our undying thanks. Verily, your blessing is a fruit of many seeds, each one a wondrous gift. But just as a seed will not grow in the absence of water and rich soil, neither can your gifts nor our devotion to you hope to swell without first purifying this wicked land." He spread his hands toward Gwyndolyn. Knowing not what to say, or even whether to speak, she remained silent while he continued. "To this end, we gather to anoint fruit born of the Hypha Tree, which has heralded the coming of our chosen one. Through her, our Blessed Daughter, a nostrum is given so that vigor may once again spring from the putrid soil of our lands and hearts. To this, we say . . ."

"Halae! Al'Haleia!" the crowd chanted.

Algus rolled up his sleeves and drove both arms into the cauldron, crushing the pulp in congress with the aromatic oil. Once a dark lavender filled the entire vessel, he lifted his stained hands before again continuing, "Through this holy wine, our baleful countenance is restored to righteousness. But these proper forms are not ours alone. Just as favor is granted, so too can it be withdrawn. I say unto you, only the most devout among us are worthy to maintain it. Let us never dwell on that which is given, for all beauty belongs to Denestra. Let us renew our pledge to serve her will."

Scarlet and Matron approached, bearing white cloth, sparkling bowl, and a flask of water to wash Algus clean. This they did, after which he dried his hands and returned the cloth. Then, taking the bowl, he dipped it into the liquid with utmost reverence and gave it to Gwyndolyn to drink. A wave of intoxication slowly percolated through her as she swallowed most of its contents.

Returning to his previous position, Algus finished the concoction and proclaimed, "Blessed Daughter, your presence makes this wine holy. Just as you have accepted it into your bodily vessel, please take it into your carafe, where it may be given to all within this congregation." With this, he extended a hand toward an ornate pillow laying neatly between Gwyndolyn and the cauldron.

This sudden request took her by surprise. She hesitated until Matron approached to whisper a reminder of her role in the ritual. Gwyndolyn nodded before moving to the pillow and awkwardly attempting to unfasten the holster at her side. It gave her some trouble, but eventually, she was able to free the tall flask by its neck. Soon, both her knees and the carafe rested upon the pillow, over which Scarlet placed a funneled colander. Algus tipped the cauldron, and together, they slowly filled the carafe.

It had a considerable heft, but a strange vigor from the wine made Gwyndolyn manage to lift both it and herself upright without aid. Long lines had already begun to form behind her, but before they would receive her gift, she was asked to administer it to Scarlet, Matron, and the rest of her disciples. Then, one by one, she carefully lifted the spout for each of the people to taste the wine. They returned to their stations, giving thanks, and soon the entire room wept joyfully out to the Holy Mother, their rightful forms restored.

Gwyndolyn was sure the flask would run dry before long, but several mouthfuls remained after all had partaken. Finally, without instruction, she eagerly guzzled the rest herself and nearly toppled over in the process. To most, it was assumed part of the sacrament, though her cadre did not seem pleased.

Next, Algus invited Gwyndolyn and her disciples to kneel with him on cushions and commune with the passions now churning within them. The euphoric crowds lowered themselves in kind, though some couldn't remain still and collapsed to the floor in fits. Clearly drunk on the wine, Gwyndolyn was also on the verge of toppling over, and so the others offered water while propping her upright. Even Algus looked noticeably flustered as his fingers repeatedly tapped the left of his skull.

After some time, he abruptly stood up and raised his hands once more. "As we graciously accept this blessing, let us always show love to Denestra, for without her, these sweet waters would surely poison our bodies and cause them to fade."

His face donned a dark, painful impression as both eyes rattled nervously about the room at nothing in particular. Pressing against the side of his brow, he calmed himself with a deep breath before speaking further.

"Tragic is the tale of any who withhold reverence from her. Hear me now! There once was a lonely fowl living in the midst of impenetrable clouds. Those familial to the tiny, black creature were long lost, though he could always hear squawking just beyond the fog. Upon searching every day, he suddenly noticed a voice calling out in friendship. The fowl was filled with joy, and for a time, the voice accompanied him wherever he went, though he could not see what it was. One day, the clouds darkened, unleashing a terrible storm that almost plucked the fowl from the sky. No matter how he tried, his cries were scattered by clamorous winds and thunderous flashes. He managed to survive the tempest, but it was some time before the voice could once again be heard echoing in the haze.

"When asked where the voice had been, it answered, 'I have always been with you, even through strong, murky winds, though you knew not.'

"However, this confused the fowl. 'You were with me then, even in the storm?'

" 'Do not lower your gaze in search of me, for I am the light above,' began the voice. 'When sound fails, rise against the tumult until you see my glow, and follow it into calm, peaceful skies. There, I will be with you, and what was lost will be seen.'

"Peace returned for a short while, but another storm inevitably separated them again. This time, the fowl climbed the currents with a raised beak, defying the squalls for so long, yet there was nothing in sight. He lamented, but trusting the voice's command, continued his battle upward until traces of light could be found on high.

"Then, with all his heart, he beat his little wings toward the shine and eventually lifted into a clearing above dark, rumbling clouds. Though grateful to be done with the storm, he searched at once for anything at all familiar to him.

"'Though my eyes are clear, I cannot see the others as you said. Will they rise to find me? I shall look downward until we meet again.' The voice beckoned to reconsider, but the fowl was preoccupied and responded: 'It matters not if I lower my gaze, for the light will always be here waiting. What good is it if I'm left alone?' And so he dwelled just above the fog, his gaze gradually dipping deeper and darker."

Algus's voice also deepened when he spoke these next words. "Soon, the fowl forgot all about his friend in the light, forsaking that which guided him all the while. Before he realized, his plumage had burned from the Solstar's rays until all the black feathers were made ashen. Crying in pain, he turned skyward, but his faded stare could no longer stand the light, which struck him blind and sent him plummeting to his demise!"

Just then, without warning, something barreled through the large stained-glass above and crashed before the altar, violently splitting the crowd. Horrific screams filled the temple as Gwyndolyn and the others shot to their feet, trying to make out what happened. Two heralds quickly descended through the hole in the wall, hanging imperiously above to vanquish the intruder with their spears. This fallen figure bore some resemblance to them, though his gloomy countenance was lackluster by comparison and bathed in waves of decay. His wings were wheels within spinning wheels, and his eyes were hidden by a gleaming band resting upon his nose.

As he straightened out, his ghastly pale likeness and silver hair came off somewhat familiar to Gwyndolyn, though she could not be certain any of it was real. Resisting Matron's attempts to pull her back, she joined at the right hand of Algus.

"Do you recognize him, Blessed Daughter?" he asked, but she was too enamored by the wine to answer. He returned his attention to the creature, who had now lifted a few feet from the ground. "You must think yourself clever, daimon. I admit you wear the guise of our keepers well, but we have been watching you this entire time. Did you think it possible to fly among us in secret? Pitiable thing. What do you have to say for yourself?"

There was no response other than the deathly gaze fixed firmly upon him. Breathing heavily, pulses of indigo grew around the floating fiend, terrifying Algus as he addressed his followers: "Hear me, believers! This frightful creature illustrates exactly what happens to those who do not pay homage to Denestra. Look upon his faded form and wail, for he has been made ashen! He is abominable in this sacred place and fated to die in her name!"

The people then cried out in supplication, striking their chests at the apparition while some tried desperately to drag him down. It was no use. Preparing his next move, the daimon rose from the masses to meet the heralds already poised to strike. They quickly descended upon him, but before either could close the gap, he enveloped them, as well as Gwyndolyn and Algus, in a bone-chilling cry, which caused each to ruefully guard their ears. This prolonged scream of rippling indigo pierced the very fabric of their perception and stripped away the heralds' ennobled visages to reveal men in similarly grayed metallic frames.

"That voice," declared Algus while gripping his head in pain. "Its cadence is deeper, and yet . . ."

"Gustav?" said Gwyndolyn, sending Algus into a fit. He took up his own pitchfork, which lay next to the cauldron, and used it to dispel the bleak resonance with some of his own. This allowed the heralds to gradually regain their saintly features and clumsily redouble their attack, but again, they were no match for the intruder. He cleverly bested one, stole his spear, ran the other through, and exited from the temple whence he came.

Thrusting his staff skyward, Algus howled: "Quickly, do not allow him to escape!"

CHAPTER

26

"We've been walking for some time," said Laerzo to General Maddock in the dark underbelly of Fort Lionel. Even without a bag over his head, he'd already lost any sense of bearing within the myriad of winding, labyrinthine roads. How could anyone hope to effectively traverse them? After some time staring at the back of his superior's thick skull, he assumed there had to be a series of markings that helped even the most simple-minded find their way. Still, there was not much for Laerzo to glean other than the outline of this brutish man eclipsing the scant light of his torch. The cadet had given up trying to differentiate one turn from the next.

"No bellyaching, you hear me?" warned Maddock, his already-short wick all but burned out.

"I'm not complaining, I'm just saying . . . You do know where you're going, yeah?"

"Like my own name. Now be quiet."

Laerzo waited a long moment before daring to speak again. "Just how far down do these passages go?"

A brief shake of the General's head made it clear he was not in the mood for idle chat. "All the way down. I'm sure your time upon the cliffside gave some idea just how far that is."

Laerzo didn't dignify this with a response, though he was unaware his time scaling the Radiant Cliffs had been made known to Maddock. The unceremonious induction into the

Alliance was a sore subject he refused to discuss with anyone, even Leopold. Still, the deed was done, and he had no intention of revisiting that death-defying feat, however clearly his superior's cruel rejoinder brought it into the forefront of his mind. Even the echo of their boots seemed to remind him now.

The rage from that day had not diminished in the slightest. He brooded regularly over the smug face of that man who'd greeted him before and after the trial, the one he begrudgingly called Master. One day, Laerzo intended to best Azacca and claim Rudra as his own. It was practically the only thing keeping him from grabbing Maybel and leaving Stolgrum altogether. He assumed this descent was somehow part of his training, that Azacca had a new trick or trial planned like before. For all he knew, Maddock was a willing participant just waiting for the chance to take him by surprise.

"Don't you usually bring Leopold down to the quarries?" asked Laerzo.

"We're not *going* to the quarries. Besides, he's busy cleaning up the mess you made in Thannick."

"I'd take credit if it had anything to do with me. Didn't have much to do with him either. At least Mr. Gibbs will put him to good use."

"And I will put *you* to good use."

"Great," muttered Laerzo in confusion. Maddock's threat made his skin crawl. "Why don't you tell me what we're doing down here?"

"Fine, but you won't like it." They continued to the end of the path, turning to a set of caged doors leading into the dungeons. As Maddock turned, a strange, growing excitement in his eyes caused Laerzo to slowly retreat a couple of paces.

"There must be some sort of mistake!" shouted Laerzo, already jumping to the wildest of conclusions. "I have committed no crime, never in my life. Don't look at me like that, yeah? What did Leo tell you? Okay, I might have worn a silly disguise to score extra rations, but he double-dared me! Please, General, I'm too young to rot behind bars!"

To this, Maddock unleashed a long, raucous laugh, which only made the young man even more fearful. "Listen carefully, whelp. There's been a lot of chatter down here lately. Something of strange encounters without much to show for it. That is, until now. We're here to investigate a murder."

"A murder?" asked Laerzo, letting loose a strange sigh of relief. He'd already slept one night too many in a damp gaol.

"That's what I said."

"I see."

Maddock's eyes narrowed. "And *you* were saying?"

"Right, never mind that."

"You almost seem giddy. Does death *please* you?"

"What? I was just—"

"Just what?"

"You were acting weird then, that's all."

"Am I *weird* to you?"

Distress lowered Laerzo's gaze down and away. "No, I mean—"

"You seem more queer between the two of us."

"Sir, I'm not—"

"Eyes to me, soldier!" ordered Maddock, watching Laerzo snap back to attention, his now-rankled face almost looking for trouble. The General coldly asked, "Got something to say?"

Laerzo's chest swelled as he returned an equally intense stare, locking their grave expressions in a silent battle. Though easily outmatched in size and stature, he nonetheless stood his ground with an apparent confidence betrayed by the sweat glistening on his face. He studied the strange stillness of

Maddock looming above him, rigid and unmovable like a wall, noted how terrifying his face was in the torchlight between them.

It became clear that neither was willing to cede his pride to the other, yet Laerzo could sense the General was hiding something. A quick deviation from Maddock's eyes revealed a small crack in the seemingly impenetrable veneer, like the beginnings of a pucker in the corner of his brooding scowl. Laerzo was suddenly embarrassed that it had taken so long to understand the game being played, and even longer to play it.

If I didn't know any better, he thought, *I'd say Maddock is enjoying this. Got to have fun somehow, I guess.*

In a strange pivot, he responded. "Does General Dietrich know we're down here?"

The question made Maddock's brow twitch and posture diminish. "Beg your pardon?"

"You and Dietrich were playing detective earlier, yeah? But he isn't here."

"And?"

"And *I* am." Standing a bit taller, Laerzo decided to press his luck. "Must not be that important if you're dragging some *whelp* around."

"Big deal!" growled Maddock; it seemed his bit of fun had ended for now. "He's too busy wasting time with that Sh'tama freak and the girl. I don't need him to hold my hand."

"Would you like *me* to hold your hand?"

And just like that, Maddock's fist punched a crack in the stone wall barely above Laerzo's left shoulder. "Maybe later, sweet pea." With his hulking arm still extended, he leaned uncomfortably close to his subordinate, staring him right in the eyes. "Before we enter, know this. These dungeons are older than Stolgrum itself. There's a lot of history here, history of the

War. There are also a lot of Gul'dani here still wasting away in cages. Back then, they would have proudly died for their god, but we spared their wretched lives out of spite for what they did to our people. As a result, their history continues in these walls, as does their hatred, and their deceptions. These nasty bottom-feeders will do or say anything to settle the score, and rest assured, they will mess with you. All you need to do is keep your mouth shut, your chin up, and when necessary, your back to mine, understand?"

A quiet acquiescence was all Maddock required for his arm to retreat into a side pocket, where it removed a busy ring of keys. The fat fingers of his free hand had some difficulty fumbling along the many similarly shaped slivers of metal, and each attempt to unlock the door caused the few features visible on his scarred face to sour. He grew ever more menacing, snarling occasionally as a warning not to speak or intervene. A palpable unease lingered in the stale air as echoes of this clamorous struggle continued.

However, after much effort and anguish, the noisy affair abruptly ended with a satisfying clack within the door. This briefly brought a rare smirk to Maddock's face before he cast the cage open in triumph.

They entered onto a pavilion overlooking an expansive cavern tinted blue, a hue that Laerzo noted was similar to both the Radiant Cliffs and Rudra's glow. It came from a giant, untapped vein of lucram ore hanging like a drop of water from the cavern's jagged awning.

Must be refracting light from somewhere outside, he thought while approaching the metal railing for a closer look. He carefully tested it before following the lucram's dusty glow into a seemingly bottomless chasm splitting the dungeon in twain. To many languishing in the lower cavities, it was their only hope, at least until dusk, where barely a trace of it could be found.

He'd just begun to make out a small source of white light at the bottom when a crash and clack practically sent him flying over the edge. Maddock's muffled laughter informed him it was just the door shutting from behind. Laerzo wondered how far they would traverse this place, what monsters awaited in the shadows. Most importantly, he wondered when they'd be leaving.

Descending the pavilion into the first block, both started along the right row of cells, which, like every part of the dungeon, guarded against the chasm with railing.

They made their way across the floor toward two lights at the end leading into what appeared to be a sculpted spiral staircase joining each subsequent level. The space was a weird combination of cave and calaboose, with its chaotic roof of glowing stalactites offering a stark contrast to the artificial uniformity of the chambers below. Judging by the smooth, consistent shapes, Laerzo rightfully assumed each path, wall, and cell must have been carefully and painstaking chiseled over the course of generations into something more befitting a gaol. Other than the occasional cough or shuffle in the distance, the quietude of this place was eerily the loudest thing about it, one Laerzo regretfully violated with every step. His glances into each cell were always met with desperate, pleading eyes.

Maddock exchanged nods with a couple of soldiers in passing, then with the one guarding the stairs.

"General," the soldier greeted in hushed tones.

"At ease," stated Maddock plainly, his deep voice an affront to the silence, though he was not the least bit concerned.

The soldier was most definitely not at ease. "I take it you've returned for the body?"

"So, he's dead? We just questioned him the other day. He wasn't in great shape, but nowhere near death's door."

"Yes, sir. I checked with the guard this morning."

"Any idea what killed him?"

The soldier's eyes seemed bothered by how casually the question reverberated through the still air. "Not sure. Recent records allege something vile feeding in the lower chambers."

"You mean the creature?" Laerzo quietly blurted, much to his partner's chagrin. He had heard vague mention of something like that in passing and hadn't forgotten it since.

"Correct," the soldier replied dismally. "Information is scarce. One account described awakening to something fleeing from his arm, followed by a bout of delirium. Nothing like what happened last night though. Echoes of the man's crazed moans terrorized the place until the air seemed to escape from his strangled throat."

"I assume that's why this place is unusually quiet?" asked Maddock, something Laerzo appeared curious to know.

"The faithful here are in mourning," explained the guard bluntly, somewhat unnerved by his answer.

Maddock nodded. "We're going down."

"Are you sure? There is no one currently—"

"Good. Don't disturb unless I call. Understood?"

"Yes, sir," the guard submitted before generously handing Laerzo one of the torches from the wall. "That thing is most likely still down there. Be careful."

Nodding, they proceeded farther into the depths. While descending the circular passage, Laerzo watched the smoke of their torches lift to the already soot-black ceiling, consuming much of the thinning air while tainting what remained. At times, his boots did not find the stairs agreeable, as some were cracked, uneven, or shorter than others. It was no wonder, considering each must have been chiseled in the dimmest light. If not for his, he likely would have sent both of them tumbling the rest of the way down.

Some number of revolutions later, the stairs suddenly ended, and they arrived at the lowest level of the dungeon. Most of the light from above didn't reach this far, but thankfully, their flames lent well to a long line of glowing lucram banisters protecting them from the pitfall.

Even more than before, the deafening silence sent chills down Laerzo's spine. His sleeve quickly rose to guard against the reek of dust and squalor, which had become quite remarkable. It suggested this block was seldom, if ever, cleaned. Indeed, the dark penumbra was a place of great sadness, no doubt reserved for the most irredeemable scoundrels that ever set foot in Stolgrum.

Of course, Maddock thought nothing of it as he fearlessly led them along the left side. They eventually approached the second-to-last cell.

"This is the one." He briefly waved his torch into and around the damp space before reaching for his keys.

Other than the rough contours of the victim's body, laying tangled in a flimsy cloth on the cold stone floor, there wasn't much to see within the cell. Nonetheless, Laerzo incessantly scanned their surroundings for even the slightest movement.

Another clack from the cage startled him as Maddock turned to say, "Here we go."

The rusty cell opened with a frightful creak, revealing an equally frightful corpse. Its stench was most pronounced here, that of filth and pestilence. Staring down at the pale body, they noticed a terrible rash covering most of the bloated neck with an unsightly blister at its center. Maddock decided against checking for a pulse to avoid popping this festering pustule, which had nearly swollen to the size of his palm. Instead, he handed Laerzo his torch before he slowly lowered to a squat and gripped the tattered sheet over the cadaver. "Keep your eyes peeled."

After a brief pause, he quickly yanked the fabric upright and snapped it like a whip. It produced a thunderous crack that echoed throughout the space but nothing else. Maddock then tossed the sheet aside and retrieved his torch.

"Who among us disturbs the dead?" a low, rusty voice with a strange accent suddenly boomed from somewhere beyond the cell. Laerzo practically lost himself in that moment. "Cursed be those who defile the fallen."

"I care not for your sleeping god, Gul'dani filth," snarled Maddock at the voice. His body pointed through the wall adjoining the corner cell. "Not one who allows such torment to take place."

"Only for those without favor," assured the man. "Nights ago, I too was set upon by a ravenous slug, but while its bane coursed through me, death came not as it did for the one lying before you."

"Good for you. Describe it."

"The creature? Nothing quite like it has ever dwelled within this darkened space. It began small and languid, barely able to best a skurat. Still, it fed often and well, for by the time its fang sank into my arm, it measured the size of a stretched hand. My life was thankfully spared while the heathen before you met his end. You should have heard him, crying like a newborn *vah*. Glory be to Avalon!" The man chuckled as if to mock the unbeliever.

"Avalon?" muttered Laerzo to himself. "But I thought—"

"What a loathsome name," declared Maddock in disgust. "I can still hear you zealots screaming it in the heat of battle.

Tell me, where is your god now? Have you two met since we tossed you away?"

"Great of you to ask," said the man. "Here even now he dwells. When the creature's venom entered me, I fell into trance the same way we used to drink Lord Judecca's blood in the glory days of the War. Then, as now, my soul met his in a vision replete with the most blessed declaration. I was to be set free! Oh, how I begged to return to Judecca, and through him, the True God, Avalon, glory be upon him. How I wished once more to become an instrument of his justice!"

"True God? Utter madness. I remember no glory days, not even decams ago when Ogden first welcomed your *salvation*. It didn't take long for the same Sh'tama, who brought word of Sancta, to deliver Avalon's fire and death to our shores!"

"A false prophet, Sancta." This statement came as some surprise to Maddock, at least as much as anything surprised him. The man could be heard spitting. "Judecca revealed a new way, one of burning pyre. It was a gift, its own blessing! We used it to purify Gul'dan, then Waldea for a time. Be thankful your sinners were offered unto its holy flame."

"Be thankful we didn't throw you from these cliffs into the Waters Emeralda."

"You mean the Sea of Gul'dan."

"You wish." Maddock's disgusted expression suggested he'd humored this villain for long enough. "Answer one more thing before I leave you to rot. Why did you suddenly turn against us after a generation of peace between our peoples?"

"An answer even more simple than its quandary. We came to purify this land, make it as holy as Judecca requires. Your stubborn people simply got in the way."

"My family and friends accepted your ways and it got them

killed, so forgive me if I want no part in your justice, or your god!"

A vein in Maddock's neck swelled as feverish laughter blasted through and around the wall. "Your bloody crowing defiles the dead, hypocrite!" His outburst caused every soul in the gaol to stir and mutter about, yet there remained a sense of reverence lingering in the air.

The prisoner's deranged laughter was followed by a bout of silence before he continued. "Those called in faith to be strong do not cry for the weak. It is right to mock and burn frail hearts that taint the world. The shrill, pitiable fool dead before you possessed one such heart. He wailed so pathetically through the night without once calling his god by name. I doubt he even had one. It utterly sickened this place into silence. Cast it into flame and leave us!"

Laerzo could tell by Maddock's grimace that any further answers they sought would not be found here. Still, watching the General pace back and forth, he understood the man a little better now. Looking back to the corpse, he asked, "What now? Should we burn the body?"

The question stopped Maddock in his tracks. "We don't burn the dead."

"But we can't just leave it here. That . . . thing will only grow if it has an easy meal."

"I know that. Keep quiet!" Maddock paused to think things through. "I'll arrange to have him brought up and examined. The bastard didn't give me a lick of information to save his life, but maybe we can learn more about how he died."

"I wouldn't do that if I were you," the voice from beyond interjected again. "Best to leave daimons in the dark, yeah?"

Maddock turned angrily toward the wall. "You would know a thing or two about that, scum!"

Something emerged from underneath the corpse.

"Sir, look out!" cried Laerzo.

"What the—" Just as Maddock spun around, it leaped onto his torch hand, which he shook so wildly he cast both creature and flame against the wall. The fleshy sac quickly rebounded with a leap, affixing itself now to the front of his armor. Spread thin, it was nearly half the size of his mail. He pounded at his chest, but the slimy mass became hard and firmly fixed like a rock in the mud. Its upper end then lifted, revealing a single fang the size of a tiny finger.

Maddock's body froze against the tendril extending terribly close to his neck, but just as the monster was about to strike, it let out a high-pitched shriek. Laerzo's torch had burned it, causing it to fall onto the boot of his prey. Maddock kicked and kicked, yet the stubborn creature remained, only detaching when his other boot came stomping down.

"Damn it!" screamed Maddock at his aching toes while the resilient leech started unevenly toward the cell door. "You're mine now!" he screamed, scooping up his torch. Laerzo went to follow him, but Maddock shouted, "Stay here until I return!"

He disappeared down the dark path.

Laerzo could hear the General's distant call to arms cause the entire gaol to hum with excitement. Still rattled by the creature's horrendous cry, he pulled at one ear and loosened his open jaw.

"You," started the man again. "Bless this old man and show yourself."

Laerzo heeded Maddock's warning and did not respond. "I know you're still there. Let me see your face, *vah*."

Still, Laerzo remained in the cell, staring blankly at the dead man as commotion continued to make its way through the dungeon. He knew his orders, and had every intention of following them, yet this strange curiosity eventually got the best of him.

I guess there's no harm in it, he thought before slowly making his way from the cell and around the corner.

"Ahhh, there you are," said the voice now affixed to a shadow. Torchlight gave the rough impression of a gangly man with lengthy, peppered hair falling next to an equally impressive gray-black beard. Two floating orbs of dim light soon revealed fierce, sable eyes as he slowly approached the bars. His rough face wore many scars and a tilted nose long since broken. The pale man wrapped a lonely sheet around his flimsy, tattered, once-white tunic barely warming his tapered frame, surprisingly sinewy for how long it lingered idle. "Tell me your name."

"Who wants to know?" asked Laerzo, still keeping his distance from the man.

"For now, you may call me Vidal. And you are?"

"Laerzo," he said after a brief pause. He could tell the man was waiting for a surname. "Just Laerzo."

"Let me have a look at you, Laerzo." Vidal waved both hands for the young man to come closer, sensing his hesitation. "What remains to fear? The beast has already fled. Surely, I cannot bring you harm."

Laerzo slowly took a couple of steps forward, close enough for Vidal to gaze upon him for an uncomfortably long time.

His black eyes widened. "Ahh, that fire in your stare. I saw one just like it once. And the tint of your skin. You are not Waldean, not completely." Vidal gasped. "Could it be? Has Avalon truly blessed me this day?"

"I don't follow," said Laerzo.

"He spoke of a young man who would lead me to freedom, a man that would be my *omar,* my son."

"That's some vision. How old is your . . . *omar*?"

"This, I cannot say. I have never known to have one until now."

"You said the man frees you, yeah? Well, I hate to break it to you, but nobody is going to do that."

"But he must!" declared Vidal, shifting forward somewhat aggressively. His hands gripped the bars just as Laerzo backed up against the glowing rampart. "It has been foretold. His coming is God-given!"

"Guess you'll just have to continue waiting then," responded Laerzo with some melancholy. "Serves you right. I heard Gul'dan did a lot of horrible things back then. You and the others deserve to be here."

"We deserved to win or die, not be locked up. It's the way of the warrior! Give us even a torturous death, not this false mercy. Avalon, thy will be done! Free me from this wretched place!"

Laerzo was so amused by Vidal's desperation that he almost forgot where he was. "Calm down, would you, buddy? Again, nobody's here to help you, but I'll tell you what. If I ever meet your son, I'll let him know you said hi."

"You are foolish to mock me, *vah*."

"Yeah, yeah. Any idea what he looks like? Your god must've shown you that much."

Vidal hesitated for a moment. "Like his father, of course."

"That's rough." Laerzo chuckled under his breath. "Do you even recall the last time you were with a woman?"

"Ahh, like it was yesterday. How could one forget something so sweet? The final days of the War, moons after sacking Thannick. We remained locked in a gruesome battle with Stolgrum day after day, neither side the victor. It was then I first crossed paths with her in the field. She was gorgeous, hazel-eyed with auburn-hair, firebrand of a woman. She was also my enemy, leader to one of the more persistent rebel forces.

"Some time later, when the tides began to turn against us, my men found the stubborn creature hiding with others in an underground cellar. They brought her directly to me along with ill news from the battlefront. Waldean forces were already on the way, quite unfortunate. I knew if our defeat was at hand, I would at least have the last laugh. The trophy so long sought after was now in my hands do to with as I wished. Would I steal her back to Gul'dan? Yes, but I had to have her then and there. Of course, her love belonged to another. I took it anyway."

"You . . . what?"

"Disobedience is quite the thrill, you see. The more she resisted, the greater my victory became. Which fool did she cry out to again? Dietrich?"

Maddock suddenly returned, completely covered in sweat, and apparently empty-handed, judging by the scowl on his face. "Damnit, soldier! What did I tell you about keeping your mouth shut?"

Laerzo didn't even notice his presence. "This must be some sort of joke," he said, his eyes flaring under the torchlight. "You said Dietrich?"

Maddock's eyes now widened as well.

"Ahh, you know the man? If so, tell him Vidal Barboa gives his salutations. I was a Commander of Gul'dan. He'll remember me."

"Quit this feeble fool!" ordered Maddock as a couple of guards approached from behind him. His posture seemed somewhat defeated. "The beast has escaped for now. I'll have additional men scour this pit until that thing is destroyed once and for all. You will join them."

The very thought made Laerzo cringe. "Yes, sir."

"I know we will meet again soon, my son," whispered Vidal before retreating back into darkness.

"Uh, General?" began one of the guards. "You wanted us to remove a body, correct?"

"That's right," Maddock replied, turning to them. "Just through there . . . What in dreadfire?"

"What's wrong?" asked Laerzo as he joined the others. All the while, Vidal could still be heard chanting "Halea!" joyously from his cell.

"You didn't drag it somewhere, did you? Toss it into the pit?"

Laerzo gave him a weird look. "The corpse? Why would I do that?"

"Then tell me where he is!" roared Maddock, throwing his torch between the two guards in the otherwise empty cell.

Connel had vanished without a trace.

CHAPTER 27

"Give it a rest, Gibbs!" barked Leopold as he groomed the kind geldtmare that carried him back to Thannick. He had been in a sour mood ever since he was ordered away from his cushy post, casting steel into this sprawling farm town.

When asked for how long, General Maddock simply said, "Until further notice."

Evidently, Gibbs had more pull with the Alliance than Leopold had originally thought, raising enough of a stink to rankle them into action, however slow their response turned out to be. The old man requested Leopold by name on more than one occasion, and eventually, the lone soldier was deployed with a couple of lousy tools in his bag. Needless to say, Leopold wasn't happy about it, not just being away from the others, but wasting away with Gibbs's in sweat and squalor. His armor had long since been tossed in a corner bale of hay, though strangely, he kept his chained hammer rapped around him, that and his orange bandanna. "We've been working nonstop since I got here two days ago."

"Quiet, you!" proclaimed Gibbs, continuing to polish divots from Bessie's battered, steel core. "Hold on, darlin'. You'll be shinin' again in no time!"

"Damn, just dragging her into this smelly shack took long enough."

"Longer to drag yer hide back here. What took yah? Expect an *old man* like me'tah do all the heavy liftin'? Could hardly git the old wagon'tah uncouple out there in the fields, much less strap on a new one."

To his credit, Gibbs had managed to swap Bessie's broken undercarriage for a sturdy metal frame. He'd even given her entire core a good scrub.

"Seemed to do just fine without me. Bolt on some new floorboards, and the job is practically already done!"

"Oh no, yah don't! You ain't gittin' outta this till she's good as the day I met 'er. It's the least yah could do!"

"Might as well call it a day then. I think you forget just how much of a heap of junk she really was when we put her together."

"Think again! Me and Bessie go further back than you know. Way back."

Leopold shot an odd look across the place. "Been burning the loopy cheroot in your golden days? I helped you build that steam wagon."

"Aye, but I knew 'er before that, in the tail end of the War. Don't act so surprised. Every farmhand in Thannick was a soldier back then. I ain't no different. Made quite the *reppertation* fer myself, I'll have yah know!"

"You mentioned something like that the other day. I don't believe it for a second. Momma never said as much."

"Yah got that right! Told me tah keep my trap shut if I knew what was good fer me." Gibbs froze abruptly, his nervous stare slowly shifting toward the look of incredulousness on Leopold's face. "Oh, drat . . . I really am gettin' old."

Leopold's brow pinched curiously low. "What else did Momma tell you to keep from me?"

"Not a thing. Now, git over here and help me fix this pretty lady! We ain't boltin' no wood on here. This chassis needs some sheet metal."

"Not until you fess up, old man!" Leopold was practically steaming. "So help me, Bessie's getting a piss wash if you don't start spittin'!"

"Yah wouldn't dare, sonny!" warned Gibbs, carefully measuring the air between them. Both knew he would never hear the end of it from Momma, but they couldn't just leave things be. "Fine. Suppose yah have a right to know, but if she hollers, yah didn't hear nothin' from me."

"Yeah, I got it," replied Leopold, patting the geldtmare as she finished her basket of spuds. The beast seemed excitable at times, but they got along well enough. He gently ran a bristle brush through the maned mullet of fur growing clear down her back. "All right, let's hear it."

"Well, I'm sure yah know yer family grew up in Thannick. Truth is, I spent my life here too. Know every person in the Heartland, yer parents included."

"You knew my father?" asked Leopold, still grooming as his head turned.

"Knew him? I gave the kid his first gig tendin' fields and gatherin' hen-cockel eggs fer the farmers' market. When it got to gittin', kid got the job done, but he was thick-skulled, always in over his head. Naturally, he fell in love with yer Momma."

"What was she like then?"

"Believe it or not, shy. Mostly kept outta trouble. Her family was a bit classier than most. Got swept up in that Sancta claptrap. Didn't care much fer the Gottas. Your pappy Gregor nearly killed himself gettin' into that lass's good graces. Just couldn't manage to win over the folks, though. Didn't matter much after he knocked 'er up. They had no choice but to give 'er hand in marriage. Sly dog!"

Leopold tried not to overthink such things. "That's fine and all, but probably not secret-worthy. Get to the good stuff!"

"Cool yer cakes! I'm gettin' there. You were 'bout three when the War broke out, and before yah knew it, we was all roped into some militia, fightin' fer life in these very fields."

"And I take it you two fought together?" asked Leopold, setting aside the bristle brush. He could tell where this was going, at least in part.

"Us and Momma, in fact."

"You've gotta be kiddin' me!" The image of her as a solider shocked Leopold, but it seemed to explain a lot the more he thought about it.

"No joke! We were all innit together, but they made me the boss. Can yah believe it?"

Leopold could not believe it. "You, a general? Get outta here!"

"Cross my craw, hope to crow!"

"But I thought Cael was the one in charge." Just the mention of her name seemed to make Leopold blush.

"Boy, she was barely a lady back then. I was the one callin' the shots! I knew the land and the people after all, so it kinda just worked out that way . . . or, at least, till it didn't." Gibbs's face grew strangely grim. "We put up a good fight, but things took a nasty turn." He stopped working on Bessie, stopped pretty much everything for a time. His sad eyes hesitated before turning toward Leopold. "I gave the order tah retreat, but Gregor wouldn't listen." He watched Leopold think hard for a moment. "It was my fault. We got spread thin, and before we knew it, zealots were poppin' out everywhere. He drew 'em away, gave us the chance to escape."

Leopold stared off to the corner of the barn, his eyes

watering. "Momma said he was a coward, that he abandoned us to save himself."

"No, Leo-boy. That's not it at all." A tear ran down the old man's face. "Truth is, yer pa saved our hides. Fought like a bravo till the end. You hear me? The man was a hero. Of course, Momma didn't see it that way. I don't blame 'er fer being mad 'bout it. We all were, but life goes on, I suppose." Both stood there a long while without much to say. Gibbs was now a bit lighter for the trouble, mostly relieved the news was better taken this time around.

"Damn it, Momma. Just wait till I—"

Gibbs saw the young man's mind wandering in worry. "I told yah not to fret. She's a tough one. Whoever she's scrappin' with doesn't stand a chance!"

Suddenly, the geldtmare cried out in pain as its two front legs shot into the air. Falling backward, Leopold scrambled to his feet several paces between Gibbs and the frenzied steed, who now bucked in circles. "Woah, girl! What's wrong?"

It only took a moment to notice something the size of a helmet clinging to the geldtmare's side. The gray-purple of its slimy, shifting hide tinted red as it expanded and contracted in violent pulses. Pure horror upon the geldtmare's face conveyed a sense of helplessness as it failed time and again to shake off the creature.

Slowly raising his hands, Gibbs inched closer to calm the wailing beast. "That's good. Easy now."

Meanwhile, Leopold carefully sidled rightward to a shovel leaning against a nearby post. Moving into position, he gradually lifted the implement, and after a brief pause, thrust it at the throbbing leech. This was meant to scoop it off, only the steel tip bounced from the center mass of the creature's veiny, leathery skin. Bruised, it let out a high-pitched shriek but continued to suck on its prey, which painfully shook about until Gibbs could again coax it still.

Leopold lined up another shot, and this time, thankfully managed to scoop right under the bloating mass, however much it bruised the geldtmare. Then, with a bit of shuffling and some leverage, he was able to detach the thing altogether. Tossing the blob upward, his swinging shovel sent it crashing into the wall.

"Good grief! What is that thing?" muttered Gibbs as the geldtmare continued to grunt and snort. She was still worked up, but her pain seemed to lessen somewhat.

"Beats me," replied Leopold while approaching the stunned parasite. "Let's see how it handles this!" Unwrapping the chains from his gut, he spun the hammer quick and brought it crashing down with a devastating swing. Blood popped every which way from beneath the force, and when he withdrew the hammer, the leech was utterly destroyed.

"Now that's something!" shouted Gibbs. "Where'd yah learn that trick?" Unfortunately, his cheering roused the geldtmare into a snarl, and her front legs kicked at both of them. "Woah, now!"

Leopold's movement across the barn seemed to antagonize the beast. She charged him, horns down, almost gutting him in the process. With a clumsy roll, he barreled upright just out of harm's way, but the attack was not finished.

"We gotta split!" he shouted, nearly trampling Gibbs in the process. They dashed outside into twilight, slammed the doors, and secured them just in the nick of time. Both were disturbed by the deranged howling and angry trotting heard from inside as hooves occasionally rapped against the walls.

"Looks like we're done fer today after all," said Gibbs,

disappointed. He pounded on the barn's exterior. "You better not goof up Bessie, yah hear me?"

"What was that all about?"

"Guess that slug's got poison innit. Girl's gone silly! Figurin' she makes it through the night. Hope we don't have tah put 'er down."

"Just my luck!" griped Leopold. "But doesn't poison make you stop moving? She's just a bit crazed, that's all. Maybe she'll sleep it off."

"Yer gonna be draggin' parts tomorrow if she don't."

Gibbs wasn't kidding, thought Leopold the next day with a great deal of exhaustion. Though relieved to find his steed resting peacefully at the crack of dawn, he couldn't rouse her, and so Gibbs lay the harness of his two-wheeled cart on Leopold instead. He'd been hauling it around town the whole morning—in full armor, no doubt, as Gibbs reminded him he was on official duty. Leopold at least had enough sense to leave his chained hammer behind and spare himself the extra heft. Granted, his stamina had practically doubled since joining the Alliance, but the burly soldier was just a man like any other, not some beast of burden. He currently struggled to load some heavy scrap on the side of the road.

"I never signed up . . . for this!"

"Yer doin' great, kid," said Gibbs unconvincingly, while riding his personal buckmule, a creature half the size of any geldtmare. Leopold did not find his words the least bit encouraging. In fact, they came off as bitter, almost sadistic. The look of exhaustion peeking out from underneath Gibbs's bucket hat suggested he hadn't rested well, though Leopold managed to sleep though the night of crazed wailing without any trouble. A good thing, too, for Leopold knew he wouldn't make it to lunch otherwise.

"Easy for . . . you to say!" Stopping, Leopold took a moment to recover. "I'm the one hauling mass while . . . you sit nice on that mule. Petty . . . if you ask me!"

"Yah don't expect an *old man* like me to walk around all day, do yah?"

Leopold shook his head while lifting another piece of scrap and tossing it on the cart with a grunt. "Do we gotta keep going . . . the long way through town? The locals laugh and wave whenever we come around. Now who's got a *reppertation*?"

"Nonsense. The people love yah!" Gibbs was definitely loving every second of it, though one could hardly tell by his tuckered expression.

"It's shameful! Besides, we got Bessie patched up well enough. Why do I got to keep pulling around town like some . . . buckmule?" With this, he sneered at Gibbs's shabby ride, who gave a silly hee-haw in response.

"Might as well put yah tah good use. Helpin' 'round Thannick don't seem like much tah city folk, but it goes a long way here in these parts. Yer doin' some fellas a solid they won't soon ferget. Neither will the Alliance if I tell 'em right. 'Sides, never hurts to have a couple of spare parts for a rainy day."

"You conniving son of a—" started Leopold, but thought twice about making too much of a stink. His reputation back at Lionel could use the commendation, after all. "Put in a good word for me. Just don't mention any of this. Fixing some grub couldn't hurt either."

"Quit gripin' and be happy with what yah git! By the way, we'd be eatin' already if yah'd quit pullin' over."

"Then get your *lady* to do the work next time!"

Gibbs's weary eyes brightened as he stared back down the

road. "Speaking of ladies, better look sharp! Wouldn't want yers to see yah slackin' on the job!"

They spotted a cavalry of thirty or so geldtmares, most carrying two men apiece. At the forefront, a pair of men atop especially massive mares led the way, pulling a decorated officer in a chariot of blackened metal. It was none other than the Regent-General of Thannick herself, Cael Tannenbaum, and the riders her sons, Cecil and Nicolo. Her current regalia was nothing compared to the classy attire Laerzo had mentioned her wearing at Grenefest. It suggested she was not to be trifled with on this or any day. A light-bronze cape hugged her slender black chest plate, hung as low as the dark chainmail dress, which she wore over matching knee guards and boots. A white scarf now housed her otherwise long, brown head of hair. On one side, her trusty spear was locked upright into the chariot's base for support and easy access. The other side secured her black skullcap in a corner fold tucked behind her boys. Her sons currently controlled the family's spoiled steeds, but even without them, Cael effortlessly guided both with confidence and care.

Her men donned much more casual garb under their Alliance armor, mostly slacks and overalls dirtied from working the land. When Cael's smoke signals were seen over town, they'd selflessly answered the call, each carrying everyday tools like rope, whips, broomsticks, spades, mallets for grinding and churning, and anything they had at the ready. Some secured more deadly implements like sickles, hayforks, and axe shovels across their backs. Many also brandished various configurations of mesh and leather slings at their side, an unsuspecting yet precision weapon for those who knew how to cast a stone. It was not uncommon for one to effortlessly strike a foe dead while riding from a hundred gallops away.

Leopold couldn't remember the last time he saw Cael's militiamen on the march. By now, they were mostly obsolete, as anything of consequence rarely happened in this Commonwealth, nothing a pack of Enforcers on the beat couldn't handle. Judging by their speed and number, he could tell they were not conducting a routine patrol. They were ready to do battle. He saw Gibbs swell with pride. Seeing them on the move again took him back to his days in the Alliance. As the riders approached, both held an overembellished salute.

"Good afternoon, m'lady—er, ma'am!" greeted Leopold much more eagerly than the occasion warranted. "Leopold Gotta, reporting for duty!"

"At ease," responded Cael with a slight chuckle. "Looks like Gibbs is puttin' you through the ringer today, soldier."

Leopold hadn't taken his eyes off her yet. The fact that Laerzo had gotten to meet her all dolled up at the festival irked him to this very day. Of all the women in Waldea, she was the one he'd yearned for the most. It didn't matter if she was a bit older than him, or was long since happily wed. He would never give up hope. Somehow, someday, he thought, she would be his to love, serve, and protect. If he was being honest, this farfetched dream was part of the reason he'd joined the Alliance in the first place.

"Yes, ma'am," he answered. "Serving the fine folks of Thannick is an honor and a privilege!"

Gibbs almost lost it right away. "That so? Differ'nt talk just a moment ago."

"Quiet, you—er, sir!"

"Don't run him into the mud just yet, Mr. Gibbs," said Nicolo lightly. "Looks like we've got official business to tend to."

"Oh?" replied Gibbs, one bushy brow lifting somewhat

under his hat. "Don't hear that much these days. Some poor kid chase his pet up a tree, or what? 'Course, wouldn't need all y'all for that!"

"Right you are," answered Cael. "Missy Bellachek rode into town this morning in a fit, said she'd spotted an encampment a few clicks east of her property."

"Yah don't say. That's not too far from my place."

"That's right, just beyond Tillman's Creek, where she likes to pick shrooms. Crowds of men and women in white robes under some strange structure. Not sure what's going on, but I rounded up a few folks to check it out."

"This what'cha call a few? Y'all look ready to rumble!"

"Can never be too careful," said Cecil.

"That's right, son," answered Cael, her eyes narrowing. "These are not our people, from what I can tell. Might just be the first we've seen from Greneva in some time. Word has it they got some Trust with 'em too."

"Them again!" barked Leopold, finally managing to drop his harness with such a crash that some of the geldtmare shuffled about nervously. "You saw them at Grenefest, didn't you, ma'am?"

Cael fielded two wary stares from her sons. "Briefly. We left early that night, but if your recent run-in was half as wild as Gibbs's report states, they are nothing but trouble. Not that you need to hear that from me. It's a shame, really. They've done right by us folk. I hope it's just a misunderstanding." Her attention seemed somewhat distracted when she said this. "Mr. Gotta! You will join us to investigate."

"Ma'am?" asked Leopold, almost forgetting to throw a clumsy salute. His gaze momentarily turned to Gibbs and the cart, then back to her. "I would be happy to. However—"

"Were you not given a steed, soldier?"

"About that. Some nasty leech attacked it last night. Got really . . . excited, so we had to lock it up."

"No kidding," answered Cecil. "Happened a few days back with one of our stock. Some strange things crawlin' around lately, if yah ask me!"

Though slightly unnerved by the news, Cael kept calm and collected. "Don't worry about it. Gibbs's farm isn't far. We can drop that off on the way." Her frown turned to a smile. "Mr. Gotta, care for a ride?"

"Hot damn!" exclaimed Leopold, perhaps a bit too enthusiastically. "Just gotta hitch this rig, and I'm all yours!"

"All right, keep it cool, soldier," warned Gibbs as he watched Leopold practically leap into Cael's chariot. "Thank yah kindly!"

"Anytime, old friend," replied Cael. When everyone was ready, she pinched thumb and forefinger to mouth and gave a hearty whistle that sent the company flying down the path.

After stopping by Gibbs's farm to ditch scrap and pick up Bessie, they continued on some ways toward Tillman's Creek, making sure to sneak through the trees for a better look up ahead. Thereabouts, just as reported, the congregation could be seen in a meadowy valley. Missy Bellachek had either understated the size of the crowd or simply gone blind. There were hundreds in attendance. They gathered downhill from something quite extraordinary in scale, approximately several stories tall. Nicolo likened it to a metallic tree of sorts, but in actuality, it was more of a giant dowsing rod with many similar yet smaller rods stacked at its center, one upon the other. Most were rotating at various speeds, some clockwise, some the opposite, and a few not at all. At the base of the structure was something shining, but it was hard to make out exactly what from that far away. It was baffling to Cael's company how something so massive had been erected without detection until now. The sheer presence of it brought their senses into doubt.

It was then Leopold felt a strange buzz in the air. The sensation wasn't quite as much an ache as pressure building within his skull, no different from what he'd experienced in the forests of Greneva. It caused his head to swim, leaving him in a bewildered, dreamlike state. He chalked this up to nervous excitement on an empty stomach, but the others seemed similarly put off as they stared at one another. Then the geldtmares started to act up, and not just one or two either. The whole lot of them displayed brief bouts of erratic behavior, some shuffling about nervously while others began to whicker and fuss. Their tone was unusually deep and aggressive, just like Leopold's own steed the previous night.

Before long, some became spooked by a rustling in the brush and prematurely cleared into the meadows. "Woah, woah!" shouted Cael as more followed suit. As their cover had already been blown, she ordered her sons to take them out into the clearing, but their mares would not budge. This they found most unsettling, given how obedient the beasts usually were, but another few snaps at the reins eventually sent them on their way. Approaching, they heard an eerily somber song from the congregation being cut short after making their presence known. Cael brought her contingent to a halt between the crowd and the base of the hill, where she scanned around for familiar faces. To her amazement, most were made nearly indistinguishable from the others by the veils and hoods over their heads. The sight of their uniformity was as unnerving as it was blatant.

"What is the meaning of this disturbance?" spoke a high,

snooty voice suddenly from behind as a flashy caravan slowly descended the hill. It was none other than Gwyndolyn sitting high upon her transport, which had become more of a gilded throne than a carriage. It was quite the gaudy display, replete with her retinue of humble Trust pulling the altar both by foot and mount. Scarlet and Matron flanked both sides, though a lone figure in white remained atop the hill to pray at the monument. Gwyndolyn's white and purple attire was now littered with gold trinkets, all reflecting brilliance of the crown of pure light newly resting upon her head. She cradled a tall, crystalline vessel of wine in her lap as she stared down at the lot of them with seething indignation.

"Dear Matron," she said, "have more come to offer themselves into blissful thralldom?"

"Perhaps, but first they must declare their intentions for all to witness." Matron then turned to address the Alliance. "You there, new among the lowly! Who stands before our Blessed Daughter, Gwyndolyn?"

"What in the—?" muttered Gibbs. Leopold could tell the man was alarmed to hear those words so brazenly spoken in broad daylight.

"I am Cael Tannenbaum, Regent-General of Thannick! From where do you hail?"

Matron cleared her throat. "We are . . . modest folks from Greneva gathering today in thanksgiving and revelry."

"To whom am I speaking? Why do you wear a veil over your face?"

"I am but a humble servant. My name is of no importance."

"That is for me to decide, woman. Why have you gathered? For what do you give thanks?"

Scarlet stepped forward with arms spread in welcome.

"That we devotees are called to join the Blessed Daughter in her most . . . special pilgrimage across Waldea."

Cael was not at all pleased to hear that word. "What say you, Gwyndolyn? Speak plainly!"

"That's *Lady* Gwyndolyn to you, reprobate!" snapped Scarlet in a bit of melodrama. "Bow, for you are not worthy to bask in her radiance!"

A quick stare from Matron across the carriage instructed her to tread carefully.

"I will do no such thing," replied Cael sternly, waving some of her men closer. Already, she'd heard enough. "Everyone, hear me! On behalf of the Alliance, I find this congregation to be in clear violation of Waldean law! Leave now, and I will let you go in peace, but this is your only warning!" Her voice reached every ear, and though the crowd squirmed and muttered among themselves, no one dared to budge. To them, she was nothing.

Gwyndolyn let out a smug, arrogant laugh befitting royalty. "I'm afraid they only listen to me, and those who speak for me."

Leopold was baffled that anybody would listen to a criminal, much less hold one in such high regard. Yet he could not deny her extravagant presentation and what it suggested. Jumping down from Bessie, he took a few steps forward, looking around just in case Momma was counted among the crowd. Sadly, he did not see her. Leopold then returned his attention to Gwyndolyn, suddenly captivated by her beauty. "Gwyndolyn, what have they done to you?"

"Sorry, do I know you?" asked Gwyndolyn derisively. She seemed somewhat disgusted he would address her in such a base manner, or at all.

"It's me, Leo! Don't you recognize me?"

Indeed, Gwyndolyn did seem to remember somebody by

that name, but before she could respond, Matron stepped forward. "Do not speak to her! She is God-given, anointed to save sinful people like you from their wanton ways. My Lady, see how his features have run pale?" Matron waved her hands, and in short order, Leopold had become almost as gray as Gibbs.

"Leo-boy, you look haggard!" shouted Gibbs in shock.

"What are you on about?" asked Leopold, but then a floating mirror suddenly appeared to reflect his faded complexion. "How in the—is this a trick? She's some sort of witch!"

"Silence, ashen!" replied Matron, signaling with her hand for Scarlet to help Gwyndolyn down from her throne. "You have but one chance at redemption. Blessed Daughter, offer Hypha's Dew just as you did the others, or he will turn rabid and strike!"

"Ashen? Bet you're just as gray under that mask!" Leopold could practically feel Gibbs's concerned look burning a hole through the back of his head. Turning, he shouted, "Don't say a word, all right? I'll be damned if I look older than you!"

"Now, hold on just a moment," started Gibbs, but Leopold had already proceeded to slowly close the gap with Gwyndolyn. "Cael, we got a plan here?"

Cael adjusted her position slightly for a clearer view. "Just wait for my signal."

"There, and no farther!" commanded Matron to Leopold, watching Gwyndolyn approach him. "Yes, child. Spread the Lutzrat far and wide. Deliver him and all who drink it into Denestra's hands."

Leopold obeyed, stopping several paces from Gwyndolyn, who was accompanied close behind by Scarlet. "Would you tell me what this is all about already?"

"You are bold to speak to me so casually," stated Gwyndolyn, her crown as dazzling as the Solstar itself.

"Cut the crap, Gwyndolyn! Maybel is worried sick about you." Leopold could tell his words were starting to reach her. "Where in Essa have you been?"

Scarlet promptly approached Gwyndolyn's ear. "Do not be deceived, Lord Sister! Go on, give him the drink."

"Yes, very well," answered Gwyndolyn, her head shaking in confusion. She stepped forward with carafe in hand to loudly declare: "Ashen, we bring gift of the Hypha Tree, oh blessed wine. Partake and be free from your wicked aberrance!" To this, the congregation began to chant, "Halae! Al'Haleia!"

Leopold turned toward Cael and the others holding steady, then back to Gwyndolyn's striking beauty. He considered the offer, but there was something odd about the whole thing, which gave him pause. "Sorry, not much of a day drinker."

Gwyndolyn watched aghast as his features continued to wither. "Fool, you must! Before the last of you fades." Her voice seemed almost frantic in that moment. "Take this drink from me at once, understand?"

"Guess I gotta, but only if you insist," responded Leopold with a slow, groggy smile. By now, he was completely enamored with Gwyndolyn as she lifted the carafe's neck to his mouth. But just when he was about to drink, the vessel exploded into pieces, driving him a few steps back in retreat.

Gwyndolyn also staggered backward into Scarlet's arms. She raised both sullied hands to a cut upon her face before letting out a terrible scream. The crowd wailed and hissed at the blatant act of blasphemy while pointing toward the discharged leather sling in Cael's hands.

"What have you done?" screamed Scarlet with wild eyes.

The carafe's destruction was devastating, yet she almost seemed to enjoy watching Gwyndolyn languish.

"Time's up!" proclaimed Cael. "In the name of Waldea, I'm placing you all under arrest!" With this, she signaled for her men to round up as many as they could and chase off the rest of the angry crowd. Unbeknownst to her, many of the worshippers came prepared to fight. They removed weapons from underneath their robes and took the militiamen by surprise. A fearsome battle broke out, and the numbers were not in the Alliance's favor, even with the aid of Leopold and Gibbs. Cael entered the fray to support some of her men who'd been dragged from their geldtmares and forced to fight on foot against the crazed mob. "Strike down those who wield blades against you, but if possible, do not take their lives!"

Leopold saw Gwyndolyn and Scarlet return to the caravan with shocked, shameful looks, watching them plead with the veiled woman before the lot of them started back up the hill. Turning his attention back to the battle, he was happy to see the militiamen had gained the upper hand, at which point Cael shifted her attention toward the congregation's ringleaders. By then, Gwyndolyn's caravan had already climbed much of the hill, so Cael had Cecil and Nicolo start after them. However, a handful of Trust guarded the base of the hill and had no intention of making way. Some of the militiamen launched stones to clear a path, but each one was repelled by the pitchforks' resonance, conjured in the form of indigo shields. The remaining men then struck their rods together and pointed them at the chariot.

"Watch out!" screamed Leopold as he and Gibbs were not far behind. Thanks to his intervention, the chariot swerved away from much of the brutal counterattack. Cael attempted to circumvent the Trust on more than one occasion, but every time she tried, more foes would suddenly appear in her path. Out of frustration, she tossed another stone, and it seemed to move right through her mark like he was an apparition. Before she had time to try again, the Trust's numbers had quadrupled in a flash of light, forcing her to circle back and rejoin the others.

"I've never seen anything like it," said Nicolo, his mouth agape.

"Sure beats tossin' rocks," added Gibbs.

"I've run into these folks before," said Leopold, thinking back to his harrowing escape from the aero-freight. "They battle with vibration. Use it to hide their position."

Cael was already beginning to connect the dots. "Hide. Or misdirect, anyway."

"Ma'am?"

"As far as attacking and defending, it seems their rods can only do one at a time. Also, they seem fairly immobile."

"Yes, we should be able to get around them just fine," said Cecil. "The hill is wide, Mother. Let's just take the long way. I doubt they would be able to catch us."

Nicolo nodded. "And if they get in our way? We'll just trample them!"

"Think again!" Leopold interjected with a wagging finger. "Did you not see what just happened? They'll pop out of nowhere if you do. Who knows just how many there are waiting? And a straight charge is too dangerous. Get hit by one of those blasts up close, and you're gonna hurt. I nearly cracked a tooth the last time they clipped me with one!"

"Got it," said Cael before shooting a disappointed look at her boys. "Don't be so quick to shortchange the enemy. Spread out and observe their actions. Once we see what they can do, it should be easier to pick 'em apart."

This time, Cael and her sons strafed along the bottom of the hill, fielding a wave of blasts just before casting their stones. Leopold and Gibbs attacked from the other end. To the shock of everyone but Cael, each went straight through the pitchforks like before. "They are illusions!" she shouted. "Strike the others to see who is real! Ignore the rest!"

Unfortunately, the next sweep proved equally unsuccessful after every subsequent stone and swing passed through their targets as well. Retracting his hammer, Leopold began to wonder if any of the figures were flesh and bone when suddenly he caught something stirring on Cael's opposite side, far away from the other targets. "Ma'am, on your right!"

Brandishing her spear, she leaped from the chariot just before it was nearly toppled by a wave of intense force. Once ensuring her boys were unharmed, she turned toward the warbling outline quickly vanishing in the distance. It was the real enemy—or, at least, one of them—hiding from plain sight until the right moment presented itself.

"We have to help her, Gibbs!" shouted Leopold.

"She'll be fine," replied Gibbs with a chuckle as he swerved Bessie past some surprise attacks nearby. "Just you watch!"

Leopold saw her charge toward the previous blast, her eyes peeled, dodging another on her flank with a clever roll. She quickly positioned herself between the two points of attack, aiming one way with her sling, only to hurl a stone in the opposite direction. This confused Leopold at first, at least until he noticed her projectile strike one of the Trust square between the eyes as his VISI goggles crumbled and his humming pitchfork fell to the ground.

"You weren't kidding!" cheered Leopold before resonance interrupted him from overhead, followed by a violent bump underneath Bessie. He looked to the rear of the wagon, where a trampled and bloodied body materialized in the dust, then to Gibbs, who briefly stared back with shrugged shoulders. His attention returned to Cael, but by then, she'd been sent tumbling hard against a nasty wave of force from behind. Hobbling upright against her spear, she realized her stones had been scattered in all directions. The assailant revealed himself to her, his brimming pitchfork rendering only the upper half of his body like a floating apparition. Thankfully, the Brothers Tannenbaum charged in, impaling him upon the antlers of both geldtmares before he could deliver the kill-shot.

Leopold was relieved to see her out of danger, though his was just beginning. Bessie was suddenly rocked by intense resonance, almost capsized as she tossed him overboard. His body hit the ground hard but surprisingly only sustained minor injuries. Struggling upright, he found himself surrounded by several foes preparing to do him in. Gibbs came back around and tried to clip a couple in passing with carriage and staff, but his efforts were in vain. Leopold knew he had no time to figure out which targets, if any, were real, and so he decided to throw caution to the wind. As the Trust closed the gap, he loosened the full length of his chain and wildly whipped his hammer around until the one true target was utterly clobbered.

At the first opportunity, he hopped back aboard Bessie, noticed Cael cheering him from afar. "You see that?" he shouted to Gibbs. "She thinks I'm hot stuff!"

"Yeah, yeah," said Gibbs. "Focus on the battle, boy! There's another line formin'—clear up the way."

Leopold fussed with the pouches strapped to his belt, mixing strange powders as he was wont to do. "No worries. I've got a plan. Get us close enough, and leave the rest to me!"

"Ah, no yah don't! I see that look in yer eye, just like before. I ain't gittin' offed today, no siree!"

"Just do it, you old coot! We don't have time to dawdle." Most reluctantly, Gibbs took Bessie up the hill, trying his best to keep a wide berth of the Trust, or at least those he could see. Leopold was not satisfied. "Closer, Gibbs! There, that should do it. Just you watch! Things are about to get spicy!" With this, he lit a fuse dangling from two of his pouches and tossed them at the line of pitchforks, ready to attack. A strange explosion of reddish haze enveloped them, and soon after, several pained men dashed into the clear, sneezing relentlessly as they removed their VISI to rub their reddened eyes. It didn't take Leopold long to dispatch them, just as Cael's crew had, with a few other emerging targets downwind.

"What did yah hit 'em with?" asked Gibbs.

"The last of my favorite seasoning, unfortunately," answered Leopold with a slight frown. "That pepper packs quite a punch, though."

Now that the coast was clear, they approached the massive obelisk looming overhead. There, Algus was tinkering with some glistening panel of knobs and buttons, not to mention his own pair of VISI resting across his face. He made one final adjustment, causing the monument to produce a wave of indigo extending through the sky along with a violent hum. Both sensations faded soon after. Standing, he stared dejectedly at the interlopers in his midst. "Must I do everything myself?"

"You have done plenty," said Scarlet. "Matron, our objective is met. Let's get out of here already!"

"Yes, let us depart back to Greneva," said Matron simply.

"Oh, no you don't!" barked Leopold as Bessie and Cael's chariot rolled up.

His VISI suddenly vanishing, Algus leered excitedly back at them with fierce, cerulean eyes. Without turning, he addressed

Gwyndolyn and the others. "You go on. I feel like having some fun for a change. Grant me this request, yes?"

"Very well, Frater, but don't get in over your head," replied Matron. "We still have plenty more to do." With this, she snapped her fingers, causing the caravan to disappear in a flash.

Leopold leaped from Bessie with an incredulous snarl. "It's you! I saw you when those monsters snatched away Momma and Gustav." Algus was taken aback by these words, though Leopold did not understand why. "Tell me. What did you do with them?"

Algus answered with a condescending laugh, removing one of several tear-shaped lucram gems from his pouch, the one called his focus. He then flicked the prongs of his pitchfork, placed this bluish stone between them, and watched it hover and glow. "Oh, those troublesome ashen ones? We don't suffer their presence in this land. They currently reside in the bowels of Mount Greneva, where they belong. Now that I mention it, you look a little gray yourself. Perhaps it's time I sent you to join them!"

"Yeah, you and what army? You're gonna need more than smoke and mirrors to take us out!"

"I may seem like just another lackey to you, and fair enough. But like most things concerning our kind, appearances can be deceiving!" Algus struck his pitchfork against the monument's metallic trunk before taking a few steps away. His lucram focus glowed even more intensely now between the prongs of the pitchfork. Then he swung it in a horizontal arc, unleashing a devastating crescent wave, which sent his foes all tumbling partway down the hill. The force of this blast was at least one magnitude greater than the Trust's previous attacks, causing even the chariot and its passengers to capsize. Given Bessie's bulky metal frame, she managed to stay upright, though Gibbs fell from his seat in a great deal of pain. To their credit, they all made a recovery and returned for more. It was at this point that Algus tapped at his temple, and almost instantly, heralds appeared from above in a blinding flash.

"Is this army more to your liking? Our power is not to be trifled with!"

Cael and the others were momentarily horrorstruck by the sight, but Leopold was more accustomed to their effulgent forms. "Not these damn things again!" he shouted while tossing his hammer at one of them.

Unfortunately, his attack missed, and before he could try again, two swooped down and lifted him from under the shoulders. Their intention was to drop him from high up, but their combined strength was hardly able to lift him a couple of feet at a time. A third went for Gibbs, who swung his staff to keep the shining fowl of a man at bay.

"Boys, protect Gibbs!" ordered Cael as she was set upon by a fourth herald. It underestimated her, however, and she soon managed to graze one of its wings with her spear. This sent the thing spiraling out of control, after which it crashed into the monument with a loud, steely clang.

"What on Essa?" Her attention shifted to Leopold dangling a bit higher in the air, but before she could intervene, another incoming arc from Algus, this one vertical, sent her diving to avoid it. She then rose with two stones, flinging one at Algus and the other at one of the heralds holding Leopold captive.

This gave Leopold a fighting chance. Pulling his left hand free, he quickly wrapped his chain around the disheveled adversary and sent it straight into the hillside. Of course, the chain was still attached to Leopold's waist, and it violently yanked him downward along with the remaining foe. He used its body to break his fall, pile driving the creature into the ground. Standing slowly, he looked down at what appeared to be a man wrapped in a bloodied frame of mangled metal. They weren't God-given at all, he discovered, just another member of the Trust in some propeller-driven flying suit.

"Leo, think fast!" shouted Gibbs suddenly as yet another herald attacked, but Cael's spear impaled the foe from afar with a masterful toss. They all watched him yank the missile from his chest, stagger slowly toward Algus in a grotesque display, and die shortly after.

Leopold spit some blood from his mouth. "That all you got?"

"Aren't we sure of ourselves?" asked Algus as he tapped his hidden VISI. At once, the others were blinded momentarily by brilliant light. When it abated, he had once again assumed his heraldic form, airborne with wings numbering seven. Incidentally, his dead companion was no longer wearing his metallic frame.

"Your eyes suggest we Trust are numbered few. This is but an illusion. As you have by now surely discerned, we are masters of perception. If we state you are tiny and insignificant, you are. If we suggest you are feral or feeble, that you shall be."

"Hah! I've seen your work back in Greneva. Neat tricks to anybody without a brain rattling between their ears!"

"We were just getting started. Every day, the Liminatum's power swells. Not just over Greneva, but even through the Heartland. One day, it will engulf all of Waldea!"

"Yet you have just told us your plan!" shouted Cael. "That will be your downfall in the end."

"Hardly. There is nothing you can do to stop us. With a strong enough impression, we can wipe our very existence from your minds. It's almost too simple, really."

"Go on then," replied Gibbs. "If yer so bold, what yah waitin' fer?"

"Well, that wouldn't be fun, now, would it?" Algus briefly held two fingers against his temple. "Speaking of which, it seems my fun is at an end for now. What a shame! But yours is just about to begin. And because I'm such a good sport, I'll give you all one chance to flee."

"Flee?" asked Leopold. "Buddy, you're flying solo! We don't gotta flee from—"

As he was about to finish, a screaming came from the militiamen down the way. They were all staring above the monument, where something was taking shape. It was among the shining, winged vessels that had been hanging over Greneva, and not just one. Soon, several vessels drifted across the skies.

Algus laughed. "I suggest you take my offer. It's the only one you'll get."

CHAPTER 28

General Dietrich stood exasperated in the conference chamber, the same one that had been used to interrogate Maybel several days prior. Littered across the lengthy table before him, as usual, was Dr. Carlyle's research. As of late, Dietrich had spent most of his time pouring through, especially after losing his only other lead into the machinations of the Trust. Yet for all his efforts, little progress had been made. Today was no different. Another morning of the same fruitless exercise had come and gone with little to show for it. Of course, this proved more difficult without Lord Lionel's presence, but the man had many matters to which only he could attend. Then there was Maddock, a most unwilling collaborator; he was still busy cleaning up his blunder in the dungeons. This left only Azacca and Maybel to lend a helping hand.

Dietrich had returned from a quick break to find Maybel dancing cheerfully in silence with the VISI goggles commandeered from Connel. White and thin, it rested over her eyes and ears like a moist towelette. "Hello? Maybel, are you with us?" asked Dietrich, his third attempt to regain her attention so far today. "Can she even hear us in there?"

"I think not," answered Azacca with a chuckle. He had been watching with great curiosity from the moment she'd powered on the mysterious device. "It beggars belief."

"Perhaps letting her use it was a mistake after all.

Who knows what this so-called technalurgy is capable of? Should've kept it locked away."

"A desperate move, surely, but regret is useless to you now. Besides, can you not see how it fills her with joy? No harm in that."

"Perhaps. How do you suppose it produces images and sound?"

"Who can say of any vision? Each one alludes me, though I hath seen my share. Nothing quite like this. I doubt hers will last much longer."

Indeed, the increasing pace and resultant sweat of her incessant dancing began to worry them.

"We don't have time for this." Dietrich walked around the table and shook the spastic girl by the shoulders. "Snap out of it, already!"

Maybel responded with a loud squeak, after which she nervously tapped buttons for the one that would return her senses. Eventually, she could see Dietrich clearly through the apparatus, though his words were all but muted. It took more time to finally hear him, but by then, he had resumed shaking her to the point of squeamishness.

"All right, sir! Please, I'm sorry!"

"Quite a stir you gave us," said Azacca. "Pray tell, what did you see?"

Maybel clasped both hands lovingly to her chest. "It was wonderful. I flew in a glowing tunnel of music, where bright, colorful notes matched the rhythm. Each one I managed to touch added beautiful tones to the melody, though this only made its composition more complex. Before long, I was completely swept away like a shooting star!" Her flowery rejoinder left the others utterly baffled. "That means nothing to you, does it? Wait, I know! One of you should give it a shot! You'd really enjoy it."

Azacca similarly clapped his hands together. "A splendid idea!"

"We're not here to play games," said Dietrich, giving them both a stern stare. He might have expected this behavior from her, but not Azacca. On second thought, he absolutely expected it from Azacca. The man always approached life with a sense of childlike levity, a bit of Sancta's grace, as he would say. On the other hand, Dietrich possessed an unfortunate penchant for sucking the fun out of a room. It was no wonder their personalities tended to clash.

"Yes, of course," responded Maybel dryly, matching Azacca's frown with her own. Still, neither could help but share a giggle for being chided by the Good General.

"Please, we need to focus. Surely, the Trust uses these devices for more than simple leisure."

"That they do, General. It's equipped with other useful information too: articles, logs, recordings, schematics, tutorials."

"Tutorials?"

Maybel returned to fidgeting with the VISI. "Like training. I saw one reviewing the fundamentals of combat, and another for technalurgical configuration."

"Anything related to Dr. Carlyle's work?"

"Hard to say. I've only begun to scratch the surface. But in a way, I understand some of his theory a bit better now. You see, the Trust is heavily invested in the concept of vibration, or what they refer to as resonance. Like ripples in water or the sound of a horn. This technalurgy is no different. It hums ever so slightly as it generates all sorts of images and sensations."

"All mere illusion, yes?" asked Azacca.

"I believe so. Everything looks real enough but a little hollow, if that makes sense. You just get the impression that something is a certain way, and in that way, well, it is! For instance, as I adjust it now, different objects and scenery appear that simply don't exist beyond my field of vision."

Maybel started walking about, staring at nothing in particular, at least as far as they were concerned. Her fingers enabled a series of additional layers that manifested over various parts of the room like ornaments upon the walls, swirling shapes in the air. Even a crowd of oddly dressed strangers gathered. They were like moving works of art, almost ancient in a way. Most were interacting with the wondrous surroundings, or each other—that is, except for Azacca and Dietrich. Both were waiting for her to come back to reality.

"Sorry," she said. "Where was I? Oh, that's right! I can also see other things, real things, much clearer than with my clunky spectacles. And this VISI is light. Why, at times I forget it's even on my face!"

It was obvious how much she adored wearing the headset. Dietrich knew separating her from it would not be easy if the situation required. "That's all well and good, but you weren't wearing it back home. None of us were. So, why did we see Mount Greneva glowing? What of these heralds and the rest?"

"Well, perhaps the Trust is able to project imagery beyond this headgear." Maybel paused, somewhat flummoxed herself. "Wait, now that I think about it, they must. I saw it in Market during their standoff with the Enforcers. Of course, they wouldn't be able to maintain the illusion for long, not without a lot of energy anyway. And you claimed Connel's attire changed once you left Greneva, right? Might that not suggest some limit to this phenomenon?"

Stone-faced, Dietrich placed both hands on the table, staring down once again at the patchwork of parchment. "But how does it work?"

"I'm not sure, exactly. That must be where this Liminatum comes into play. It has the ability to impress, right? And if the Trust deals in resonance, they likely use it in such a manner. That's about as much as I can gather from the research."

"I suppose we don't need to know all the specifics. Only how to stop it."

"Waves spar upon the waters," interjected Azacca. "Some sounds as well."

"What do you mean?" asked Maybel inquisitively.

Azacca laughed for no reason apparent to them. "I know a few things of sound. Ancient things. The right tone can beget visions of events once lost or yet to come. Play another, and it vanishes. Ah, yes. Sound of this nature is well known to . . . my people."

Maybel seemed especially intrigued by the last part of his response, but before she could pry, a sudden bout of dizziness caused her balance to falter. "Oh dear."

"You look a bit pale," said Dietrich, pointing to the chair closest to her. "Why don't you take a seat?"

"Thanks, but I'm fine. Must've overdone it with the dancing earlier." Maybel went to pour some refreshment from her service cart nearby, but the shiny, metallic pitcher ran dry. She then lifted a hand cloth to her mouth as a brief tinge of malaise drained all color from her clammy face.

"Best not to push yourself too hard. Sit down, and I'll go fetch more water—"

"You're very kind to offer, but that's my job," she replied with a smile before rolling the cart with her to the door. "Please don't worry on my account! I'll be fine after a quick break, really."

Some time later, Maybel started back from the kitchen, pushing her replenished cart with one hand and finishing a tasty snack with the other. It was crumbly and sweet, something the kindly cooks were happy to spare from the cupboards. Ever since she started working there, they always attempted to fatten her up every chance they got. It had become a challenge of theirs, one born out of sheer amazement at how slender her figure remained. She wasn't complaining either. If her time at Common Ward had taught her anything, it was to never to pass up a meal, no matter how small. Some made a wise crack or two at the VISI still resting upon her nose, but it was all in good fun. Before saying thanks and farewell, she made sure to down as much water as she could bear.

Perhaps a bit too much. Halfway to the conference room, she stopped suddenly to a strange twist in her stomach. This dull, painful churning had been bothering her on and off for some time now. Such persistent squeamishness was never a problem for her before, definitely nothing this intense. For the life of her, she could not explain why, and she assumed it was a lingering side effect of her prior illness. That or some other perfectly normal explanation.

I am still growing, after all, she reminded herself. *Maybe this is just part of becoming a woman.* Still, the pain would not relent, and she felt a sudden need to rush back to the others. Her aching body ruled out that possibility a few steps later. As another wave of dizziness swept over her, she gripped the rim of the cart and dragged it—tray, pitcher, and all—down with her in a spectacular fashion.

When she came to, there was a mess of water spilled everywhere, as well as a blurred figure standing several paces away. He was yelling something she could not hear, so she tried to toggle the settings to her visor like she did previously. This time, it was actually her head that needed adjustment, which it did gradually. Soon, Azacca came into focus with anger—or was it disgust?—strewn across his face. Then she noticed the knife in his hand. He hurled it at her, and she leaped upright in horror, but it landed a few feet short. Following his gaze, she looked slowly down upon a putrid, sluglike monster pinned firmly dead to the floor.

"The vola," declared Azacca. "How ominous to see it here. This foretells of dark times ahead."

Those were the first words to reach Maybel then, though she still couldn't make out their meaning. "What just happened? Why have you come?" she muttered, barely loud enough for him to hear.

"Dietrich had me follow. We could tell something was amiss, but this!" Azacca studied her carefully. "But you know not."

"I was returning with the water, and then—" she stopped, her head suddenly pounding.

"So, you remember nothing?"

"Only you standing there." Maybel had never seen anyone so disturbed. His eyes revisited the creature as if he was afraid to look at her. "Mister Azacca, tell me what's wrong."

Slowly, his eyes rose to meet her. "This wretched parasite, Maybel. It came from you."

Maybel fought back another wave of revulsion. "I—I don't understand."

"Your mouth expelled it just now!" Azacca let the words sink in before continuing. "Listen well. Never wise am I to speak of scripture in this land, yet it must be said. We Sh'tama recount an ancient fiend such as this, one from deep within the heart of Essa, *Quu'cana,* or the Quartzcore. There, since the beginning, it hath steeped in the World Blood, or *Lutzrat* in the tongue of my people. Like all others, this vola slain before you shares the Lutzrat's very essence, secretes it from every pore. So hath your blood been tainted."

Maybel's lower lip began to tremble. "But how? I've never seen anything like it in all my life."

"Neither hath most. Long, long ago, Holy Sancta and her disciples drove them from the land, yet some claim they dwell ever still in the Great Chasm. If the vola hath risen, then Lutzrat bubbles from the Quartzcore once more. And if *that* be true . . ."

"Then what?"

Azacca shook his head. "For another day. Let us focus on the now. The girth of this swollen spawn does not bode well for the size of its mother. Surely, it hath been feeding for some time."

"The . . . Mother . . ." It took one terribly long moment for Maybel to connect the dots. By then, she was trembling. "You're . . . you're saying . . . it's still inside me?"

"I'm sorry, my child." Despite his sadness, traces of hope twinkled in Azacca's eyes. "You would not succumb to it directly, but rather by what courses through your veins. Lutzrat be a blade of dual edges; it grants strength in bantam and death in plenty. First and foremost, the vola must be excised. A way exists among my order, but time runs short. We must return to them before it overwhelms you."

They stared silently at one another for a long while.

"Do you trust me?" he asked.

"I'm . . . not sure who to trust anymore." Sniffling, Maybel lifted her VISI to wipe a tear from her eye. "But I do know one thing. I don't want to feel like this anymore, like a burden! I've always tried to help others when I can, but these days, I'm the one who needs it more than anyone. If possible, I want you all to lean on *me* for a change. It's the least I could do. To show thanks."

"You wish to serve others?"

"Yes. It means more than the world to me. So, I can't die here. I just can't."

Azacca approached her with a tender smile. "Blessings, Maybel. You hold the very likeness of Saint Remora. Your boundless love be a light upon the world! Fear not, for Sancta hears the cries of the meek. She will not abandon you. Belief be told, our meeting hadst been ordained long ago. For this very reason do our paths cross! So, you see, we will drive that beast from your belly, or I hath no right to be called Godsend. I swear it!"

At once, Maybel embraced the gracious man, her eyes filled with tears of joy. Unfortunately, their tender moment was interrupted by an explosion that shook the entirety of Fort Lionel. This was quickly followed by blaring horns sounding the alarm in the distance, which caused the creature within her to stir. Within seconds, all chaos broke loose as soldiers dashed every which way through the halls to answer the call. Initially, the commotion caused her to hold on to Azacca more tightly, but no longer overcome with emotion, she eventually withdrew. "What's happening?"

"I know not. We must return to the others!"

"Azacca, is that you?" a voice shouted from a crossing at the end of the hall. It was Dietrich with Lord Lionel and a contingent of troops.

"Yes, over here!" shouted Azacca. "Are we under attack?"

After a quick exchange, Lionel bid them farewell and took his men in the other direction. "I believe so," said Dietrich while approaching. "We still haven't figured out from where just yet. Our lord has taken eastward to the ramparts above the entrance. He told me to cover this end of the Fort. We will head to the upper levels and take a look."

"Why surveil the seaside? None dare risk being struck blind by the Radiant Cliffs."

"I realize that, but we have to cover all our bases first."

Dietrich then noticed the mess nearby in the hall, followed by Maybel awkwardly scanning downward. "Maybel, what's this all about? What's wrong?"

"That shaking. I think it came from the lower levels," said Maybel with some surprise. "It's hard to explain, but when I look to the floor, there's a strange glow, like fire."

Azacca turned to Dietrich with a grave stare. "That would be—"

"The quarry, armory, dungeons." Dietrich's eyes shot open wide. "The dungeons! But it can't be. Maybel, are you sure?"

"That's what the VISI shows me. I don't know what else to make of it."

"All right. We'll take it from here. Hurry back to your room, and don't leave until somebody comes to get you. Understood?"

Maybel shook her head so hard her visor almost fell off. "But I can help you!"

"No, it's too dangerous."

"So is running around unattended! What if intruders have made it up here? The Trust could be anywhere." Maybel looked to Azacca for some support, but at the moment, he seemed preoccupied in thought. "No, I won't cower anymore! Not while everyone else puts their lives on the line. Besides, Laerzo is down there! Let me lead you to him."

A few of Maddock's men came running around the way and approached as Dietrich continued. "Out of the question. Now, go! I don't have time to argue with—"

"She will join us," declared Azacca suddenly. "If need be, I will protect her."

Dietrich already knew better than to question the man's intuition. "If you say so." He then turned to the soldiers awaiting nearby for new orders. "Men, scout around the western ramparts. If anyone asks, we're heading into the tunnels. I'll join you shortly, assuming all is well below. Move out!" The men saluted before quickly departing. Dietrich then returned his attention to the others. "Come on. Let's get moving!"

Without delay, they made for the lower levels of Fort Lionel. Once into its belly, they pressed deep through numerous winding corridors, which Dietrich was fairly accustomed to by now, or at least enough to keep them from wandering aimlessly or getting turned around. Other than an occasional whisper, they shared few words. They searched for distant noises, displaced shadows, anything out of the ordinary, but there appeared to be nothing of import aside from the same heated signatures on Maybel's display.

That was, until the line of torches normally mounted upon the walls suddenly came to an end. The path ahead was now rendered pitch-black. No one could sense anything from it except for the smell of lingering smoke, which suggested the torches had been there until recently. They quickly concluded that someone had taken the time to remove them, an ominous sign of what was to come. This would have made the cavernous passages nearly impossible to navigate further, but thankfully, they had brought a most useful, if not unassuming, ally.

The moment they stepped into complete darkness, Maybel's VISI illuminated their path in an instant, though she did nothing to prompt it. She marveled at how even the most minute details of every nook and cranny had been revealed. It was as if the cavern had been exposed to the very light of day. The others were impressed to be sure, but wishing not to waste time, Dietrich instructed her to keep it fixed to the path and continue forth. She reluctantly took the forefront and led them along, a couple of cautious steps at a time, until her confidence improved.

Some time later, they arrived at a split of many paths, one of the only intersections down here. It didn't take long for them to notice the wafts of smoke sifting from the path leading to the dungeons. Maybel confirmed this to be the location of the explosion. They were about to investigate when Azacca pointed out the streams of footprints upon the dusty floor, most of them exiting the dungeon into the port down at the bottom of the cliffs.

Dietrich quickly took off down that trail, while the others followed close behind. Soon after, they heard screams and clashing metal. A distance farther, they encountered a bloodied figure hobbled up against the wall.

"Soldier, what happened?" asked Dietrich.

The man shrank from the VISI's glare, slumping farther down the wall in clear distress. "I'm glad to hear your voice, sir. There's been a gaol-break. Dozens of Gul'dani suddenly quit their cages and toppled some of our Enforcers."

"Brother," said Maybel despondently.

The soldier coughed up some blood. "We managed to quell

most of the uprising, but the last of them armed themselves and escaped this direction."

"They fight to return home," declared Azacca. "Or die at sea."

"Yes, sir. I was injured while trying to stop them, but General Maddock and the others continued without me."

"Bruno," whispered Dietrich, looking down at the bloodied man.

"I'll be fine. You must hurry if you wish to catch them."

"We'll come back for you soon, I promise!" said Maybel as Dietrich motioned for her and Azacca to get moving.

Leaving the soldier, they tore through the passages, keeping their eyes peeled. They rushed down and around many pivots in the path, eventually spilling out into a salty cavern tucked beneath the Radiant Cliffs. At this point, the light from Maybel's VISI ceased as she and the others looked around the docks. A confrontation played out around the largest of several boats resting upon the water. It became apparent the Gul'dani men had the upper hand, as they'd already boarded safely and were in the process of weighing anchor.

Maybel and the others scrambled down the stone path and approached a dozen or so soldiers left on the dockside, many of them visibly battered and exhausted. One tended to Maddock, who knelt, gripping a bloody mess at his waist. Maybel was the first of the three newcomers to spot Laerzo on the large vessel with a blade to his throat. "Brother!"

"Maybel!" shouted Laerzo, shocked at his sister's presence, though slightly relieved to see Dietrich and Azacca close behind. "Stay back!"

"Do as he says," ordered Maddock with a pained grunt. His pride appeared more wounded than his body. "Sorry, Sigurd.

That creepy cadaver blew the dungeon wide open, got the jump on us."

"Well, well! If it isn't Dietrich here to clean up poor Maddock's mess!" shouted a pale, wily man wiping a bloody dagger on his stolen Alliance uniform. "I told you we would meet again."

"Connel!" shouted Dietrich in disbelief. "But they found you lifeless in your cell."

"That man is no more! There is only Ichabod now." Indeed, he exhibited the same devious demeanor and dual-toned voice they had observed briefly during interrogation—Connel's other self, his Aspect. "It so happens the rumors of my demise were premature. And deliberate. You see, this vessel, though without breath at the time, was anything but expired! In fact, I am stronger than ever, thanks to the creature which now dwells within! It is one of the many new friends I've made since my incarceration. But where are my manners? Vidal, why don't you say hello to the others?"

"It can't be," started Dietrich, his eyes widening all the more.

"Blessings upon you, Dietrich!" exclaimed Vidal with a delightfully crazed stare. "When I was promised emancipation by my god, nothing could prepare me for just how magnificent this moment would be. Not only do I stand with my brothers on a *carraque* from my old fleet—one wonderfully maintained, no doubt—but I have also been reunited with my *omar,* long-lost fruit of my seed! And I suppose his mother's cuckold as well. How serendipitous to see you again!"

Dietrich angrily lifted his shaking fist. "Let him go! This is between you and me!"

"What, and spoil all the fun? I think not, old friend! Besides, you have failed this boy in more ways than one. He will fare much better at my side, where he belongs."

"Like I'd join you!" defied Laerzo, only to be mocked by his captor's ridiculous laughter. He was further embarrassed by the disappointed look on Azacca's face. "Sorry, Master! Things got a little out of hand."

"Worry not, *galante*," replied Azacca in a strange calm. "This distraction will pass, and when it does, I will make a warrior of you yet!"

"*Galante!*" shouted Vidal in amusement. "Azacca, you old fool! He stands before you a hero to none!"

"Hold on!" shouted Maybel frantically. "We'll save you somehow!"

"Perhaps sooner than you think," replied Ichabod, shifting his focus to Maybel. "Girl, how would you like to strike a deal?"

Maybel took a step back, repulsed by the man's vicious gaze, sullied by his question. "Who, me?"

"Yes, you! Hand over the VISI, and I will relinquish your brother. Now, how does that sound?"

Vidal turned to his fellow conspirator with a wicked sneer. "That was not part of our pact. The boy is mine!"

"Forget him," said Ichabod. "That visor is of incalculable value to me and your prophet!"

"Then you should've stolen it while you had the chance," answered Vidal. "We will not suffer another moment in this repugnant land."

"But—"

"Stay behind if you wish, but we are leaving now. Men, hear me! We depart for Gul'dan!"

With a raucous cheer, Vidal's men dropped the ship's sails as it began to inch from the dock.

"Hold fast!" shouted Ichabod, but none paid him any mind.

Vidal turned one demented eye toward Dietrich and the others trailing helplessly along the pier. "You want him, Dietrich? Come and get him!"

With that, the ship cleared the docks, disappearing into blinding light cast down by the Radiant Cliffs. For one grueling moment, Dietrich stood with the others at the edge of sea, downtrodden and defeated.

"What are you idiots waiting for?" barked Maddock as his subordinate helped him stand. "Not just going to let them get away, are you?"

CHAPTER 29

"Perhaps more Lutzrat is required," said Algus in the manor's darkened shrine, once again kneeling at the base of the Hypha Tree.

Its brilliant white light had become noticeably faded, in small part due to the humming pitchfork standing upright between them through some trick or invisible force. The tree's lackluster appearance was of some concern, though his mind was currently drawn to more personal matters. A trance gripped him now, evidently self-induced by the syringe clasped tightly in his hands. He was by his lonesome in that vestibule, and yet he was not alone. "Father, why can I not find you?"

"Just focus," spoke a voice through his VISI. "Imagine him before you."

Algus shook his head. "Imagine asking a blind man to muster his father's image. It was no easier trying to conjure my brother."

"Don't get smart. You know what I mean. Let's start again." The silvery tone of a small bell rang within the headset. "Try to remember his presence. What did he smell like? How did his voice sound?"

Another ring of the bell caused Algus to dip his head. "He was always very cleanly, never produced a strong odor. Part and parcel for physicians, I suppose. What I sensed was more sterile, like if static was a smell. I never cared much for it." He took a deep breath. "His voice was gruff, as deep as he was tall. It towered over me, though I was only a child then."

"Good," said the baritone voice. "Explore some fond experiences together. What did he like to talk about? How did you feel when he was around?"

"We didn't share as much time as I would have liked, but every moment was memorable. We would toss a whistle ball back and forth while he described every aspect of our surroundings in painstaking detail. How high the fences were, petal formation of the flowers, where the fowl made their home in the trees, what existed beyond our vista. That sort of thing. Other times in our residence, he would beckon for me to find him from different parts until I memorized every single dimension. Sometimes he would just hold me close while it rained so I wouldn't feel afraid. In a way, he was my portal to the world. I felt . . . connected when with him, like I wasn't just some dim figure wading in the void."

The voice paused. "Is there anything he used to say when you were feeling down?"

Algus took another moment for himself before continuing. "He used to say, 'Better to see right than light.' "

The man in the VISI waited patiently for these words to simmer, and simmer they did. Algus's breathing quickened, growing erratic as something tested his focus. Judging by the sweat dripping down the wrinkles pinched across his forehead, he was failing that test. And when the pressure became too much to bear, he sent his pitchfork crashing to the ground. This wave of discord caused the Hypha Tree to curl, wither, and fade for a terrifying moment before returning to its previous dormant state. "Damn it! I was so close, and yet—"

"These things take time. Finding the one I sought was no easy exercise either."

Algus gripped the back of his neck. "I swore I could feel him. But he never says a word. Why does he refuse me again and again? Does he not want to be with me?"

"What do you think?"

Dropping the needle at his side, Algus stood to retrieve his pitchfork. "I think you're trying to mess with my head again, *Doctor*! Don't forget who's in charge here. We had a deal!"

"Haven't you demanded enough of me? Managing the Liminatum is taxing enough without having to oversee every thrall toiling endlessly within the Mount to fuel it. Besides, reuniting you with your family was Gebhardt's promise, not mine. I can only work so many miracles."

Just then, footsteps approached.

"We'll try again another time. Algus, out." Turning, he saw Matron enter the shrine. "Good day."

"Pray tell," said Matron. "Who were you speaking to just now? Surely not the Hypha Tree."

"As a matter of fact. You no doubt heard my frustrations from afar. I'm afraid every frequency from my pitchfork was unable to boost Hypha's vitality."

"Of course you already knew this. While I admire your efforts, no amount of resonance alone can sustain her." Matron glanced briefly at the bloodied syringe on the floor before shooting an accusatory stare at Algus. "Or *medicament*, apparently. For her or you, I wonder?"

"I was just—"

"No matter. What I'm trying to say is as basic as it comes. Everything that lives in this world must feed."

"I just don't want to feed her needlessly."

"Or at all. Silly boy, it's time you finally faced facts. Without *proper* nourishment, the Holy Tree will stir and claim it one way or the other." There was a harrowing earnestness in her voice, as if she had seen this come to pass before.

"The proper nourishment . . ." echoed Algus sadly. "You mean blood."

"Yes, I mean blood. You know Hypha could not have grown to such a size without it. And must I remind how you and the Madam kept it nice and fed all this time? She tells me naughty wards make for tasty snacks."

Algus had tried just about everything to forget it. "Surely, there must be another way."

"Must we go through this every time?" Matron knelt before the Hypha Tree. "If you have any fresh ideas, I would be interested to hear them."

"No, I suppose not. Apologies, Matron. I don't mean to be difficult. Something just doesn't make sense to me. Now that the reactor has been activated, why bother with the Hypha Tree at all?"

"The Liminatum may be sufficient to control the masses; however, even trace amounts of Lutzrat make them more impressionable to our illusions. The more we possess, the more that can be possessed. It's quite that simple, really."

"But to what end?"

"Perhaps you should ask that voice from before, the one whispering in your ear." Matron preempted Algus before he could respond. "Don't. The Madam has already made it abundantly clear that she will deal with him exclusively. You would do well not to contact him again. Or sap the life from Hypha to fuel foolish pursuits." She paused long enough to keep her temper in check. "As far as your question, you know Waldea can only be won over amicably with the tools at our disposal. And so, Hypha must feed. I know this unsettles you, but it's the only way to avoid greater bloodshed. Do you understand?"

"Yes," answered Algus, trying his best to ignore the blatant contradiction in her words. Just as much as ever, he naively hoped to avoid any real sacrifice, but wishing not to push the matter further, he joined her kneeling before the Hypha Tree.

"Your heart wavers," said Matron after a time. "You have not lost faith in her, have you?"

"I suppose I have. She's been quite distant as of late."

"Now how can that be? When you met her as a blind, scared, little boy with nowhere to go, did she not care for you without so much of a fuss? Were you not provided for?"

"That's right."

"And when you wished to learn of the mysterious sounds and shapes around you, did she not divine their true nature?"

"She did."

"And when you cried that you could not see the world—"

"I had no faith then either."

"Until she restored your sight."

Algus nodded solemnly. "Yes. Seeing is believing, after all."

"So why, after all this time, do you struggle now?"

"Because she promised the impossible and has not yet delivered."

"And you do not think her capable?"

"I hope against hope that she is, but for the life of me, I have no clue how such a thing could ever happen. Can she truly raise the dead, Matron? Will I ever meet my family again?"

"Yes. In fact, that is the crux of our faith. It is said that when Lutzrat covers the planet, all those dearly departed will once again walk upon this land. This is what the Holy Mother desires above all else."

Algus fell silent for another spell, praying that her words would prove true. He wanted it more than anything in the world. Then, for reasons he couldn't explain, the thought of it suddenly drew his attention elsewhere.

"Matron, do you remember the daimon that crashed into the temple?"

Matron suddenly stood. "Yes, child. Why do you ask?"

"Like most things, I have never laid eyes on him, yet strangely, I cannot shake the impression that we have met before. And how the Liminatum parted when he cried out—"

"Think nothing more of that man. He is nothing but an aberration playing tricks within the illusion. He will be dealt with in time."

Algus stood then, took his pitchfork in hand, and flicked it ever so sweetly. "Indeed, he will. I will see to it personally."

CHAPTER 30

Gwyndolyn had been in the worst of moods since her embarrassing encounter back in Thannick. After returning to Greneva, she'd castigated Scarlet, Algus, and Matron for their disgrace, questioning how such a thing could even happen to her, the chosen one. Just as the Alliance had shattered her crystalline carafe, so too did they destroy her veneer of infallibility, her supposed protection by the divine. She felt bare, exposed to be as weak and pathetic as those around her, even more so when she could do nothing but flee. Everything about her had been cast into doubt, and a scant few began to take notice, though she quickly banished them for daring to question her holy favor. As for the rest of her adherents, she was relieved to see the flames the zeal stoked in their eyes and hearts. They swore justice would be delivered against such humiliation.

In the coming days, she felt increasingly isolated by her handlers, who had barely exchanged a few words with her since. They weren't the only ones. When Gwyndolyn took some time for herself in the garden, none of the people outside seemed to even notice she existed—not the droves of workers connecting the manor to the castle underway, not the swelling ranks of soldiers on patrol around the mountainside, not even the afflicted hunched in their makeshift camps outside the gates. It was as if she'd been made invisible to them. The sudden silent treatment was unsettling and almost felt like a punishment in its own right.

Once more wine could be procured, she and Scarlet were summoned before the Hypha Tree and ordered to resume their usual mission. Before they left, however, Matron informed them of a couple of changes. First, they would be sent out without the glamour of the gilded throne in order to keep a low profile, at least until the blessed wine could be fully replenished. Gwyndolyn protested vociferously, claiming it had been taken as recompense for being so careless in Thannick, but her words fell on deaf ears. Matron then presented Hypha's Dew in a pouch composed of stitched hamhern guts. Of course, Gwyndolyn protested this as well, but Matron insisted it would serve as a suitable container until another proper vessel could be crafted.

"Humility is a good thing every now and again," she added, which only served to infuriate Gwyndolyn further, almost purposefully so. Still, the grotesque vessel was handed over before both she and Scarlet were sent on their way.

A few days later, around high dawn, Gwyndolyn brought her entourage to an abrupt halt in the middle of a narrow avenue leading into Greneva's town square.

"Why have we stopped?" asked Scarlet, pulling up with a light-red hood covering her charred, peeling complexion. It seemed she had finally heeded Matron's advice after traveling carelessly one too many times. She noticed Gwyndolyn's arm pulling uncomfortably around her waist. "Are you not feeling well?"

"Do not dote on me. I need only a moment." Gwyndolyn turned and drank exorbitantly from the unsightly pouch as a sweet cringe shivered through her body. Then she inconspicuously lowered it back at her side, though it was no secret she had taken quite a liking to the sacrament as of late. When previously confronted on the matter, she angrily declared it perfectly permissible, that Denestra herself had given Gwyndolyn the right. She was the Blessed Daughter, after all, the one who transformed poison into wine. If anything, she claimed it would bring her and the Holy Mother closer together. No one had mentioned it since.

"The pouch seems a bit light today. Perhaps we should take our fill of water instead? There is a fountain not too far from here."

"Is your concern for me or the wine?" asked Gwyndolyn, her defensive, slurred tone and stare noticeably deadened by the drink. "Either way, it is misplaced."

"So I pray, though you do look a bit *pale*." Like most of Scarlet's words as of late, Gwyndolyn interpreted her seemingly innocuous observation as a deliberate attempt to antagonize. And it worked.

"You would do well to keep your mouth shut," snapped Gwyndolyn at the veiled threat.

Do not let this one damage you, my dear, the voice inside her was quick to console. *Her duplicitous barbs are ones of simple jealousy.*

Indeed, thought Gwyndolyn, by now all too accustomed to how Scarlet and the others diminished her holy station. Their meek admonitions were too frequent to deny. At best, they made her feel small, coddled, put upon; and at worst, smothered and isolated. What was the point of being chosen if her supposedly inviolable will was challenged at every twist and turn? Most days, she refused to let it bother her, but this was not one of those days. Her confidence had already been too greatly shaken.

"No offense was intended, Lord Sister. I wish only to follow Frater's will. Let us give unto the people what is theirs."

To this, Gwyndolyn suddenly smiled. "You are absolutely correct."

"I am?" asked Scarlet, shocked by the calm concession, and slightly suspicious of it.

"Yes. His will *shall* be done. Perhaps I am a bit parched after all. Let us stop at the fountain."

Scarlet nodded silently as they resumed a quiet trot up the avenue. The day was cool and calm without much in the way of goings-on, a testament to just how many had been saved. With each passing day, more folks took leave of their lives in the city to join those already laboring up the mountain. The time demanded of them was excruciating to a fault, but all were overjoyed to do Denestra's bidding nonetheless. To them, nothing else seemed to matter, not even their well-being. Of course, there was always need for people to run shops and others to patronize them, but Greneva had slowly lost its steady bustle in exchange for something greater.

Gwyndolyn barely saw a single soul until they reached the square, where a group of faithful gathered at the opposite end, worshipping a stone statue of her twice their size. She didn't recall commissioning it, and wondered whether they had taken it upon themselves to erect it. Though beautifully chiseled, she felt it was a waste of effort that should've been used to complete the castle in the mountains.

Speaking of which, her eyes gazed longingly at the Mount, as they often did now, marveling at how much progress had already been made. It was no wonder, considering how many had devoted every waking moment toward its completion.

Work was the only true worship, she reminded herself, not simple lip service. Anything less would fail to deliver what she truly desired: a home worthy of a goddess. She could not wait to live there with her mother once it was finished.

Once her cadre of pitchforks formed a perimeter around the fountain, Gwyndolyn positioned herself behind it to hide from the crowd. "Do not bother me until I beckon," she ordered after servants helped lower her from the geldtmare.

They turned their backs out of discretion, after which Gwyndolyn began to drink of the water, yet she found it tasteless and unacceptable. Glancing over her shoulder, she uncorked her hamhern pouch and took another generous swig, causing another wave of exhilaration to course through her body. Then she did something she knew was a bit careless, if not completely forbidden. She filled the pouch from the fountain.

"Are you feeling better?" asked Scarlet suddenly as she peeked over the wall of guards.

"What did I just say?" shouted Gwyndolyn, her hands suddenly lifting from the waters. "I'm fine, Scarlet. Great, in fact. So, please be so kind as to grant me some privacy for a change."

Scarlet shoved past the guards. "You are modest to a fault! Why not lean on me every now and again? We are sisters, after all. Here, let me help you up."

Gwyndolyn resisted, but Scarlet dragged her upright by the arm, only for the pouch to hit the ground with a swish. Both were relieved to see the fleshy container intact.

"What is this? Why is it soaking wet?" asked Scarlet.

Gwyndolyn shot her a wicked sneer. "Never you mind, nosy girl! I must've spilled some water on it while cleaning myself up." She was startled when Scarlet snatched the vessel from

Gwyndolyn's hands. "You fool! You know you're not supposed to—"

"It's been completely filled! You couldn't have—"

Gwyndolyn smiled deviously. "Halae! A miracle, no doubt. Now, come! Let us offer it up to the people."

"Hypha's Dew must not be diluted. What would Frater or Matron say if—"

"They won't say a word because you will not tell them. And do not speak like you know the inner workings of this wine. If I've sanctified it before, I can do it again."

"Lord Sister, please reconsider. What would happen if the Dew fails?"

In a sudden fit, Gwyndolyn wound back her open palm. "It is not the sacrament. I am! They will have it and rejoice!"

"But—"

"Be silent!" erupted Gwyndolyn, her voice humbling all around her as it reverberated throughout the square. "That is all I require of you."

Scarlet lowered sorely in compliance, her red hood obscuring the pained look in her eyes. It was then that the curious crowd of faithful left the statue and approached the fountain. One overly eager worshipper in particular practically sprinted over to the line of Trust standing guard in their white robes.

"I beg you to let me through!" the girl shouted desperately past their humming pitchforks. "Oh please, I must see her! Lady Gwyndolyn, it's me, Bethany!"

"Bethany," whispered Scarlet with a warm, reminiscent look on her face. With a wave of her hand, she parted the guards to reveal a frantic girl wearing a simple white tunic and frazzled brown hair. Her skin was pale and eyes cloudy. "Is it really you?"

"*Obviously*," responded Bethany in her usual dismissive tone, though never before to Scarlet. "Take me to see her at once!"

"Don't you remember me?" asked Scarlet, suddenly agitated by Bethany's infatuation with Gwyndolyn. "I suppose it matters not. Do not disturb her. She will deign to meet with you all in due time."

"Out of my way!" shouted Bethany as she shoved Scarlet aside. "Please, I have gone too long without blessing!" The Trust was about to squelch this incessant pleading when Gwyndolyn begrudgingly emerged from around the fountain. "Thank you for seeing me. Your most devout disciple stands before you now. Please save me!" Humbled by the look of disgust on Gwyndolyn's face, Bethany quickly dropped to her knees. "Don't you recognize me? Many days ago, in the forest, I graciously received your wondrous gift and was healed! Ever since, I have been singing your praises, but fear I may have done something wrong, for my features are again beginning to fade."

What a pathetic little girl, no more worthy to behold you than a bug! spoke the voice inside Gwyndolyn.

"So it seems. What wicked deeds have you committed in my name?"

"Nothing. You have my word. I would never do anything to betray you or the Holy Mother."

She knows me not.

"And yet you bow before me, nearly ashen," scoffed Gwyndolyn. "What makes you twice worthy of my love? Is this pitiable form all you show for it?"

"Please, if you would only give me another chance. Drive away this sickness, and I will pledge myself to you always!"

"You swear this to me now?" asked Gwyndolyn, her words

bleeding with arrogance. She intended to offer them all drink eventually but reveled in the girl's needless groveling all the same.

"Oh yes, I swear my very life."

And she will give it, the voice promised.

Gwyndolyn bore down on Bethany a painfully long time before finally lifting the pouch. "Very well. I cast away your sin. Serve me now and forever!"

She was pleased to see Bethany's pale countenance slowly brighten as she administered the diluted drink.

Likewise, Bethany jumped upright and proclaimed, "Halae, my vigor has been restored! Oh, you are good, my lord, so very good! Halae Al' Haleia!" Though uplifting for a short while, her relentless reverence quickly became insufferable to those patiently waiting in line. With an aggressive tilt of the head, Gwyndolyn motioned for her to be removed, and a couple of the Trust did just that. Bethany could still be heard wailing as the others drank the diluted wine, and so each attempted to outdo her jubilance with their own praises.

"You sniveling, good-for-nothing traitor!" shouted Scarlet out of nowhere, seething with vitriol. Thinking the words were meant for her, Gwyndolyn became quite incensed, at least until Scarlet pushed through the clamorous crowd. Scarlet looked all but ready to wring Bethany's neck when the girl suddenly collapsed in her arms, even paler than before. Not long after, Bethany's eyes clouded to the point of blindness, and every bit of brown drained from her hair like dirty water from a rag.

It was not long before Gwyndolyn and Scarlet crashed through the heavy double doors of the shrine on the Mount, hysterically bickering all the while. Gathered before the Hypha Tree were Matron and Algus, who twirled abruptly toward the commotion. They watched the Trust file into the chamber as well, one of the men carrying a frail, shrouded figure who was placed before the Hypha Tree.

"What is the meaning of this?" asked Matron, clearly startled. "Do not bring your squabbles into this hallowed place."

"I told her not to, but she wouldn't listen!" sobbed Scarlet as she threw her finger in Gwyndolyn's direction. "She wouldn't listen!"

"Be calm and explain yourself."

"There's nothing to explain!" answered Gwyndolyn, her quick defense suggesting the complete opposite. "This wicked soul rejected my blessing and caused the whole crowd to go ashen. She made me look like a fool!"

"That's because you are!" screamed Scarlet. "Bethany would've been fine had you never split the sacrament!"

Gwyndolyn squirmed slightly. "You see, there wasn't much left—"

"Because you drank it all!"

"Enough!" boomed Algus, his skull pained by the shrieks echoing through the chamber. He stared over to Matron, expecting some reaction, but she would not speak. Turning back to the others, Algus stroked his chin. "How long has the girl been like this?"

"Just under an auram. When the crowds turned rabid, we were forced to flee." Scarlet's face pinched dreadfully. "We can still save her, right?"

Algus shook his head in despair. "Her hair has already fallen completely white—"

"No! There has to be a way." Scarlet turned to her sister with fire in her eyes. "If you're so high and mighty, beg the Holy Mother to intervene."

"I will be made to beg for nothing."

"Do it, you disgusting wretch. This is your fault. Your fault!"

This whole affair had given Gwyndolyn's ego quite the hit. "Even if I did as you said, she only speaks while I am heavy with wine."

Algus shot Gwyndolyn a strange stare. "She . . . speaks to you? Do you hear her now?"

"Not since we fled. You have prepared more of the sacrament, correct?" asked Gwyndolyn, though she took his silence to suggest they had not. Turning to Scarlet, she pompously asked, "Why do you even care to save her? She is a monster among us."

Scarlet, apoplectic by that point, seemed poised to attack when Matron finally intervened. "Be still, my child. Gwyndolyn is correct. I fear this girl is beyond saving. She must be destroyed at once."

"You cannot be serious," lamented Scarlet. "Bethany was always sort of a wet sponge, but she was my friend!"

"Are you certain, Matron?" asked Algus with a subtle discomfort in his wavering voice.

Matron nodded. "You know all too well those who turn ashen are to be sacrificed—"

"Or driven into the Mount," said Scarlet.

"Not this time. She would never survive exile, anyway. Let her blood nourish the Hypha Tree so its fruit may save the many."

"Goddamn it!" wailed Scarlet, falling on one knee with both hands wrapped over the back of her skull. Her despair rang loudly through the dimmed halls of the shrine, so much that members of their order starting poking heads into the chamber. Her sorrow only worsened when an unsolicited chuckle suddenly escaped from under Gwyndolyn's breath. "What is so damn funny? Does her demise truly please you?"

Gwyndolyn was equally surprised by her own reaction, but she simply could not help herself. With a twisted expression, she laughed again and again, her amusement becoming bolder, more heinous. Soon it caused the entire shrine to shake as all her subjects gathered to behold what had become of their Blessed Daughter. After finally stopping, she addressed Scarlet before the congregation in a deep, menacing cadence overlapping her typical tenor tones: "We see nothing wrong with letting the girl bleed out. In fact, we will it."

"That's too depraved, even for you," muttered Scarlet, numb with disbelief.

"For Gwyndolyn, perhaps, but not her Holy Mother. Behold your goddess, Denestra. At last, I have come."

Nary a soul could believe what they'd just heard, including Matron, who almost collapsed on the spot. Awkwardly staggering forward, her dark veil could no longer obscure the emotion underneath. "No, my lord. Please, you must save your strength. And hers. It's still too soon."

"Matron, what are you saying?" asked Algus. "I thought Denestra was just part of our—"

"Our patience grows thin," proclaimed Denestra through Gwyndolyn. "Butcher the child so Hypha, this blood-sucking whore, may produce what we require. Let her Lutzrat flow into us so we may regain our worldly throne. If you don't, Gebhardt, we will devour every last bit of her here and now!"

The name sent a chill across the entire space as Matron was forced to finally lift her veil. Algus's sour expression suggested he, too, had been deceived this whole time, that this revelation was beyond his awareness.

Scarlet slowly rose to her feet, sorting out some mental haze that appeared to have misguided her as well. "All this time, it was you. But surely, I would have recognized you."

"Daughter, I did not wish to hide from you," began Gebhardt softly. "Believe me when I say a certain dissonance was required to maintain the tapestry of illusion we have woven throughout Greneva."

"Madam, you know well not to ignore us!" boomed Denestra, the echoes of her voice a dreadful violence within the space.

Gebhardt turned to her master. "Denestra, I hear your words, but you mustn't do this. That body has not yet been completely broken. Gwyndolyn has not yet been fully conditioned."

"The eternal pessimist. You will make a fine Aspect one day. We feel just fine. This body takes quite well to the Lutzrat."

"Too much at once will prove fatal."

"So you keep insisting. Why don't we test your theory?"

With a possessed stride, Gwyndolyn's body slowly sauntered toward the Hypha Tree with both hands gravitating toward Gebhardt's neck. She, or rather, the cruel persona within, had half a mind to end the woman right then and there, if not for something gleaming under her robe. It was Gwyndolyn's dagger, her Wicked Slight. With a simple flick of the wrist, it inexplicably returned to Denestra's possession.

"What a fitting turn of events. To think the Fatima Dagger, one which belonged to my oldest and worst enemy, would find its way back to me yet again. I will relish it forever, but first, we will do away with this ashen girl ourselves. What better way to commemorate this gift, not to mention our joining?"

Scarlet threw herself between Gwyndolyn and Bethany. "This isn't you! Please stop this, I'm begging you."

Gwyndolyn stood balefully over the ashen with a wicked smile and casually shoved Scarlet aside with her boot. Then, with dagger in hand, she lowered to prepare for the slaughter, but when the time came to strike, a rigid hesitation stopped her hand. The more she tried, the sooner all joy faded from her face. Shaking and snarling, she turned ever so slightly toward the others with frightful, confused eyes.

"I—I don't want this."

The menacing voice returned in the next breath. "Who cares what you desire? I am your goddess!"

Gwyndolyn's head shook wildly, her mind beginning to split. "I don't want it!"

"Insolent sack of flesh. I am your everything! You will do as I command! Kill the girl at once!"

"No, not like this! Someone, please help me!"

Denestra's attempts to bring the dagger down renewed a few times more with the same result. All the while, amid this struggle was a warmth burgeoning within Gwyndolyn. And with it came the kindly remembrance of the one that, once upon a time, expressed to her the deepest of devotion. She found herself again as a child awash in the setting of the Solstar like in her dream, nestling her mother with all the love in the world.

"What is this?" spoke Denestra with bitter venom. "A presence. Gebhardt, this body has been claimed by another."

"That's not possible," insisted Gebhardt. "I have wrenched every ounce of goodness from her heart. She is a perfect vessel for you to do as you will."

"There is no mistaking it. An Aspect has risen, one familiar to us both. I would remember this presence anywhere. She irks me to no end. Almalinda! Even in death, you stand in my way. Your daughter and dagger are mine now, do you hear me?

Curse you!" Denestra turned Gwyndolyn toward Scarlet with a deathly stare. "Perhaps you would serve as a better host."

"I don't understand," answered Scarlet, turning to her mother. Gebhardt was startled half to death by Denestra's sudden pivot.

"Yes, I can sense it. There is great covetousness in you. All this time, you have sought to take her place. How did I not notice before? Listen, darling. Everything I promised to Gwyndolyn, I will give to you. Rip the life from this girl, and it is yours."

Scarlet lowered to Bethany's side now with a sordid, intoxicating stare of her own. "Everything . . . promised," she began to mutter in a trance, once and again. "Everything . . . promised."

Gebhardt immediately dragged her daughter upright. "You mustn't! I offered up Gwyndolyn in order to save you. Please do not give yourself in this way."

"Everything . . . promised."

"Selfish woman," said Denestra. "It is not for you to decide."

"Scarlet, is that you?" Suddenly opening her eyes, Bethany reached up and clasped Scarlet's hand into hers. "It's okay. Do what she says. To be ashen means to die, after all. What else is there to say? Maybe we can still help each other. So, please do me this one favor: End my miserable existence."

"Everything . . ."

"I want you to be the one. You said we were friends, right?"

". . . promised."

"Let my life give you what you desire. Let it help the people."

A tremendous weight suddenly lifted from Gwyndolyn's body. At the same time, Scarlet's body whipped backward as if something had collided with her, possessed her, darkened her demeanor.

"Do it, my darling," commanded Denestra, this time in

concert with her new vessel as she conjured Fatima into Scarlet's hand with the sheer force of her will.

Now utterly exhausted, Gwyndolyn fell to her knees before them all, her vision blurring. Trembling, she struggled to make out what was right in front of her, namely Scarlet tearfully looking down at Bethany's feeble, withering body. Gwyndolyn was so confused, so tired, she couldn't even remember returning to this place. It seemed more and more like a dream, its dimensions vacillating between the shrine and that of her former estate. For one terrible moment, basking in the Holy Tree's light, she watched in silence and horror as Scarlet drained all the life from her one and only friend.

To be continued in Book II of "War of the Faith."

Compendium of Terms

Planet – Essa

Time
- **Auram**—hour
- **Annum**—year (28 days per moon, 13 moons per annum)
- **Decam**—decade
- **Fortnight**—two weeks
- **High Dawn**—noon
- **Moon**—month
- **QE**—Quarnal Epoch (as in Quartzcore, Qua'cana, etc.)
- **Solstar**—sun

Locales
- **Archeim**—eastern land located somewhere beyond the Great Chasm in the mainland
- **Egress Island**—tropical island in the Waters Emeralda, home and refuge of the Sh'tama
- **Great Chasm**—a vast stretch of jagged wasteland connecting Waldean Plateau with the larger mainland and Gul'dan to the south
- **Greneva**—northestern commonwealth of Waldea, forest city at the base of Grenevan mountain range, closest to Great Chasm

- **Gul'dan**—vast desert nation south of the Waters Emeralda, former kingdom turned fanatical regime
- **Ogden**—southern commonwealth of Waldea, wide port city lowering into the Waters Emeralda
- **Quartzcore**—center of the world (see Qua'cana)
- **Stolgrum**—western commonwealth of Waldea, largest city and capital of the Waldean Alliance
- **Thannick**—central commonwealth of Waldea, rural expanse of heartland including Tuley to the north
- **Waldea**—Plateau of Commonwealths connected to the mainland only by the Great Chasm
- **Waters Emeralda**—emerald-colored sea shared by Waldea to the north, long stretch of Great Chasm to the east, Gul'dan to the south

Players
- **Enforcer**—colloquial title for soldier of the Waldean Alliance during peacetime, Man of the Law
- **Gul'dani**—citizens of Gul'dan
- **Militiaman**—voluntary fighter under Regent-General Cael Tannenbaum in Thannick
- **Pitchfork**—member of the Trust wielding a two-pronged vibrational rod by the same name
- **Polity**—elected council of any given commonwealth
- **Sh'tama**—an ancient religious order known to worship Sancta, often conflated with radical faction in Gul'dan, who worships Avalon
- **The Trust**—purveyors of Technalurgy from beyond the Great Chasm

- **Waldean Alliance**—military force representative of Waldean Commonwealths

Terminology
- **Aero-freight**—aerial ship, technalurgical mode of transport for the Trust
- **Carraque**—Sh'tama word for "sea vessel/boat"
- **Galante**—Sh'tama word for "hero"
- **Metalurgy**—study/application of metals/elements
- **Mechalurgy**—study/application of mechanical contraptions
- **Omar**—Sh'tama word for "son"
- **Qua'cana**—Sh'tama word for "Quartzcore"
- **Technalurgy**—study/application of advanced mechalurgy unknown to most in Waldea
- **Vah**—Sh'tama word for "boy"
- **VISI/VISI goggles**—technalurgical headgear worn by members of the Trust

Wildlife
- **Buckmules**—sheep donkeys raised for milk and wool
- **Cockel/Hen-Cockel**—rooster/chicken
- **Fengalin**—larger, feral felines with some foxlike features
- **Geldtmare**—larger, six-legged, horse-like creature with a beaked snout and tall, pointed, narrowly spaced antlers
- **Hamhern**—beastly boar with mighty horns
- **Skurat**—forest creature, much like a cross between a squirrel and a rat

- **Vola**—gelatinous, blood-sucking parasite which multiplies from inside hosts, excretes Lutzrat

Flora

- **Cheroot**—plant dried and smoked for its medicinal/relaxing effect
- **Chillybeans**—hearty whitish/blue beans harvested during colder climes
- **Chokeberry**—bitter blackberry used for tinctures
- **Chuteseed**—tall, golden crop lined generously with lengthy pods of nutritious seeds
- **Jiccam berries**—orange, juicy, plum-sized fruit with pits
- **Lavabeans**—oily, combustible bean used for lanterns and lubricants as well as Leopold's secret sauce for Bessie
- **Lemelon**—sweet/tart melon, typically colored green to yellow depending on age
- **Lutzrat**—mysterious, intoxicating sap bubbling up from deep within Essa
- **Sour Palm**—larger variant of chokeberry the size of one's palm, more sour than bitter
- **Star fruit**—sweet, pink, star-shaped fruit, which grows on trees farther south
- **Tellia weed**—a plant of various colors processed into potent dyes
- **White amaranth**—moderately thick, flowery stalk, milky inside but can be dried and processed into flour
- **Wildenberries**—flavorful red berries found in the forests of Greneva

About the Author

Bob Vacanti Jr.'s love of fantasy in video games and books started very young and continues to this day. In college, he decided to try his hand at storytelling, as he found language fascinating and was drawn to epic fantasy adventures like *Dune* and *Lord of the Rings*. *War of the Faith: Into Liminatum* is his debut novel and is the first book in his *War of the Faith* series.

Bob lives in Omaha, Nebraska with his family.